Also by Richard A. Kirk

The Lost Machine

NECESSARY
MONSTERS

RICHARD A. KIRK

Arche Press

This is A007, and it has an ISBN of 978-1-63023-050-0.

Library of Congress Control Number: 2017936817

This book was printed in the United States of America, and it is published by Arche Press, an imprint of Resurrection House (Sumner, WA).

The stories are tragic, of course . . .

Edited by Mark Teppo
Cover Art by Richard A. Kirk
Book Design by Mark Teppo

First trade paperback Arche Press edition: June, 2017.

www.archepress.com

For Elaine and Emily, with love

In memory of Allen Keith Love

NECESSARY MONSTERS

I am the black shadow
of chaos, whose pallid face frightens
the heavens with confusion;
I the dark prison: I the mournful veil
that conceals the formless nothing
and covers its stuff with its wings.

— Pedro Calderón De La Barca

TADPOLE IN A JAR

MEMORIA TURNED IN HER SLEEP. EVERY LIMB ACHED. SHE PICTURED Moss as a boy many years earlier. With this scrap of memory, she opened a doorway into his dreams, and stepped inside, unseen.

Two children faced each other in the compartment of a horse-drawn coach, separated by a shaft of unexpected sunlight. Moss, just past his eleventh birthday, had been instructed to accompany Memoria to a mansion in Hellbender Fields, where she would perform that evening. They sat on threadbare seats, Moss in a black suit, Memoria in a black dress. Memoria had a fair complexion accentuated by color at the extremities of nose, chin and ears. A band held her hair back. Moss was wind-burned. His hair was uncombed and full of static. A pencil line of dirt ran beneath his ragged fingernails.

It was late in the day on October 29. In spite of the season, they had not been provided with a blanket for their knees lest the clothing be spoiled. Memoria sat with a book closed under her gloved hands. Her eyes were also closed, but she was not asleep. Moss removed his own gloves and used them to wipe the condensation from the window to get a clear look at a dog, which had come loping across a lawn.

"Why do you think we've stopped?" asked Memoria.

"There's a dog blocking the road," said Moss. The tip of his nose squeaked against the glass. "It's frightening the horses." His warm skin fogged the window, obscuring the view. "It's enormous."

"In mythology, a dog guards the entrance to the underworld," said Memoria.

"Then what's it doing running around out here?" Moss slid across the seat to the window on the other side of the coach. "It looks mad."

3

"The driver will see it off." Her breath was white when she spoke. "It will be dark soon, and I'm cold. I want a fire, some supper and a hot water bottle in a warm bed." She opened her eyes. "I don't want to perform. I hate the way I feel when they look at me. It's like being a moth on the end of a pin."

Since August, her self-proclaimed guardian, John Machine, had arranged private gatherings in the drawing rooms of Hellbender Fields. For a fee that soon vanished into his pocketbook, Memoria was compelled to exhibit her gift. While he sat in the dim corners of high-ceilinged rooms, she levitated stones, marbles or whatever trinkets the audience might produce. Each night she had suffered John Machine flouring her face and darkening her eyes with crushed charcoal. Once he had even stained her lips with a berry juice that had made her ill. She shied from his impatient hands, coarse with freckled skin and copper hair, and especially the touch of the battered gold ring with the dark ruby. Once, mellowed by brandy, he had told her the stone was a symbol for blood and identified him as a member of the Red Lamprey, a secret society. She had seen similar rings among her patrons.

"I despise them," she said.

Moss sat back from the fogged glass, exasperated, and faced Memoria. "If you give them what they want, they will only want more. The answer is simple."

"To you, maybe. Everyone expects you to be rude and disappointing. You're an uncouth boy, which means I have to work twice as hard just so they won't have a bad opinion of John." Memoria shoved her book into a pasteboard suitcase.

"Who cares about their opinion?" said Moss. He pedaled the air with his feet. "My feet creak in these horrible boots. I might take them off."

"Don't you dare, or you'll never get them back on."

Moss fell back into the seat and worked the toes of his pointed black boots against Memoria's seat.

"Behave." Memoria threw a cushion at him, but it bounced to the floor. The driver's voice came through the walls of the coach, commanding the horses. It was followed by an erratic clopping of hooves, and much snorting. The coach lurched backwards, then forwards. Moss pivoted to the window in time to see the dog loping off across a wide lawn. Memoria, looking out the opposite window, watched a brittle reef of ornamental gardens drift by the coach as it lurched over the uneven road. At a bend, the mansion they were to visit swung into her field of vision. The coach heaved, returning her attention to the gardens and trees.

"Is he trying to kill us?" Moss gripped the seat. Memoria did not answer. She had felt off all day. Her vision seethed with the onset of a migraine. Unlike Moss she found the confinement of the coach soothing. Moss's chatter was ceaseless. She held her tongue, understanding that he was frightened by the prospect of the performance and the presence of refined people. During the slow coach ride through the City of Steps she had tried to read, discovering that although she loved to read when relaxed, it did not follow that reading would ease her into that desirable state. Her eyes had skipped around the lines of print, forcing her to re-start sentences, which Moss interrupted with random comments. She had tried to sleep but the frantic parade of images behind her eyes further eroded her mood. She longed to escape the performance and be sent to her room so that she could take her headache medicine without notice.

"One of these days I am going to paint your portrait," said Moss. "It will be a great unsmiling thing with squinty eyes so everyone will know what I had to put up with."

"One of these days I'm going to tell you a secret that will put you in the madhouse," hissed Memoria. Moss looked at his companion with wounded eyes, until he could no longer bear her gaze and turned away. She took his hand.

Memoria held the jam jar up to the June sunlight. They were behind the old house called Fleurent Drain. John Machine had brought her to live there a year earlier, with Moss and his mother. Tadpoles wriggled in the green water, much fatter than even two days ago.

"It's like they think that one of these days, if they keep trying, they'll be able to swim right through the glass. They don't understand glass. To them it's magic."

Moss, who was watching Memoria, and was not at that moment interested in tadpoles, nodded. Memoria's face was still thin from a bout of fever, but the bruising had gone from around her eyes. Her hair hung about her sunburned shoulders and over the straps of her swimsuit.

"Well," said Memoria. She lowered the jar.

"Well?"

Memoria made a face as she tried to twist the lid off the jar. "It's a big day in Tadpoleland." Her wet hand slipped on the tight lid, sloshing the water, and panicking the tadpoles. She thrust the jar at Moss. "Here, can you?" Moss took the jar and twisted the lid. It came off with a loud pop.

"Let them go," said Moss, his face betraying his anxiety that Memoria was about to do something horrible. She took the jar and lay belly-down on the warm dock. She lowered it into the canal, letting the water slip over the rim. Moss lay down beside her. She saw him look at the healed scars that encircled her arms. Moss switched his attention to the jar. He had never summoned the courage to ask her about them. The tadpoles continued to wriggle against the glass until a large one made its way to the rim and slipped into the canal.

"That's the clever one," said Memoria. In a few seconds the jar was empty.

It was October again. John Machine and Memoria had argued. She had run away and John had chased her to the edge of the city where it met the sea. Moss followed, angry with John and afraid for Memoria. Memoria had reached the end of the path near the Irridian Sea and climbed onto a seawall. She fought the wind to pull herself upright, keeping a hand on the wall as long as possible while gulls swept around her. A gust caused her to stagger. She shrieked. Moss's breath caught in his throat. She regained her footing. The ocean crashed at the bottom of the fifty-foot drop behind her. Watching John approach, she stood in that strange, slightly k-legged way of hers, hands on hips. John bellowed. Memoria shouted back, gesturing with her arms. Despite the danger, Moss half smiled. He knew what was coming next; he had been on the receiving end of it many times. A handful of stones lying loose on the seawall popped into the air, like the click beetles he kept in a jar under the house.

"Don't," said John, walking forward. "I'm warning you." The stones rose into the air. "Memoria, you'll be sorry." The stones flew at him, as if in retort.

"God dammit." John stopped less than twenty feet from her, his skin raw. He raised his arms to cover his face and twisted away. The stones bounced off his upper body and scattered around his feet.

Moss felt a twinge of pity. John was ill dressed for the elements. His worn overcoat flapped around his limbs. His socks had drooped to expose bare ankles. A fresh haircut had left a band of raw skin on the back of his neck. It struck Moss as poignant.

"I'm not going with you," shouted Memoria. "I don't want to live with that monster."

"Come on," John said. "Nobody is asking you to do anything but your share. Do you think your food is free, your clothes? That man is our benefactor."

"Liar. You've never asked me what I wanted."

"What do you say we go get a cup of cocoa and talk about this reasonably?" John worked his way closer. He lifted his hands, palms out.

"I don't want to. You'll say anything to get your way."

"We've all got to do our part, Dove. You're no different. You have to earn your keep like the rest of us." John's voice had grown calm.

Moss was now within a few feet of them. "Don't listen," he shouted. Memoria looked at him. He had always been in awe of her unusual, pale-blue eyes. The corners of her mouth dropped. Time slowed. Moss's face burned with embarrassment at the thought that she understood the feelings he had never dared to reveal.

"What?" he whispered. It was as if just the two of them stood there. "Memoria, what?" She shook her head in wonderment. She had guessed his secret. He was sure of it.

"Get off the seawall," said John, in a voice wrecked from too many hand-rolled cigarettes. He pointed an ochre-stained finger at her. "If you don't get off that wall I'll knock you into the middle of next week."

The spell was broken. Another stone flew from Memoria's side. Moss winced at the sharp crack against John's head. The hand with the ruby ring pressed a whitened patch on his brow. When he pulled it away blood dribbled down a crease in his face.

"You little bitch," he said. He lunged toward her. Moss cried out when Memoria skipped backward on one foot, close to the outer edge of the wall. She was quick, but John was strong. He grabbed her ankle, causing her to fall on her side with a shrill yelp. John pulled against a welter of blows from her other foot. Moss threw himself at John's back. He flailed his fists at the man's head and shoulders.

"Let me go. Let me go," screamed Memoria.

John turned, grabbed Moss's hair with his free hand and sent him sprawling.

"Stay out of this." John returned his attention to Memoria. He slapped her face and told her to shut up. In return she windmilled her legs. A booted heel drove into John's face. He staggered back with a hand over his eye, releasing Memoria's leg. She screamed, and then she was gone. Moss felt a sensation that he had never experienced before. It was black and unyielding, plunging under his ribs into his organs. His scalp prickled as the blood rushed from his head. He wanted to be sick. John sprawled across the seawall, hands grasping as though Memoria had somehow become invisible. Moss rose to his feet, but he could do no more than stand with his fists clenched.

"No, no, no," John yelled. He ran up and down the seawall looking over in disbelief every few steps. At the spot where Memoria had fallen, John picked something off the wall and clutched it in his fist. He turned to Moss. His bloodless lips quivered. "You see what you've done? This is your fault, you little bastard. Yours." John grabbed Moss by the upper arm and shook him. Moss thought his teeth would shatter. "What have you been telling her?" John struck him, making his head ring. "Do you know what you've done to me? Do you? You've ruined me."

"We have to find her." Moss tried to pull away.

"I'm finished," John bellowed. "That should be you down there." John's face was inches away. The reddish-grey stubble congealed with blood, his teeth, ivory but for one that was grey, the reddened eyes, these things would be etched in Moss's memory forever. A thought took hold in the one quiet spot in his mind as he fought John's grip. *I should have done more. I killed her.*

John Machine was right. Moss had been telling Memoria things. This morning, Moss had woken to find Memoria staring at him from under the cowl of her blanket. He learned that the previous night she had been taken to see a strange man who had spoken to her from behind a screen. After seeing a demonstration of her gift, the stranger asked if she would like to come and live with him in his mansion in Hellbender Fields. He had said that she deserved an education, a better life, and promised to give her both. As Memoria lay propped on a pile of stained pillows drinking tea, Moss told her that this was what came from demonstrating her abilities too readily. The stranger's offer was a snare. The more she accommodated him, the sooner his curiosity would turn to boredom or worse, brutality. She would be miserable. Moss's warning was well-intentioned, but he had set a tragic chain of events in motion. When John arrived in the late afternoon, hung over and foul-tempered, Memoria had refused to go with him. He had grabbed her hand in anger, but Memoria had slipped away and run from the house.

Moss perched on the edge of the seawall until dawn, numb from the cold and the shock of what had happened. When the waves struck the wall, spray rose before him as though a bomb had detonated on the sea floor. Whirlpools sucked at the foundations and smooth patches of water suggested broken masonry in the depths. Moss's heart ached at the thought of Memoria's body at the mercy of the cold water. Nobody had come. Moss knew that John's involvement meant that there would be no police or rescuers searching the dark water with arcs of torchlight. Moss tried to summon the courage to slide off the wall. He imagined what it would feel like to drop into the sea. One thing stopped him from doing it: the thought that maybe Memoria had survived. He remembered the tadpole. Maybe she had managed to slip away. The more he thought about it, the more certain he became. She was, after all, the clever one.

SMOKE

A PIEBALD CROW LOOKED DOWN ON NIGHTJAR ISLAND. IT WOULD be winter soon. The clouds would close in for days at a time, and the forest below would be limned in frost. For now, the air was warm, and he meant to enjoy every moment.

Two days earlier, the wind had stripped the trees. This morning, sunlight patterned the forest floor. A line of white-tailed deer moved along a trail, rooting for apples and mushrooms. The ground was covered in leaves, from staghorn sumacs, white birches, oaks, trembling aspens and maples. The crow recalled their names like lines of poetry. The evergreen trees had names as well, tamarack, jack pine, black spruce, balsam fir, red and white pine. The boy, the one that the women of the order called the Monster, had once spoken these names out loud as he stood in the deepening snow in a courtyard. At the time, he had been drawing in a book with a sharpened nib made from one of the crow's feathers. Ink had fanned in the fallen snowflakes. The deaf Attendant, a special role conferred by the order, had stood nearby, shivering and holding the bottle of ink in a cold, spattered hand. The crow had listened and remembered the names, because he had a remarkable memory, but he did not know which name belonged to which tree. The line of deer became untidy as they nuzzled dried stalks and seedpods. Names. Words. They fell easily from the mouths of men and monsters. Their meanings gave them agency over all things.

The crow soared higher, angling his wings to take advantage of the thermal. The air pressed the feathers against his skull. He cawed for no reason but to celebrate the glorious morning, and reasserted his grip on a twitching mouse. The crow was missing a toe on his left foot, and the adjustment gave the mouse a fortunate opportunity. It flattened its body and fell, as though it had turned to sand.

Watching the plummeting rodent, the crow followed the rising air in a lazy arc. He was neither irritated by the loss, nor inclined to follow. Mice were plentiful.

In the north end of the island, the forest dwindled, becoming meadow and then hardpan where little grew except lichen. Past the barren land, the empty city of Absentia was visible as overlapping shades of blue. The city appeared lifeless, but the crow had flown among the wind-sculpted domes and towers and seen the choking ivy, honeysuckle and nightshade. He had also seen survivors of the Purge, fewer every year, searching for anything useful in the ruins. Absentia, abandoned and ruinous, did not suit his mood this morning. He was light of heart and more than happy to turn his gaze to the west.

In this direction, a turbulent body of water divided Nightjar Island from the mainland. Along the coast, the forest broke into copses and scrub, and ended in prominences of limestone. At the foot of the cliffs, pitched slabs of rock were home to seals and cormorants. Testing the limits of his vision, the crow could make out the landscape across the channel and felt a familiar longing to fly there. His reverie was interrupted. There was something unexpected in the air, a trace of smoke. The crow swiveled his head, scanning the forest. He was flying over the low-lying center of the island, the great crater, where the rains had collected on the clay-rich soil and flooded acres of land. Curious, he angled his wings and spread his tail feathers.

He dropped through the trees into a different world. Here, the air was heavy with fungal damp. Tangled branches and the glitter of sunlight on pooled water obscured visibility. He skimmed over a horse carriage, its wheels and axles caked in mud. A second later it was lost behind him. As the crow flew through the forest, the taint of smoke became pronounced. It was the crow's fifteenth autumn. He was still agile on the wing and proud of it. He moved with grace through a maze of branches that would have confounded a younger bird, ignoring the rodents scattering among the roots, and the warnings of a blue jay. Now the smoke was all around him, a layer of blue, acrid and warm. He dipped under it. Seeing movement ahead, he alighted on a tree limb with a soft slap of feathers against the air.

Driven by curiosity, the crow had entered the part of the forest that made him tremulous with dread. Here, the old-growth trees, blanketed with moss, muffled all sound. Water dripped into hollows formed by fallen branches and roots thrust from the earth. The ground was higher than the surrounding landscape, forming an island in the swamp. A shuttered building rose out of a confusion of rooftops, casting a deep shadow. It was known as Little Eye, the Monster's prison up until the time of the forced evacuation at the war's end. That had been several years ago. The crow never knew the fate of the Monster. He knew only that the boy had lingered after the summary execution of the dwindling members of the order. The soldiers, eager to be away from this haunted place, had overlooked him in the mayhem. Whether the Monster had died, taken by the harsh winter that followed, or found some way to escape the island was impossible to know. The crow was aware that the reason he could feel badly about this was the Monster's gift of consciousness, given one day with a touch as soft as a petal.

Smoke poured from a brick furnace. The snap and hiss of burning wood sounded closer than it was. The furnace's conical shape was blackened at the top and mottled with lichen at the base. Concrete walls spread out from the foundation and disappeared under a heavy growth of deadly nightshade, a sign of a once greater industry. A pile of dead branches leaned against the chimney, a green layer on top of one much thicker and darker. Sacks and wood blocks, iron implements and mounds of shattered green glass surrounded a work area.

A girl opened a grate in the side of the furnace, unfazed by the blast of heat and a shower of sparks. Nearby, seven human-sized puppets sat knock-kneed on a wall, each wearing an animal mask. The crow was familiar with the shapes of a bird, a fox and a frog. They were a part of his world. The others he found unsettling. Staring in different directions were four disturbing amalgams of multiple creatures, with split snouts, multiple eyes and bared teeth, no less frightening because they were carved from wood. Although there was no puppeteer to be seen, the group's hands and feet twitched. A black dog lay panting before them, its tongue hanging like a ladle. The girl was as indifferent to the puppets and their fidgeting as she was to the breath of the fire.

She wore a leather apron over a ragged dress and mud-caked boots. Her tangled black hair was tied back with a strip of cloth. She worked a blowpipe through the grate into the flames, turned it for a few seconds, and then pulled it back. A globule of molten glass clung to the tip of the pipe. The crow, which had sidestepped his way along the bough, stood with head cocked, watching with a beady eye.

The girl turned, squinting against the smoke. Climbing onto a stump, she whispered to herself. With the pipe held vertically she lowered the glass through the opening of a wood mold that sat on the ground. She blew into the end of the pipe, causing steam, or smoke to pour from the mold's seams. The crow smelled burned cherry wood and felt excitement in his breast. The pipe came away on a ribbon of smoke. Resuming her whispers, the girl let it fall into the mud and stepped down. She knelt before the mold and pried the halves apart, releasing a glass form. It looked like a large moth pupa. It squirmed, a living thing of glass, as she retrieved it with tongs pulled from the belt of the apron. The crow cawed and hopped on the branch. He could not help himself. The girl paid him no mind and carried the magical thing back to the furnace, where she placed it on a cooling ledge.

What was this? The pupa had joined several other miniature writhing glass pupae. Each one was iridescent and irresistible. A beautiful prize, thought the crow. He sidled further along the bough, flapping to maintain his balance. One pupa was nearer to the edge than the others. It seemed to beckon to him, an illusion brought on by excitement no doubt. The girl had returned to the stump and now sat with her face in blackened hands, as though depleted by her work. She had shed the apron on the ground. Taking advantage of her distraction, the crow leapt and crossed the clearing with three surging wing beats. He landed on the ledge and seized the object in his beak. It clinked against the brickwork.

"No," screeched the girl, as she jumped to her feet. "Idiot bird."

The crow, a master thief, was already in the air. He flapped his wings, plunging through the trees. But from the start something was wrong. The pupa was heavier than expected and threw off his center of gravity. He misjudged his movements and twice came close to dropping the prize. The girl's angry shouts followed him, but then stopped as he shot free of the forest. A few more strokes carried him away from Little Eye. It was when he was once again in the great vault of the sky that he understood that back in the forest something had been forming in the air above the glass pupae. He understood now, the girl had been performing a summoning magic. What had he gotten himself into?

"Echo," the girl said to the air thickening in the clearing. "Echo, you will never be complete now."

The form coalescing around the glass pupae, drawing into itself a rind of forest detritus, leaves, lichen and scraps of tattered wasp's paper, answered with a voice of howling fire. "Elizabeth, undo this. Unmake me."

Elizabeth laughed. "That I cannot do. You must be whole to be sundered, and that silly crow has stolen your heart."

PICKPOCKET

THE SONGBIRDS OF NIGHTJAR ISLAND WAS A SMALLISH BOOK. MOSS lifted it from the museum display case and ran a finger over the embossed cover illustration, a thistle head bowing under the weight of a finch. Restless hands had long since worn away the gold.

He opened the book, wincing at the spine's protest. The endpapers and the title page were foxed. *For S. The emissary of dreams.*

Strange, thought Moss. He believed he was aware of the few people who played a significant role in the author's life. S was a mystery. He checked the sewn binding and found it well used but sound. When the book was held just so, it fell open to the stained impression of a plant. Deadly nightshade, *Atropa belladonna*, it grew in profusion along the walls of Brickscold Prison. Moss paused as he considered the significance of the impression. The author had made a tea from the root of the plant, ensuring a release that no authority could rescind. Moss's fingers moved through the book. Tissues covered the engravings. The raised typeface could almost be read through the fingertips.

On the other side of the display case, Mr. Tern, the Head of Collections, sighed and fidgeted with a key ring. Moss opened his eyes expecting to meet Tern's gaze, but a young woman passing several feet away distracted the man. Had the woman had been looking at Moss? She averted her eyes too soon for him to be sure. Sensing he was unobserved, Moss slipped the book into his coat and pulled out the facsimile that he had spent the past week constructing. He opened the new book and closed it with a slap.

"Did you find what you were after, Mr. Woods?" asked Tern, returning his attention to Moss. He glanced at his watch and swept his hand over his balding head as though he had lost his hat.

"Yes, thank you. There's no question that it's the signed first edition." Moss put the book in the case with care. "It's a nuisance, but the insurer was insistent that the location of the book be verified in person. I apologize for the inconvenience."

Tern shrugged. He lowered the glass lid and locked it. "Allow me to once again express our heartfelt thanks to Judge Seaforth, for his generosity in allowing the book to be displayed in the museum." The man retreated. "Now, if you'll forgive me, I have a meeting of the board."

"Of course," said Moss, smiling. Tern spun on his heel and walked away. Moss looked down the front of his coat to ensure that there were no suspicious lumps or creases. There should not be. He had spent almost as long sewing the pocket and practicing the deft movements needed to steal the book as he had on the creation of the facsimile.

The Museum of Natural History's central hall was as large as an airship hangar. Even the suspended skeleton of a right whale seemed insufficient to command the space. Opposite the entrance, a reception desk sat on a marble floor. Wall murals, sparkling with efflorescence, surrounded staircase openings, which led to the collection galleries. Few people were around due to the hour. A group of museum employees argued in whispers behind the desk. Visitors meandered through the hall or sat in chairs flipping through exhibition catalogues. No one paid attention to Moss as he paused against a pillar to rein in his excitement.

Confident that his theft would not be discovered, Moss decided to wait for the weather to clear. He had arrived an hour earlier, moments ahead of the rain, and now had a practical reason, even a responsibility, to avoid a drenching. He could not risk getting the book wet. After visiting the lavatory where he wrapped the book in cloth and transferred it to his shoulder bag, he decided to kill time with a visit to the beetle lithographs.

The Coleopterist's Society's Special Collections Room, or Beetle Room, was deep within the building. Moss turned left and followed the wall beneath a row of portraits. At the foot of a staircase, he noticed a world map affixed to a bulletin board. A sign invited visitors to insert a pin at their birthplace.

He searched for the places his life had taken him so far, a depressing exercise. For a start, he had never left the continent of

Irridia. He picked a brass pin from the tray below the map and stuck it in the City of Steps, a fading bruise on the northeastern coast of the continent. A centimeter to the north, his finger found the Chimneys Institute where as a man of twenty-two he had been an assistant professor of literature. Two centimeters above the institute and slightly to the left was Brickscold Prison where, following his brief career, he had been incarcerated for twelve years before escaping into the wilderness.

Moss stepped back, dismayed by the possibility that he would see just a tiny portion of the world during his lifetime. As a fugitive he lived in a different kind of prison, its walls now defined by a lack of official stamps, papers and passports. Depressing indeed, but one day he would break free of it, just as he had broken free of Brickscold Prison.

He climbed the stairs reworking a well-worn plan to leave the city forever, in the hold of a cargo ship. It would be a fresh start on another continent, where nobody was looking for him, and where memories would be buried under new experiences. Moss's friend Irridis had developed the ability to travel clandestinely. Irridis bore danger and privations that would finish a lesser man, things that Moss longed to test himself against. Eventually Moss came to the doors of the Beetle Room, and found them locked.

He set his bag on the floor and rattled the handles, even though he could see through the window that the room was deserted. The only source of light was an ellipse cast by a barrister's lamp. Moss was disappointed. As a boy he had been an avid collector of Buprestidae, metallic wood boring beetles. The lithographs would have to wait. As he turned to retrace his steps, he collided with a young woman in a rust-colored coat. She swept around him, head down, muttering. It was the same woman who had distracted Tern. Surprised, Moss watched her disappear down the stairs. He shook his head and took the same route at a more thoughtful pace. When he entered the central hall, he realized that he was not carrying his bag. He knew what had happened. The woman was a pickpocket. She had walked into him to create a diversion. With her back turned she had concealed the bag from his view. In a moment she had taken the book he had spent weeks planning and preparing to steal. He raced back up the steps to confirm with his eyes what he already knew in his gut.

"Think, think," he said, as he paced before the Beetle Room doors in a cold sweat. Would she have left the museum immediately? Surely she would be afraid of being seen and confronted. Unless she had seen Moss's crime, in which case she would know he would never risk publicly exposing her. It was more likely that once she realized there was nothing in the bag of apparent value, she would dispose of it. To the uneducated eye—and he had to hope she was simply an opportunist—the stolen book would appear unremarkable. Unburdened, she might stay to work the mid-day crowd, already trickling into the museum. He realized this plausibility was his only hope. If it proved true, then he had to find the abandoned bag before it was turned into the Lost and Found or discovered by a member of the museum staff.

An hour later, he stood in the museum's Hall of Time, waiting, blended into the background. He had walked through the collection galleries peering into waste bins and under benches. As he did so, he had watched for the thief. He could not shake the feeling that she had just vacated each room as he entered, that they were playing a private game in and among the oblivious crowd. Convinced that she had not dumped the bag in any of the public areas—it was early in the day and the bins were low—it occurred to him that remaining in one place might be a better way to find her. Needing a prop, he had bought a small notebook and pen from the gift shop. He had then taken up a spot in front of a mounted pterosaur skeleton with a good view of the hall.

It was now early afternoon. He was beginning to think the woman had made her escape after all. The hall rang with voices and the air was sticky with the humidity from rain-dampened clothing. Moss was alert as he sketched. He had always been poor at drawing but it was a simple and convincing role to play, the amateur naturalist with more enthusiasm than talent. It rendered him invisible. If he needed proof, it came in the form of the numerous shoves he received as visitors pressed against the velvet ropes surrounding the exhibits. Moss sketched the same skeleton three times, scanning the crowd with each upward glance. And then, she appeared, so abruptly it took him a heartbeat to recognize her.

"There you are," he said to himself. It was obvious from her direct gaze that she had seen him first. She had probably known of his whereabouts the entire time, and was now, for reasons of her own, revealing herself. He remained still, meeting her eyes through the barrier of mounted bones. She backed through the throng and vanished. Moss pretended to return to his drawing. She would show herself again, he had no doubt. He frowned as he drew, chewing the inside of his cheek. He looked up and searched the slow-moving crowd of visitors. She was not among them. He closed the notebook around the pen and put it in his coat pocket. Someone bumped his shoulder from behind. He took a deep breath before turning to see her several feet away. The strap of his shoulder bag was twisted around her hand.

"Wait," he said. "Let's work something out."

There was amusement in her brown eyes. He reached for her, but she evaded his hand. She ran, pulling the strap of the bag over her neck. Moss gave chase, pushing between people. He could sense curiosity spreading through the crowd as he pressed forward.

"It's nothing," he said, holding up his hands. "My apologies, excuse me please." He stepped over the rope that surrounded the diplodocus exhibit and, ignoring the shouts of a guard, took off down the length of the hall. He watched for her rust coat. At last he spotted her running up a staircase, his bag thumping against her backside with each stride. This was the route to the central hall and the museum's exit. The slap of the guard's boots approached. Moss plunged into the crowd of amused onlookers.

She stopped at the top of the stairs and leaned with her back against a column. Hair hung across her face in damp strands. She whipped it back over her head, smirking. Now at the bottom of the stairs, Moss understood that she was waiting, giving him time to close the gap. With a hand pressed to a stitch in his side he took the steps three at a time, conscious of the spectacle he presented.

"Wait," he called out. The woman sprinted across the marble foyer. Moss reached the top step in time to see her push through the revolving doors to the outside. Lightning lit the windows.

MASTER CROW

THE CROW LONGED FOR THE MORNING'S SERENITY BY THE TIME HE reached Absentia. The air was cold and briny. Fish flies occupied every square foot of the sky, blown in from the ocean before a curtain of fine rain. The wind was an invisible terrain, a distorted reflection of the land below. It had its own paths and obstructions, cliffs and valleys, but they were made of vortices and perilous changes in pressure. Any miscalculation or distraction from his purpose would send him plummeting. The crow's head ached from concentration and the muscles in his breast and wings cramped with every downward thrust. The foot missing a toe curled inward. Seeking relief, he let it trail, but this further destabilized his flight.

Absentia was a city of war ruins. The library's domes and cupolas, the caverns of the theatres and the opera house were home to the birds. The halls of governance and religion were the domain of bears, elk and wolves. The Monster had told him about the destruction of the zoo and how the animals had gone out into the city and terrorized the survivors of the war, and later the Purge. He could be an eloquent storyteller and had heard many things from the order of sisters in Little Eye. Though they were forbidden to speak to him, the Monster had sharp ears.

Fog drifted from the countryside into the avenues and squares. The crow was overwhelmed with a need to protect the squirming thing he carried in his beak. He struggled to understand what drew him to the city, until he realized he needed the reassurance and silence of its unmoving walls. The riot of the wild made him feel ill. The crow sensed that something followed him on the wind, leaping and running like a sprite along the calm trails between the cascading walls of air. A sibilant whisper, audible even over the rush of air, urged him toward desperation. The sound had become trapped in the three chambers of his ears, and no amount of exertion would dispel it. He was sure it was the girl's voice. The crow's sense that the pupa was somehow alive, and that he was bound to protect it, drove him forward. The magic of it held him to an unspoken obligation.

Vertigo, which had threatened to upset him for the past hour, now affected his flight. He came to within a wing beat of striking a chimney pot. Veering from the rooftop he aimed for a canal, looking for a safe place to alight. He spotted the ruins of a bridge. The road had collapsed on either side, leaving three arches in the middle of the canal to support a flat, weed-covered expanse. It was inaccessible to all but the most ambitious of predators and the weeds would provide some cover. Once the promise of landing took hold, all ambition fled. Fatigue enveloped him and he stopped flapping his wings. Gliding over the black water of the canal, he thought about dropping the pupa. He had the unsettling thought that if he did it would continue the trajectory to safety while he fluttered to his death. He swallowed it. He did not know how or why, it just happened. The pupa slid into his gullet, a fat prey.

He aimed for the middle of the approaching bridge, where a sapling had rooted in a crack. The ground was covered in leaves and clumps of grass. It would provide a cushion of sorts, a place to rest and think through the consequences of what he had done. He swooped toward it, too fast, too aggressively and misjudged the distance, hitting the sapling with his left wing. Centrifugal force whipped him around the trunk and he struck the road with one leg outstretched and his head back, beak pointed skyward. A sideways tumble snapped the bones in his left wing, as if they were no more substantial than the reeds that grew in profusion beneath the bridge.

Evening came early. He was aware of the cooing pigeons around him as he rested, feathers fluffed and his beak buried in his breast. His left wing stretched to the side at an angle that told him he would never fly again. The pupa was inside him, emanating warmth as though the heat of its creation had not dissipated. When the light dwindled to a streak in the west, the frogs in the canal began their courtships. Overhead, bats feasted on moths. Something large splashed near the rotten pilings of a nearby dock. As the crow absorbed these impressions, the nictating membrane of his eyes moved over his irises and remained. His heart slowed, and the lapping of the water against the bridge's footings soothed him. There were worse ways to die, worse places, but the thief felt that he had swindled himself nonetheless.

The moon appeared between the clouds. The crow lifted his head, surprised to hear the beginning of the dawn chorus. Already? Could he have slept? The thread of his wandering thoughts seemed unbroken, but the light was rising in the east. For the first time since the theft of the pupa, the whispering voice was no longer in his ear. It had been replaced with something else, a creak from within his body, felt as much as heard.

His drowsiness disappeared. Alarmed, he tried to fold his outstretched wings, but they would not cooperate. Instead, his pinions vibrated in the dirt as though no longer under his control. The sound that followed was the dry splintering of feather shafts and the strain of bones twisting within the constraints of his flesh. Pain and pressure grew in his wingtips, until there was a paper-like tear and slender digits emerged from beneath the skin. They flexed in the cool dawn air, pushing feathers back like a coat sleeve. The crow tried to stand but his legs had grown inadequate for the weight of his head, which had become enlarged and bulbous. He tried to caw, but it came out as a stutter of strange vocalizations. Words.

Sharp teeth bit into a tongue that fluttered in the unfamiliar cavity that was now a mouth, no longer a beak. There was a pause. He shivered against the ground, snorting dust into his nostrils. Then came the greatest pain of all as the keel in the center of his body throbbed. The bones and flesh within pushed the skin outward as if he was now an expanding bubble. Ribs twisted and stretched, riding folds of swelling muscle and ligament into new positions. The pain became too much and he succumbed to a greying of consciousness. He was no longer a crow as he watched a shower of rain wash the ashen residue of his black and white feathers into the soil. He had become something bound to the earth, something that had fingers, toes and teeth. Words? The Monster had long ago given him the ability to understand them; now it seemed the witch's magic had finished the job. She had given him the anatomy to shape them.

The crow awoke beneath the mid-morning sun to find himself carried like a human child. The man holding him waded across the canal through waist-deep water. It was warm and pleasant on the crow's dangling feet. Lily pads and seething masses of tadpoles slid over his toes. The man chose his route with care, looking for safe footing amid the submerged rubbish. When he mounted a staircase leading out of the canal, leopard frogs darted past. The man stopped and looked down at the crow's feet. There were lines around his eyes and touches of grey threaded through his red beard. His exposed skin was wind-burned.

"You seem to be short a toe." At the top of the steps the man laid the crow in the grass. It was earthy and buzzed with insects. The crow lay on his side with his new hands curled toward his chest. The rough hands of his benefactor massaged his legs and arms. As he worked, the man whistled. After a while, the crow's muscles loosened, and he sobbed into the grass.

When he awoke for the second time, sensation had returned to his hands. The pupa was on his mind, the residue of a dream. He imagined it as transparent green, like the water of the canal. He felt it turn within him, a compass needle oriented to the direction he had flown from, to Little Eye. One by one, he opened his fingers and the image of the pupa receded. He became distracted by the details of his new digits, knuckles, fingerprints and nails. He opened the last finger and panicked. The crow scrambled to his feet, his eyes screwed shut. He stood thus for a few seconds and then opened one eye, and then the other. He lifted an arm and wiggled his fingers.

He was clothed. The outstretched arm was enclosed in a green jacket sleeve, with an embroidered cuff. Looking down, he saw boots, pants, and a rough sweater. The jacket extended to his knees, had two rows of brass buttons, and was embroidered in painstaking detail with gold thread and tiny sequins on green velvet. All in all, thought the crow, it was bloody marvelous.

"I'm sorry about the clothes, Master Crow. It was all I could find that'd fit you. I dug them out of an old theatre wardrobe in a building back along the road a bit. They're not too musty I hope? At least, they weren't completely eaten by moths." The man who had carried him from the bridge sat on a wooden chair a few feet away. His voice was deep and unhurried, melancholy but not unkind.

"A theatre?" Master Crow's voice was hoarse.

"The building was a theatre before the war. It used to have beautiful murals." The man rubbed his scruffy chin. "I think that the clothes belonged to a monkey in one of the shows."

"A monkey." Master Crow thought about this. "What is a monkey?"

"A monkey in a production," said the man, ducking the question. "Yes, I'm sure of it. Nothing to be ashamed of."

"I'm not ashamed. They are very fine." Master Crow smoothed the coat against his sides. He smiled. It was a very unusual sensation.

"Indeed they are." The man fixed Master Crow with a curious gaze, turning a large ruby ring on his finger. "Now Master Crow, where are you from?"

Master Crow watched the swallows flitting over the water. The bridge sat in the shimmering autumn heat with mallards gliding on the oily eddies between the arches. Master Crow, yes, that would do. He must have a name if he was going to talk to people. He was pleased.

"Here, and there." Master Crow indicated the sky. "Who are you?"

"My name is John Machine. I'm from the City of Steps. It's a long way from here. I haven't been home for a few months." He smiled, without humor. "Have you heard of it, the City of Steps? It's a very old city, several days south of here. It sits on the coast of the Irridian Sea."

"Yes," lied Master Crow. There was no point being thought provincial. The questions made him uncomfortable.

"I'm looking for an old black carriage. Things have grown up so much since I was last here. I barely recognize the place now. Such a thing would stand out on Nightjar Island. Have you seen anything like that?"

"Yes!" Master Crow remembered his flight through the forest. "It was in the same place that I saw the girl and some odd creatures wearing animal masks."

"Oh?" John stiffened. He raised his eyebrows, which revealed a pink scar at his temple. "Where?"

"And a nasty-looking dog with a long tongue."

"Where?" John Machine's tone had become pointed.

"In the forest." Master Crow shrugged.

The man sat forward, twisting the ring. "The forest covers fully two thirds of this island, my little friend. I would appreciate it if you could be just a little more specific."

"In the great crater in the middle of the island, quite far from here. Is that specific enough?"

John laughed, settling back. "I can't decide if you are guileless or just a sarcastic little prick. What was she doing, this girl?"

"Magic."

The man considered this. "What kind of magic?"

"Making glass things, living things. Things that change things."

"What do you mean?"

"Pupae blown from glass, brought to life with her breath." Master Crow shrugged. "I stole one."

"You stole one of these pupae?"

"Yes."

"That explains a lot." John Machine looked him up and down. "Can I look at it?"

"I swallowed it." Master Crow looked at the ground and indicated his body with his hands. "Then this."

"I saw," said John, not without sympathy. "It's quite a predicament you find yourself in."

"Yes." Master Crow's eyes grew wide. "You're not supposed to be here. It's forbidden. The Purge."

"Well," said John after a long pause, "I suppose that's true, if one chooses to recognize a certain authority, but you see, I am a collector. I don't feel it's right for one person to tell another where they can go, or not. I find things for people, special things that I can only get here on Nightjar Island. If I didn't find them, they would be lost forever. That's why I want to go to the place called Little Eye. I think I might have some luck there. I did once. That's where you saw the witch, isn't it?"

Master Crow swallowed hard, and nodded. In truth, he wished he had not mentioned the girl, or her companions. A knot of mistrust had formed in his belly, despite the apparent kindnesses John Machine had shown him so far.

John Machine looked into Master Crow's eyes and then glanced away as though he had come to a decision. He slapped his still-damp knees and rose to his feet. "I have to go. I daresay you had better not follow. If you stole from who I think you stole from, well, let's just say she's not a forgiving type." He pulled a dusty pack over his shoulder and walked away without another word. In a moment he would disappear between two bombed-out buildings.

"John Machine," shouted Master Crow in a high voice. "What should I do?"

John's voice floated back. "Find a woman named May. If you're lucky, she'll help you. And look for some new clothes. You've grown three inches since we started taking. Until we meet again, Master Crow."

Master Crow sat down on a piece of machinery protruding from the ground and put his hand over his stomach where the pupa moved. What now?

Half an hour passed. Hunger overtook his thoughts. He walked to the edge of the canal. In the water below, minnows darted through the weeds. Below them, a carp drifted with lazy gestures. The frogs had returned to the steps to warm themselves in the sun. He stared at his reflection. It would take some getting used to. Everything seemed to have a place except him. He looked into the sky, but that was no longer his home. He flapped his arms. What did this new body eat? What could it do? It seemed cruelly limited. It occurred to him then that he had three benefactors. The Monster had given him the gift of consciousness, the witch the gift of a body, and John Machine the gift of a name. A sick wave spread through his stomach as he remembered his earlier thought of how men and monsters had agency over things by giving them names.

Master Crow walked, surprised that his head did not bob. His feet made impressions in the earth still damp from the overnight rain. The ground was his home now and he had made his first marks on it. Crouching down, he grabbed a frog from the stairs before it could escape, and swallowed it whole.

LAMB'S MILK

THE STORM MOVED INLAND FROM THE IRRIDIAN SEA TURNING THE sky a dirty yellow. Thunder came through Moss's soles and for a moment he was taken back to the day twenty-five years earlier when Memoria had fallen from the seawall. A flash of lightning brought him back to the present. Black walnut trees swayed, littering the grass with leaves. Moss swore. The stolen bag would not repel the rain for long.

From the vantage point of the museum's entrance he watched the woman run down a hill in the direction of Leech Lane where coffee houses and bookshops were crowded and bleached to a common hue. Behind Leech Lane lay Hellbender Fields with its historic mansions and lush gardens. The City of Steps' smoke-veiled northern reaches faded into monochrome undulations. She slowed, turned away from Leech Lane, and instead followed the natural curve of the ground toward a ravine. Seeing an opportunity, Moss followed. The vegetation would slow her. He would be able to collar her out of public view.

The rain intensified. He splashed across the lawn shielding his eyes with a forearm. His glasses fogged and he ran almost blind as he tried to thumb the lenses clear with his shirttail. When he pressed them to his nose, he was startled to see the woman watching him from the edge of the ravine. Her breathing was rapid, but she bolted when he came within shouting distance.

Moss entered the ravine with trepidation, following an animal track. Stepping over roots, he cursed the fact that he had left his gun at home. The path soon became a washed-out bed of loose stones. He slid down a decline, snatching at branches. They ripped through his palms leaving him with hands full of leaves that smelled of decay. He hit the bottom of the slide with a spine-jarring impact.

Lightheaded, he stood astride a rill, staring into the mouth of a drainage tunnel. A brick opening obscured by vines left a keyhole-shaped entry point that was impossible to see beyond. Moments ahead of him, the woman had left cloudy footprints in the streambed. He caught his breath, resting his hands on his knees, and tried to recall what else was in the bag besides the book. There was a newspaper, an empty sinispore bottle, an assortment of pens and pencils, an eraser, a notebook, and some cigar cards illustrated with various fish that had caught his fancy in the market at the Cloth Hall. With renewed anger he plunged into the tunnel.

A few strides took him beyond the reach of daylight. As his eyes adjusted he became aware of a glow. It revealed slimy cobbles and trash. Rot burned in his nostrils. The sound of the rain faded, replaced by his breathing and the trickle of the stream. The light, he soon discovered, came from a candle sitting beside his bag on a makeshift table. The woman watched him from the shadows. Moss snatched the bag. The weight was wrong.

"Where is it?" he asked. His ears whined. Tinnitus flared when he was angry, a consequence of a childhood in the ship-breaking yards. The woman stepped forward, ringed fingers twirling hair that hung in rat-tails. Her lips were tinged plum from the cool air. Candlelight distorted her beauty with liquid shadows.

"Don't make this difficult for yourself," she said, meeting his eyes. She followed this with a burst of phrases in an unfamiliar language and stepped to the side. There was movement nearby. *So, an accomplice*, thought Moss.

The man who stepped forward was tall, maybe seven feet. He wore a beaver top hat that came close to scraping the roof of the tunnel. A black lace veil covered his face. A coat with an ermine collar hid the contours of his body. The only visible skin was on his large, scarred hands. Faded indigo tattoos crisscrossed his knuckles. The fingers ended at the second joint, the head of the phalanges. The man's sleeves, also trimmed with fur, were matted with the pulp and mucus-like secretions of the tunnel walls. Moss did not see a gun, but guessed that one was hidden in the folds of the disgusting coat. The man moved his left arm and *The Songbirds of Nightjar Island* slid out of the sleeve into his hand.

"My book," said Moss. He had decided on reasonable calm and tried not to be distracted by the woman, who had moved behind him.

"Your book?" asked the man. The voice was sonorous and accented. "I think we can at least agree," he cleared his throat, "that it's not your book."

"What, it's yours now because she stole it from me?" asked Moss.

"You stole it from the museum. And, unless I am misinformed," said the man, "the judge who donated it stole it from the infamous ornithologist and serial murderer Franklin Box. It was Franklin's book."

"It was, once." Moss saw no point in lying. "It was his personal copy."

"He wrote but one book during his career, did he not? But what a book, do you agree?" The man swayed, making Moss think of the walnut trees outside of the museum.

Moss shook his head. "I'm no expert."

"*The Songbirds of Nightjar Island* was a masterpiece of scholarship. It would have made him a household name, at least among ornithologists. But he murdered and dismembered several prostitutes over the course of his career. A thing like that can cast a long shadow on an academic career. Many of those women were endeared to the Red Lamprey."

"You seem well informed," said Moss.

The other man shrugged. "Judge Seaforth, the same man who sent you up, understood the book's importance. It had value as a work of scholarship, but it came with quite a story attached. Tainted by association, a conversation piece. He had it confiscated on the day Box was chained and sent to prison. Franklin had been in Brickscold for what, twelve years when you met him? And then he told you his unfortunate story. That very day, you promised him you would steal it back. You would exact a small, but sweet, measure of vengeance for you both."

"How do you know all this?" Moss's voice was thick with incredulity.

"One knows things," said the man. After a moment, he added, "People call me Lamb." He set the book on the table with care, touching the corner to the wood and then laying it flat. He extended his right hand. The backs of the fingers were carapaced with rings, rubies set in dull gold. Taken off guard, Moss thought he was meant to shake hands but Lamb opened his stubbed fingers and something fell onto the table. It was a tarnished silver pendant, a running fox, with filthy red string threaded through its curled tail. The hair on Moss's arms rose.

"Respect is important," said Lamb. "It's the only thing we have to prevent us from tearing each other apart like animals, no?" He waved at the book. "Take it. I've no use for books. It was simply to draw you here." Moss lifted his eyes from the pendant.

"Please," said Lamb. Moss returned the book to his bag.

"Now then, Mr. Moss, respecting your time and mine, let's get to business."

"I don't have any business with you," said Moss.

"But I have business with you. Do you know who I am?"

"I have an idea. You said your name was Lamb."

"Yes, they call me Lamb, but I meant in a broader sense." He clasped his hands behind his back, straining the buttons down the front of his coat.

"I know who you are," said Moss.

"Now, you know who I am, and I know who you are. So when I say we have business, I don't expect you to waste my time with your—" Lamb hesitated, "obfuscation."

Moss was angry and afraid. Now that he had the book, he could run, but somehow these people knew him, knew how and where to find him. How long had they been watching him? There was no choice but to listen. He had first become aware of Lamb in prison. Lamb was one of those storied creatures of the underworld that everyone whispered about but few had seen. He was nicknamed partly as a reference to the birth defect that had left him with tiny bead-like eyes and a face elongated like a sheep's. There was also irony in the name. Lamb was a lion, and not to be trifled with. He was rumored to be an assassin for the Red Lamprey.

Lamb continued. "I'm a believer in straight talk, Mr. Moss, so I won't dance around the issue. We must discuss your obligation." The man pointed to the fox.

"My obligation?" This was not the first time Moss had seen the pendant.

"You know what that is?"

"Where did you get it?" Moss was far from sure he wanted to hear the answer.

"I've carried it in my pocket for many, many years," said Lamb. "As a reminder." He felt around the table, picked it up and settled it in his palm. He turned it with practiced ease, like a gambler with a worn charm. It vanished into his sleeve. "It belonged to a little girl. You knew her by the name of Memoria. In fact, you gave her this as a gift, didn't you? You were in love with her."

"Who told you that?" asked Moss. The cicada-like sound in his head threatened to split his skull.

"I didn't get the little fox from Memoria," said Lamb, as though he had not heard Moss. "I got it from a man who owes me a large sum of money. A man named John Machine."

"I can't see what this has to do with me," said Moss. "Memoria is dead and I haven't seen John since she died."

"Let me be clear. She did not die; she did not drown. It was a fluke, but she survived the ordeal."

"I've thought about her fall nearly every day since it happened," said Moss. "The ocean was wild. I see no way she could have survived."

"I know for a fact that she did so. She was caught up in the chain of an old, unexploded mine. It buoyed her up, even though she was unconscious. Later, the low tide deposited her on the mudflats. That's where the mudlarks found her, more dead than alive. I can't imagine that she would have lasted long if they hadn't. So, make no mistake, Memoria is still alive now, a grown woman obviously. But nobody seems to know where she's gone and there's the rub. I desire to find her, as soon as possible."

"Why?" Moss's mind raced as he tried to process the implications of what he was hearing. Lamb's swaying ceased.

"When I saw her beauty, the things she could do, I knew without question that she was that most exquisite of beings. A true super-natural being, a light, a cleansing spirit, that could lift me from the dross of this world." His voice dropped to a growl. "She's my property. I bought her from John Machine and he cheated me."

"What do you want from me?" asked Moss, sickened by Lamb's delusions.

"It's simple. I want you to find her. You know her nature; the places she is likely to frequent."

"That's unreasonable. I knew her as child."

"You will do this discreetly, and once you have verified her where-abouts you will report it immediately."

"And why the hell would I do that?"

"Because if you do not, I will see that you are sent back to Brickscold Prison for the rest of your life. I have many associates inside its walls, not all of them inmates. It would not be an easy time, Moss." The man chuckled, but the resolve underlying the threat was unmistakable. "Your task, when the time comes, is to provide the information to Oliver Taxali, the antiquarian book dealer. You know this man? I am told you do. He will see it safely to me. This is Oliver's obligation."

Moss opened his mouth to protest, when something stung his neck. He slapped at the spot and felt his hand come away wet and already numbing.

"We are finished talking now. You will speak of this conversation to nobody. I hope it will not be necessary for us to meet again, but do not make the error of thinking you can leave your obligation unfulfilled. Enjoy your book." Lamb walked into the darkness of the tunnel.

Moss turned to see the woman backing toward the tunnel entrance. In her hand was an apparatus consisting of a needle and a deflating rubber bulb. A pressurized stream of milky fluid sprayed toward the ground, turned to a dribble, and stopped. The tunnel darkened. Moss's knees buckled. He dropped to a squat and mumbled an entreaty to the woman now blurred in front of him. She spoke to him in a reassuring tone, but the words were jumbled. He lifted his hands and they flailed in unexpected directions. He spoke but the words were wooden blocks in his mouth.

Moss opened his eyes in a strange bed. The pillow smelled of dust and cinnamon. Something warm and heavy lay across his feet. He propped himself on an elbow and looked down the length of his naked body. A purring cat looked back with glowing, impassive eyes. Moonlight fell through a skylight, washing the scene in blue. The room was just large enough to contain the bed. His weight tilted toward the center where the woman who had stolen his bag lay, also naked, snoring gently. Her body was covered in scrolling tattoos, fantastical creatures: demons, trolls and fairies. Realizing his stare had lingered, Moss turned away, head swaying as though it contained an unbalanced brick. A flick of his foot sent the cat on its way. Holding his breath, he rolled out of the bed.

He found his stiff clothes hanging on a wooden drying rack in the adjacent room. They smelled faintly of puke. His bag, with the book in place, lay between the legs of a chair. A kerosene lamp burned low on a kitchen table where three smeared glasses sat amid empty liquor bottles and spoons. He picked up a glass and smelled it. Absinthe. It was then that he noticed the tattoo on the inside of his wrist, a coiled red lamprey eel. He touched the center of the design, a yawning mouth filled with tiny teeth. An elongated body spiraled counter clockwise. Raw skin surrounded the tattoo. Of all the indignities that Moss had experienced in the past few hours, this was the most infuriating. He started for the bedroom door, but stopped after two steps. Memoria was alive. Whatever had happened here, however unsettling, was irrelevant before this possibility. He needed to sort his head out, privately.

Moss dressed, jamming his arms into the sleeves of his shirt, haphazardly buttoning the front. He pulled on his pants and stuck his bare feet into muddy shoes, not wanting to waste time looking for socks. Once he had fastened his coat and pulled the bag strap over his head, he checked the bedroom. The woman was still asleep, with the cat nestled into the small of her back. He pulled the door shut, trying to ignore the raw tattoo on his forearm. Before leaving, he piled kitchen chairs in the doorway and stole her shoes.

When he pulled the outside door open, the kerosene lamp fluttered. He stepped onto the landing of a wooden staircase. The apartment was located on a mezzanine overlooking a large interior space. Moonlight, filtered through a row of filthy skylights, revealed a room almost as large as the central hall in the Museum of Natural History. Although it was difficult to differentiate the jumble of objects spread out below, Moss thought that he could make out the form of an elephant. Shaking his head in wonderment, he threw the shoes as far as he could.

METEORITES AND MOTHS

MOSS LEFT THE BUILDING AND FOLLOWED A LINE OF LINDEN TREES to a nearby street. Concealed in shadow he looked back at the Cloth Hall, a landmark building that faced the sea. It was miles from the Museum of Natural History. During the day it served as a busy market, but at night it was less hospitable. Three men in butcher's aprons smoked below an entrance arch. Fresh fish were being unloaded from a truck some distance away, the clanking of the activity reaching Moss's ears with a dreamlike lag. Seeing the building did not stimulate any memories of the past few hours. Somehow the woman had brought him across the city. The third glass suggested she had help.

Leaving the building had felt like an escape, despite there being no sign that he was being held. After descending the stairs from the mezzanine apartment, Moss had navigated through the attic of the Cloth Hall, winding through centuries of clutter. The sound of running water and a cold glow from elsewhere in the room had piqued his curiosity, but there had been no time to investigate. His purpose had been to get out of the building. The woman could have awoken at any time and he was too disoriented by the narcotic to confront her. Another time, he promised himself. Instinct had led him to a stairwell.

With his back to a tree, Moss searched his bag. Most of his possessions were there, but somebody had emptied his wallet. With no money for a taxi he had little choice but to walk. He set off, cold and angry, through the empty streets. At dawn he reached Judge Seaforth's apartment house, where he had held a live-in position for the previous three months. Passing through the foyer he was conscious of every creak in the ancient wood floor. It was Moss's habit to conceal his activities and he did not want his arrival noticed.

34

Overcome with tiredness, no doubt another lingering effect of the drug he had been given, he climbed the main staircase, forcing each step. At the top landing, he dug out his key and entered the judge's apartment. He closed the door with care, as the familiar smell of books and antique furniture enveloped him. A grandfather clock ticked, but the apartment was otherwise silent. Without removing his shoes and coat he passed through the richly appointed suite to the servant's room in the back. He collapsed on the bed amid a thrumming of springs. Ten dreamless hours later he woke thinking someone had whispered his name, but it was only the distant vibration of an airship's propellers that seemed to recede forever.

From the warmth of the bed he listened to the rain against the window. As he often did upon waking, he lay still, reconstructing the recent past from memory. Three months. It seemed much longer ago that he had responded to an advertisement in the paper for the position of a live-in academic instructor. He had appeared at the office of Seaforth's solicitor with a secondhand briefcase filled with false references. He had not expected to be hired. It was curiosity that motivated him. He wanted to know more about the man who had sent him to prison on circumstantial evidence. The solicitor made no attempt to disguise his impatience. He conducted the interview in a harried manner, giving the impression that the task was a waste of his time. He might also have been a little drunk. He had seemed to have an almost conspiratorial willingness to be taken in by Moss's act of convivial good manners and cardboard backstory. To his surprise, and dismay, Moss had left the interview with a contract, the key to Seaforth's apartment and an advance on his salary. During a contemplative drink or two in a nearby bar, Moss's determination to drop the key into a public toilet gave way to a dangerous plan. Later that night, Moss let himself into the empty apartment.

The solicitor had told Moss to settle himself in preparation for the family's eventual return from their country estate. From the three rooms put at his disposal he had picked a former maid's bedchamber. It was smaller than his prison cell. With the family absent, he could have slept in Seaforth's large bed, or even the children's. Instead, he preferred the close walls and the firm mattress of the domestic's room. He had not intended to stay. The plan had been to explore the apartment, search for Franklin Box's book and perhaps empty a bottle of brandy or two in the process. It was an opportunity to fulfill his far-fetched promise to Box and indulge in a bit of childish mischief. But there had been no sign of the book. One morning he looked in the mirror at his gaunt, bearded face and realized that he looked nothing like the man who had sat in Judge Seaforth's courtroom. Moss's plan sprouted a new branch. He would stay, play the role he had taken on, and eventually learn the whereabouts of *The Songbirds of Nightjar Island*. Time passed. Moss became comfortable in the apartment, and then, three weeks ago he had come across the museum's Deed of Gift in the middle drawer of Seaforth's dressing table.

Moss's thoughts also led him to the events of the previous day. He rested in the furrow of the bed, with a single-action revolver tucked under the blanket near his thigh. He tried to piece events together, beginning at the point when he had stolen the book, but his memories were confused, their sequence untethered. The drug the woman had injected into him had been pharmaceutical grade. She could have lopped off a limb and he would have been none the wiser. He lifted his arm. The muscles beneath the tattoo rippled as he unfurled his fingers. *Not what I would have chosen*, he thought. He let it fall and squinted in the dust produced from the mattress.

The Red Lamprey. John Machine had been a member. Lamb's comments confirmed what Memoria had somehow known many years ago. Moss sat up as a realization struck him. Lamb must have been the man that John Machine had taken Memoria to see, the cause of the argument on the seawall. Moss cursed himself for not picking up on what should have been obvious from the moment Lamb showed him the fox. Memoria said that John had taken her to see a man who had spoken to her through a woven screen. He had remained hidden but at the end of the conversation put his eye to the weave. Its gaze had disturbed her. And what about Memoria? Could Lamb be right? Moss had thought of nothing else during his long walk from the Cloth Hall.

The memory of her fall, though relived countless times, had lost none of its horror. It seemed impossible that she could have survived. How many times in his fantasies had he imagined seeing her? The sea had been too powerful, too cold, that day. The submerged rocks had been like giant molars. Yet it was clear that Lamb believed what he said. Why else would he threaten Moss in person? Producing the fox had been a skilled manipulation. Lamb knew the gesture would be more powerful than words. Memoria had never known her real birthday. So they had made one up, September 7. Moss had given her the fox to mark the day. It had a flaw in the silver, where the eye should have been. In the tunnel Moss had noticed this detail immediately, even though he had not thought of it in years. Still, the fox's reappearance was hardly proof that she was alive. Moss had always wondered what John had palmed that day. Now he knew. The fox had broken free in the struggle on the seawall. Lamb had not been interested in providing proof. His intention had been to catapult Moss back in time, where emotion was the most intense, to clear his mind of all else.

It worked. He wanted to believe. The sadness of Memoria's death was a burden he had carried for years. The thought of that intelligent, mischievous child missing out on life was a heavy weight. He berated himself for not being able to fend off John long enough to prevent the accident. Everything had happened too quickly. Now, he felt foolish for being manipulated by Lamb, who had found his weakness. Moss had never been able to let Memoria go. His inability to change the events of that day had wounded him in a way that no amount of rationalizing could heal. He fell back on the bed. Maybe now there was a chance to change that.

Facing a cooler part of the pillow, Moss wished he had a hit of sinispore. It would have sharpened his thinking. He had started using the drug in prison to focus his mind on study, and a wall of defense against the tedium. Once it took hold it proved a tenacious foe to dislodge. Sinispore would have taken the edge off his nerves, but the thought of leaving the apartment to find it was a strong deterrent. He had taken the last of his supply to amp his clarity for the theft at the museum. Leaving Seaforth's apartment required him to be an impersonator. He had trained himself to adopt the character of Joseph Woods, but it took concentration. The craving for sinispore was perilous and distracting. It compromised his ability to watch the critical details. In a fragmented state of mind, a casual glance on the street felt like an interrogation. A casual encounter with the police could be catastrophic. Ironically, the effects of the sinispore would help him to fall back into the role of unassuming Joseph, but he had none. Moss closed his eyes and drifted into a restless sleep.

Moss woke late in the afternoon surprised to find himself feeling somewhat restored. The effects of the woman's drug had retreated from his muscles and joints. He cast the blankets aside and sat forward on the edge of the mattress. He was distressed at the thought that Lamb might have others looking for Memoria as well. A man like Lamb would have many contacts and numerous associates who could access places and produce results where others could not. If there was truth in Lamb's words and Memoria was alive, Moss had to find her first. The nature of Lamb's obsession was not clear, but it was hard to imagine it would end happily for Memoria. Watching the stirring drapes over the window, Moss was vexed, knowing that the urgency he felt was what Lamb intended.

He looked at the aged wristwatch he had taken to wearing. It had once belonged to the real Joseph Woods. From it, Moss had crafted his ruse. He had found the watch a day before his interview with the solicitor, pawing through a box of clutter at the flea market in the Cloth Hall. Its faint inscription had led him, by way of the Hall of Records, to an overgrown plot in Hellbender Cemetery. There, on the steps of a small mausoleum, he had written an imaginary biography for Joseph Woods in his notebook, and committed it to memory. From that point on, Lumsden Moss, escaped convict, had become Joseph Woods, an introverted literary scholar who supported himself as a private instructor. The reflection in the watch crystal revealed that Moss had slipped out of character. His beard was untrimmed and his tangled hair needed to be washed. He thought about taking a shower but settled on washing his hands and face instead. In the bathroom he let tepid water pool in his fingers. He poured it over his head and leaned over the drain as it streamed from his face. The grandfather clock ticked. He knew what he had to do. He had known since he had opened his eyes.

Moss had not visited the house on Fleurent Drain since his escape from Brickscold. Regardless, he decided that this was where he would begin his search for Memoria. However remote, a chance existed that she might have come back to the house at some point in the intervening years. From a walkway he considered the familiar shapes, the peaks and chimneys, the ink-black shadow of the house on the water. Though the house was technically still the property of John Machine, a lawyer paid its taxes from account set up by Moss's mother. John had never been declared dead.

The canal was just as he had remembered, water choked with lilies, and air that vibrated with a ceaseless amphibian chorus. From a distance, the house seemed in reasonable condition, considering that it had sat empty for years. The shutters were intact. The roof was only missing a few tiles. Moss's mother had named the house Insomnia—she had found no rest there. The house's real name, Fleurent, was still legible on the pillars that Moss had passed through to enter the property.

Moss came to the end of the walkway and picked his way through the untended garden to the house. A welcome breeze stirred the air as he knocked on the door. He waited, but there was no response. It was not all pantomime for any observers that might happen by. He half expected squatters. Jiggling the handle, he found it locked. The key had been lost years ago. Turning, he looked out at the yard where a column of insects, illuminated in the setting sun, swirled above the weeds. The first bats of the evening made crazy stitches over the canal.

At the back of the house Moss forced his way through an overgrown forsythia bush to a bay window. Years of neglect had left the glass murky. He cleaned a patch with his shirt cuff, dampened with saliva, until he could see a room on the other side. It was lit a watery green by the last of the sun's rays. He could make out a long table covered with books. Curious, Moss worked himself between the branches and the window, hoping for a clearer view through the next pane. Instead he found the glass broken. It looked as though it been that way for some time. Dirt and mildew had accumulated along the cracks, the putty had fallen away, and the sill on the other side was weathered. A dagger of glass pulled easily away from the frame. He set it on the ground and tried another. Soon he had cleared an opening large enough to crawl through. Moments later, he stood in the parlor, feeling like an intruder in his childhood home. It was the room where many years ago he had found his mother lying on her side on a couch, still holding a tea towel, its corner dipped in arsenic.

"Hello?" His voice rang in the empty room. As before, there was no answer. He walked to the antique dining table where his mother had once sat to do the household accounts, and the secret accounts she maintained for John. Her chair was pushed against the wall. He sat on it, taking comfort in its contours as he looked around. Somebody had been using the room, recently. The books, stacked haphazardly on the table and floor, were relatively free of dust. Rolled charts and maps leaned against the walls. Moss stood and walked around the table to where a large map had been laid out. Its corners were prevented from curling by the same large trilobites that his mother had used for paperweights, a rare and inexplicable gift from John. Moss examined the map of Nightjar Island. It was hand-labeled and difficult to read in the failing light. The abandoned city of Absentia followed a section of the coast and had been hand-annotated in pencil. The interior of the island was relatively unmarked, an expanse of stained yellow paper broken by lines meant to indicate forest. "Here be monsters," said Moss. He picked a book at random from a nearby stack. Its subject was celestial impacts, as was the one beneath it, and the one beneath that. He shook his head, perplexed.

Moss left the room and entered the hall. It led to a foyer and a staircase. Forgotten details jumped out at him, the long ornate carpet with a bald path down the center, a painting of the City of Steps from the vantage point of the sea, and a storybook mouse-hole in the wainscoting. He was about to look into the dining room where he had eaten countless meals, when he heard a sound like rustling paper from the top floor.

"Is someone there?" His voice was flat in the dead air. The sound was repeated. Moss climbed the stairs. His feet remembered and avoided the worst of the creaky steps. At the top he followed the noise to a door at the end of the corridor. He rapped on the wood. When there was no answer he opened the door and stepped into the room.

Inside, he was greeted by fluttering wings as Luna moths settled on his clothing. Trays of black walnut leaves were spread on a table beneath a shuttered window. Under the leaves lay the cocoons of *Actias luna*. Several moths had recently emerged. Amazed, he was tempted to feel their quivering wings but knew better. Instead, he unlatched and pushed out the shutters. The sound of a thousand trilling frogs filled the room. Sensing their freedom, the moths flew into the evening and vanished from sight. Moss took a glass atomizer from the window ledge and misted the trays of leaves. His hand was trembling. Raising Luna moths had been Memoria's hobby as a child. When he was finished spraying the leaves he returned the bottle and looked down at the canal. A strange figure stood at the edge looking into the water where pulsing fireflies and bats skimmed the surface. Moss pulled back far enough that he could watch without being observed. It took him a moment to realize that what he was seeing was a girl sitting on the back of an enormous black dog. After a few minutes she meandered along the canal wall and vanished among the weeds.

THE MAN WITH THE GLASS PIN

MOSS PULLED AN OVERSIZED ATLAS FROM A SHELF IN TAXALI'S secondhand bookshop and thumped it down on a table. The shop assistant at the front desk shot him a caustic look, seemed about to speak, but then returned to counting money. An untidy stack of similar volumes sat to Moss's left. Most had damaged bindings and loose leaves. Some had ship's names printed on the covers and were filled with marginalia describing things like water depth and cartographic coordinates. He opened the cover and felt the tickle of leather dust in his nose. The strange child he had seen the previous evening occupied his thoughts, and he was unable to pick which book he wanted to buy. He turned the pages without registering their content.

She was gone by the time he had made his way back through the house. He had lingered at the canal's edge until the sky was dark and the moon lit the water. He had followed in the direction he thought the girl had gone, but found only footprints. He gave up when the darkness made it impossible to see any additional evidence.

The presence of the Luna moths was a far more compelling sign that Memoria might be alive than the fox pendant had been. He tried to imagine a world that once again included Memoria, but could not feel the reality of it. What he believed about Memoria and his role in her death was a scar on his mind. And then there was the girl and her dog. What was he to make of this severe straight-backed child, so unlike the young Memoria, glimpsed for a few seconds in poor light? Why had she been alone near the abandoned house late in the evening? Moss's thoughts had been circular for hours, with little to build upon.

"He's not coming down," said the clerk, whose name was Croaker. "It was half past five when he came in. Right langered he was. He won't be in a fit state until this afternoon, and then he'll just want the company of his bloody parrot. You're shite out of luck, my friend."

"I just came for a book," said Moss, not looking up.

"Oh, my mistake, yeah," said Croaker, rolling his eyes.

Moss sighed, and slumped into an armchair that was blanketed in cat hair. The book was heavy in his lap. He was damned edgy. His left eye felt as though there was a grain of sand under the upper lid. No amount of rubbing would dislodge it. A muscle twitched under his right eye, the result of lying awake for most of the night. Other than Moss, the bookshop was empty of customers. He had arrived early enough to watch Croaker unlock the door and follow him in. He preferred Taxali's bookshop to Seaforth's apartment. Taxali's book-crowded rooms were less imposing than his employer's. They were smaller, and the jammed shelves absorbed sound. He felt at home among the piled books, where a mottled cat named Mouse patrolled in an unhurried fashion. Judge Seaforth detested cats. Moss took grim satisfaction in laying his cat-hair-covered coat across the purple velvet of the man's settee. He drummed his fingers on the chair arm. Exasperated, he closed the atlas, rubbed his eyes again. He chose another atlas he had set aside earlier.

He approached the cluttered counter. Annoyed, Croaker emerged like a moray eel from around the reef of an antique cash register. When he saw the book that Moss held, his pupils sharpened.

"Ahhh, a first edition of *The Golden World Traveler*," he said. "I wasn't aware we had it. You do know that it was published pre-war, I suppose?"

"Yes," said Moss. His stomach grumbled. He was anxious to leave. "Do you have a bag? It's raining."

"Mm." The man fished beneath the counter while Moss looked at the shelves wedged with books behind him. The old joke was that the books held the building up. Remove them, and it would collapse. Behind Moss, the shop door opened allowing in a gust of damp air and the hiss of rain that had come overnight. The cat, Mouse, which Moss had not noticed, stirred on the counter near his hand.

"It's just that many of the place names on the map of Nightjar Island will be incorrect," said the shop assistant, taking the book from Moss's hands. Moss was more interested in the older names than those imposed by the surveyors that had followed the military withdrawal. The name changes had been salt in the wounds to those who had been evicted from their homes. Moss had decided not to remove the books and charts from Fleurent Drain, and risk startling Memoria, if indeed she was the one using them. In buying an atlas, Moss hoped to glean some clue to the intruder's interest in the place.

"I understand, thank you." Moss watched the man as he fussed. Croaker had been correct in his assumption. Moss had hoped to see Oliver. It was not unusual for the man to crawl home at dawn. He was an inveterate womanizer. Moss had hoped to encounter him before he staggered to bed. He had some pointed questions about Oliver's connection to Lamb. Now that Oliver had made it to his bed, he would be comatose for hours.

Croaker opened the cover of the book and inserted a bookmark, thumbing through the pages as he did so. His eyes widened. "Look, I rest my case, Nightjar Island is still pictured as it was before access was forbidden. See all the little roads and towns, so pretty. I'm sure that the island's not so pretty now. Lovely endpapers though, and you just don't see typographic decisions like this any more. A lost art really." He ran his fingers along the edges of the book boards. "I'm afraid this won't be a great deal of use to you. Are you sure I can't interest you in something, ah, more practical?" He closed the book. A puff of air ruffled the cat's fur.

"I'm fine with this," said Moss, and passed the man a crumpled bill. With his lips pursed, Croaker slid the book into the bag with his ink-stained hand. He shoved it at Moss.

"Well there you are then. I certainly hope you appreciate it." Moss took the book, shaking his head. He had just turned away when he felt a touch on his arm. A heavy man in a camel overcoat swept around him and grasped his hand before Moss could react.

"Gale. My name is J. Hart Gale. Unless I've made an unpardonable error, you're the teacher hired by Habich Seaforth. Yes, no?" The man looked Moss up and down. His watery, pink eyes were surrounded with folds as soft as petals. A small mouth, nested in a full salt and pepper beard, was filled with crooked teeth.

"Hired by his solicitor actually, but yes, that's right," said Moss. "I work for Judge Seaforth."

"I see you've bought an atlas! Is it for the children?" Gale clapped his hands together.

"Do you know the family?" said Moss, taken aback.

"Yes, I do indeed. The judge is a dear friend."

"Then you'll know that the children are—" began Moss.

"Out of town, of course, how stupid of me." He slapped his forehead, leaving a red mark on the freckled skin. "They always accompany Habich to the country. It's all right for some, I suppose." He indicated the book with his hand. "You'll have bought it for when they return to their lessons."

"That's right, Mr. Gale." Moss paused, unsure what to say next. "Well, it was nice meeting you, but if you'll excuse me, I was just leaving." Gale frowned, his forehead pleating.

"Before you go," he said, moving between Moss and the door, "there's one thing I wonder if you might just help me with?"

"What's that?"

"Well, this is a bit awkward, but Habich, dear, forgetful fellow that he is, was to leave me a book. I'm a collector, you see, a bit of a bibliophile, and he acquired it on my behalf. We were to meet before he left so that he could give it to me, but well, you know how it goes. Last-minute things and all that."

"I'm sorry, Mr. Gale, but I'm sure you'll understand I can't just give you a book from his collection without permission. I've only just met you and I don't have any way of reaching him. No offense." Moss edged toward the door. He only succeeded in moving that much closer to Gale.

"I would be disappointed if you did," roared Gale, laughing. "Good lord! But happily I have a receipt from Habich himself, which should authorize the exchange. If I'd known there was any chance of running into you today I'd have had it with me. I did call last night and you were out."

"I suppose it might be all right, in that case. When were you thinking?" Moss was twitchy with rising suspicion. Gale seemed oblivious, or chose to ignore it.

"Is tomorrow evening too soon? Say seven?"

"That would be fine, Mr. Gale. What's the book? I'll try to have it ready."

"It's called *The Songbirds of Nightjar Island*. Here, let me write it down for you. Habich is mad about books on birds." Gale produced a tortoiseshell fountain pen with a deft sleight of hand and inscribed the title of the book on Moss's shopping bag in perfect copperplate.

Moss used the distraction to center himself. He focused on a glass pin piercing the man's lapel, a tiny ruby, like a drop of blood, affixed with a gold clasp. "Now then." The pen vanished into Gale's overcoat. "We are all set. Good day to you, Mr.? I'm terribly sorry, I didn't catch the name."

"Woods," said Moss, taking his hand. "Joseph Woods." Moss shot a glance at Croaker, but the man was busy arranging a shelf of erotica behind the counter, humming and moving his head from side to side like a simpleton.

"Tomorrow night then," shouted Gale. With a tight smile, Moss left the shop with the bag under his arm.

The rain dwindled to an acrid mist. Moss did not go straight home. To walk off the unease of the encounter, he tucked the book under his arm and traveled several blocks east to the vast staircase that gave the city its name. Carved from the limestone cliffs through some unimaginable feat of ancient engineering, the steps formed the city's bulwark. At the foot of the steps lay the Irridian Sea. To either side, the steps ran for miles, vanishing into the mist. Moss came here often. He took the air into his lungs. Moisture settled on his face, cooling his burning skin. The vast sense of space allowed him to feel anonymous as people rushed past, focused on their errands, heedless of another soul staring into the grey.

Was it a coincidence that Gale would ask for that particular book? According to the Deed of Gift Moss had found in Seaforth's desk, the book had been given to the museum six months ago. Moss felt his stomach constrict. He had to play the character. He would meet with Gale at the apartment and recall that his employer had donated the book in question. Hopefully that would be the end of the matter. If not, it might flush out any ulterior motive Gale might have.

Moss left the Steps and entered the pedestrian traffic around the Cloth Hall. His eyes swept over the people in the square, watching for the tattooed woman. With the uncanny ability of the human eye to pick a familiar face out of hundreds of others, Moss found himself staring at Gale who stood about two hundred feet away. The other man was not looking at him but Moss was sure that he had turned his face away at that very moment.

Moss worked his way around the edge of the square to a dilapidated telephone booth. He stepped inside and pulled the door shut, blocking out the street noise. The enclosed space reeked like a latrine. Hypodermic needles littered the floor. The plastic receiver dangled on a stretched cord like a fetus. Moss averted his eyes. He pulled out a red pen and looked at the writing that covered every plane of the booth. Choosing a spot with a clear patch, he drew a small bird and put five dots above its head. Moss pocketed the pen and left. Leaving the sign was near hopeless. It had been months since he had seen Irridis, but he needed to talk.

AN EMPTY MAP

"Why's the map so empty at the top?" asked Andrew. The morning sunlight fell across the boy, his armchair, and the heavy atlas open on his lap. Two days had passed since Moss bought the book from Taxali's bookshop. He had spent long hours in the Central Library studying everything he could find on Nightjar Island and celestial impacts. The most fascinating account was under his nose, which he had discovered at 2 a.m.

> *Ten thousand years ago, an asteroid exploded in the atmosphere over the Irridian Sea. The largest remaining fragment ended its journey in the heart of the island that would later be known as Nightjar. The crater was almost eight miles in circumference. The impact flattened and burned the forest to the island's ragged coastlines and obliterated all life. Beneath the crater, ancient limestone voids collapsed, revealing the island's bones to the stars.*
>
> *Over the centuries, the ruined island was reshaped into a much different place, smoothed by the elements and the returning forest. Many species of birds returned to the island. Nine and a half thousand years after the cataclysm, the first human explorers, a cabal of women, found the epicenter. To their surprise, a small island had been formed there, surrounded by a dark swamp. They called the island within the island Little Eye and declared it a sacred place, the spiritual home of their sisterhood.*
>
> *Working in conditions that killed many of them, the laborers brought in by the women built a great*

monastery house. The foundations and walls were constructed from the stone that the asteroid had left behind. They pulled the trunks of the ancient trees from the swamps and used the remarkable wood to create the floors, balconies, staircases and tables for the house. The house itself became known as Little Eye and was from the first, a melancholy place, though it is said, many caged birds lit the rooms with song. Within a few short years only the women of the Sisterhood of Little Eye remained. All others had fled or succumbed to disease or suicide. The sisters conscientiously rubbed the wood with beeswax, and stared often over the black waters of the swamp to the impenetrable forest as if waiting for something to emerge.

—Introduction to *The Songbirds of Nightjar Island* by Franklin Box

Was the intruder's interest in Nightjar based on some connection to Little Eye monastery? The books on celestial impacts led in that direction. By the time he had reached the end of the passage, Moss wondered if he had found an important clue to Memoria's story. For the moment, though, he was stymied.

Gale had missed the agreed-upon appointment. This angered Moss. Despite the inevitable discomfort the meeting would entail, he wanted it over with. He did not want to leave the business unresolved, only to have it pop up again at some less opportune time.

Moss was also worried that Lamb or the tattooed woman were watching the house. It was not a good combination of circumstances. He was pinned down and such confinement led to dubious coping mechanisms.

His eyes ached at the brightness of the atlas pages. Too much brandy, he thought. Andrew shifted the weight of the book and leaned forward, bringing the smudged lenses of his glasses close to the northern region. On the couch opposite, Moss rubbed his face. He rinsed his mouth with brandy from a tea mug and sucked the drops from his beard. It flowed down his raw esophagus like a bolus of molten glass.

Andrew was a street kid. Moss had collared him several weeks earlier attempting to break into the apartment through a door in the attic. He had grabbed the boy intending to send him out the way he had come in, but when he saw how thin Andrew was he invited him to have something to eat. The something ended up being a tin of sardines, and toast, but Andrew had not minded. He was more interested in the books in Seaforth's library. He was an intelligent boy, and they had soon struck up a surprising friendship.

"It isn't, not really. There's just not a lot of manmade things there," said Moss. "Not any more. Nature swallowed it up after the war." He half smiled at the boy. "Maybe someday you'll go. When you get back you can fill in the map." Andrew searched Moss's face for a moment. He returned his attention to the book.

"What would it look like? If I was there, in the empty part?"

He thinks I know everything, thought Moss. "Grasses, sedges, boreal forest, a lot of coniferous trees. It would be windy. In the winter, the sky would be so clear you might see stars in the daytime, some of them anyway. The ground was left very polluted after the war, unexploded shells, abandoned weapons, those kinds of things."

Andrew sat back in the chair, his eyes wide.

"It sounds awful," said the boy.

"Places like that have their own beauty," said Moss, shrugging. "The earth heals."

"Who do you think lives there?"

"Very few people live there now. You'd get sick, I imagine, if you stayed too long."

"I mean other things."

"Animals?" Moss massaged his temples. "Let me see, small mammals like martens and foxes, birds, lots of birds. Fish." Andrew slumped. Moss sat forward. "But in the fjords I imagine there's still a killer whale or two. Did you know they can toss a grown seal forty feet in the air?" Andrew grinned. Moss rolled a cigarette of tobacco taken from a humidor pulled from his dressing gown. He picked small pieces of apple from the tobacco and set them on the table of burled wood. The boy fixed Moss with a direct gaze.

"I thought you said nobody lives there? How do you know so much about it?" He watched, attentive, as Moss licked the edge of the rolling paper and curled it inward.

"That's not exactly what I said. I'll tell you a secret," said Moss, squinting as he lit the cigarette with a candle. Smoke streamed from his mouth. He swatted it away from his face. "And no matter what, you can't tell anyone."

"I won't," said Andrew.

"I was sent there once, to prison, a miserable place called Brickscold. Nothing but forest for miles around."

"No shit," whispered Andrew, after a moment of reflection. They both burst out laughing. When they had quieted down, Andrew pointed to a pale blue line of longitude where the green gave way to grey and then white. "I'd like to go there one day and see what it's like. Do you think I could?"

"Of course," said Moss. "How old are you, eleven, twelve?"

"Ten."

"Well, first you have to attend to your education. You'll have to study the sciences so that you are prepared."

"What do you mean?"

"You must be educated, to understand what you are seeing, to see the patterns and hidden connections. It's not enough to look. You have to see."

"What about courage? I think it would be a scary place."

"That can't be taught in school." Moss grew serious. "Courage is something you have to teach yourself."

"How long would it take to get there?" asked Andrew.

Before Moss could answer, there was a knock on the apartment door. They froze and exchanged glances. The grandfather clock ticked. Moss knew that it was risky to ignore Mr. Morel, the building manager. It just made him that much more inquisitive. For weeks, Morel had used every opportunity to interrupt Moss's day. Every small drama within the walls of the building was cause for an immediate and exhaustive consultation. Moss put a finger to his lips. Andrew giggled.

It was Morel's often-expressed belief that Moss, as the instructor of Seaforth's children, was the de facto family representative during their absence. As such, he was to be accorded, or at least appear to be accorded, the same respect due to the family. While arguable, this belief had one positive side effect. It precluded Morel from entering the apartment out of respect for Moss's privacy. It also meant that Morel was forever knocking on the door to impart informational updates from the threshold, which Moss had to hear with a certain amount of grace.

51

"Don't move a muscle," Moss whispered.

The previous day had been a cascade of minor catastrophes. Apparently, Morel was intent on making a pest of himself today as well. Earlier in the morning, Moss had removed the newspaper and a milk bottle from the landing. Morel, ever vigilant, must have interpreted this as a sign that Moss was awake and available to receive the first report of the day. It was easy to imagine Morel standing inches from the door, head cocked like a terrier, waiting for any sound that might confirm his conclusion.

Seeing Andrew about to open his mouth, Moss made a zipping motion. The boy shrugged, happy to play along. Moss glanced at the clock. *It's conceivable that I might have gone back to bed,* he thought. Had Morel heard them talking? He might imagine that he had heard a radio. There was another knock, but it was half-hearted. Moss scratched his chin and ran his fingers through his hair. He stubbed the cigarette in the bottom of a cup where it sizzled aromatically.

"You'd better go," he said in a hushed voice, as he slipped the humidor back in the pocket of his dressing gown.

Andrew remained where he was. The empty milk bottle sat on the cushion beside him, a bluish film forming on the inside of the glass. He leaned against one armrest, leaving half of the chair empty. His skinned knuckles and bruised shins jutted from the suit that he had stolen from a manikin in the high street. Scuffed brogues dangled on bare feet, held on by knots of shoelace. He was the antithesis of Seaforth's privileged brats, or so Moss surmised from the smug portraits scattered throughout the apartment. Moss felt an affinity for him.

Under Moss's stern gaze, the boy relented. He closed the book and put it on the cushion. As he jumped to his feet, Moss stopped him with a hand on his sleeve.

"Quietly," he said. The boy's wrist was like a piece of smooth driftwood. "You can't come back here for a while; do you understand me? It's not safe." Andrew nodded. He pulled his sleeve from Moss's grip and ran. The boy ran everywhere. "Go the back way, and don't let Morel see you," said Moss over his shoulder. Andrew was already gone, flowing over the sill of the lavatory window and up the gutter pipe with feline agility.

Moss pulled the atlas onto the coffee table and opened it to Nightjar Island. As a boy he had spent hours imagining what it would be like to sail through the mine-infested waters that surrounded the island

and walk through the empty streets of Absentia. He had shared these fantasies with Memoria. As children they had lain side by side watching the canal reflections on the ceiling, or leaning out of the window as she levitated unsuspecting frogs in the moonlight. He had talked with excitement about Nightjar and the ghosts he imagined there. Memoria had always been too busy laughing at her own mischief to take in what he was saying. He thought about the stacks of books in the house, the map and the Luna moths. Perhaps she had heard more than he thought. Was she alive, right now, somewhere in the City of Steps?

A final thump from Morel preceded the creak of retreating footsteps. It was a temporary victory. Beside the atlas, an empty glass medicine bottle cast an oscillating point of light on the tabletop. The word *sinispore* was hand-printed on its label. The bottle's tiny cork, itself made of a bark containing several halluci-nogenic alkaloids, had dropped through the neck and rolled loose in the bottom where it had accumulated a coating of the narcotic residue. Lost in thought, Moss stared at the light on the table until he became aware of a soft cooing. He turned his head and followed the shaft of sunlit dust to the window. On the other side of the glass, a pigeon paced back and forth. Like a prison guard, Moss thought. He drank now from the open bottle of brandy that he had kept out of Andrew's view beside the couch. As it once again bathed his throat with fire, he was seized with a conviction. It was obvious. The books, the maps and moths were not accidental discoveries. Someone, maybe Memoria, intended for him to find them. They were leaving a trail of breadcrumbs.

THE RETURN OF THE BEES

JUST AFTER 7 A.M. THE NEXT MORNING MOSS HEARD A DOOR SHUT in the attic. It was barely audible, but in the isolation of the prison Moss had trained his ear to pick up and interpret subtle patterns of sound. Judge Seaforth's building was number 2 in a row of seven houses. The sound meant that someone had entered the vacant building at the end of the row, number 7, accessed the roof through the broken skylight, and made their way, building by building, to a door that opened into Judge Seaforth's attic. The purpose of this exertion was to enter the house undetected from the street. The route was complicated enough that the probability of someone chancing upon it was remote.

Moss opened his eyes, assuming that Andrew had returned, despite being told to stay away. Footsteps, too heavy to be the boy, passed overhead, creaking toward the ceiling of the next room, the judge's library. A pause was followed by the thump of the counter-weighted ladder sliding from the ceiling. The visitor descended. Moss felt a cool draft on his skin from under the door.

Irridis, he thought, sitting up on the couch. Moss had hoped for this visit since drawing the bird inside the telephone booth. The bird was a private symbol. It meant *check public locker 12 in Central Station*. The locker was a method of communication they had established before Irridis left the City of Steps months earlier. It was a way for him to find Moss, who was, of necessity, untraceable. In the remote train station locker, Moss had left Seaforth's address, written in a private code, along with a note describing how to access the house via the rooftops. Moss had placed the instructions in a sealed envelope a short time after taking the job. The system had seemed comic when they devised it, but Irridis had as many reasons as Moss for discretion, so it stood.

54

Moss concealed the sinispore vial in his robe and kicked the empty brandy bottle under the couch with his heel. The ladder in the other room rumbled in its tracks as it withdrew into the attic. Footsteps crossed the library floor to the closed door separating it from the living room. Moss waited, elbows on knees. Between his fingers, he twirled a pencil stub left behind by Andrew. The door slid into its side pocket and Irridis entered, tracking mud.

Water dripped from Irridis's coat onto the acanthus-patterned carpet. It ran in rivulets from the hood that shadowed his face. Finger by finger, he removed tight-fitting gloves, and dropped them on an antique sideboard. Moss flinched. Irridis pulled back his hood. The milky-blue translucence of his skin appeared ghostly in the dim room. Moss, never at ease with Irridis's appearance, tried to look past it. Five glass stones, called ocelli, floated above Irridis's head. They were a source of spectral light.

Moss stood up and shook his friend's hand, knowing that an embrace would be unwelcome.

"Irridis," said Moss. "It's wonderful to see you. How are you?"

Irridis broke his gaze with a faint smile. "Desperate for sleep. The sea was rough and I haven't slept since I arrived. I found your sign in the telephone booth just last night." Irridis looked around the room, frowning at Seaforth's curios. "How long ago did you put it there?"

"A few days," Moss said. "God, it's great to see you."

"And you too, Moss."

"Where did your travels take you?" Irridis's inexhaustible thirst for knowledge often took him away for months at a time.

"I spent some time in the Minnows, an archipelago in the far northeast, studying the biome. It wasn't an easy journey."

"I've heard of them, a scattering of tiny marks on the map. Almost the end of the world."

Irridis nodded. "Trust me, there is no almost. You couldn't find a more barren place. It took some time to learn the moods of the land, but I had help in that. At first I found the aboriginal people in the remote fishing settlements wary of my appearance, especially the ocelli. I told them I was a religious pilgrim, which seemed to put the matter to rest. After that, they were willing to offer me assistance, although somewhat reservedly." The ocelli drifted through the room throwing odd shadows. "Their own spirituality steers toward the supernatural, so maybe that had something to do with it. Nevertheless, I didn't stay in any one place for long. I spent most of my time hiking in the wilderness far from settlements. I followed the hunting corridors, resting in huts. It is a desolate and beautiful landscape. Caribou and seals are stolid company. Timber wolves and brown bears, less so."

"Yet here you are," said Moss.

"The season was changing. By sheer happenstance I found a privately operated ship willing to take me on. It's been anchored here for two days. I would have looked for you sooner, but I had other business to take care of." He picked up a glass paperweight containing a sea urchin.

Moss sat down, waiting for an elaboration that did not come. He had so many questions, but he knew better than to ask them so soon. Irridis would tell his stories in his own way, or not at all.

"How have you been?" asked Irridis.

"Something has happened, and I need your help."

"Go on." Irridis held the paperweight to his eyes, squinting out of one and then the other as he turned it. One of the ocelli swept behind it to provide illumination. "These are protected, you know. Harvested nearly to extinction to satisfy the demand for paper-weights." He put it down on a polished hutch with a hard knock. "Sorry, go on."

"I think Memoria's alive."

Irridis leaned against the hutch, arms folded. "You told me that she drowned."

Moss nodded. "Yes. That's what I thought. For so many years, I've had this horrible image of her falling off the seawall. I—" He pulled out his humidor and rolled a cigarette. He rolled it too tightly and started again. "Sorry, I'm not making any sense. She's been dead to me for so long I can't get my head around it."

"What's happened to make you think otherwise?"

"I went to the old house on the canal. You remember, I told you about it once. Fleurent Drain? It's where John Machine moved my family after he brought Memoria to live with us."

"Yes, with the frogs. I've seen it."

"Exactly. Nobody has lived there for years. When I checked on it a few days ago, it was vacant, but in one of the rooms I found a setup for raising Luna moths. It was a hobby she had."

"Hardly conclusive. Something left from years past."

"No. These were live moths, Irridis. Someone was tending to them very recently, somebody who knew what they were doing. It's too much of a coincidence." Moss lit the cigarette. The smoke eddied in a diagonal band of sunlight creeping across the room.

"Unless someone wanted you to make that assumption."

"I thought of that. But why?" Moss had dwelled on this possibility. If Lamb had contrived such a thing to convince him of Memoria's existence, it was smart. But, to do so depended on knowledge of a trivial detail from Memoria's past.

"I don't know," said Irridis. "Did you see anything else?"

"Some books, maps of Nightjar Island. I know it sounds peculiar but I can't help thinking that these are clues that she left for me."

"If she were alive, why wouldn't she approach you directly? Why be so mysterious?"

"Think of our bird symbol. Maybe she has something to hide, or maybe she is afraid."

"Of whom?"

"John Machine exposed her to a lot of strange people. They were excessively curious about her, because of her so-called gift, as if she was something to be possessed."

"So what are you going to do?"

"Find her, of course. Irridis, I need your help."

"Well, even assuming that you are right, how would you recognize her? It's been years. Do you even have a photograph of what she looked like then?"

"I'll recognize her, no question. I'm going to go back the house for a start and see if she's been back since I was last there."

"Moss, you are a fugitive from the law, an escaped convict. It's one thing to play dress-up here, but if you're spotted coming and going around the family home, someone could identify you. It's an obvious place for the police to watch."

"I'll take the risk. Besides, I look so different. Who's going to make a connection with my past?"

"Well, if the Luna moths are a setup, presumably someone already has. You might be walking into a trap."

"Which is exactly why I need your help." He felt guilty withholding information from Irridis, but falling into Lamb's snare had been stupid. Being drugged and tattooed had been fucking humiliating.

He was not ready to share, not yet. "I just need to do this. Will you help me?"

"It strikes me as a big assumption to think that random things you've observed are signs she's left for you."

"It's the kind of thing she'd do," said Moss, with conviction. "She had a taste for puzzles."

"Your urgency will put you in danger," said Irridis.

"What?" asked Moss, a little sharper than he had intended.

"Trying to find someone in this city, who may want to remain hidden, means making enquiries. That kind of behavior is going to expose you eventually. If the wrong person makes a connection, you'll be sold out and arrested in no time. I advise you to leave it alone."

"No. She left me signs, Irridis."

"Signs." Irridis waved his hand. "How much of that brandy have you had, Moss?"

"She's out there. How can I ignore that? I have to do what I can."

"Because you're to blame for her falling into the ocean?"

"I hated the way she was being used, but what I did that day was stupid." Moss paused and rubbed his eyes, as though that could erase the image of Memoria falling.

Irridis paced the carpet. The ocelli moved around the room in an agitated manner. Moss knew that Irridis could experience and process multiple sensory inputs from each stone. He could not begin to imagine what a cacophony the man's consciousness must be.

"Here are my terms," said Irridis finally.

"Name them."

"You stop the game you're playing here, for one."

"Done."

"And you leave this house immediately."

"That was a given anyway."

"There is a house in Hellbender Fields. An old friend, a shipwright, owns it. I make use of it sometimes. You can hole up there while we figure this out."

Moss nodded. "Those are your terms?"

"For now. You look awful. Haven't you slept?"

Moss fell back into the couch without answering. Dust sparkled around him. Irridis continued. "The man who owns the house is aboard his ship the *Somnambulist* and isn't expected to dock for another seven weeks. You will have complete privacy. You can stay in the house without fear of discovery. There's a key under an urn at the back door. Don't expect to be comfortable, though. He's a man of simple tastes."

"Is that a crack?" Moss smiled. "Thank you, my friend."

Irridis ignored the question. "I went by the house a couple of hours ago to check on it. It's sitting empty. Even the neighbors seem to be away."

"It'll be worth it just to be shut of Morel. He's been banging on the door already this morning. Probably found an earwig in his bed or some similar crisis."

"Morel?"

Moss rolled his eyes. "The building manager. The man's a nightmare."

Irridis walked to the window. "The air is stale in here." He turned and leaned against the radiator in front of the window. The ocelli had relaxed and now drifted around the room like bumblebees in search of pollen. Moss swatted at one that had begun nosing at his pocket. "How are you going to extricate yourself from this—grandeur?"

"I'll submit my notice by letter. I'll say that I have been called home for family reasons. I don't want to do anything too sudden and risk Morel smelling a rat. When Seaforth returns, it will be an annoying dereliction, nothing more. By that time, I'll be long gone to your shipwright's house."

"Was it worth the effort?" asked Irridis.

"I promised Franklin Box that I would get his book back. I found it, too, in the Museum of Natural History. It's over there in my bag."

"That's it? A book?"

Moss shook his head. "I wanted to show Seaforth that his shell has a soft spot, that he is as vulnerable as anyone. I wanted him to feel violated. One day he'll figure out what I've done." Moss glared. "I wanted to punish him for sending me away and ruining my damned life."

Irridis nodded, a familiar flicker of a smile in the corners of his mouth. "Well played, Moss, well played."

They exploded in laughter. When it had drifted off, sounds of the city welled up from the street. Irridis flicked an ant off his sleeve.

"I need to sleep before I help you fix your life," Irridis said. Moss nodded, grinning and closing his eyes. Irridis took off his coat and laid it over the high-backed chair that Andrew had vacated. He moved the empty milk bottle to the table. "It's not a good idea to feed strays."

Moss stretched out on the couch and pulled his sleeve over the tattoo. The sinispore bottle dug into his leg. Irridis closed the curtains to block out the morning sun and returned to the chair. They rested while the pigeon cooed and paced. *Strays*, thought Moss. He opened his eyes. How long had Irridis watched the house?

BOOKCASE

AN HOUR LATER, WHILE IRRIDIS SLEPT, MOSS TUGGED HIS WEATHERED shoulder bag from behind the couch. The ocelli had deprived him of restful sleep. Lying on his side, he had watched through slit eyes as they moved around the room. Relentless in their curiosity, they darted, formed a cluster and then darted some more. It was damned unnerving. Left uninterrupted, the ocelli would come to know the apartment in every detail. All that information would be transmitted to Irridis, who would draw from it conclusions that might never occur to Moss. Pulling the bag over his neck, Moss decided to seek relief from their intrusiveness on the roof.

He entered the library, shutting the door before the ocelli could follow. With a hooked staff, he pulled the ladder from the ceiling. It was a creaky contraption and he had to climb slowly to avoid noise. At the top he stepped into a long attic filled with bundled court documents and unused pieces of furniture. The door was at the far end.

Moss stepped onto a flat roof. The base of a telescope was bolted into the tarpaper. It looked heavy and military. He had always wondered if it had played some role in the war. He shuffled around it, balancing against the cast iron until he reached a chair. He tipped a puddle from the seat and dried it with his cuff before sitting down. The chair offered an excellent, if unstable, perch to view the surrounding neighborhood.

He set his bag between his ankles and pulled out *The Songbirds of Nightjar Island*. He was pleased to have kept his impetuous promise to Box. Years ago as they sat in the prison courtyard feeding bread crusts to the sparrows, Box had lamented the way Seaforth had taken his book. It had been taken as "evidence" but Seaforth had kept it for himself. Box knew this because the judge had bragged about it to the warden; the information had trickled down. Box had seemed so crushed. When Moss made the promise to steal it back, Box had put his hand over Moss's arm and given him a patronizing smile. Moss had burned with embarrassment. He had felt the pressure of the murderer's hands for hours after.

Moss remembered later watching Box sitting on the damp floor with his trays of blown eggs collected from the gutters and crevasses of Brickscold, and realizing that the man was operating in a different reality. Nevertheless, Moss had been determined. He would find the book and one day Seaforth would understand what had been done. The book was heavy in his hand.

He faced the direction of the sea and read passages until the wind came up and the first droplets raised spots on the paper. Blinking himself back to his surroundings, he closed the cover. He returned the book to the bag, and hurried back around the telescope base. Standing in the shelter of the doorway, watching the rain on nearby rooftops, his thoughts returned to Memoria. Was she hiding somewhere close to hand? Watching him from a distant window? He smiled at the fantasy. If he found her, he would give her the book. Hadn't she always loved birds? He was sure Franklin Box would approve.

It was late afternoon. Across the chessboard Irridis's features had grown indistinct. Moss switched on a lamp. Its filament sizzled and brightened. A streetcar passed, sending a rumble through the apartment house. Glass rattled in the front of a bookcase, causing something inside to thump over.

"That sounded expensive," said Irridis dryly.

Bathed and dressed in clean, if rumpled, clothes, Moss hunched over the game board, trying to work out how Irridis had humiliated him yet again. He turned the black queen in his fingers. Like everything Seaforth owned it was of the finest craftsmanship. The handmade board and chessmen were made of snowflake obsidian and ivory. Each piece had green velvet on the base so that game play could be conducted in silence.

In Brickscold, the prisoners had made their own chessmen out of cork and bone. The games were played in a hall filled with clamor. Earlier, Moss had commented that he quite enjoyed the luxury of

Seaforth's game board and the coziness of the room. Ever contrary, Irridis had remarked that he preferred blindfold chess, thereby eliminating the need for any board, which had irritated Moss to no end. Moss was about to tip his king when there was a knock at the door. They exchanged looks.

"I'll see what he wants," said Moss, rising from his chair.

Irridis restored the pieces to their starting positions and then walked into the adjoining library. The ocelli concealed themselves within an unlit chandelier. Moss straightened his clothing, adjusting the tuck of his shirt and smoothing the pocket flaps of his jacket. At the last moment, he took his revolver from a console table. He stroked the blue barrel. Another pounding on the door snapped him out of his reverie. He aimed the gun at the door.

"Bang," he whispered. He tucked the gun into the waistband at the back of his pants where it was concealed by the tail of the jacket.

Moss fiddled with the latch, and opened the door. Mr. Morel stepped forward to present himself. The man had a habit of knocking on the door and then retreating to a position several feet away where he would stand with his hands clasped behind his back. When the door opened he would then step forward in a crisp, officious manner. Small and misshapen, he reminded Moss of a root vegetable, all odd lumps and unappealing growths. He was dressed, as usual, in filthy moleskin pants, a tight jacket with greasy cuffs and thick-soled black shoes. Pinned to his lapel was a badge that he had made for himself that read Building Manager. His dog, Fits, named for her frequent epileptic seizures, sat at her master's heel, a muscular hobgoblin.

"Ah, you're in! You must have slept late." His eyes roved around the room behind Moss as if they were tracking a housefly.

"It's four in the afternoon," said Moss. Another streetcar rumbled past. The apartment house shook as though it might collapse at any moment.

"Yes, indeed it is, I can't argue with you there. Up late studying those heavy books, were you? My father always said reading will spoil your eyes. He always encouraged his children to get their noses out of a book and go outside for some fresh air. Not, I hasten to add, that one can find fresh air in the city. My father's point was a philosophical one."

"I have trouble sleeping."

"I dare say you do. All of those big thoughts tumbling around in your head, like so many rocks in a polisher," said Morel.

Is he mocking me? Moss wondered. *Unctuous little prick.*

"I am sorry to bother you, sir," said Morel, with an air of getting down to business, "but there is someone at the foot of the stairs. A not entirely unattractive lady, rather striking in fact, with airs to match." Morel followed this snide comment with a flourish of his hand as if to transport it to Moss's ear. He looked over his shoulder, and sheltering his mouth with his hand, commented sotto voce, "She doesn't seem quite right in the head, if you know what I mean." He pulled down the corners of his mouth like a carp.

"I'm sorry," said Moss. Suppressing the urge to slam the door. "I don't have any idea what you mean."

"Well, eccentric, I suppose. And not at all disposed to be forthcoming to the likes of me. Such disrespect for my station. By hell, it's a rare display of cheek for someone turning up unannounced on the doorstep."

"Mr. Morel," interjected Moss. "How can I be of assistance?"

"Yes, well, right then, I was wondering if you might go and see the lady, and I use the term with reservation, for yourself. She was dropped off by the streetcar, unaccompanied, and walked through the foyer doors as if she had business. She was scanning the names on the intercom when I spotted her during my rounds. But when I asked her what she wanted, she just stared at me as mute as a mop handle for nearly five seconds before finally asking for you."

"For me?" Moss, who had drifted into a trance, snapped his attention back to Morel's face.

"Indeed, though not by name. She asked for the instructor in Judge Seaforth's employ. A strange one. You'll understand when you meet her, sir. Not the kind that Judge Seaforth would suffer in the building, not at all. Judge Seaforth is careful who he lets in."

"All right, Mr. Morel, your point is well taken. I'll take care of it." Moss held up his hands in surrender.

"Well done. I thought you might. Find me if you need me. I'll be in the basement, cleaning out the mousetraps." Morel left, clutching a small burlap bag. Fits hesitated for a moment and then followed her master.

Moss glanced at the chandelier, and then entered the hall. Irridis would not risk sending the ocelli after him. If trouble arose, he would have to deal with it on his own. A visitor was unprecedented. Moss rubbed the tattoo on his wrist as he walked.

Despite his dread of the device, Moss took the elevator, rather than the stairs. Inside the cage, a mechanical and aesthetic monstrosity of brass tendrils and birds, he fastened his jacket and straightened his sleeves. Descending, he adopted what he hoped was an authoritative demeanor. He rehearsed a few words in his head, brisk but not unkind, something to send the stranger on her way with a minimum of questions. The elevator stopped and Moss opened the cage gate.

Lamb's accomplice waited across the foyer. Her left hand rested on the finial at the bottom of the staircase. Reflections from the street-facing window moved over her. At the sound of Moss exiting the elevator, she turned, as though her thoughts had been interrupted. She was dressed in a black coat with tortoiseshell buttons over a grey skirt and knee-high leather boots. At his approach, she folded her kidskin-gloved hands and raised her chin. A case sat at her feet, antique wood with an ox ring handle and brass fittings.

Moss walked toward her, his speech quite forgotten. "What do you want?" he asked. His heels clicked on the parquet floor. The revolver prodded the small of his back.

"I need to talk to you," she said. "And Irridis."

"I'm Joseph Woods, Judge Seaforth's instructor," said Moss, his voice raised. "His children's instructor, that is." With a bemused smile, the woman removed a glove and offered her hand. It felt cool and slender. The effect was immediate and erotic. The image of her body naked in the moonlight flashed through his mind. He refocused.

"What the hell are you doing here?" Moss said under his breath.

"My name is Imogene. Is there somewhere we can speak privately, Mr. Woods?" Her voice had a slight northern accent. "I'd be most appreciative." Relieved that she was willing to play along, Moss nodded.

"You won't need your gun," she whispered. She raised her eyebrows at Moss's confusion. "Behind you." She pointed around him. Moss looked over his shoulder and saw the obvious shape beneath his jacket, reflected in a large framed mirror. "Now, can we go up, or should we talk here and risk being overheard?" A lamprey pendant hung on a chain around Imogene's neck. It was identical in design to the one that itched on his wrist.

"Come with me. We can take the elevator."

"Would you mind helping me with this? It weighs a ton." Moss nodded and took the case by its handle, realizing a beat too late that she had just disadvantaged him by occupying his hands. The case was heavy but he was able to move it on two reluctant metal wheels. Gesturing with his head, he indicated that Imogene should lead. In the elevator he tipped the case back with relief. He closed the gate, hoping that Morel was still engrossed in his mouse-catching activity. They stood in awkward proximity not speaking as the elevator ascended to the third floor with creaks and groans. When the elevator stopped Moss pointed to the apartment door.

"There. Go in. I'll follow with this." Struggling with the case, he wondered if he was making a terrible mistake.

COMMON INTEREST

Moss locked the door and directed Imogene through the apartment to the library. Even Morel would not be able to hear their voices from there. Moss was relieved to find that Irridis had left the room, though he did notice the ocelli resting innocuously among glass paperweights on a shelf. At his invitation, Imogene sat in a wingback chair facing the cold fireplace. Moss leaned against the mantelpiece and invited his visitor to speak first.

"Why don't you sit down, Moss?" She removed her left glove, revealing a slender hand. Moss's eyes lingered on the simple ruby ring on her index finger.

"I'll stand, thanks."

Imogene sighed. "Suit yourself." She laid the gloves across her knees. Beneath her eyes the skin was purplish.

"I haven't found Memoria. It's only been a few days."

"That's not why I'm here."

Moss pulled up his sleeve, exposing the lamprey tattoo.

"I was wondering how long it would take for you to bring that up," said Imogene. "For the record, I didn't do it. It was done at Lamb's insistence."

"A member of the Red Lamprey?" asked Moss, wearily.

"No. You have to admit it has a certain quality of line."

"Hilarious," said Moss. "That night, when you drugged and kidnapped me—"

"I was supposed to watch you, make sure you didn't stop breathing. That drug I gave you in the tunnel was dangerous and unstable. That's why you were there with me, to sleep it off. I did you a favor."

"A favor? I'll pretend you realize how completely insane that is. Besides, you were asleep when I woke up," Moss said, incredulous.

Imogene shrugged. "Sorry, two glasses of absinthe and—" She shut her eyes and tilted her head.

"How did you find me?"

"Don't worry. Lamb doesn't know I'm here. I was careful."

"It's hard for me to believe anything you say."

"Of course, you don't trust me. Why would you?"

"Well?"

"I wanted to see you privately. I couldn't ask Lamb where you were so I went to see Oliver Taxali. We'd never met, so he didn't connect me with Lamb."

"Oliver told you where I was?" asked Moss.

"Not at first. My father knew Oliver's father years ago. They were both members of the Red Lamprey. That's Oliver's connection with Lamb also." She paused. "Very clever of you, by the way, to focus my attention on the fireplace. Limit my view of the rest of the room. Is he here?"

"Is who here?"

Imogene smiled and then continued as though the question had not been asked. "I knew the Taxali family had a reputation for buying and selling rare books of questionable origin. I thought with the right inducement, like a rare antique book, he might be willing to trade for some information." She leaned forward conspiratorially. "And I was right."

Moss felt drawn into her familiarity, despite his wariness, as if they had just shared a private joke. Curse Oliver. God help him, he would kill the idiot. "Why don't you want Lamb to know you're here?"

"You'll find out soon enough." Her eyes looked toward the door. "Anyway, Oliver liked my offer." She pulled Taxali's business card from inside her glove and turned it so Moss could see the address on the back. "You'll want to visit Judge Seaforth's apartment," she croaked, in a spot-on imitation of Oliver Taxali.

Moss took the card from Imogene. "Oliver should be more discreet," he muttered.

"You look nothing like your portrait in the paper," said Imogene. That ironic smile again. It took Moss a moment to understand what she was referring to. Then it clicked. The newspapers had run his photo for days after the "Brickscold Situation" had been discovered. The mug shots of twenty-three escaped inmates had appeared on the front page. The papers gave the impression of a mass breakout. In fact, a disease had ravaged the prison, killing guards and inmates without prejudice. By the time Moss walked away, there had been nobody in a condition to stop him. In the following weeks, twenty of the inmates had been captured, or killed in the process. By then, the wretched photograph of his younger self, taken during his processing into the prison population, all Adam's apple and protruding ears, had ceased to be news.

Moss's patience was gone. "Is that some kind of veiled threat? What do you want?"

"Oh Moss, I'm teasing you."

Moss dropped the card into the fireplace where it landed with waft of ash. He looked at Imogene, the movement of her lips, the curve of her neck, and the red flush of the skin beneath her collarbone. Her cultivated manner was so at odds with his first impression that he wondered if she had a twin. She unbuttoned her coat. He looked away.

"Do you mind? It's warm in here." Moss hung it on a stand near the door. His hand lingered in its folds feeling the residual heat of her body. He let it go. Back at the fireplace, he stirred the card into the ash with a poker.

"Now that you've found me, are you going to tell me why you are here?"

They heard footsteps. Imogene stood and turned toward the door. "Do you remember me?" Irridis stood on the threshold. The ocelli flew across the room and took up a circular formation above his head.

"Yes," he said. His voice was unwelcoming. A faint sequence of opalescent lights ran beneath the skin on his skull. Moss's gut tightened. It was a tone that did not bode well.

"I hoped you would. It makes this easier," said Imogene. "I didn't know what to expect. We only met once, and for such a short time. But I never forgot it."

"You'd better explain yourself quickly," said Irridis.

Moss remained silent. He needed time to process this new development. Imogene chewed the inside of her cheek and seemed to come to a decision. "Can I show you something first? It might help you understand what I have to say." Irridis looked at Moss, who nodded. Rising, Imogene produced a key from a cord around her wrist. She crouched in front of the case. Moss reached behind his back and closed his hand around the grip of the revolver.

"Slowly," he said.

"Easy, Moss," she said, as she turned the key in the lock. Two doors opened outward. "There we are." Moss let go of the gun.

The interior was divided into small compartments. At the top, a row of miniature books was held in place by a strap. Most were leather-bound and tied with stained ribbons, but some were bundled signatures, or even single sheets of paper, folded and sealed with wax. Under the shelf of books was a row of bottles containing tinctures and specimens suspended in a yellowish medium. The lead-sealed bottles were set into ingenious holes in a shelf, which prevented them from knocking together. Eight small drawers with hand-printed labels lined the bottom of the case. A folio was attached to the inside of the left door with bone clips. It was tied with the same type of ribbon used on the books. It was this bundle that she removed and handed to Irridis.

His expression was unreadable as he pulled the ribbon, releasing four pieces of thick paper. He took them to a desk and arranged them side by side.

"Where did you get these?" Irridis asked. The threat had left his voice. Imogene did not answer, instead she watched as he examined the works. On each sheet was an elaborate ink drawing. Irridis did not touch the paper, but moved his hand as if replicating the artist's strokes. Sections of human anatomy merged with animal and plant forms. There were fungal shapes; others were marine or even prehistoric forms of life. Moss lifted a large magnifying glass from the desk.

"Strange," he said, looking up at Irridis. "The detail continues even under magnification. It seems to go on forever. Who could have had the hand or eyesight for something like this?" He set the magnifier on the table and turned to Imogene. "They look very old."

Imogene looked down. "There was another one. It was stolen from my room in the Cloth Hall. I was stupid. I took them out to look at and fell asleep." Moss watched her profile. "A noise in the room woke me. There was someone else there. I chased them but they got away." Her face had a look that Moss recognized from the tunnel, amused and lethal. "Lucky for them, not so for me. I treasure these drawings, having meditated on them for years."

"Where did you get them?" Irridis turned one of the drawings over, and examined the back.

"When I was a girl, our family home was set on fire. I lost my mother in the blaze. Years later, I returned. There was very little there by that point, just some foundations sticking out of the weeds. I knew of a place where my father used to hide his most secret things. I worked out the location from memory, and a lot of luck. The case was buried near the foundation, where the wine cellar used to be. That's where I dug it up."

"How did you know about the hiding spot if it was his secret?" asked Moss.

"You can't keep secrets from your children," said Imogene.

"What do you know about them?" Irridis said. He returned the drawing to its place among the others.

"I know that they are, as Moss said, old. They were in the bookcase when I found it. I know the bookcase was stolen."

"Why are you showing them to us?" asked Moss.

"I'm coming to that." Imogene turned to Irridis. "I remember, Irridis. Do you? The one time my father brought you to the house. We were banished to the garden while my parents argued. Do you remember what you showed me that day?"

"Yes," he said.

REVELATIONS

AT IMOGENE'S REQUEST, MOSS POURED HER A GLASS OF SEAFORTH'S whiskey. She took it, holding the tumbler in cupped hands, but did not drink. Moss was wary and stepped away from her. The memory of her standing in the tunnel with the expiring poison bulb was still vivid. She was a dangerous associate of Lamb's. He would not be lulled. Moss was glad of Irridis's presence, but puzzled by this evident connection. Irridis had not yet answered her question. To break the uncomfortable silence Moss asked Imogene to explain.

"My father didn't have an easy life," said Imogene. "Circumstances led him to become an opportunist, a thief. He stole antiquities. He made secret forays to Nightjar Island and sold what he found in the ruined libraries and museums to underground dealers and collectors here in the city. The Red Lamprey lined up the buyers. They got a generous cut of everything."

"Wait, are we talking about a man named John Machine?" asked Moss. "John is your father?" He watched her body language. He prided himself on his ability to spot a liar, another skill honed in Brickscold. She was composed, but her eye contact was direct. Had John ever mentioned a daughter? Moss knew next to nothing of the life John had led when he was not at the house on the canal.

"That's right," said Imogene. "Whatever else he was, John was resourceful. He found a back door to the island, so to speak. We lived well for a time, but I didn't understand where the money came from until much later. Honestly, at the time, I didn't think about it at all. What child does? Things are as they are." She rested her head on the chair back and closed her eyes for a moment, as if seeing her younger self.

"What happened?" prompted Moss.

She opened her eyes. "Before her death, my mother, Sylvie, confided that for years John had been obsessed with a monastery he'd found in the interior of the island." She circled her palm with her finger as she spoke and then tapped the center. "He'd been a military surveyor during the Purge, and had stumbled across the place during his work. He kept it to himself. There were signs of a massacre at the hands of the military. He reasoned that anyone involved would be more than happy to let the place return to nature."

"I didn't know John was in the military," said Moss.

Imogene nodded. "He was a contracted surveyor. It was a way to stay out of the fighting. The monastery was called Little Eye, but he only found that out later. A few months after the war, he traveled back on his own. The trip nearly killed him, but he found Little Eye again, consulting the maps he'd made earlier. The monastery appeared to have been undisturbed since his first encounter with it. This bookcase was one of the things he brought back from that journey. He knew there was a strong underground market for occult items. The case and its contents were a trove. Lamb later told me that when John got back, he circumvented the Red Lamprey to deal directly with the collectors. When things inevitably became dangerous, he stashed the case."

"Fool," said Irridis, who to this point had remained silent.

"It was a naïve plan, one guaranteed to piss off the Red Lamprey, but there was a worse consequence of his expedition." Imogene stopped and took a deep breath. The rims of her eyes had grown red.

Now we get to it, thought Moss. "Go on."

"Despite appearances, Little Eye was not completely deserted. Someone had survived there."

"How? From what I've read, the Purge was thorough." Even as Moss spoke he felt the hair rising on his arms.

Imogene's laugh was bitter. "If only. On that return expedition, John camped there overnight, sleeping in the open. He was woken in the morning by a little girl." Imogene faced Moss. "It was Memoria, as I'm sure you've already guessed."

"What happened?" he asked, flashing a glance at Irridis.

"He abducted her. There's really nothing else you can call it, though I'm sure he rationalized it as a rescue."

"Despite the fact that she had somehow survived. She must have had help," said Moss, angry.

"He saw what she could do. After that, his concern for her welfare was inextricably linked with how he might benefit."

Moss folded his arms. "And he had to pretend she was his daughter or face difficult questions about where she came from."

"That's right. Of course Sylvie was horrified. She was having none of it, which is how Memoria ended up living with you and your mother."

"I don't know what to say," said Moss. "This all sounds incredible."

"Anyway, Lamb knew that John was cheating the Red Lamprey," said Imogene. "He had John watched. When he learned about Memoria, he knew right away that she was unique and wanted her for himself. It became an obsession."

Imogene sipped the whiskey but the glass clinked against her teeth. She held it out to Moss. He took it and set it on the desk. "After Memoria fell into the ocean, Lamb came to our house with several members of the Red Lamprey. Aside from Lamb, they were all men we knew as well-regarded members of society. They beat John senseless. Lamb demanded the case, which he had heard rumors about. John insisted that it didn't exist, that people had misinterpreted things he had said. Lamb never believed him. All this happened the year before I was born. According to my mother, after that incident, things seemingly went back to normal. John was away a lot but I was well provided for. It was an almost idyllic childhood."

A long silence followed. Moss poured himself a generous glass of whiskey from a crystal decanter.

"But, do you want to know what kind of man Lamb really is?" Imogene's voice had grown hushed, her eyes far away. "Twelve years later, Lamb burned our house to the ground and took me in Memoria's place. It was a delayed punishment for John's lies, his disloyalty and debts. I was forced to live in Lamb's house, supposedly to work off the debt that John owed. Lamb told me that John would be killed, as my mother had been, if I didn't comply. He didn't tell me that John had already vanished. After a while, I knew no other life. I became a daughter of the Red Lamprey. Now, to outward appearances I live a relatively normal life, but I am bound to the Red Lamprey and can be called upon at any moment to do

Lamb's bidding." She looked at Moss pointedly.

"I want my freedom. I've come to you because I have no one else and we are all linked, whether we like it or not." Imogene pressed the heels of her hands to her forehead. Her lips pursed and tears rolled down her cheeks. Moss laid a hand on her shoulder but withdrew it when she flinched. "And I want rid of that." She indicated the case. "I don't want any of it. Lamb and his cronies know that it exists and have spent years looking for it. It's been hidden in the apartment he arranged for me in the attic of the Cloth Hall, right under his nose. It must be hidden where it will never be found."

Irridis stood by the window. Moss looked at his feet, deep in thought. Imogene bowed her head for a minute, but then rose and gathered the drawings from the desk. Her face was pale.

"Leave them," Moss said. The air was charged. Although still disturbed by Imogene's role in the meeting with Lamb and what followed, her account had changed his perception of her. It had made him more sympathetic. He strode to the window where Irridis stood beneath a halo of ocelli, watching. "I need to talk to you privately."

Irridis turned away from Moss and addressed Imogene. "There is a bedroom next door. Would you mind giving us a few minutes?"

When the door closed, Moss told Irridis about his encounter with Lamb. The story came around to waking up beside Imogene in the Cloth Hall, and the discovery of the lamprey tattooed on his wrist. Irridis listened to the account without interruption.

"You should have told me about this before," said Irridis.

"What does it mean? Not the tattoo. It's the obviously the emblem of the gang. What does it mean that they've given it to me?"

"The mark indicates that you are under the eye of the Red Lamprey. It is a warning to others. How much do you know about them?"

"Not much. Just stories I picked up in Brickscold."

"The Red Lamprey is a secret criminal society, a brotherhood, with roots that go back to the earliest days of the city. It began with a family called Lamproie that originally came from, interestingly enough, Nightjar Island. They are still at the core of the organization but the membership extends far beyond, to all levels of society. Lamb, the man you met, is, or rather was, one of their most notorious assassins. The tattoo is a warning that you are conducting business on their behalf and therefore fall under the aura of their protection. It is also a death mark. Typically, those who bear the mark are executed when their business is concluded."

"Oh, good, I was worried it was something bad," said Moss. "Imogene said that Lamb didn't know she was coming here. Do you believe her?"

"Do you?" asked Irridis.

"Yes, given what she told us."

"Strange bedfellows," said Irridis.

"Now you need to talk to me," said Moss. "What did she show you in her parents' garden?"

"Wait here," he said. Moss sat in the wingback chair vacated by Imogene. It was still warm from her body. Irridis left the library and walked into the main sitting room. He returned with a folded piece of paper and handed it to Moss.

"What's this?" Moss unfolded it. "I see." He stood up and carried it to the desk and laid it beside the drawings from Imogene's case. It was done in the same style, though much less aged.

"Explain," said Moss. "You had this?"

"I drew it. This is what she was referring to. That day in the garden, I showed her this drawing."

"But these other drawings are ancient. They must have been done decades, even centuries before you were born," said Moss. "You heard what she said. They were found in a monastery."

"Yes, a mystery. I don't understand it either. Years ago when I was very young, the shipwright on the *Somnambulist* saved me from drowning in the sea off Nightjar Island. I have no memory of my life before the moment when I revived onboard the ship."

"The same man whose house I am going to?" asked Moss.

"Yes. On return to the City of Steps, it was impossible for him to look after me and eventually gave me to another man to square a gambling debt. I have since forgiven him this. The other man promised to see to my needs. I don't remember much of that time," said Irridis. He reached down and picked up the drawing.

"And who was this stranger that showed such largess?"

"You've not guessed?"

"Say it."

"John Machine."

"When was this?"

"Thirteen years ago."

"Years after I last saw him," mused Moss.

"He was not unkind, at first, but he tried to exploit my differences. He took me from theatre to theatre, stage to stage, put me in freak shows as the Glass Boy. From the start it didn't go well for him. Audiences accused him of fakery. People have long memories. They remembered that he had once done something very similar with Memoria. Then something happened. He came to the dilapidated building, where he hid me when we were not traveling. He was covered in blood, hysterical with fear. I sat for a week in that building behind locked doors, like an animal, while he came and went by night."

"So you knew about Memoria all along?" asked Moss.

"Only a little. I had heard the stories. I'm sorry, I too should have been more forthright."

Holding the drawing, Irridis moved to the window and looked out. Moss watched his face in the reflection. "One morning, without warning I was put on a train and sent north. That's how I ended up as your pupil at the Chimneys Institute. Two terms, prepaid."

Irridis turned and held up the drawing. "When it came time to put me on the train, he found my drawing and took it, saying that if anyone saw it, I would be in grave danger. He never explained what kind of danger. He was furious. He didn't realize that I stole it back out of his pocket. Before we parted he did something he'd never done before, he struck me, on the side of the head. Then he spat in my face and said that I'd ruined his life."

"Well, that certainly sounds familiar," said Moss.

"It was like he had gone insane with fear before my eyes."

"I believe Imogene," said Moss. "She's right: for better or worse, John Machine has linked us all."

"She has just given me a clue to my past. Maybe I can find the answer to the questions that have bothered me for my entire life."

"Which are?" asked Moss.

"Who am I, and what am I?"

"Then our path is clear," said Moss. "I have to deal with Lamb—"

"And then we go to Nightjar Island. I believe it is there that I'll uncover my past, and we have good reason to suspect that Memoria would return there, given what Imogene has told us."

Whether it was because of the whiskey or her unburdening, Imogene was asleep when Moss entered the room to tell her of their decision. They left her undisturbed and talked until a late hour. Irridis remained in the library long after Moss had gone to bed. He sat accompanied by the ticking of the clock, and the occasional rumble of the streetcar outside. The drawings sat on the desk behind him. He had no need to hold them. The ocelli had already recorded them in every detail, making the information available to him. He was not just able to examine them sequentially in his mind's eye but to experience a full awareness of the information in the moment. Irridis took his augmented cognitive powers for granted. He knew his memory and degree of mindfulness far exceeded those around him, and for all of that, there remained a room he could not access. The time before he was rescued from the icy Irridian Sea was blank, a locked door. Whether through trauma or design, he had no way of knowing. The ocelli, which he believed to be sentient servants, remained mute on the topic.

When the clock chimed 3 a.m. Irridis rose and walked over to the still-open traveling bookcase. It sat as Imogene had left it, and for some time a pinprick of light had attracted his eye. He reached down and pulled a bottle from its recess. It was filled with small shells and bones; the kind of things you would expect a child to collect at the seaside. He held it up and turned it in his hand. Sure enough, something inside glinted. The lid unscrewed with a dry rasp. Irridis emptied the contents onto the desk. Amid the small collection sat a glass oblate ovoid. Its interior was smoky but a faint light could be seen. When he picked it up, it fit in his palm. When he moved his hand away, it remained in the air. It rose to join the five ocelli that were moving towards it like a group of curious fish.

TAXALI'S BOOKSHOP

THE NEXT MORNING MOSS DECIDED TO PAY OLIVER TAXALI A VISIT. Irridis had gone out sometime in the night, and Imogene was still asleep. It was the first time he had left the apartment since Irridis's arrival. In a borrowed leather coat and wingtips, Moss maintained a brisk pace, avoiding the faces of the few people he passed. He rubbed his hands together for warmth. It was early and a light frost lay on the nearby rooftops. A streetcar would have been quicker but he wanted to travel unobserved to the extent possible.

The backstreets were paved with bricks worn smooth by centuries of traffic and inset with sewer covers molded with a bas-relief fish. The smell of baking bread filled the air, intermingled with coal smoke. From a railway bridge Moss could see workers in a bakery yard wheeling loaves into delivery wagons. Horses stamped in the cold. The privations of the war had brought back many of the old ways of doing things. A further walk of fifteen minutes brought him to the bookshop, which dominated a traffic circle webbed by tramlines. In the middle of the circle there was a park. From Moss's approach he could see the façade of Taxali's bookshop through a jumble of rusty playground equipment and a bronze monument to a forgotten hero.

Croaker did not deign to lift his eyes as Moss came to the desk. No doubt he was still sulking about the atlas.

"I need to talk to Oliver," said Moss.

"Mr. Taxali is at bath," the man intoned, rolling his eyes. "I hope you're looking after that atlas, Mr. Woods." Moss climbed to the second floor. The walls were lined with signed photographs of authors famous and obscure. He came to a door and rapped a brass knocker mounted at eye level.

"Get lost," shouted a voice from within.

"Oliver, it's Moss."

"I'm having my bath, damn you."

"You're always having a bath. Let me in before I suffocate out here." Moss was growing hot in the close air.

"Leave me be," said Oliver.

"Oliver, open the door before I kick it in."

"Blast you. Very well. You'd better come in then. I can see there will be no peace otherwise. It's unlocked. Don't let the hot out."

Moss entered a large bathroom of cracked tiles, grout like strips of black licorice, and a floor covered in fungal growth. Oliver Taxali wallowed in a cast iron tub on a raised platform. Mingled with the general fug of steam and mildew was the headache-inducing smoke of his cigar. A moth-eaten top hat sat on his head and before him a book of pornographic woodcuts lay open on a bath desk. A housemaid poured scalding water from a kettle into the bottom end of the bath. Then, as though agitating a grotesque soup, she distributed the pocket of warmth with a laundry paddle.

"Well?" he demanded. "Make it quick. I'm not a well man."

This was not Moss's first tub-side meeting, but he vowed it would be his last. As the book dealer lolled, red-skinned in the grey water, Moss averted his eyes from what his imagination had already conjured.

"A woman came to Seaforth's house yesterday afternoon and she said that you had given her the address and my name. My real name."

Oliver scowled, pondering Moss's words. "She already knew your real name."

"That's hardly the point, Oliver."

"She went there, did she?"

"What did you think she would do? Why would you expose me like that? What happened to loyalty?"

"Hmmm. Well, why didn't you just lie? Tell her you'd never heard of Moss." Oliver laughed, showing his stained teeth. The disease that accelerated Oliver's aging had taken a terrible toll in recent months. He looked twice as old as Moss, despite the fact that they had once been inseparable childhood friends.

"But if he'd done that then she'd have come back here." The maid's voice, as soft as the patter of mouse feet, caught them both by surprise.

"What?" Oliver looked at her out of narrowed eyes.

"I just thought she might have come back and caused a fuss," she said.

"Stop editorializing, woman. It's damned distracting. Can't put two and two together around here for all the mumbling and chatter. Make yourself useful and pass me my legs."

"Yes sir, of course. Please forgive my impertinence." The maid removed the bath desk, set it on the tiles and then ran to an antechamber, lifting her dress clear of the floor.

"Come with me," said Oliver. With a great deal of splashing and swearing, the man heaved his substantial bulk upward until his buttocks, as red as boiled ham, rested on the edge of the bath. His legs, terminated at the knees with puckered scars, paddled the air as he fought to maintain his perch. Moss once again averted his eyes, pretending a sudden interest in the sagging plasterwork overhead. He counted long seconds before the maid's return, hoping that Oliver could maintain his balance without assistance.

The maid brought the prosthetic legs to the bath side. Instead of approximating a human foot, Oliver's legs were fitted with mechanical bird's feet. Three articulated toes were splayed forward, while a fourth curved backward, providing balance. Each toe was tipped with a silver claw. The shaft of the legs had been worked in an imitation of scales. When the long-suffering maid had finished belting the legs onto Oliver's stumps, he took a few tentative steps and to Moss's relief accepted a bathrobe.

"Give me your arm," he said, reaching out to Moss.

He took Oliver's elbow and led him away from the bath. They entered the room from which the maid had retrieved the legs. It was smaller than the bathroom, and furnished with a rolltop desk, lamp and chair. Oliver sat with a grunt, leaving Moss to stand in front of the desk. He felt that he might pass out from the humidity waiting for Oliver to shuffle through the contents of the drawers.

"Where the hell is it?" Oliver shouted.

The maid appeared at his side and removed the top hat, handing it to him as though it contained something unpleasant.

"In your hat, sir."

Oliver snatched the hat from her fingertips and plunged his hand into the interior. "There is a hidden compartment," he mumbled as he fought with something. "Ah-ha!" He produced a small, leather-bound book. "This is a treatise on magic. A grimoire. Hold it a moment." Oliver thrust it at Moss. His heart quickened. It was no forgery. His educated eye had already determined that much. It was older than any of the occult books already housed in Seaforth's substantial library, but matched those in the traveling bookcase.

"She gave me this. It's the real deal. Nightjar Island. Look at the mark on the cover."

"You think it's real," Moss asked.

"Of course it is, you idiot. Take it," he snapped.

Moss's fingers closed around the book.

"Possession of that book you're holding," said Oliver, "is enough to get you done for." The bookseller licked his thin lips and ran his tongue around the space between his lower teeth and cheek. "I'd have sold my own mother to the devil to have it." He snatched the book out of Moss's hand and wagged it in the air. "Selling you out was nothing. You were small change, chum."

"You sold me out for a book," said Moss. "We are friends, or so I thought." Oliver came around the desk on his avian feet. The maid rushed to his side.

"Mind now, you'll slip," she said. She held him as he returned the book to the interior of the hat.

"There are bigger things afoot than your problems, Lumsden. Speaking of which, any news for Lamb? That lot will be bothering me soon."

"Not yet," said Moss.

Oliver returned the hat to his head with a pat. "Do you know what the secret to catching a fly with your hand is, Moss? You strike not at the fly but where the fly will be next." With that, he turned away, cawing. "Friendship, be damned."

THE BUTCHER'S WINDOW

Stung by Oliver's betrayal, Moss left the bookshop and entered a side street. He stopped in front of a butcher's window and rolled a much-needed cigarette. Even the quiet street seemed overwhelming to his mind, already crowded with thoughts that threatened to boil into a rage. In an effort to block outside stimulus, he raised his collar and faced the window.

On the other side of the glass, three skinned rabbits landed on a bed of fresh snow. The red-eyed bodies, pink-muscled and footless, appeared to squirm, but it was only the result of the snow crystals melting beneath their ebbing warmth. A collection of other animals, in part or whole, was arranged around the rabbits: a pig's head with soft lashes and a split nose, a skinned lamb, a cow's tongue, blue at the tip and covered with polyps of ascending size. There were hanging ducks, lumpy with pores and stiff with subcutaneous fat, hardened like soap. Chickens, songbirds, fish, mollusks, octopi, squid and the aged fetal piglets were arranged on the snow, a harvest of horror laid out like a parody of the treats in the chocolatier's shop across the street. The flaw to the diabolical ordering of this fleshy exhibit was the group of rabbits, until a scarred hand shot into the snow and rearranged them with practiced efficiency.

Moss looked at his reflection. His blue eyes were reddened. He had lost weight and his face was lean. Sweat glazed his high forehead and his hair seemed to have grown overnight. His hands were held over his stomach like two arachnids clasped in death. Smoke from the cupped cigarette seeped around his fingers. *Relax*, he thought, *you look every bit the escaped convict that you are.*

Moss looked down at the lamb curled in the ice. Leaving Taxali's he had seen a lithograph on the wall that showed the muscles underlying the human face. For a nauseating moment he imagined his own skinned face lying among the animals, with a halo of snow and a lacework of bloody fluids. He imagined Lamb growing impatient somewhere in the city. How long had it been since the talk in the tunnel? As Moss did the calculation, he shifted his gaze to read the scene behind his head. Shops were jammed together, a pattern of windows and doorways. Behind the peaked rooftops and chimneys there was a dark sky that threatened winter. In the street, the passersby seemed almost of another world, knobs of imperfect flesh animated by some unfathomable spark. He saw each shifting form as a piece of flesh that began a process of decay the moment it came into the world. They were worms, swaddled and perfumed, devourers that chewed the world into a paste and shat out the indigestible remains. Their bodies lay heaped in the cemeteries, fouled the waterways and clogged the sewers. Their names were scratched in blocks of ancient limestone and granite millions of years old, the vainglorious declarations of worms, ticks and burrowers that were born and dead a moment later. He fiddled with the bottle in his pocket. *For God's sake relax*, he thought.

Moss refocused on the display in the window and the arrangement of livers that looked so reminiscent of a woman's private parts. He turned away and put a hand to his mouth and discovered he had bitten his lip. The coppery taste of blood rose in his sinuses. He flicked the spent cigarette into the street, noticing that he had caught the attention of a large dog. It was the dog from the canal. He had no doubt.

Moss did not know much about dogs. He had grown up with the collection of mongrels in the ship-breaking yards and its adjacent town, but he had avoided the wild dogs of the city. Every dweller in the City of Steps was familiar with the packs of curs that dragged the garbage into the street during the night and often had to be cornered and shot for reasons of public safety. Morel's dog Fits was representative of this kind of animal. The beast that faced him now was not. It was something else, massive, with muscles that moved like liquid beneath a coat that had a racehorse's sheen. Intelligent eyes watched him from the folds of its face. Its ears were pricked like horns. Moss felt awe as his hand reached to the side for the handle of the shop door, preparing to step inside if it became necessary. Then, without warning the dog left its position on the pavement and trotted down the left side of the street.

On impulse, Moss followed at a distance. There was an aesthetic appeal in the dog's fluid gait. It seemed careless of the shoppers that crossed the street to avoid a head-on encounter or those that simply turned to stare. He followed it down the winding street to the end, and then entered a passage. It stopped once and turned to look back. At the end of the passage it vanished from view. Curiosity overcoming sense, Moss broke into a jog, passing through the shadows. He emerged into an abandoned railway roundhouse. All that remained was a large circular yard covered in clumps of grass, goldenrod and late milkweeds. The yard was defined by a curved wooden building, with empty doors and sagging walls.

A windowless black horse carriage was drawn up in the center of the yard. The dog had settled on its haunches in the shadow of an iron-shod wheel. Moss stopped. What he saw next drove all fear of the dog from his mind. In the place of a team of horses stood a towering figure. Its head was hooded in weather-beaten canvas. Its body was covered in a heavy coat, which appeared to be encrusted with lichen and fungus. A massive yoke hung around the creature's neck, joining it to the carriage with chains. As Moss registered these details, it turned with an elephantine lugubriousness.

Moss staggered backwards. With all his being, he did not want to see the creature's face. In a panic, he turned and ran. He tripped on a piece of buried rail tie but recovered his balance and fled back through the passage. With each step he was certain he would feel the weight of the dog against his back, but moments later he had returned to the quiet backstreets without incident. He walked unnoticed out of the street in the direction of Seaforth's apartment.

AURA

HE DID NOT REACH THE APARTMENT THAT MORNING. WHEN traveling on foot, Moss preferred to vary his route to avoid notice. He entered an unfamiliar street, agitated by what he had seen in the roundhouse yard. The conversation with Oliver had shaken him. Although they had grown cagey with each other over the years, at root they had always been loyal. Their relationship had taken a new turn. Moss was at a loss to say why. He knew his emotions were intensified by the symptoms of sinispore withdrawal, which he had unsuccessfully tried to ameliorate with brandy. He was sweating and self-conscious. Every stranger seemed to look up at him at the last moment, as if startled by his presence. It puzzled him, until he realized that they were probably reacting to his own stare. A group of children playing quoits stopped to jeer at him. Under normal circumstances such behavior would have been forgotten a moment later. This time, the children's voices remained with him, like an echoing chorus.

Moss leaned against a wall to clear his head, several feet from a row house. Through the front window, past a sprawling aspidistra, he could see a parlor occupied by an upright piano. It was covered with framed photographs. Beyond the piano was a doorway, and within that, another. At the end of this succession of openings was a kitchen door leading into a tiny garden with a shed and a rose bush. Sparrows chased something invisible across the path. A sharp rap on the glass brought him back to the street. Moss jumped. An elderly woman, with a pale powdery face and a nest of hair held by a scarf, gestured for him to move on. Without argument, he resumed walking. He wanted no trouble.

The street was lined on both sides with red brick row houses like the one he had just looked into. The left side of the street was a mirror image of the right. He half expected to see a doppelganger walking along the sidewalk on the other side. This thought so seized his imagination that he could not help looking. When he did, he saw a child pushing a doll in a rusty stroller. He turned back to find yet another child, a girl of about five years, standing in front of him.

"My dad says strangers aren't to be trusted," she said. Moss froze, somehow unable to pass. "My dad says that's how Mum got knocked up with another little one. He's going to kick that man's teeth out if he ever catches him. There might be blood, you'll see."

"Let me past, please," said Moss. His voice sounded odd to his ear. It was high, impatient.

"I'm not stopping you. Have you seen blood? Real blood?" The girl stepped toward him. Her face was filthy and her hair crawled with lice. Moss walked around her. "You will soon." He hummed as he walked, attempting to drown her out.

A jagged seam of light appeared in his field of vision and slid on the diagonal. The back of his head throbbed and his skull was heavy, as though filling with sand. In the window of a post office, a riot of typography dizzied him, pulling him into a vortex of language. Letters shimmered, dissolved and then reappeared elsewhere when he tried to focus. He kept walking, convinced that the movement and the air would calm him. His vision deteriorated. To his left, a green gate led onto a narrow space between the houses. In this alley, old lumber warred with cans of overflowing garbage. A cat, with Imogene's amber eyes, slunk past, its tail low. He needed to vomit and shit at the same time. Terrified that he was about to have a humiliating accident, he rolled against the gate with his shoulder. It swung inward, stopping with a loud smack against the wall.

The alley was chill and damp with a welcome, concealing shade. Moss stumbled forward clutching his belt buckle, ready for any eventuality. By now the visual snow that had all but robbed him of his sight glowed like a cascade of embers. He gulped air and expelled vomit. It poured from his throat like magma. He looked toward the end of the alley, his eyes filled with tears. The sentinel-like creature from the roundhouse towered against the light. Embers flew from its head, on a wind that seemed to rise through the creature as though it were a chimney. Moss turned away intending to go back the way he had come, but another form blocked the route. This time it was a man. When the boot heel hit his sternum he flew backward into darkness.

They rooted through his pockets, and he was powerless to prevent it. He was detached, lost within himself. Had his heart stopped? Was he dying? They were not gentle, these hooligans. They rolled him over and over, grinding gravel and granulated glass into his hands and cheeks. They tore open his coat and shirt. They pulled his pants down to his knees and when they found nothing, kicked him for sport. He felt his sleeve being pulled up and Wood's watch fall away. There was a moment of argument as though they had become afraid, and then they were gone in a flurry of booted footsteps.

Hours passed. The wind rose as the light died, setting the leaves of nearby poplar trees ticking. Poplars, with their distinct smell, woody and ancient, reminded him of his childhood. He would escape from his sisters and their claustrophobic house near the strand where ships were broken, and climb into the poplar copse far down the beach. In the spring the buds were sticky like the blood that was now drying between his fingers. He wanted to cry out, but still, he could not move.

A dog came by. He could not tell if it was real or a dream. It licked his hands with a rough tongue that curled around each finger. At intervals it would stop, make a soft rhythmic sound with its mouth, and then begin again. How much time had passed? The night came and for a time the dog lay alongside him, its fur coarse but warm. Eventually, Moss became aware that the dog had left him. Had he blacked out again? He looked at the stars for a long time before he realized two things. He was shivering, meaning he was moving, no longer paralyzed, and somebody was standing nearby. He turned his head as much as he dared, and saw a pair of child's boots. A fetish was twisted around the ankle of the left foot, a chain woven with black feathers and small vertebrae in place of beads. He had found similar bones in pellets beneath the poplars.

"Moss," said a girl's voice.

Help me, please. It was no use; the words would not come.

The dog panted nearby. So, it had not left.

Rain.

At dawn he was lifted from the ground and carried to a running car, a taxi by the smell of it. He must have cooperated in some manner, but he had no memory of it later. A male voice spoke to him, giving gentle instructions and asking questions that Moss was unable to respond to. When he came to it was in his bed in Seaforth's apartment. He was alone and guessed by the intensity of the light in the window that it was midday. Kicking aside the blankets he found that the blood and grit had been washed off. The bruises and scrapes that remained were sore, particularly his knees, which were raw, as though he had been dragged over a pavement. He settled back onto the pillows and slept for a while longer. When he woke the second time he climbed out of bed and dressed in his own clothing.

Irridis sat in the kitchen, eyes closed, his head lit by the slanting light of the evening. Moss lowered himself into the chair on the opposite side of the table. When Irridis was in this meditative state, Moss had no idea if he was aware of what was going on around him. The ocelli hung motionless on the air in no discernible pattern. Their arrangement reminded Moss of a child's mobile. He cleared his throat to speak and then thought better of it.

GLASS SKELETON

"He was a painter with no talent." J. Hart Gale had grown even more whiskered since their first encounter. The change gave him a grandfatherly aspect at odds with the duplicitous undercurrent Moss sensed. He put his empty brandy glass on the mantel over the library fireplace and clapped his hands. His face was creased and raw, as though he had spent several days outdoors. Its texture reminded Moss of pomegranate skin. Gale had spent the past hour opining on a murder that had occurred in the Cloth Hall.

"You'd often find him at the Cloth Hall, where he was working on the mural of a whale, painting in an apron over a full suit, never a spot on him. His work had all the soul of a diagram in a schoolbook, accurate enough scientifically, I suppose, but lacking in that ineffable quality that makes a work truly great. I think he was doing the current leviathan to scale." He snapped his fingers. "If I am not mistaken, that deplorable episode in the Cloth Hall made the paper, the morning edition. Did you see it? Horrible when a man is murdered in cold blood, even a man of middling talent."

Moss shook his head, and lifted himself from an armchair. He winced as the muscles in his legs and shoulders complained. Only a few hours had elapsed since he had awoken bruised and scraped. "I don't read the paper."

"No?" said Gale, regarding Moss with watery eyes. "A curious thing for an educated man. I'd have thought you'd want to be up on things, current events and such. These are changing times, sir."

"Of course I will, when the children are here," said Moss, scrambling. "But when I'm alone I prefer to direct my attention to books, focus on the deeper analysis, if you know what I mean."

"I suppose so, you have a point." Gale took his coat from the back of the chair he had been sitting in. "It's nothing but spectacle at any rate. 'Twas ever thus." Moss wasn't sure if the man was referring to newspapers in general, the painter's murder, or his work. "Well, thank you, Joseph, for a most agreeable evening."

"It was kind of you to drop in, Mr. Gale," said Moss. "I am sorry Judge Seaforth wasn't here to greet you himself. Nevertheless, I enjoyed our visit. Your knowledge of antiquities is very impressive. Are you sure I can't get you another brandy?"

Gale chuckled. "No, no. I think we have abused that bottle well enough for one night. Well, I hope that Seaforth will shed some light on the whereabouts of the book when he returns. It amazes me to think he misplaced it. I've been looking for that book for several years, and he knows it. He should be more careful. It's quite a nuisance."

"Maybe he took it with him. Since it's a rare book, he might have wanted it for his stay, to look it over before passing it on. I'll be sure to mention it to him when he arrives back." He helped Gale into his overcoat.

"I shall remind him myself, the old son of a bitch." He raised his voice, wagging the air with his finger. "Where is my copy of *The Songbirds of Nightjar Island*, you old rogue? That is what I shall say. Ah, but at least he left the key to the liquor cabinet, Joseph. It made enjoyable what would otherwise have been a disappointing visit. In all seriousness, see that you do ask after the book. I paid a hefty price for a similar volume on ichthyology. In unscrupulous hands, the plates alone would be worth a fortune." He rested his hand on Moss's forearm. "They cut the illustrations from the binding and sell them framed. I've seen it done. Barbarous practice. I would hate to see the book placed in the wrong hands."

"I am sure it's in good hands," said Moss.

Gale made his unsteady way past a glass-topped table. One of Seaforth's odder curios, a three-foot replica of a human skeleton, made of red glass, stood on its surface. Moss held his breath as Gale stumbled toward it. With a lurch in his stomach, he became conscious that the angle of the skeleton's arm pointed to Moss's atlas, *The Golden World Traveler*, which sat a foot or so away. Gale did not notice this alignment, but for Moss it presaged what happened next. As Gale balanced himself on the carved edge of the table, he was brought up short by the atlas.

"Ah, the book you purchased the other day. Delightful." Before Moss could protest, Gale lifted the cover to reveal one of the drawings from the traveling bookcase. Moss had been studying it when Gale arrived unannounced and hidden it in his haste to answer the door. Gale opened the cover fully, his demeanor serious.

"Oh my, this is quite something. May I?" he asked, already picking up the drawing. Huffing and puffing, Gale squinted at it under his glasses, and then dropped it as if it had come to life in his hand. "How did you come by this?" His cheeks were ashen.

Cursing his stupidity, Moss struggled to maintain a neutral expression. "Is it important? A dealer gave it to me on speculation. Do you know something about it?"

"On speculation? Forgive me, Joseph. Pull the other one. Something like this, on an instructor's salary? Please."

"Of course," said Moss. "I'm joking. What do you know about it?"

"It looks very much to me like a drawing that might have been used in ritual occult practice, such as was once practiced on Nightjar Island. Ah, there's our proof. Do you not see that watermark? Papers made on the island were tightly regulated and made under the strictest guidelines. The guild required a watermark on each sheet. By God, this must be three hundred years old if it's a day."

Moss laughed. "Now you're pulling my leg. I think you have had too much brandy, sir. It's only a drawing. An interesting one, yes, but as to your explanation, well, you'll pardon my skepticism. Besides, it's a felony to have art from Nightjar in one's possession."

"If Seaforth has a mind to sell it, I would compensate him generously." Gale's eyes had hardened.

"It's not his to sell, unfortunately," said Moss, panicking. "The rub is that it's actually on loan, but as you rightly guessed, to Judge Seaforth, not me, and he's seriously considering the purchase. I am sorry that I deceived you just now, I was just trying to protect my employer's privacy." *And this lie is becoming quicksand*, he thought.

"If he does not purchase it, does there exist a possibility I might have an opportunity?" The greed in Gale's expression was naked. The man wanted to negotiate.

"I really don't know," said Moss, keeping his tone breezy, hoping to dissipate the tension.

"Preposterous," said Gale. "Let's not deceive each other, Joseph. You're no fool; surely you know how this looks. If the wrong person knew this drawing was in Seaforth's possession it could ruin the judge. You may not read the papers but others certainly do. Let me take it from you. Save the man from himself, Joseph."

"Mr. Gale, that sounds like a threat," said Moss. "I'm sorry. I cannot do as you ask." Gale's eyes moved around the room and returned to Moss. "I see. Well. Let's part company with the understanding that should you change your mind, my offer stands." Gale squeezed Moss's shoulder with a hand that felt like something used to remove tree limbs.

"I'll keep that in mind."

"Yes, you do that," said Gale. Moss walked him to the apartment door. He opened it and stepped into the hall for the final goodbye. Gale shook hands, turned to leave, and then stopped.

"Sober second thoughts?" asked Gale.

"Don't forget your hat, sir. It's still raining."

"Come now," said Gale, taking his hat by the brim. He explored Moss's face, lifting his glasses for a closer look. His breath reeked of expensive brandy and worn teeth. "Have it your way, then. I don't understand your reasoning. Good night." With that, Gale weaved to the head of the stairs. Morel was sweeping dead flies from the window ledge on a lower landing, eavesdropping.

"I won't take the elevator," said Gale. "Never could stand being trapped in a cage, if you know what I mean. By the way," he added as an afterthought, "you must come to my club for dinner before too long."

"Thank you, sir, I'll consider it."

"Goodnight then." A lesser man, thought Moss, would throw him down the entire thirteen steps to Mr. Morel's feet.

"Damn," said Moss. Back in the apartment he paced the floor in front of Irridis. "He knows who I am. He was toying with me there at the end, the smug prick. That remark about being trapped in a cage."

"He's a bad actor," said Irridis. "The mistake was in letting him through the door in the first place."

"He showed up unannounced," said Moss. "What was I to do? I've been on edge since Imogene arrived. I'm not thinking clearly."

"I thought you'd lost your mind," said Irridis. Moss's expression darkened, as he emptied a prodigious measure of brandy into a fresh glass.

"It's quicker if you drink it from the bottle," said Irridis. "I couldn't believe that you asked that gasbag if he wanted another drink."

"I was trying to put him at ease. You should have seen his face when he saw the drawing," said Moss. "Pure covetousness."

"I don't think you should underestimate him." Moss could see the twitch of dark orbs beneath Irridis's eyelids. As always, he was reminded of a certain type of toxic amphibian he had owned as a boy. "I find it hard to believe that his encounter with you in the bookshop was an accident."

"It just underscores what we talked about. It's time to leave."

"Yes, it is."

"Something must be done about Lamb." Moss looked at Irridis, meeting his eyes.

Irridis understood. "What is your plan?"

"I'm going to see Oliver Taxali tomorrow and tell him that I've located Memoria. I'll tell him that I'm planning to bring her to the Cloth Hall at midnight the day after tomorrow. He'll know it's bullshit, he loves a bit of trouble and will play along." Irridis started to speak, but Moss shook his head and continued. "Imogene not only lives in the Cloth Hall, she actually works for the Museum of Natural History."

"How do you know that for sure?"

"I found her employee card in her coat pocket." He shrugged at Irridis's mock face-palm. "I've done some research. The attic of the Cloth Hall is where the museum stores their mothballed collections. I just need to convince Oliver to arrange a meeting there, with Lamb."

"That will be unpredictable," said Irridis. "When Lamb discovers he's been tricked—"

"It doesn't matter. The whole point is to draw Lamb out. He won't be able to resist."

"And then you will kill him?"

Moss nodded. Prison had inured him to the occasional necessity for violence. It had been an undercurrent to everyday life. He was equally aware that enacting violence was not the same as contemplating it in the abstract. Therein lay the reason for the tightening in his gut.

"Yes, and we'll have to move quickly after that. The Red Lamprey will be looking for retribution."

Irridis looked thoughtful. "Politics in an organization like the Red Lamprey are complex. From what I understand, certain members of the group, who see Lamb as the last of an old guard, revile him. He's made a host of enemies over the years. The power vacuum that you will create will distract them. They are a surprisingly traditional organization. The loss of Lamb will initiate an arcane sequence of rituals that will keep them tied up for a time. The last thing they will be worried about is some snitch of Lamb's, with all due respect. By the time they return their attention, you'll have dropped out, taken a new identity. The real danger is surviving a confrontation with Lamb himself. Are you sure this is what you want to do?"

Moss twisted his arm until the lamprey tattoo was visible to them both.

"You said it yourself, Irridis. This is my death warrant as long as Lamb is alive. He doesn't leave loose ends. If we leave with Imogene, he will stop at nothing to track us down. This is his contract with me." Moss dropped his arm.

Irridis looked up. "Yes, he has chosen you and you are bound to him as tightly as Imogene is. As long as he is alive, you could both be hit at any moment, at his whim."

"He chose me because he thinks I can be turned. It's that simple, Irridis, he thinks that I can be turned." Moss felt rage building in his breast. "He believes that I will be highly motivated to produce Memoria to save my own skin." Moss stepped backward and swept the glass skeleton off the table. It shattered on the floor. He stood for several minutes amid the mess.

"I will help you do it," said Irridis. His voice was flat. "Lamb is a trained assassin and he won't come alone. It won't be easy."

"He will underestimate me," Moss said. "That is his blind spot. Tomorrow night I'll leave here and move to the shipwright's house." He emptied his drink into the broken skeleton, where it ran like blood.

The ocelli orbited Irridis's head, color shifting through the visible spectrum. As each one passed behind, Irridis was imbued with an amber glow not unlike the spilled brandy. "It's settled," Irridis said.

"Fine, I'll talk to Oliver in the morning."

"Good," said Irridis. He aligned the drawing with the table edge. "I'm going out. You should check on Imogene. She was barely conscious yesterday when I spoke to her." Moss had been surprised, on waking after his ordeal in the alley, to learn that Imogene had fallen ill.

"I'll look in."

"And clean this mess up before Morel sees it." Irridis winked.

His heart heavy with the prospect of what lay ahead, however necessary, Moss wandered through the apartment, distractedly examining various pieces of bric-a-brac and pulling books from shelves. He found and lit a poisonous-looking green cigar. It proved foul, and he stubbed it out in the kitchen sink a few minutes later. He picked up the drawing that Gale had examined and carried it back to the room where Imogene lay asleep.

Seaforth's bedroom had the same high ceilings as the living room and the library but it was smaller and more intimate. A chandelier in the form of a jellyfish cast spots of light across burgundy walls and dark wainscoting. A small fire ebbed behind a decorative grate, and the remains of a meal sat on the mantel, reflected in a slab of gilded mirror. A space between the voluminous taffeta drapes offered a peek at the city behind the building. Moss pressed his forehead to the window's cool glass. Realizing that he could be observed, he pulled the drapes shut.

Imogene lay not in Seaforth's bed but on a comfortable couch. As he pulled a blanket over her shoulders, his hand brushed her cheek. She had developed a fever. With skin so pale, she might have been non-human like Irridis. Although the fine wrinkles around her mouth and eyes argued otherwise.

"Everything's changed," he said. Her eyes moved behind their lids and her chest rose and fell in a gentle rhythm beneath the blanket. He placed the drawing in the traveling bookcase with the others. As his hand lingered over the case preparing to close it, he thought about looking through some of the books. Who knew what lay within those bindings? He imagined a movement in one of the bottles and decided it would be an exploration best left for daylight. He wished that he had a vial of sinispore to clear his head. But he did not. So he eased into an armchair and passed the time watching Imogene, until he too drifted toward sleep. His eyes popped open as his subconscious tossed up something he had noticed in the heat of his discussion with Irridis. Six ocelli?

THE ALLEY OF BIRDS

THE NEXT MORNING MOSS WOKE FEELING PURPOSEFUL. HE BATHED, and examined himself before a mirror framed in cherubim. His face had been spared the worst of the abuse that the rest of his body had endured. Red nicks on his eyebrow, and some marks on his cheeks were the only visible evidence of his beating. He dressed in clothes from Habich Seaforth's ample wardrobe, a white shirt, a slate-grey tie and creased pants. Over this outfit, he donned a black suit jacket and an overcoat. He trimmed his beard as an afterthought and polished his glasses. When his transformation into Joseph Woods was complete, he looked in on Imogene, who was still asleep. He closed the bedroom door so that his departure would not wake her. He did not intend to be gone long. He would set the bait and return.

Moments later he stepped from the apartment house into the cacophony of mid-morning. The street in front of Seaforth's building was just wide enough to support two streetcar tracks and a pedestrian walkway. A similar three-story row house with a limestone façade stood opposite. Both ends of the street were brightly lit and busy. Turning right, he set off at a brisk pace, noting the dramatic transition from summer to autumn that had occurred over the previous week. The air was cool, scented with coal smoke and the sea. Plants in the urns on the sidewalk were overgrown and yellowing. It was a peaceful morning.

He thought back to his mental state in the alley. He reasoned that it had been some kind of seizure, triggered by the sinispore withdrawal or the culmination of stress. The signs had been with him for days. He had not acknowledged them and paid a price for his carelessness. All of the dream fragments and visions could be explained thus. What could not be dismissed was the question of

his savior's identity. Who had rescued him in the taxi? To whom
did he owe his gratitude? It was not Irridis. Irridis had cleaned him
up and put him to bed, but another had delivered him home to
Seaforth's lobby, where Irridis had found him.

He walked toward the sunlight, where Devonian Lane inter-
sected with Sperricorn Avenue. He passed several shops, including
a boarded-up art gallery and a tobacconist. On the avenue he
pushed into a crowded streetcar that had just rumbled to a stop.
Moss was forced to stand in the aisle as the streetcar lurched
and sparked toward the market district. It was all he could do
to keep his balance. After several blocks he realized that he had
not checked for police agents before leaving the building. It had
been his practice since he started working for Seaforth. He took
this as a warning that his sense of purpose was overtaking his
caution and resolved to take his time, and be more attentive to his
surroundings.

The columns and blackened statuary of the Opera House slid
past, followed by the Maritime Museum and the Art Gallery. The
previous night's rain lay in puddles on the pavement but the sky
was now clear. Moss stepped off the streetcar near the Memorial
Gardens within sight of the market. As it trundled on with a
clanging of bells, he stopped to look at the Cloth Hall, an imposing
architectural landmark. It was not yet his destination. Turning
away, he traveled west to an old street behind the Art Gallery,
dodging trucks, dray carts and steaming piles of horse manure. He
was going to Bird Alley.

Bird Alley was a slime-covered stretch of cobblestones between
the gallery warehouse and the armory. Laundry lines had been
strung between the walls so that visitors could hang birdcages.
They swung in constant motion, housing a bewildering variety of
birds that showered feathers and seed husks into the air. Entering
the alley, Moss ducked to avoid a collision with a crowded line of
cages. The fluttering occupants filled his ears with pretty songs and
less pretty squawks as he navigated between the tables where old
men gathered to trade birds, stories and chess strategy. He circled
around a stall that served bitter coffee from a samovar. The smoke
of lamb skewers and chestnuts thick on the air reminded him that
he had not eaten. It would have to wait; he had spotted the person
he had come to see.

Oliver Taxali sat at his usual spot. A cage of sticks sat on a table in front of him. A small green parrot with a red beak stuck its head through the rungs and took a sunflower seed from his teeth. Croaker, also at the table, watched the performance with mild interest.

"This bird has a softer touch than the girl I spent last night with," said Oliver. The clerk snickered. He sat across from Oliver, in a black suit and a white hat, pouring red wine into a dirty coffee cup. Oliver sat with one leg crossed over the other, dressed in striped pants and a white shirt. He also wore a hat, charcoal grey with an emerald feather tip set into the band. Between them, Andrew leaned back on a chair avoiding Moss's eyes by thumbing through a dog-eared stack of boy's adventure comics. Oliver continued to attend to the parrot as Moss came toward the table. He knew Oliver would not be alone but Andrew's presence was a shock.

"Oh, you again," said the clerk. "How dreary. There's no peace, is there? Are you bringing me the atlas, Mr. Woods, Moss, whoever you are today?" The clerk hid a laugh in his handkerchief. He was drunk. Moss shook his head.

"Ah." Oliver spoke around the sunflower seed pressed between his lips. "It's the teacher." He gestured to the boy. "Andrew, run and fetch Mr. Mossy-Woods a cup of coffee."

"Good morning, Oliver," said Moss. "I didn't know you knew Andrew."

Oliver laughed. "I have many Andrews, Moss. Sit down. You obviously know Croaker?" Moss nodded at Croaker who was licking at spilled wine on the back of his thumb. Oliver served the bird another seed, this time with yellow-stained fingers. Croaker swallowed his wine in a gulp and looked at Moss with an inscrutable expression.

"Yes. How are you today, Oliver?" asked Moss.

"As ever. Pissed. Things haven't been so well. I invested heavily in a ship and last night I learned that the twat of a captain has run it up against a sandbar in the southern sea. Everything, glub, glub, at the bottom." He made a horizontal settling motion with a ring-heavy hand. The parrot cocked its head.

"Pity the fool of a captain when he returns," chuckled Croaker, showing his wine-stained teeth. Andrew returned with a tiny cup of something that looked like steaming sepia ink. Moss gave him three hexagonal coins as Oliver continued. "Enough of my sad story. What brings you to the alley? Didn't have enough yesterday? Are you here to buy a bird? Maybe listen to some old men talk shit? Have any more strange women showed up at your door?"

"I have something private I need to discuss." Moss had decided to act on a hunch.

"Croaker, Andrew, plug your ears," said Oliver.

"What do you know about a drawing that was stolen from the woman who gave you the book? I'd like to get it back." Moss darted a look at Croaker.

"Stolen?" Oliver made a face as though he had just put something sour in his mouth. "A rather strong word. Where was it, ah, stolen from?"

"I think you know."

"The Cloth Hall," Croaker supplied. "I know it well." He scratched his balls through his suit. Oliver cracked a sunflower seed and ate it, spitting the shell at the clerk. "Croaker, you should be more discreet." He looked at Moss. "And she should be more careful." Moss sipped the coffee and shuddered. Oliver laughed, causing the bird to flutter against its cage. "Come, man, it's only coffee." He shook his head, the smile leaving his face. "Your query is uninteresting, accompanied as it is by empty hands." He sighed.

"I haven't come with empty hands." Moss reached into his jacket pocket and pulled out *The Songbirds of Nightjar Island*. He laid out one of Seaforth's silk handkerchiefs and set the book on it. Croaker's eyes betrayed a flicker of interest, a movement that did not go unnoticed by Oliver.

"It's of greater value than the drawing," said Moss.

"I'm sure," snorted Oliver.

"*Songbirds of Nightjar Island*," Croaker said, as he snatched the book up with unconcealed relish. He opened the cover to the title page. "Rare."

"Careful with it, you fool," said Moss. "It's the author's personal copy."

"Pfff." Oliver waved his hand as if shooing a fly. "It could be a facsimile."

"It isn't," said Moss.

"He's right," said Croaker, cooing over the volume.

Oliver took a hand full of seeds and let them fall from one palm to the other. The air separated the husks. "How can you be sure?"

"Because, Oliver," Moss lied, "I met someone with great interest in the book and he confirmed its value. He was desperate for it. I thought you might want to see it first." Moss glared at Croaker who was holding the book in one hand as he reached for his wine with another.

"It's true," said Croaker ruefully.

Oliver fed the parrot another seed. Croaker slid the book across the table at Moss. Moss picked it up and held the book out to Oliver.

"You can see the authenticity by the marginalia." Moss slipped his finger into the book and opened it to a spot where he had written *I am bringing Memoria to the attic of the Cloth Hall tomorrow at midnight.* He angled the book so that only Oliver could see it. The man gave no indication that he had. Instead he picked up a tiny cup and sipped. "If I am able to produce the drawing you'll bring the book back to me as a trade. Agreed?"

"Yes," said Moss. He looked at his childhood friend's hooded eyes. When had the boy that he had knocked around with for long summer days become this frightening, cold man?

"Hey," said Croaker, "let me see that." Moss returned the book to his coat.

"Screw off, Croaker," said Moss.

"Write down the name of the book and its particulars," said Oliver. He produced a small notebook. "No offense, but I'd like to make an independent assessment of its value. I'll make inquiries about the drawing, see if anyone knows anything." Moss did as he was instructed, noticing the names of desperate souls that had come to Oliver for help. Croaker hissed petulantly through his nose.

"Very good. Now, is there anything else you would like?" A small brown vial with a tiny cork had materialized on the table. Moss's pulse quickened. He looked around the alley with its forms, huddled over tiny cups. Over their heads hundreds of birds fluttered like an oneiric manifestation of their thoughts. A thumping sound seemed to rise from somewhere deep underground, but it was only his heart. A welter of images from the previous day came at him and for a moment he thought he detected the presence of the seam of white light.

"No thanks." He stood up and smoothed his borrowed clothes. "Best not." The vial vanished beneath Oliver's palm, like an object in a trick of misdirection.

"Goodbye then, Lumsden," said Oliver, smirking. "We'll be in touch with you soon."

Moss left the alley shaken, but pleased. The unexpected presence of Andrew had rattled him from the start, but it was the appearance of the sinispore that had set his hands trembling. Moss had gone to the Alley of Birds knowing that anything like the stolen drawing would find its way to Oliver. There had been an even chance that Oliver would choose the drawing over the book. Moss had gambled and won. When the moment came he would take the drawing at gunpoint if necessary. It was an act that would have been inconceivable even a year ago. It would be something if he could return it to Irridis.

In the lane behind the Art Gallery he stopped at a loading dock and leaned on a pile of straw to roll a cigarette. His skin felt clammy and the beginnings of a headache throbbed in his temples, triggered by the acidic coffee.

"Are you all right, sir?" The voice was stentorian. Moss looked up to see a mounted police officer blotting out the sky. The officer was dressed in black, high boots, an immaculate greatcoat and a peaked cap. A gun hung off the man's wide belt. Moss could smell its oil from where he stood and it did not help the churning in his gut.

"Just a little too much to drink last night." The horse shuffled back a few steps. The sun blinded Moss.

"I understand, sir, but you cannot stay here. This is no place for a member of the public. Only the gallery staff members are permitted."

"Sorry, I'll be on my way then. Goodbye." Moss walked around the horse, which had chosen that moment to become as immobile as a bronze war memorial.

"A moment, sir."

Moss turned. "Yes?" A truncheon moved towards him and brushed his shoulder.

"A feather, sir."

"Thank you, officer." Moss felt like he might puke as the horse and rider moved away like a single, well-lubricated machine.

THE SCRATCH

"Don't take your coat off. You have to leave." Irridis dropped the lid of Moss's steamer trunk as Moss walked through the apartment door.

"What's going on?" asked Moss. His hand fell from his coat button. The apartment was in disarray. Clothes were strewn over the backs of furniture, dirty breakfast dishes sat on expensive wood surfaces. The curtains had been pulled back as far as possible to let the daylight in. Having made his decision to leave, knowing that his time there was at an end, Moss had grown impatient and less fastidious about the finer domestic details. More than ever, he saw the place for the grotesque museum to its owner's vanity that it was. Every surface was a curated still life that crowed, look at what I have, look at me. Moss felt no envy, and took satisfaction at the pile of shattered red glass swept against a baseboard. He cared nothing for an orchestrated exit. Let Seaforth know a convict had pissed in his treasure box.

"Morel came knocking for about the tenth time since I arrived back," said Irridis. "He was rattling his key ring and I thought he was going to let himself in. So I talked to him through the door, pretending to be you, using the convenient excuse that I was dressing. He told me that he had received a call from Seaforth's secretary this morning."

"Damn," said Moss, anticipating the worst. "He's back?"

"Not yet, but he's on the way. Apparently he asked after you. He wanted to know if you were still here. Not if you'd be here, but if you were still here. Morel could hardly contain his excitement."

"Someone's tipped him off." Moss's first thought was that Gale had alerted Seaforth, but it did not sit right. Gale would have more to gain playing a slow game. Lamb? The approach seemed too indirect.

"Then he might be on his way with the police," said Irridis.

Moss shook his head. "I don't think so. If he's suspicious, he'll want to deal with me personally. I imagine there are things in here that he wouldn't want prying eyes to see."

"Maybe. The secretary asked Morel to make sure that you will be here when Seaforth arrives."

"Okay, let's go. We can be long gone before he gets home."

Irridis pulled his hood over his head. "I ordered a cab. It's waiting in the yard at the back. I'll tell the driver to radio for another car, for you, and have it sent to the front door. I'm leaving now." He handed Moss a piece of paper. "Go to the shipwright's house. I'll see you tomorrow night at the Cloth Hall at 10 p.m."

"Wait, Imogene?"

"In the other room," Irridis said. "Waiting. I haven't filled her in, but she must suspect something is up."

Moss considered his friend, the person who had shown him more humanity than any human being ever had, even in his criticism. Irridis had been true, and even now stuck by him at enormous risk. He looked as alien and formidable as anything Moss could imagine, dressed head to toe in black, the lethal ocelli tumbling around him. He had waited for Moss to return and even packed his trunk, despite approaching danger. Turning on his heel, Moss started for the bedroom.

"I'm taking Imogene with me," said Moss.

"I had a hard time waking her. She still has a fever and she was talking in her sleep. When she woke and saw me, she started to thrash around. I got her to take a sedative. Eventually she calmed down and slept. I couldn't have her carrying on like that with Morel hanging around."

Moss turned the doorknob and entered the bedroom. Imogene sat near the hearth staring at the embers of a coal fire. Her eyes were sunken and her skin pale and clammy.

"You're cold," he said. "I am sorry about that. Irridis doesn't feel the cold the way we do. It can be very irritating actually. Are you still sick?" Imogene shook her head. Not wanting to provoke her annoyance by contradicting her, he busied himself with the grate, stirring the embers. Sparks jumped onto the hearth and smoke rolled up the wall. "Not my area of expertise." He turned his attention back to Imogene. She was trembling.

"I didn't tell you everything," she whispered. "Look." She pulled her blouse up to reveal a scratch, a puckered and raw diagonal line across her stomach.

"What happened?"

"Not what, who. Her name is Elizabeth," said Imogene distantly. "A girl that never ages. She rides a dog. She is a witch." Imogene stole a glance at Moss. "She claims that the traveling bookcase belongs to her and she is obsessed with its return. She scratched me before I came to see you. She confronted me in the market. I escaped, but not before she did this to me. I think it's what is making me sick." She covered the wound.

"Why not just give it to her then?"

"Precisely because she wants it so badly. It's evil, Moss. You didn't see her eyes. They were horrible, piercing. There was a terrible want in them. I can't properly convey how they made me feel, but every-thing in me rebelled against giving in to her lust for the bookcase. I knew in an instant that with the knowledge in those books, she would be capable of great evil. I could not live with myself if I submitted to her will."

"I am going to help you. Can you walk? We must leave."

"Why, what's going on?" she asked.

Moss took a deep breath. Imogene was obviously delirious. A rumble came from the other room as Moss's trunk was dragged across the floor. It was followed by a thump. A hoarse voice, which Moss guessed to belong to the cab driver, negotiated a transaction.

"They'll be gone in a couple of minutes. And then we have to go too."

"Answer my question."

"I can't right now. No time." More thumping punctuated his words. "Can you move?"

"I don't know. I feel so weak."

Moss retrieved her boots and worked them onto her feet. She emanated a heat that made Moss want to bury his face in her stomach.

Imogene closed her eyes. "Oh, I really am not well."

"Let me help you." Moss picked her hands out of her lap and pulled her to her feet. She stood, swaying.

"I'm so cold. She'll find me again. I can feel her near. I simply don't feel like I can run again. I don't have the strength."

"We'll have you somewhere warm soon." Moss thought back to the first time he had seen Imogene, mischievous and quick in the halls of the museum, lethal and wicked in the tunnel. The thought of someone who could change her so quickly gave him pause, and then anger, as he recognized a begrudging admiration of those earlier qualities.

"I'm not a child, Moss," she whispered.

"No," he said, "you're not."

He needed to get her moving. He could not afford sympathy now, not with Seaforth on the way. Somehow he needed to motivate her.

"We're going to another house," he said. "In another part of the city, out of the way. Lamb, or this Elizabeth, won't know about it. We'll drop out of sight, but we only have a few minutes. Come on, there's a cab downstairs." Moss cleared his head of the image of the girl and the dog by taking Imogene's arm more roughly than intended. He led her from the room. Irridis, the trunk and the bookcase were already gone.

"What's the matter, Moss? Are your troubles catching up to you as well?" Imogene said, her voice mocking but faint.

"Keep walking," said Moss.

Imogene did not resist as he guided her out of the apartment. In the hall, she turned toward the elevator but Moss shook his head and steered her to the staircase. They descended. Tightening his grip on her arm, Moss kept her upright, knowing that if she sat down he would not get her up without a struggle. When they reached the main floor they heard Morel above them.

"I see you. Stop there!"

"There's the cab coming," said Moss under his breath. "Ignore him and keep moving. Don't stop." Moss pushed open the front door of the apartment building, timing their exit to the arrival of a dilapidated taxi. The driver, cigar wedged in the corner of his mouth like a woody growth, took note of Moss and Imogene and then looked away to leaf through sheets on a clipboard. Imogene hesitated. Moss collided with her.

"What are you doing?" he asked. He fought his irritation, knowing it was the harbinger of panic. The driver looked toward the apartment entrance, squinting through smoke, as though impatient to be away. "Let's go." Moss started, but Imogene pulled her arm free, stopping him.

"Where are you taking me?" she asked, confusion in her eyes.

"I told you, to a house." He clenched his lips and shook his head. Only specific information would dislodge her from the vestibule. "It's a house in Hellbender Fields."

"Your house?"

Moss hesitated. "No, of course not. Do I look like someone who could afford a house in Hellbender Fields?" His voice rose.

"Whose then? Lamb's house?" Imogene's lips blanched and her hands tightened into fists.

"What? No," said Moss, astonished. He wondered if the effect of the scratch was making her paranoid. "I told you, it's a safe place. It belongs to someone that Irridis knows. They're out of town for the next few months. The place is empty. Nobody will know we are there. You can rest and we can sort out what to do next." He hoped his smile was more encouraging than it felt.

"She's found me again," said Imogene. She looked around as though she expected the strange girl to leap from behind a planter. "Echo is with her."

Desiring to be anywhere else, Moss shot a glance at the cab.

"Why do you think she has found you?" he asked. He never received an answer. A second, newer car, covered in dust and crusted insects, lurched onto the curb behind the waiting taxi. A rear door flew open and a lean man with swept-back grey hair and black-framed glasses fought his way over suitcases and climbed from inside. He jammed a hat on his head as he emerged and pulled an expensive-looking overcoat after him. The hat cast a shadow over his face but it did not hide the angry set of his jaw. A radio patrol car marked with dents and bullet holes pulled up behind the first, and a second man jumped from the passenger seat. His gloved right hand held a revolver. The first man was Habich Seaforth; the other, judging from his gun and weather-stained raincoat, had the air of a plainclothes detective.

Moss swore and grabbed Imogene around the shoulders. He forced her into the shadow of the vestibule. Telling her not to move, he dropped to his knee and pretended to lace his boot. He was banking on his beard and the presence of a woman as his disguise. Although Moss knew Seaforth's face well, his employer had not seen him since the trial years earlier. Both men rushed past. Seaforth bumped Moss's shoulder.

"Out of my way," Seaforth said, as he pushed against the interior door. Then the two men were gone, thundering up the stairs in a cloud of dust.

Moss stood and grasped Imogene's sleeve.

She tore herself free. "Don't touch me."

"We have to go, now," he said. "They'll be back any second."

"Who are they?"

"We don't have time for explanations," said Moss.

"Who are they?" she insisted.

He lifted his hands. "Look, the one with the glasses owns the apartment. The other one is a cop." Feet rumbled on the stairs, accompanied by muffled shouts. "They're looking for me."

"He had a gun," said Imogene, dazed.

"Come on," Moss said. He grabbed Imogene and dragged her from the vestibule. She moved with him in an awkward dance. The sound of feet on the stairs was like a racing heart. The men were coming back down. Morel cried out at the top. Fits barked in hoarse whoops. Moss prayed that the man did not think to slip the dog from its leash. The vestibule door closed behind them. Moss and Imogene lurched forward. Halfway between the door and the curb she stopped. Her face was stricken.

"Where are the drawings, the books?" She reversed her steps. "I have to go back for them."

"No, Imogene, no," yelled Moss. "Irridis has them." The two men appeared in the doorway. Moss reeled back across the cobbles toward Imogene, arm outstretched. The detective drew aim with his revolver. A shot cracked in the narrow lane and a slit, like a red thread, opened across Imogene's throat, sending her pendant flying over the cobbles. Moss grabbed her as she slumped. As he eased her to the ground a bullet tore through the collar of his shirt making a sound like the slap of a flag. Imogene was on the pavement, still and pale. Moss held the sides of her head and shook. "Imogene, get up," he shouted. A third shot hit the ground beside her head and sprayed her face with sparks and shards of cobblestone. He lifted her eyelids but the pupils were unmoving.

The detective attempted a tackle. Some animal instinct alerted Moss and at the last second he rolled to the left, smacking his forehead against the ground. For a second the white pain blocked all other sensations, and he came close to losing consciousness. A hand on his ankle kept him scrabbling across the pavement. He rose to his haunches and kicked the cop square in the face. There was a stomach-churning pop as the man's septum split. The detective buried his face in his hands and shrieked, rocking back and forth as blood spurted between his fingers. Moss staggered to his feet. With a last glance at Imogene's unmoving form, he fled.

He barged through the crowd that had gathered. Hands grabbed at his clothing. He lost the remains of his shirt collar. Someone tried to trip him. He landed on the side of their ankle. The bystanders pulled away, shouting. A sharp pain from his left calf told him that another bullet had found its mark.

BLACKRAT BAKERY

THE LAND BEHIND SEAFORTH'S BUILDING WAS A WARREN OF alleys connecting scrubby railyards, gardening allotments and crumbling buildings from centuries past. Moss knew that his best chance of escape lay in that direction. He had made a point of walking and internalizing the main arteries in his first few days in the neighborhood. If his leg held out, he could slip away unseen into the ever-narrowing capillaries of nameless access lanes and canals.

His calf burned as he limped along a wall in the shadow of a fire escape. Intersecting alleys channeled excited shouts. The pop of gunshots continued, which confused Moss. Who were they shooting at now? He paused and looked up at a hinged fire escape ladder, trying to block the image of Imogene's expressionless eyes. It was too much. He rolled the back of his head against the brick, his own eyes tearing with the pain. The agony he felt at having to leave her became one with the pain in his leg and head.

He cursed and kicked at the wall. A single thought ate at him. What if she wasn't dead? What if he had made a mistake and abandoned her to Seaforth and the detective? In the moment, he assumed a bullet had caught her from behind, but had he actually heard a second shot before she fell? Events had unfolded too quickly. If she had survived, she would be held complicit. It would go hard on her. He winced as he looked for options through sweat-smeared glasses. More than anything he wanted to double back and check on Imogene, but it would be suicide after what he had done to the policeman. He lifted his glasses and rubbed grains of pavement from his eyelashes. The elegant pants were now soaked with congealed blood. Pink foam rose through the weave. His knees were rubber and his vision swam.

A boy rounded a corner, running so hard that his shoes threatened to fly off his feet. He was coming from the direction of Seaforth's house. It was Andrew.

"What are you doing here?" asked Moss. "Go away, you shouldn't be here, it's dangerous."

"I saw what happened," said the boy, breathing hard to catch his wind. "They're right behind me."

Moss groaned. It was impossible to think that he could outrun his pursuers in with an injured leg. He grabbed Andrew's shoulder. "Andrew, I need somewhere to hide. Can you think of anywhere, nearby?"

The boy thought for a moment. "Follow me," said Andrew, pulling at Moss's jacket. Moss followed, reasoning that the boy would be familiar with every bolthole in the neighborhood. "It's not far. Hurry, over here." They had entered an alley beside a large blackened building. It looked familiar to Moss. Andrew ran to a recessed coal cellar door. It opened with a dry metal rasp. Without a second thought, Moss hobbled across the road. He patted Andrew on the shoulder and ducked into the black opening. The boy slammed the doors behind him, loosening a shower of wood and rust. Moss slid down a steep chute and landed in a pile of coal with a violence that winded him. He lay on his back in the dark, sucking in the dust raised by his entrance. A group ran past in the street above. Their voices and footsteps waned. For some time, a dog pawed and whined at the cellar doors, but nobody seemed to notice or care, and then it too stopped.

Moss worked into an upright position. The room had a floor of packed earth and walls constructed from a jigsaw of stone. A wooden crate sat to one side and a stack of clay tiles to the other. In the center of the room a mound of coal and straw formed a bed for a pale lettuce-like growth. It was as unpleasant a place as any, but he was happy to be in it. He stood, testing his weight on the injured leg. The pain was excruciating. A few minutes later he gathered the nerve to pull up his pant cuff. His calf was cut on the inner side. It was raw, but not life-threatening. The bullet had not pierced an artery or shattered the bone. He squeezed a flap of skin over pulped flesh and dry heaved as the pain throbbed through him. The wound was not bleeding as it had been, so he lowered and tented the material. It was a mess, but it could have been much worse.

He wiped the tacky blood from his fingers on his clothing as he pieced together what might be happening outside. There was no sound to suggest that anyone remained near the chute entrance. Andrew seemed to have drawn off Moss's pursuers, but how long would it be before they backtracked?

He had to alert Irridis to his disastrous exit from Seaforth's. If Andrew returned, he would have the boy take a message to Irridis at the Cloth Hall. The boy would find him. Moss had full confidence in Andrew's resourcefulness, if not necessarily his forthrightness. As soon as possible Moss had to find out what had happened to Imogene. If she was alive, he needed to know so that he could devise a way to help her.

He sat on the crate and rested, head in hands. It seemed his luck had grown worse with every move. He pulled back his sleeve and rubbed the red lamprey tattoo as if he could erase it with his thumb. Had Lamb tipped off Seaforth? Maybe Lamb had somehow discovered that Imogene had gone behind his back and was punishing them both. If Moss had not escaped, the result would have fulfilled Lamb's promise, a return to prison. Moss dismissed the theory. Using Seaforth as an unwitting participant was too indirect for Lamb. A man who would set fire to another man's house would not work in such an elliptical manner. The money was on Gale. The collector had the most to gain. Exposing Moss would make Gale a hero to Seaforth. In Gale's fantasy, Seaforth would no doubt be more than willing to reward him for his diligence, with a prized book or perhaps a rare drawing. Having arrived at a plausible theory, Moss lay down on the crate. The straw smelled of cat piss, but he fell asleep as if were fresh cotton.

Scratches against the wall woke him. He had slumped to the ground with his head at an uncomfortable angle. He straightened his neck, which felt as though it had a thick, resistant wire at its core. The realization of his predicament returned. He hawked and spit into the corner while he pulled at his clothing. He deplored the damp. It penetrated the cloth and covered his skin with a clammy sheen. His hands smelt like mushrooms. Flexing his fingers, he resolved to wait no longer. Anything waiting beyond the door was better than becoming a medium for the rank growth in the cellar. As if to under-score the point, three rats, no doubt the source of the scratching, ran along the wall in single file. They stopped every few seconds to sample the air, whiskers twitching. They were accustomed to his presence, a disconcerting reminder of how much time might have passed. A curse sent them skittering over each other, but not as far as he expected, or would have liked. How long had he been lying on the ground? Thick sinuses and heavy limbs suggested hours, but he knew that isolation and discomfort could fool the body.

Using the chute for support, Moss pulled himself to his feet. Ambitions of climbing to street level were put to rest. Even if his leg was fine, the chute was too steep, too dusty. He looked for an alternative and found a rough door where several coal bags sat in a line. Five steps would get him there, five determined steps. He took a deep breath, filling his mouth with acrid dust. Five steps. He lifted a leg to take the first, and swore, pressing a fist to his forehead.

"Yeeeeooow," he yelled. Flaring his nostrils, he pitched himself toward the wall and gripped the stone. The pain from his calf flared and knocked inside his head in a way that made him hesitate, eyes wide, waiting for something of surpassing neurological awfulness to follow. When it did not, he exhaled and shuffled toward his goal, using the wall as a support. The calf muscle eased but the pant leg peeled from the friable wound and blood ran down his ankle. He persevered and reached the door. Yellow light shone through the gap beneath it, but listening, an ear pressed to the wood, he could not hear a thing from the next room. One, two, three. He seized the latch. The door opened like a gummy mouth. Warm kitchen air enveloped him.

Generations of baker's slippers and a permanent dusting of flour had worn the floors to a surface that undulated like a limestone riverbed. Walls of the same stone used in the cellar were cluttered with blackened pots and pans. Knives, rollers, spatulas, spoons and ladles were hung in untidy rows or scattered on the ground. A cast iron coal range was set into a brick fireplace that was taller than Moss. Its numerous small doors, grates, and pipes twisted away with biological complexity. It was a gargantuan troll with multiple mouths, and its febrile breath was the source of the heat on Moss's cheeks.

Oliver stood in front of the stove, a pipe smoldering between his lips. The smoke hung around him like a noxious, personal atmosphere. The skin beneath his eyes bagged. He wore black pants, a white shirt and a dove-grey overcoat. In spite of his affected posture he was in a state of repressed conflict, edgy, even nervous. His body gave the impression of being held upright by a supreme act of will. His fingers drummed on his thighs and his left bird claw rattled like a sewing machine treadle.

Moss limped to a chair and gripped its back. His first impulse was to throw it at Oliver. He settled instead on using it for support, easing his weight onto his good leg. He could only imagine how much Oliver was enjoying his predicament. Seaforth's fine clothes were ruined. The delicate weaves and detailed stitching had not been designed for gunplay and coal chutes. The pants bagged at the knees, the jacket was torn across the left shoulder and the shirt was soaked through with sweat, stained with blood and coal dust. Something below his left eye itched, making it run, but he was too spent to care.

"Oliver. What a coincidence," said Moss. His mouth was dry, and there was coal grit between his teeth. "Just happening by?"

Oliver exhaled a stream of blue smoke that ended with an impatient sigh. "The boy got the shellacking of a lifetime. He was confused about his loyalties. But eventually, he told me where you were hiding. Under my nose, no less."

"You're a prick."

"I'll not be lied to."

"You beat him."

"You have a soft spot, Moss. You always did. And where's it got you?"

"It doesn't matter to you that he's a kid? How can you be so callous?"

"How can you be so ridiculous? He's a guttersnipe, just as we were all guttersnipes at his age. You'd do well to remember where you came from, Moss. Besides, what do you really know about that damned boy? Nothing. Confusing him with books, that's what you're doing."

"That's a strange opinion from a bookseller," said Moss.

"Bah, books are a commodity. Ideas come and go; the world never changes in its essentials." Oliver drew his head back in challenge. "Don't think I don't know what you've been doing. Books. Where have your damned books got you?"

"He deserves better than the life you are offering him."

"Oh really?" said Oliver with mock seriousness. "I think you're making assumptions. You think you know everything about the boy."

"I didn't say that."

"Well, did you know that he's been going to Seaforth's apartment to keep an eye on you and your friend? Very naïve." Oliver wagged the stem of his pipe. "Did you think your silly lessons—oh, never mind, it's not important anymore."

"So what did you learn? Chicken on Monday, shellfish on Friday night? That must have been a scintillating revelation."

"Don't mock me. You never know when a little inside knowledge is going to come in useful."

"What do you want, Oliver?" asked Moss.

"I want Imogene's bookcase and everything in it. The contents will be very interesting to the right people."

Moss spit coal grit.

"Oh yeah, I know who she is, Lamb's little criminal protégé. That's why I had Andrew sniffing around her apartment at night. He would have grabbed the bookcase then, but it was too heavy."

"Of course, Andrew."

"Like smoke through a keyhole," said Oliver. "But not very strong. So, we decided to watch her and see what she was about."

"Always after the big prize."

Oliver shrugged. "Andrew scared her. Imagine my surprise, though, when she came to the shop the next morning. She dangled that book under my nose, not knowing that I knew there were many more." Oliver chuckled. "And then she asked for you, very direct, no small talk. That woke the curiosity in me, I can tell you. I mean, given what you are supposed to be doing for Lamb."

"You followed her?"

"Well, not in person." Oliver widened his eyes and tugged his pants by the sharp creases.

"So you had Andrew do it."

"She didn't set a foot toward Seaforth's building for two days. I thought she'd thought better of it."

"You could have stolen the case while she was out," said Moss.

"Yeah, but then I remembered that Lamb had approached my father looking for a traveling bookcase many years ago. So it started to feel like a double-cross on the girl's part. That being the case, forgive the pun, the potential of the situation became that much more interesting."

"She knows I work for the judge," said Moss. "She wants to sell the books to him and asked me to broker the sale. I wanted the drawings to be the complete set. You of all people should understand that, hence my request to trade for the bird book."

"I knew it." Oliver tapped his temple. "Little bitch assumed he'd give her a better price."

Moss let go of the chair. Vertigo threatened to overcome him. He wondered if he was concussed or had lost too much blood.

"But Seaforth and the cop fucked it all up by trying to shoot you and the woman in the street."

"Trying? Is Imogene alive?" said Moss.

"Seaforth is incandescent that you, an escaped convict, were living in his apartment, and touching his precious first editions." Oliver put his hands over his face, and then looked at Moss through parted fingers. "To think you nearly taught his little darlings." He dropped his hands, becoming serious. "Seaforth is telling people that the good detective was aiming to wing you. I'd recommend that you lie low, Lumsden Moss, late of Brickscold."

"Oliver, for fuck's sake, where's Imogene? Is she alive?"

"Yes, idiot, she is alive. While you were leading a merry chase, it seems she got up, dusted herself off and capitalized on the confusion to escape in the cab," said Oliver. "The driver panicked when he realized she was hurt and dumped her off somewhere near the steps. Fortunately Croaker was there to lend a hand."

"So, where is she?" asked Moss.

"Somewhere safe, if not altogether comfortable." Oliver drew on his pipe. "I'd like to know where the case of books got to in all of this." He expelled smoke. "She doesn't have it. I assume even you weren't stupid enough to leave it behind, which leaves our good friend Irridis."

"I don't know where he is."

"But you can find him. So here's the offer, Lumsden. Bring me the case before you go to the Cloth Hall to meet Lamb and I'll give you Imogene. You'll need her, I assume, for whatever stupidity you're planning next. Lamb doesn't have to know a thing about any of this. He'll be distracted and he thinks the bookcase is long since lost.

You can find me in the Bird Alley."

"Don't screw me on this."

"I won't," said Oliver. "But if you don't show up, I'm going to turn her over to Lamb and tell him the whole sorry story. At least I'll get points for going to him. I'm taking a huge risk in withholding, so I need to get something sweet out of this. I'm giving you a chance, for old times' sake. Bring me the case, get the girl."

"You think of everything," said Moss.

"Strike where the fly is going." Oliver looked around as if he had heard something. "We'd better get out of here. The cops will be searching every cellar and attic for you. It's just a matter of time before they check here. Can you walk?"

"Barely. A bullet sliced my leg open," said Moss.

Oliver reached into his pocket. He tossed Moss a vial. "For the pain, on the house. Nothing better."

Moss caught the vial of sinispore and put it into a pocket without a look. Grimacing at the pain, felt simultaneously in his heel and knee, he followed Oliver through the abandoned bakery, leaving the warmth of the kitchen for a progression of cooler and dimmer corridors. They emerged through a service door into a wet night where every surface was dark or reflective, as if everything had been transformed into crude oil. They stopped in a space beneath a corrugated overhang, which was dominated by a giant food mixer with a fire-blackened motor housing. Moss had difficulty seeing Oliver's face. It was a blob of folded dough moving from side to side. His shoulders were hunched.

"What's the matter with you?' Moss asked, raising his voice to be heard over the hiss of the rain.

"We aren't the only ones with an interest in Imogene," said Oliver.

"I know, Lamb—" began Moss.

Oliver shook his head. "No, I don't mean Lamb. Another."

"Who?"

"Someone has been stalking her. Somebody uncanny."

Moss forced a laugh, but his arms had gooseflesh. "What are you talking about?"

"A witch."

"Oliver, are you resorting to frightening me with phantoms now?"

"A word to the wise is all. I'd hate to see you run into problems before I get my prize." Oliver tapped his pipe bowl against a wall.

Tobacco embers sizzled to the ground. He stared into the night. *The man is shit scared*, Moss realized.

Something nudged his foot. Moss looked down to see a pale slug larger than his hand, moving in fluid contractions up his leg. It had a crest of waving tendrils that were probing the blood-stained cloth. He kicked it off in disgust. It landed nearby, a glistening knot of tissue crusted in dirt. Moss winced, touching his calf, now streaked with iridescent mucus. "Did Imogene mention the witch to you?"

Oliver's pale face ran with water. He had stepped outside of the roof's protection. A curtain of drops now separated them. He hesitated.

"No," he said, finally.

Moss raised his palms. "Okay, let's say you are right. What does your witch look like?"

"Don't patronize me." Oliver turned on him, jabbing the air with the pipe stem, his affected composure gone. "I didn't see it. The damned thing entered me. Felt inside me, like a long cold hand stirring my organs. I never want to encounter it again. Which is why you are going to find that case in a hurry."

"Tell me what happened."

"I saw the woman, Imogene, in the Cloth Hall on the day she came to the shop," said Oliver, staring into the middle distance. "It was night. She was alone. Most of the stalls were closed. I was with Andrew in the corner where they sell fruit. All of a sudden I felt sick."

Oliver was rattled. He stopped talking for a moment and scraped at a still-glowing ember on the ground with one of his metal feet. "I could feel something, invisible, working at me, like it was trying to get into my body. At first it wasn't able, then all of a sudden it found a way in. It slid into my mouth and ears, even the corners of my eyes. It probed anywhere there was a hole, for God's sake, like invisible fingers. Once it was inside, it was warm, a presence. It only lasted a few minutes. After that, it left me and I woke up on the ground. It had gone to the woman. I could tell by the strange expression on her face that she felt as I did. I don't know what happened after that because I fainted again. Andrew claimed that I had some kind of seizure and that I was raving about strange lights. He said that while I was kicking around on the ground he saw a demon, shuffling through the horse stalls, a giant covered in dust.

I tried to beat a more accurate description out of him, but that's all the boy would say, a giant." Oliver spat on the floor.

"Are you really sure you want that bookcase, Oliver?" asked Moss, his voice low.

Oliver raised a fist. "Patronizing bastard. I don't give a shit if you believe a word of it, Lumsden, just bring me that case." Moss limped away through the dark. "Make no mistake, I will hand her over to Lamb," Oliver shouted after him.

Moss stepped into a recessed doorway and watched Oliver leave the bakery yard. As soon as Oliver rounded the corner, Moss hobbled after him. In his current condition it would be impossible to track a person walking at normal speed, but Oliver moved slowly and deliberately on his bird legs. Perhaps he would lead Moss to Imogene.

Oliver's route led to the front of the bakery. The façade of the building came from an age when even industrial buildings were given the countenance of authority. A black sedan rumbled against a backdrop where wide steps led to hidden doors and towering columns with elaborate capitals supported heavy cornices. A signature of exhaust rose from the car up through the rain. Moss stopped in time to see Oliver climbing into the back of the car. Oliver ducked under an umbrella held by the same woman who had stirred his bath. She folded the umbrella and climbed in after him. The door closed with a solid thump. A moment later, the car roared away, its engine echoing off the surrounding buildings.

Moss found a stairwell. It was full of trash but otherwise empty. One image filled his mind, the towering figure he had seen harnessed to the black carriage. At the time it had seemed a frightening apparition, one that he had stumbled upon in his curiosity about the dog. Oliver's story put things in a new light. It was clear that the witch stalking Imogene was also stalking him. He had to warn Irridis.

Witches and giants. *Great*, thought Moss, *just great.*

SAWDUST AND GLUE

DURING HIS FIRST YEAR IN BRICKSCOLD PRISON, MOSS WATCHED a young man, older than but not unlike Andrew, die of sepsis. During a rough game of football, the youth had been knocked into a drainage ditch that ran along the side of the exercise yard. Climbing out of the murky water, he had cut his foot on a piece of rusty culvert submerged in the soft mud. Within hours, what had at first seemed a superficial gash had begun to swell and show signs of infection. Through the night, the youth became fevered and the wound spread red tributaries along his pale legs. Some of the older men brought him blankets and tea, but the infection was relentless and despite the rough words of encouragement, the outcome was never in question. In the morning, Moss saw the guards drag the body, rolled in mildewed canvas, into the yard for cremation.

The makeshift shroud against the prison floor had made an unforgettable sound. The memory roused Moss to leave the stairwell, fighting the pain, and walk to the shipwright's house. The house promised a dry, warm and hidden place to ingest the sinispore. He would find Irridis, as soon as his strength was restored.

t took him an hour to reach Hellbender Fields. The ill-lit avenues and treed gardens provided welcome concealment. He came to a marble fountain at the center of a deserted square, dwarfed by the silent, facing houses. Inclement weather had driven the residents to the warm hearts of their homes. Moss shivered in the shadow of a sea deity, a diminutive figure before its scaled limbs and tentacles, wreathed in stylized fish, all gaping maws and rolling eyes.

He located a winding cut between a mansion and its carriage house. A summer's growth had thrown up rustling walls on either side to obscure what lay beyond. A river of bricks led him to a crisp house surrounded by rattling weeds. A rusting anchor declared that he had found the home of the *Somnambulist*'s shipwright. Moss had never seen the house. There was a vulnerability about it that gave him pause. The fastidious attention to architectural detail might have suggested pride, but Moss saw in it the unbearable agony of being away from the sea—the need for constant distraction.

The house was a tower set in a walled lot, with a gnarled apple tree huddled in each corner. Moss skirted the front door and made for the back of the house. The gate opened onto a path through untended herbs to a door that was a minor masterpiece of joinery. Snail shells snapped beneath his shoes as he shifted from foot to foot to ease his injured leg. The door was unlocked. Moss paused, uncertain whether to proceed.

"Irridis?" Inside, moonlight patterned the floor. He was in a kitchen. There was a nutty odor of cardamom and cloves. It was a simple, clean room, with a concave chopping block, a modest gas cooker and a larder. The only furniture was a wooden table with a single chair. Ship shape, thought Moss.

In the next room he felt leaves and grit underfoot. Someone had preceded him, but who and when? A faint glow emanated from a single window. A few steps took him to the foot of a spiral staircase. From there he could see the front door where a tea tray sat beneath the letter slot, catching a card house of scattered post. Lumpen shapes of draped furniture and bookshelves lurked in the shadows like sleeping beasts. A clock face above the fireplace reflected Moss's distorted form as he moved about the room.

At the foot of the staircase he listened for sounds on the upper floors, but there was only silence.

"Irridis?" There was no response. "Irridis, are you here?" Again, nothing. He started up the stairs. Halfway to the top he heard the creak of a heavy body walking across the kitchen floor.

He rushed to the top, gritting his teeth against the throb in his calf. He took in a workshop laid out around a bench covered with an assortment of plans. Lumber leaned in racks against the walls. Carpentry tools dangled from hooks in the ceiling. A model of a rigged ship, perhaps the *Somnambulist*, rested on a table. Odors of sawdust and glue filled the air.

Kneeling on aching heels, he watched the room below through the open staircase. A now-familiar figure moved between the furniture. Its head, disproportionately large, swayed from side to side. Wisps of leaf smoke reached Moss's nose, threatening to make him sneeze. The creature, for it could not be described as human, crashed furniture to the floor in its passing. It gave a bestial snort, exhaling a cloud of hot gas and embers, like a bog fire disturbed by a sudden wind. Moss hardly breathed. He fought an impulse to retreat deeper into the house's recesses. The creature moved out of sight.

A cool hand covered Moss's mouth. He twisted away and found himself staring into a man's deeply shadowed face. The creature's sudden roar shook the house. The stranger put a finger against his lips. Moss glanced at the room below, but the creature was still out of view. The reek of scorched tinder faded. When he turned back, he saw the man walking toward an open door where an overhead pulley was silhouetted against the night sky. He was short and lean, barely taller than Andrew. Scraggly black hair swept over a high forehead and spilled over the man's coat collar. When he turned, Moss could see a narrow nose, a dab of white between close-set eyes, thin lips and a pointed chin.

Moss joined him, and together they looked down on the garden.

"What is it?" Moss whispered.

The man shook his head and raised his hand to silence Moss. The fingers were as thin as sticks and unusually long. Moss was aware of a terrible heat in his core, and an uncomfortable loosening of his bowels. The air sparkled around him. Damn, not again, he thought. He looked back at the garden.

The creature had moved outside and stood in a rising mist. A heavy coat concealed its form. Its shoulders and arms were covered with bioluminescent lichen and fungi that seemed to grow up and die back, shedding a fine but ceaseless plume of spores. The creature's covered head smoldered. Without warning it walked from the garden, exhibiting the strange elephantine agitation that Moss had witnessed in the railyard.

The man turned away from the door. His eyes were bright and piercing. "His name is Echo." There was sadness in his voice. "He is Elizabeth's servant. Her demon."

"It'll be back," said Moss. He was growing confused, weak. The air around the man's head seemed to swirl.

"Not tonight."

"I latched the door behind me. How did it get in?"

The man's smile was barely perceptible. "There's no lock that can slow Echo."

The room spun. Moss stretched hand toward the wall to steady himself.

"Who are you?" said Moss.

The man took his hand. "We've met before, though I am not surprised you don't remember. I am a friend of Starling's, the one you know as Irridis. My name is Master Crow."

"I know Starling." It had been a long time since Moss had heard Irridis's real name.

"You're bleeding," Master Crow said. He was looking at the floorboards. They were covered in dark smears. Moss's soles were tacky.

"Oh," he whispered. His vision darkened and he fell against the wall. Master Crow's arms caught him, but he was too heavy. He landed hard, losing consciousness. He whispered something inaudible to the floorboards.

He woke to an ache in his shoulders, a consequence of spending the night unconscious on the floor. A blanket had been laid over him. The room was quiet except for a blue jay calling in the garden. Master Crow was gone. Moss was quite alone. The floor smelled of wood shavings. He was thirsty. The wound on his leg had become a distant ache. He sat up and discovered that his calf had been cleaned and stitched. A bitter salve had been spread over the wound. Moss tapped the stiches gingerly. The swelling around the cut had gone down and there were signs the skin had begun to regenerate.

Scrounging, Moss found some old clothing in a wardrobe. He shed Seaforth's clothes like a foul skin, stepping gratefully out of the heap. Fortunately, the carpenter was close to his size. Moss pulled on a pair of work pants, a threadbare T-shirt, and sweater of unfortunate, homemade construction. He satisfied his thirst from a cast iron pitcher pump in the kitchen. Wiping water from his beard, he shoved the kitchen door open. The sun and a gentle breeze mellowed the early morning garden. Other than some broken plant stems, there was no sign of the creature the Master Crow had called Echo. There was no sign of Master Crow either, which was unfortunate as Moss had a thousand questions.

He sat on the step and lit a cigarette. The tobacco burned with a satisfying crackle as he inhaled. He blew the smoke into the sunlight. A grackle hopped into the path with a yellow snail in its beak. It tapped the shell against the flagstone until it broke, and then gulped down the constricting morsel. Moss thought of the slug he had seen the previous night, which triggered a cascade of fragments from his conversation with Oliver.

"Hello," said Moss. The bird eyed him, cocking its head before flying away. A moment later it returned with another snail and repeated its performance. After swallowing the snail, it flicked pieces of shell with its beak. Satisfied that nothing remained, the bird squawked at Moss. He ducked as it flew past him, through the doorway and into the house. Startled, Moss tossed his cigarette into the garden and hobbled after it.

He found the bird in the room with the fireplace. It was scrabbling on the marble mantelpiece, working an envelope from under the clock. Moss shooed the bird away. It flew to the back of an armchair where it bobbed and screeched at him. Moss snatched the envelope free of the clock. His initials were printed on the front. Inside, he found a piece of stiff paper with a note tidily printed in the same blue ink. *A gift from a mutual friend*. There was no signature, merely an *X*. He flipped it over, but the other side was blank. The bird screamed. Moss turned, still holding the note in front of him, while the deranged bird filled the air with dust and feathers. Then he saw it. Peeking from behind the chair was the traveling bookcase, with his shoulder bag slung over its corner.

THE ATTIC OF THE CITY

ON THE DAY HE WAS TO MURDER LAMB, MOSS ARRIVED AT THE Cloth Hall in the late afternoon. Earlier, he had gone to the Alley of Birds to look for Oliver. As a precaution, he had left the bookcase at the shipwright's house, hidden behind stacked lumber in the workshop. Oliver was not in in the alley, and Moss could not risk asking around. He called the bookshop from a callbox, but there was no answer. In frustration, he finally walked to the shop itself, only to find it locked up and dark. Of course Oliver might be inside, but Moss had no way of entering. By that time the hour was late. Moss had returned to the shipwright's house and retrieved the bookcase. After camouflaging the case, using a roll of canvas and some twine from beneath the carpenter's bench, he walked to a taxi stand, dragging it on squeaking wheels.

By the time the cab deposited Moss at the Cloth Hall, most of the day's activity around the market had dissipated. Farmers and vendors were tidying stalls in preparation for the next day or standing in groups talking. Moss entered the loading doors unnoticed, despite the squeaking wheels, and found his way to a freight elevator. He pulled the safety gate across the opening and pressed a worn button. Beneath his feet the elevator floor heaved, dropped slightly and then ascended at a crawl.

The floors above the main hall appeared deserted. Two levels were littered with broken crates, skids, and other market detritus. The third was a wide-open expanse of hardwood, a dancehall in years past. A raised bandstand occupied the far end of the room, and chairs lined the walls. A heavyset man swept the floor with his back to the elevator. He moved in a lazy, lateral shuffle as though listening to music. In a moment the view was gone. Thinking about Oliver's unexpected absence as the elevator climbed, it occurred to

Moss that once he had killed Lamb, he would be in a very different negotiating position to deal with Oliver. The elevator arrived at the attic with a clang.

Moss pulled the gate back on a vestibule lit by flickering sconces. Split boxes, rubber tubes and bags of salt were stacked in a corner. Opposite the elevator, the ruins of a mural surrounded a door twice Moss's height and nearly as wide. It depicted animal life across the millennia. Above it, scrolling calligraphy declared *The Museum of Natural History—Collections Repository*. Cetaceans were generously represented. Moss wondered if the mural was the work of the late artist that Gale had derided.

A peephole was set into an eye painted on the door. Moss pushed a button dangling on twinned wires, wondering if he would have been wiser to enter by the stairwell. Shifting the bookcase, he knew that it would have been tiring and noisy. He stepped to the side as machinery within the walls screeched, metal on dry metal. The door opened inward. A tin monkey wearing red tails moved arthritically into the doorway and extended its hand.

"Natural welcome museum to visitor the history!" said a high, confident voice full of static. Moss was still parsing the odd syntax when he realized that the monkey had not lowered its hand. "Visitor museum the welcome to history!" The monkey's cracked face was expressionless. The glove had long since worn off, exposing wire fingers with encrusted metal joints. A grinding came from within and the monkey trundled back along a rusty floor track, to a space hidden beyond the entrance. The door moved but Moss stuck his foot into the opening, causing a thump, which was followed by a sound like cascading sand within the wall, as the resistance backed up along the hidden chain of machinery.

The hall was approximately fifty feet high and two hundred feet long. Moss could see no immediate sign of Irridis's presence. The elephant, which he had last seen in the dark, towered in front of him, swathed in plastic sheeting. Collections of bird nests, eggs, teeth, fossils and every other imaginable relic once belonging to a living creature sat on shelves, minutely labeled in a complex system of organization. Surplus cabinets and large animal displays occupied the center of the main floor creating a labyrinth of dream-like juxtapositions. Seen over the labyrinth, at the far end of the hall, was an empty aviary, a ruin of metal and glass that extended into the pitiless elements above the city. The repository had once held tours for interested members of the public, but it did not look like it had seen a visitor for decades. Moss lifted the canvas on the bookcase and tore a package free, which he had secured earlier with tape. Laying it on the floor, he pushed the bookcase into a deep alcove between two fossil cabinets. *Where the hell is Irridis?* he thought as his fingers worked.

Moss had left his gun behind in the rush to get Imogene out of Seaforth's apartment. Left without a means to kill Lamb, a new approach had to be devised. One had occurred to him earlier that day, as he inspected the shipwright's collection of tools. Kneeling on the floor in front of the elephant, Moss unwrapped a piece of sailcloth to reveal a cobbler's awl and hole punch. It had a smooth wood handle that fit as neatly into Moss's palm as a missing appendage. Two metal prongs emerged from the handle. The longer was about the length of his index finger; the shorter was a metal claw the length of his baby finger. Both prongs were lethally sharp.

Lamb was a cunning and dangerous man, but he was handicapped by a great desire. Moss had invented a story. He would say that he had found Memoria in the house at Fleurent Drain and after a joyous reunion had managed to convince her to come with him to the Cloth Hall, on the pretense that he lived there—as Imogene actually did. On the way to the Cloth Hall, Memoria had become spooked and leapt out of the cab at an intersection. The story was tissue-thin, but he just had to get close enough to Lamb as he spun it to lunge at the man with the awl. He would drive the tool into Lamb's temple and destroy the artery beneath. Moss was not particularly adroit with tools but he had seen this done in the prison lavatory with devastating effect. Moss had never killed a man before, but he had killed a rabid dog, and knowing what he did of Lamb, he saw no distinction.

Moss tossed the canvas to the side and pocketed the tool in his coat. As he stood, his eyes strayed to the staircase that led to Imogene's mezzanine apartment. There was a light on. At the same moment, Moss again became aware of a burbling sound he had heard the night he had escaped from the attic. He squeezed between a number of taxidermied animals and fossil-laden cabinets. Following the sound he eventually came upon a large open space, occupied by a glass tank as large as a upended railway car. It rested on an iron stage, accessed by wide steps. The ironwork belonged to the previous century, dark and overwrought. The top of the tank was stabilized from the ceiling by chains. Hoses snaked from inside the aquarium and disappeared into the overhead shadows. The tank's pumps and filters were the source of the sound. The water glowed, cool and blue, with bioluminescent light shining from countless marine animals.

Schools of fish and solitary creatures moved behind thick glass. Jellyfish undulated drawing lengths of stinging tentacles through living corals and anemones. At the bottom of the tank, something moved on frond-like limbs, emitting pulses of light as it nosed into the substrate. Moss was absorbing this wonder when Imogene appeared from a slop room to his left.

Her hair was pulled back. She held industrial grade rubber gloves under an elbow. An expired fish was draped in her hand. It was a pale pink, with milky eyes and gills that expanded around her fingers like chrysanthemum petals. She moved stiffly. The line on her neck was livid.

"You're here," said Moss, stupidly. He was stunned.

She looked up abruptly at the sound of his voice. Her expression changed from shock to rage. She walked toward him shaking her head, lips pale with anger. Moss fell back a step, just as the dead fish came flying at him. It sailed past, close enough for him to smell its flesh. There was no time to see where it landed. Imogene tried to slap his face. He ducked and she struck his right ear instead. Her raised foot caught him in the wounded calf.

"Imogene, stop. What are you doing?"

"What the hell are you doing here?"

"What's wrong?"

"You left me lying on the fucking road."

"I thought you were dead. They were trying to shoot me."

"Shoot us." Imogene paced, breathing heavily. The exertion had freed her hair and it hung over her face. She pulled it back behind her ears. "Well, obviously I wasn't dead." She snatched the rubber gloves from where they had fallen on the floor.

"I didn't have a choice," said Moss. "If I'd stayed I wouldn't be here now."

"More's the pity, asshole." The rubber gloves hit his face, leaving a trail of fish slime and scale. Wiping it from his face with his coat sleeve, he tried again.

"What are you doing here?"

"I live and work here. Where else was I supposed go?" Imogene glared.

"Oliver let you go?"

"I don't know what you are talking about, Moss."

"Oliver Taxali. He told me that he'd kidnapped you."

A hint of amused confusion crossed Imogene's face. "Did he?"

"I just said he did."

"And you believed him?"

"Again, I thought you were dead. I was so relieved to hear that you weren't that I wasn't thinking. What happened?"

Imogene stared at the fish on the floor. Moss tensed. "I woke up on the ground, with that ugly house manager slapping my face, and telling me to get up. He kept saying that I was going to jail. The two men with the guns ran off after you making a lot of noise. They thought they saw you, but it was just someone checking out the commotion. It was absolute chaos. That man kept yelling at me, calling me all kinds of names." She picked up the fish.

"Imogene, I am sorry—"

"So I punched him in the trachea."

"You what?"

"I managed to get up and get into the cab, despite his dog trying to tear my leg off. By that time more people were arriving. I told the driver to get me out of there, which he was more than happy to do. I had him take me to a club called Leviathan's."

"That's a dangerous place."

"Is it? Well, there is a woman there named Estelle. She does a lot of under-the-table abortions and surgical work in a suite of rooms on the fourth floor, what the Lamprey likes to call patchwork. A lot of weird activity goes on there. Anyway, she knows me—she did my tattoos. She's the one who tattooed your arm and supplied the drug I used on you. She sorted me out, but the downside is that Lamb will certainly hear about it, and so basically I'm fucked."

"That's why I'm here."

Imogene frowned. "What?"

"Lamb is coming in a few hours. I intend to give him some bad news."

"That sounds like a euphemism." Imogene dropped the dead fish and the gloves on a utility cart that was laden with scrub brushes, tubing and other paraphernalia.

"I arranged it."

Imogene's lips tightened as she took a sweater from a chair back and tugged it over her head. "Well, that was rash. I came to you and Irridis for help."

"And we will help you."

She looked past Moss, eyes widening. Moss turned to see what had caught her attention.

The girl that Moss had seen by the canal stood before the towering aquarium, her upturned face washed by the light of the life within. Her raven hair coiled onto the shoulders of a soiled red velvet dress. There was a distant look on her face, lips parted, eyes limpid and unblinking. It was an odd thing to notice under the circumstances, but she did not swallow. She seemed oblivious to their presence, as though they were beings outside of a dreamer's singular focus. Her milk-white hands, with their colorless nails, were pressed to the surface of the aquarium glass where hungry organisms crowded and followed her trailing fingers.

The bottom-dwelling creature that Moss had noticed earlier rose to meet her with rows of blue lights moving along its length. The smaller fish, darting at her hands through the glass, were agitated by its interest. They were shredding their fins in a struggle to be ever closer to her, damaging even more delicate animals in the process, like the spider-limbed shrimp and seahorses. The flashing creature moved inexorably through the chaos, drawing its barbels like a train.

"It's her, Moss. It's Elizabeth," said Imogene, stepping forward. Moss took her arm to draw her back, but she remained as she was. Her face was blanched. Elizabeth's attention shifted. The impassive expression changed to annoyance, but with several odd shifts in between. The word that came to Moss was *sorting*; a person shuffling through a series of masks until they found one suitable. It was subtle and occurred within a couple of seconds. She stepped back. The platform's railing prevented her from falling. Imogene pulled her arm free but stayed beside Moss. The mass of marine creatures had moved to the middle of the tank, where they hung suspended as a single writhing mass.

Imogene looked at Moss. "What's happening? How the hell did she get here?"

"I don't know," he said. "Maybe she followed me."

The water was clouded with silt, torn fins and scales. A loose form took shape as the animals struggled to gain a position at a core dominated by the flashing creature. Individuals became indistinguishable in the frenetic whole. Moss saw a humanoid form. A gasp from Imogene confirmed that this was not merely his imagination. Seconds passed while the form found equilibrium. An elongated arm, composed of hundreds of panicked fish held by an uncanny force, reached out to touch the inside of the glass where Elizabeth's hand had left a smear. The glass bulged.

Moss, transfixed, had not noticed Imogene leave his side until he saw her come around the tank behind Elizabeth. She had a raised gun, which he recognized as his. She must have stolen it from Seaforth's apartment while he was out.

"Wait," he said, sensing the knife-edge they were balanced upon. While there would be a cost for lingering, sudden action would break the spell, perhaps leading to unmanageable consequences.

Imogene did not respond. Her eyes were locked on the girl's face.

"Get out of here," she said. Her voice was husky with suppressed anger. Elizabeth narrowed her eyes into inhuman slits, and settled her weight as though planning to leap.

"Now!" Imogene edged closer, the gun at shoulder level. She fired at Elizabeth, catching Moss off guard. The bullet passed through the girl's raised palm and lodged in a stuffed ibex with a puff of dust. Blood was slow to come. The doors to the attic opened. He could not see it from where he stood, but heard the automata roll into the opening and begin its garbled greeting. It was silenced mid-sequence.

"Over here," shouted Moss. Seconds later, Irridis appeared in an opening between two plastic-shrouded displays. Imogene dropped the gun to her side and offered no protest as Moss eased it from her hand. Over Irridis's head, the ocelli flew in a tight circle. Elizabeth remained motionless, clearly waiting for the form in the tank to reach an apotheosis.

The creature had elongated and now looked down on them. The ocelli left Irridis and flew to the glass, where they hovered and dodged near the handprint. The bee-like behavior of the ocelli struck Moss, once again. He had seen the ocelli used to deadly effect in the past, though what they could do against the thick glass and the creature suspended behind it was uncertain. Without warning one of the ocelli darted away and struck Elizabeth, who had turned her back on the creature to look at Irridis. She pitched forward with a deranged scream that echoed through the hall. The form in the tank immediately lost its cohesion, leaving the dazed creatures to scramble or swim away as best they could through the blood-tinged water.

Imogene ran toward Elizabeth, clearly thinking her dead. The girl struggled to her feet, clutching her shoulder. A dark fluid pooled in the hollow of her clavicle. Imogene reached forward and grabbed her arm. Elizabeth cast her off with surprising strength. Imogene recoiled at this preternatural display of power, balling her fists, but uncertain how to proceed. In the meantime, Irridis had recalled the ocelli to him.

Moss raised the gun while his mind raced, trying to make sense of what had happened.

Elizabeth crossed the floor until she stood a few feet from Irridis. She looked up, examining him quizzically. Irridis was trapped by her gaze, his expression one of intense scrutiny as though he could see through her to some almost attainable greater truth. His features were marble. Elizabeth inhaled and opened her mouth, speaking words in a sibilant language Moss had never before heard. Her eyes rolled under their lids. Irridis's skin was more translucent than ever before, but he remained calm in the face of this bizarre onslaught. The stream of words trailed off. The girl opened her eyes.

"Who am I?" asked Irridis. It was not what Moss expected him to say. He felt the hair rise all over his body.

Moss had followed Elizabeth at a safe distance and now moved to the side. This was to prevent a bullet from passing through her into Irridis.

"Aurel," said Elizabeth.

Irridis's expression darkened. He turned his face from Elizabeth. Moss could see that he was deeply affected by the name she had spoken.

"She has a knife," whispered Imogene, who had come up behind Moss. Moss cleared the few remaining paces and pressed the gun against Elizabeth's temple. "Drop it."

Elizabeth rolled her eyes toward Moss. Her tongue wagged obscenely as she laughed.

"For God's sake Moss, pull the fucking trigger," said Imogene.

Moss was an instant from complying with her wish when he heard the footsteps of several men spilling from numerous narrow corridors between the stored museum collections. Irridis was seized around the neck and jerked backwards in the opening gambit of a coordinated strategy. Even as two men dragged him out of sight, the ocelli were attacking.

The sweeper from the dance floor ducked through an opening, followed by Lamb and three others in succession. Behind them Oliver lurked, clutching a hat, his face blood-smeared. The sweeper lowered his scarred head and made for Imogene, arms outstretched like a man rushing through waist-deep water. Something in his purpose told Moss that he had been instructed to attack her specifically. Moss fired at his head but succeeded only in shredding an ear. Elizabeth had thrown off his aim as she shoved past him. He was peripherally aware of Lamb seizing Elizabeth by the wrist as another man thrust a bag over her head. Valuable seconds had been lost. The sweeper seized Imogene by her hair and struck her across the cheek. She crumpled without a sound. Moss had almost reached her when the sweeper turned to face him. He felt the man's fist come down on his head, fast and hard. White light exploded, as blood and mucus sprayed from Moss's mouth and nose. He lost balance. A booted foot caught him in his injured calf on the way down. Moss rolled onto his back and fired the gun to the left of the man's sternum. He rolled out of the way as the man toppled. The wind of the sweeper's fall covered them both with sparkling dust from between the floorboards.

Moss laid on the floor, semi-conscious, and unable to move. The handle of the awl dug into his ribs. He heard a nearby struggle and several voices shouting. Oliver's in particular rose up in panicked protestation and pleading. It was silenced with a gunshot that left Moss's ears ringing. Jolted, he clambered to his feet, skating in blood. Oliver lay on the ground dead, eyes half open. The three men who had killed him were throwing plastic sheeting to the side in order to leave. Moss chased after them. The first two disappeared from sight, but he body-checked the third against a crate. He struggled to pin the man, but lost his grip. The man danced backwards and ran after his accomplices. After several steps Moss realized that even if he caught them, he was in no shape to fight three armed men.

He turned around to look for Imogene. He expected to find her unconscious, but she was already sitting forward, spitting blood into the V formed by her legs. There was no sign of Lamb or Elizabeth.

Moss checked Imogene for wounds. She had a red mark on her face from the sweeper's assault, but otherwise her injuries were minor. The blood came from a bitten tongue. He sat down with his back to the aquarium base and made her lie against him with her head in his lap. He held her hand, fingers entwined. Before him the sweeper lay prone, face pressed to the floorboards. Rivulets of dark blood followed cracks in the wood. Oliver was on his back, the holes in his head forming a neat colon. It was his blood Moss had slipped on. He rested his head against the base and closed his eyes. In a low voice, he told Imogene of the events following their chaotic exit from Seaforth's apartment house, about the deal and Oliver's fears about the witch. By the time the ocelli whooshed ahead of Irridis's return, Moss was unconscious.

SQUEALER

IMOGENE WIPED DRIED BLOOD FROM MOSS'S FACE WITH A moistened cloth. The daylight was unbearable. Shading his eyes, he tried to make sense of where he was. Oliver's body was suspended in the aquarium. With a larval hunch, arms tucked, the bookseller turned on gentle currents, trailing a reddish plume. Precious little remained of the softer tissues; a marker of how long Moss had been unconscious. Oliver's avian legs lay on the bottom of the tank. Moss pressed a palm to his forehead and for a few seconds his world became the coolness of its pressure. His thoughts turned to Irridis. He looked around but his friend was nowhere in sight.

"Moss," said Imogene. She pointed at the tank without looking at it. "I'm sorry, Oliver came to a bad end."

"Who did that?"

"Irridis. I helped," she said. "It was the quickest way to deal with the bodies. It looks gruesome but it's really not that much different than what happens if you bury a body in the ground, or at sea."

Moss looked at her with incredulity, but she turned away chewing her cheek.

"Where's Irridis?" asked Moss, at last, trying not to look at the floating body.

"He's out there," said Imogene. She pointed to the end of the hall where daylight fell between the doors leading to the aviary. Moss groaned as he stood. Imogene watched him carefully. "Thanks for what you did. That goon would have killed me." She stood up, wringing the damp cloth in her hands.

"I'm sure he thought he had," said Moss. "I have to talk to Irridis." He walked toward the aviary. Imogene followed.

The aviary had been the pride of the museum repository, a geodesic glass and metal dome that had been used to raise specimens for the Hall of Birds. Hundreds of birds from all over the globe had lived among the lush vegetation. From the ground, the aviary's glass and copper flashing had glowed in the sunrise like a captured star. Since the war, it had fallen to ruins.

Moss and Imogene walked between the doors onto a large deck that glittered with broken glass. The view was spectacular. The Irridian Sea was a calm sheet of blue. Closer in, the great staircase swarmed with people going about their early morning routines. Cable cars positioned at intervals along the steps were moving people and goods back and forth from the city to the docks hundreds of feet below. Scars from the war were still in evidence on the steps. Craters in the limestone, slopes of rubble, and the ruined artillery fortifications visible from the top of the Cloth Hall offered a view of the city's history not available in the innumerable books written on the subject. Erosion had softened many of the scars, carving the stone into whorls and caves. In places they had become reservoirs for marine life, replenished with each tide. Irridis stood against this panorama. He was dangerously near the edge of the deck that jutted out over the rooftops of the Cloth Hall.

Imogene remained by the door. The air was raw on the open deck. Hearing Moss's approach, Irridis turned from the city to face him. His weathered coat was splattered with blood. It was the same coat he had worn on the day Moss had met him for the first time, outside Brickscold Prison. Back then, Irridis's head had been concealed under black cloth, but now it was bared to the intense daylight.

"Irridis, what happened?"

"I freed myself of the two men who grabbed me from behind and tried to follow Lamb, but he escaped."

"I meant, what was all that with the girl?"

"I'm still trying to understand that myself." A breeze came off the ocean. Irridis's coat flapped around his legs. "I wanted to be outside. I came out here to look."

"At what?" For the first time, Moss had a clear look at the sixth ocellus. It was darker than the others; smoky was the word that came to his mind.

Irridis reached up and took the dark ocellus between his fingers. He placed it in Moss's hand. It felt warm, like an egg taken from a nest.

"I want you to take this, and protect it." Irridis folded Moss's fingers around the ocellus. "I found it in the traveling bookcase. I don't yet understand what it means, but after what happened today, I need to place it with someone I trust." He squeezed Moss's hand. "You are the only one I trust, Moss."

"I'll look after it," said Moss. He placed it in his pocket. It seemed like an insufficient gesture, but he was at a loss what else to do.

"I came out here to look at the ocean," said Irridis. Moss stood for a long time beside his friend before he felt Imogene's hand on his back.

"We have a visitor," she said.

Andrew stood in front of a cabinet filled with brachiopods. He was dressed in a shabby, oversized coat. His blue eyes tracked around the mess created by the fight with Lamb's gang.

"A shambles," he said.

"You said you had something to tell Moss," said Imogene.

Andrew ignored her and addressed Moss directly. "He sold you out." He pointed at Oliver's body floating in the aquarium.

"I put that together," said Moss.

"I was with him when Mr. Lamb came to the old bakery last night. Croaker told him that's where Oliver hid when people were looking for him." Andrew sat on the edge of a chair and crossed his legs, seemingly inured to the streaks of dried blood on the floor. This was not a squeamish boy.

"Oliver told him everything, about the case of old books and how he'd bullshitted you about kidnapping this lady." He thrust his thumb at Imogene. "Just to get you to give it to him. It didn't work, though. Mr. Lamb said he never could abide a squealer."

It made sense. Moss believed the boy.

"Where's Lamb now?" Moss asked.

"They took that weird girl back to the bakery. Mr. Lamb thinks she's a witch. He said that she might know something about some other lady he's looking for." He levelled his gaze at Moss. "Is she?"

"Is she what, Andrew?"

"The girl, a witch?"

The word rankled. Witch was not a word that Moss liked. His own sister, Jenny Sugar, was a healer, a student of magic as well as science. She often called herself a witch, without irony. Moss knew there were many others of her ilk. He also knew that he did not have time to parse the meaning of the word for this wide-eyed boy.

"The evidence would seem to support that conclusion," said Moss with a sigh.

"Fantastic!"

Andrew left with scarcely a backwards glance at Oliver Taxali. Moss sat on the chair vacated by the boy, pondering the exchange with Irridis. The ocellus rested in his pocket. Irridis had remained where they had left him. While Moss was looking in the direction of the aviary, trying to decide his next move, he felt a weight drop into his lap. He knew without looking that it was a gun.

"It was on the floor. I'm surprised one of them didn't take it," said Imogene.

He picked the gun up and balanced it in his hands thoughtfully. "I have to find him. By now his men will have told him that we are still alive. You know he won't let this stand."

"I know that better than anyone," said Imogene. She sat on a stack of shipping pallets.

"That's just it, isn't it? Lamb is a threat to all of us, you, me—Memoria."

"For the moment, he's distracted by Elizabeth, but that won't last. Thanks to Oliver he also knows the bookcase still exists. He'll want that too. Where is it?"

"Hidden, near the entrance. They ran right past it."

"Then we need to leave, and take it with us," said Imogene. "As much as I don't want it, I want Lamb to have it even less, and we can't afford to let it fall into Elizabeth's hands. At the house I overheard you talking to Irridis about traveling to Nightjar Island to look for Memoria. I'm coming."

"I have to kill Lamb first," said Moss. "How else can I be sure that he will leave us alone and never find Memoria?"

"Then kill him," said Imogene. "He's a monster, and he turned me into one too."

"You had no more of a chance with Lamb than Memoria had under your father's influence. It's not just one person you're fighting, it's your whole reality in the moment. You're no monster. You were just trapped in a maze with one."

"I'm coming with you," said Imogene.

"You should stay here. Gather what you need. We'll have to leave quickly—after. Talk to Irridis if you can. Something has happened. He's not the same."

A LETHAL SUSPENSION

AFTER HIS CONVERSATION WITH IMOGENE, MOSS LEFT THE CLOTH Hall and stepped into the biting wind of the streets. He longed to stand on the great steps, in the mist and glare of the sea, to calm the roil in his mind. Instead, he walked by backways and gardens until he emerged near Taxali's bookshop. The shop was dark, the contents beyond the glass indistinct, like a groping memory.

Moss trotted to the rear, following the slope of a lane barely wider than a delivery van. Standing in the cardboard detritus of the back entrance, he thumped on the door with a hand reddened from the cold. He waited for several minutes, wind blowing at his back, conscious of the heaviness of the gun and the awl in his coat. Eventually Oliver's maid opened the door. She heard the news with no greater display than the clenching of a handkerchief in her chapped hand.

"You better come in," she said.

For half an hour, they sat at a cluttered table breathing the smell of gas and stale cooking oil. It was covered in toast crumbs and pressed to the wall of a tiny kitchen. Moss drank tea that tasted of dish soap as the woman wept, pinching her thin cardigan against her throat. Oliver's parrot sat in a cage that hung from the ceiling, grinding grit in its crop and occasionally shrieking.

"Thank you," she said. "He wasn't as bad as you might imagine."

Late that afternoon, as the light was dying, Moss returned to the Blackrat Bakery. It loomed, fractured by shadows that felt like a sly reference to Lamb's presence within. Moss kept to the narrow arteries of darkness as he approached. He had no wish to revisit the coal cellar. Plashing through puddles that reflected the sky like polished steel, he dodged surreptitiously to an adjacent administrative building. Several stories above the ground, a pedestrian bridge connected it to the bakery.

A fire escape ladder led to the third floor, where a rusty padlock proved no match for the awl. Inside, he navigated dusty offices as much by touch as by sight, and soon located a central staircase. He ascended, stepping at the edges where the boards were least likely to squeak, with his hand on the bannister rail. At the head of the stairs he encountered a warren of offices strewn with moldering paper, upended furniture and raccoon droppings.

Moss searched for an opening to the bridge. He had not brought a light, which would have broadcast his movements. Instead, he relied on the building's internal logic and whatever clues his exploration revealed. A current of air led him to the last of several interconnected offices. The bridge entrance lay behind a wall of splitting records boxes and a hand-lettered admonition not to enter. Moss took hold of the nearest box and hurled it to the side. In ten minutes of sweaty work he had cleared a space wide enough to squeeze through. On the other side, less a button on the shipwright's peacoat, he confronted the pedestrian bridge.

The bridge, exhibiting a state of advanced neglect, spanned nearly thirty feet. Moss's first thought was to revise his plan, but the idea of approaching Lamb from the cellar struck him as a disadvantage, something easily anticipated. A hole in the bridge's floor gaped in the moonlight. The wood splintered and sagged around its fringe. Moss wondered if someone had fallen through, necessitating the closure. Closer inspection revealed the entire structure was rotten. Broken glass covered the floorboards. Innumerable bats colonized the ceiling above conical accretions of guano. Moss would have to leap the hole by a generous margin, with unlikely athleticism.

He toppled more boxes out of the way to widen the opening. Walking back into the office, he felt for the gun in his coat pocket and ran his finger over the safety. More worrisome was the jagged awl. This he threw to the other side of the bridge. He considered his aching calf and tried not to imagine his legs breaking through the boards.

Ignoring the rustling bats, he took a deep breath and sprinted. When he reached the bridge, the boards sagged beneath his feet. He jumped, causing the bats to panic. They raced around him, making for the hole in the floor. Moss twisted midair and landed awkwardly. Flying forward, he drove his palms into the floorboards. He lay winded as bats darted chaotically above him. Eventually they escaped, or settled. He sat up to assess the damage. His palms bled from a dozen nicks and punctures. A scrape ran the length of his left forearm. Beneath its dressing, his calf felt wet. He had lost another button from his coat. He could not help being pleased with himself as he stood and shook the guano from his clothes and hair. He picked up the awl. The bakery was open to him.

The upper floors were deserted. He descended warily to the lower level, pausing periodically to listen for movement. He had been searching rooms for ten minutes when a rhythmic thump led him to Andrew in a long corridor. The boy kneeled, feet splayed to the side, his concentration fixed on a rubber ball. It bounced off the floor, struck the opposite wall and arced neatly to his waiting hands.

"Andrew," said Moss in a low voice. The boy looked up, acknowledging Moss with wide eyes. He stood up and walked in the opposite direction. At the end of the hall, he looked over his shoulder before disappearing around the corner.

"Andrew, wait," Moss said. Dead air absorbed the words. He reached the spot where Andrew had been playing. A trail of footsteps led through the dust and the ball rolled along the intersection of floor and wall. He pulled the gun from his pocket, clumsy with adrenaline. Lamb had to be nearby. He released the safety.

Rounding the corner, he saw a swinging door and heard the boy's receding footsteps. He flattened himself against the wall. It would be foolish to blunder forward. Was Andrew leading him to Lamb, or into a trap? His breathing slowed. He was decided. He would place his trust in the boy.

Moss pushed through the swinging door, leading with the barrel of the gun. He assumed the space beyond would be a continuation of the corridor. Instead, he found a lit, open area filled with worktables and blackened oven racks. It was larger than the kitchen he had been in during his previous visit. The walls opened into extensive galleries filled with vats and stacked equipment. Flour dusted every surface. Andrew's footprints led between towers of pans and trays, enormous mixers and paddles. Moss scanned for clues that would reveal his hiding spot. When the time came to shoot, he wanted to know Andrew's precise location.

Moss sensed something large falling from overhead. It struck the table inches from where his hand rested. Flour filled the air. Two more strikes came in rapid succession. Moss looked up to see Croaker in the process of pushing a fourth sack of flour over the rail of a mezzanine. Andrew ran from under a nearby table coughing. Moss swept the gun overhead without aiming, squeezing off two shots before a sack hit him in the shoulder. It knocked him off his feet. His shoulder was seared with pain, but it was not broken or dislocated. The sound of the shots still rang in his ears. He looked up, as he tried to scuttle under the lip of a table, but there was no fifth bag to come. Moss found his footing in a blanket of flour and waved the gun in all directions. Had he killed Croaker? He had no time to investigate. Lamb had appeared in front of him, standing between two long tables. The fox pendant was entwined around the stumps of his fingers. Elizabeth was draped across his arms, unconscious. Her head lolled against his chest. Lamb was otherwise alone.

"What have you brought with you, bastard?" shouted Lamb. Confused, Moss aimed the gun at his adversary's grotesque bared head. Lamb walked toward him, sniffing the air, heedless of the danger. He dropped Elizabeth to the ground, as though she had suddenly become of secondary importance. Moss hesitated on the trigger. Lamb seized the advantage. With uncanny accuracy, he leapt, striking Moss high in the chest with a knee. Both men were carried over. Moss worked to free the gun that had become tangled in the other man's clothing. The twisted material forced his fingers around the barrel until he thought the bones in his hands would snap. In desperation, he pulled the trigger as Lamb rained blows on his head. The man bellowed and disengaged from Moss. He lurched in a tight circle clutching at his stomach, his mouth agape and his tiny blind eyes rolling in agony.

With strength he did not know he possessed, Moss brought a boot up under Lamb's jaw. The other man staggered backwards and fell to the ground. Crazed with rage, Moss straddled Lamb and forced the barrel of the revolver between Lamb's jaws. Strands of blood smeared his teeth and ran down his chin. Even as Moss slammed the back of Lamb's head against the ground he felt detached, euphoric; free. It was no longer about the personal threat; it was for Memoria, Imogene, even Oliver. It was for everyone whose life Lamb had destroyed. Moss closed his eyes. Holding the gun with one hand, and covering Lamb's face with his forearm, he pulled the trigger.

A familiar roar filled the air. Moss stood. Dazed and deafened, he stumbled backward and felt his way around tables. Echo's form materialized out of the haze of flour dust. So this was the source of Lamb's panic. Moss emptied the remainder of the cylinder into the creature's massive head, with no discernible effect. Echo's lumbering raised even more dust until its form was reduced to a swaying shadow. Moss hurled the empty gun at the creature, and tripped backward through the swinging door. As he struck the floor, he saw the creature open its cowl and send a fountain of sparks into the dispersed particles in the air. The flour exploded. The blast wave blew the door back and rolled Moss across the floor. Still conscious, he crawled on his hands and knees until he reached another door that opened into a storage room. He stood up in the dark among the brooms and mop handles, and peered through the door's tiny window. A heartbeat later, the creature passed, carrying Elizabeth's squirming body in its arms. She was now awake. She swiveled her head and caught Moss's eyes through the glass. He jumped back, nearly losing his balance, but his gaze never left the monster's retreating back.

Echo's body had suffered from the explosion. Fibrous clumps hung from tendrils of a dried, vine-like material down the creature's left side. It moved along the hall, listing to the right while the body knit itself back together. String, small machine parts, bones, what appeared to be masses of smoldering animal nests, and even yellowed pages of an old book, twisted and folded into an emulation of muscle and sinew. The resulting forms burrowed into Echo like animals anxious to escape the light, releasing a miasma that made Moss dry heave behind the door. The release he had felt when venting his anger on Lamb was gone, replaced by an unexpected empathy for the man as a human being. He gripped the door handle, smearing it with Lamb's blood, but through some magic perpetrated by the monster in the corridor, he was unable to turn it so much as a degree. Cold sweat ran down the furrow of his back and something swept across his cheek causing the hair on his body to stand on end. Something was probing his ear canals, his nostrils and mouth. An invisible presence shared the tiny room with him, grotesque, intimate and terrifying. Moss looked down and found the fox pendant clutched in his other hand. He shoved it in his coat pocket with the ocellus Irridis had given him, not bothering to wipe away Lamb's blood. The presence abandoned Moss in the dark among the spiders and fusty rags. He pulled out the awl and smashed at the door handle until it fell to the floor leaving a circular hole.

Echo and Elizabeth were gone. Outside the custodial closet the floor was littered with debris and a fine layer of flour. Moss realized that he was also covered. He shook it from his hair and clothing and made his way back to where he expected to find Lamb's body. The explosion had spent itself almost immediately, but it had still devastated the bakery's workroom. Tables were knocked on their sides. Bowls and pans littered the floor. The stone was blackened from smoke that remained in the air. Lamb's body lay on the ground horribly contorted. Thankfully, he saw no sign of Andrew. Moss had no desire to check the mezzanine to see the results of his indiscriminate shooting. Standing amid the aftermath, he could only shake his head in disbelief.

The street was empty. He left the bakery by the same door he had passed through with Oliver not so long ago. It was difficult to reconcile the utter chaos inside the bakery with the lack of police or even members of the Red Lamprey outside. Watchful, he began the long walk back to the Cloth Hall, favoring his injured leg. The effects of the explosion were still with him. He was lightheaded and half deaf. The road seemed to swell and roll beneath his feet, but his footsteps were deliberate and he managed to pass several doorways without stumbling. He worked through the facts. They were simple enough to relate, but how did one explain a living thing not made of flesh? Lamb's words, *what have you brought with you?* haunted him. The image of Echo's reconstituting form looped in his head.

The sky opened, sending down a cold rain that darkened the bricks and completed his misery. Entranced by the rivulets moving between the cobbles, he did not notice the girl until he was mere feet away from her. She stood on the hump in the road. The red velvet dress, now soaked through, was the color of dark venous blood. She seemed oblivious of the sheeting rain. Though to appearances a girl of nine or perhaps ten years of age, her wry expression was mature and superior. Her skin was pallid. Strands of black hair moved across her face, animated by the downpour. Her lips were blue.

"What do you want?" asked Moss, stopping.

"So direct." She twisted a strand of hair around a finger, in an eerie gesture reminiscent of Imogene in the tunnel. The pupils of her eyes were like keyholes.

"What do you want?" He wiped rain from his face with his sleeve. "What the hell do you want with me?"

"I'm here to give you the only warning you will ever get from me, Lumsden Moss. You no longer have a part to play. Memoria is long gone, and Irridis soon will be. I have no ill will towards you, however if you persist you will suffer for it."

Moss snorted. "Part to play in what?"

"Retribution." A stream of soft clicks came from her throat.

Moss spat. "You're talking in riddles."

"Irridis is searching for meaning, but he will find only torment. He will look for the truth about himself, but I'll be waiting for him, to finish what should have been done long ago."

"Fuck you," said Moss. His voice was almost swallowed by the roar of the rain.

Elizabeth laughed. "What a curiosity you are! And who are you to speak up for him, a friend of five minutes, a fugitive? The differences between you are not superficial, Lumsden. Your friendship isn't sufficient to hold his attention. He cannot form relationships. He cannot love you." She tilted her head, mockingly. "Are you angry? Cheer up! He is lost to you. It would have happened sooner or later anyway." The girl shook her head as though stating what should have been obvious. "Life is a string of dark beads. We spend our lives adding to them, one by one, stringing them together, our little beads of torment. Then one day the string dissolves and they all roll back to the shadows. That's when you realize how futile it all was."

He became aware of the dog sitting in a doorway observing the discussion. The girl clucked her tongue without taking her eyes off Moss. The dog ambled into the rain toward her. Moss fervently wished he still had the gun. She opened her small fist and a firefly crawled over her knuckles and took to the air, flashing before it vanished.

"Remember what I said, one warning. Let them go."

"Never," he said.

The girl laughed and climbed onto the dog as though it were a pony. She turned the animal away from Moss and trotted through the fog that had begun to drift into the street, from over the rooftops and out of the mouths of alleyways.

"Never," shouted Moss hoarsely at the disappearing monstrosity. "Never! Fuck you."

RHINO BUILDING

THE RAIN HAD A FEROCIOUS INTENSITY. A PAIR OF HEADLIGHTS exposed Moss in the middle of a single-lane bridge. There was no escape. It was a drop of thirty feet to the railway below. He shrank against a metal truss. An antiquated military cargo truck braked, sending vibrations through the bridge deck. Moss coughed in a cloud of diesel exhaust. He edged along the truss to the cab and read *Museum of Natural History* in letters stenciled over a painted-out military insignia. The passenger door swung open, almost hitting him in the head.

"You getting in, or not?" Imogene shouted. She leaned across the seat, using the steering column for support. Moss climbed onto the running board and pulled himself into the truck. He slammed the door and dropped into the seat. The cushion was hard and split down the middle but it felt good to sit after an hour of walking. A heater blasted hot air and diesel aromatics. His soaking clothes lay over him like a lead blanket.

"What are you doing here?" Moss shouted over the engine.

"I took a chance you'd be coming back this way. I don't know what I would have done if you hadn't. We have to leave the city. We can't stay here now." The truck started rolling.

"Where's Irridis?"

"Gone," said Imogene.

"Gone? Where?"

"No idea. He didn't tell me that. He just told me to tell you that he couldn't wait. Your things are in the back. A cab company delivered the trunk after you left. Irridis had arranged it beforehand. There are some clothes. The traveling bookcase is back there too, along with your bag and the bird book." Imogene gestured behind her without taking her eyes from the road. There was a tarp-covered opening leading into the cargo area. Moss nodded but stayed seated. Imogene glanced at him. "I went down to the market to look around. There were Red Lamprey guys hanging around. Irridis was gone by the time I got back to the attic. I gathered up some things and cleared out. Then I mailed a letter to the museum and told them I was finished, and that I was heading south to visit family. By the time they figure out that it's bullshit, and that I stole this truck, we'll be long gone in the opposite direction."

"You seem quite restored," said Moss.

"Don't sound so disappointed."

Moss watched the road. The state of mind that had led him to murder Lamb had not returned. The image of his arm over Lamb's eyes was burned into his mind. He replayed the sensation of his finger's pressure on the trigger; the sudden collapse of Lamb's skull beneath his palm; Oliver in the aquarium, floating like a deformity in formaldehyde. His anger exploded. He punched the dashboard, swore, and elbowed the side window while Imogene withdrew against her door. She stopped the truck. He pulled his arms to his sides with his fists clenched, white-knuckled, and screamed a profanity at the windshield. He felt her hand on his arm, but he could not look at her. Instead, he turned toward the passenger side window and stared into the darkness.

Imogene pushed the clutch pedal down and moved the transfer case shift lever forward. She released the hand brake lever and the truck moved forward. For several minutes they traveled in the direction he had just come from and then swerved north. Moss was numb. His forehead bumped against the glass. Imogene divided her attention between the gearshift lever and the wheel, casting periodic glances at the oil pressure gauge on the instrument panel. After several miles they turned left onto a wider road and headed inland. The built-up city core gave way to mansions on tree-covered estates where woodlots grew to the edge of the road. Moss fell into a dreamless sleep.

A sudden loud noise woke him. He rubbed his hands over his beard and eyes. His clothing was dry and stiff over the front of his legs and torso, but still damp against the seat. Although his lower back and calf throbbed, he felt somewhat rested. Patches of light sky appeared through breaks in the cloud. He looked at Imogene.

She stared straight ahead, biting her bottom lip as she avoided the worst potholes. Her hair was a tangled mess, and there were smudges under her eyes. She leaned across the steering wheel and swerved around the hump of a dead animal.

"Where are you going?" he asked. His voice sounded unrecognizable to his own ears.

"Somewhere where we can catch our breath. Sort of." There was peevishness in her tone, so he did not pursue his question. "I thought we were being followed for a while, a black car."

Moss looked in the large side mirror, but could not see a thing.

"They're gone, if they were ever really following us. It might have been a coincidence," said Imogene.

He gripped an overhead strap as the truck heaved on its suspension. They pulled into a neglected gravel drive. Imogene eased the truck to a stop in front of a tall iron gate.

"This damn truck is killing me." Imogene stretched with her hands in the small of her back.

"Let me drive," said Moss.

"We're here."

"Where's here?"

"The City Zoo. This is their back door. Nobody uses this access road." She leaned forward without further explanation and fished in the pocket of her leather jacket, producing a ring of keys. She sorted through them. "This one."

Moss took the ring by the key she had separated out. The open door of the truck cab let in a pungent odor of wet hay and manure. He jumped out of the truck and unlocked the gate. Imogene nosed the vehicle through and Moss jumped back in. Ten minutes later, she slowed the truck to a crawl, skillfully guiding it down a rutted road to an area at the back of a building. She stopped the truck on the dry side of a partially flooded yard.

"Tell me what happened," said Imogene. "I want to hear all of it."

"I'll be right back," she said. Leaving the engine running, she climbed down and ran through the rain. Moss watched her enter the building. She had remained mostly silent as he recounted Lamb's death, the explosion and Echo leaving with Elizabeth. He told her about the ocellus Irridis had given to him to protect. At the end, she folded her arms and made him describe Echo in every detail. If she felt one way or the other at the news of Lamb's demise she concealed it well. Two large doors opened from within and Imogene emerged. He allowed himself a smile when she bowed. Mission accomplished. Back behind the wheel, she steered the truck through the opening. The engine rumbled like a locomotive in the large bay before she killed the engine.

"Interesting hideout," said Moss. The inside of the cab suddenly felt intimate, awkward.

"It's the old Rhino Building. Back when the zoo had rhinos they were kept here when they weren't on display. It hasn't been used for that since they became extinct fifty years ago. Poaching dropped the numbers perilously low and some kind of respiratory disease finished them off. Since then it's been a place to dump old equipment. The museum used to keep an office here." She looped strands of wet hair behind her ears. "John shared a room in the back with a senior zoologist named Philip. Philip was the person who got me the job in the repository, under some pressure from Lamb. He was one of the few people that actually liked my father. He's dead now. John used the office until he up and vanished. Philip still came here after that, to work on his field notes. It's still there, I think. Nobody ever bothered to clear it out. I thought we could hide here."

"I want to leave in the morning for Nightjar," said Moss.

"Okay," she said. "It's a long trip. Won't be easy."

"Everything points there. The books and charts at my old house were one thing, but knowing what you told us, about John kidnapping Memoria, convinces me that she would try to get back there."

They climbed out of the truck and watched the rain fall on the pool of foul looking water in the yard. Trees encroached on all sides. The overhanging boughs and yellowing leaves formed a barrier dense enough to hide the road they had followed. It seemed a safe place, at least for the moment. Moss breathed in damp air and smelled a trace of smoke. He turned to find Imogene with a hand-rolled cigarette held in one corner of her mouth. She flicked the dead match into the yard.

"Hashish," she said, holding the cigarette out.

Moss took it from her. The smoke made his head spin but it made him relax. He exhaled. "Thanks."

"Philip's idea of tobacco. He and his cronies used to smoke it. Does the job. There's an appreciable amount in repository, stuffed in a taxidermied ostrich. Kind of a sideline for the Red Lamprey."

Moss shook his head and took another drag. This time he felt a rush as it hit his blood. It felt strange to be standing here with Imogene as his unlikely ally. He stole a glance. She was quite beautiful. To distract himself, he watched a family of crows arguing in a tree.

"You're sure he was dead?" said Imogene. Her face grew serious.

"Yes." Uncomfortable under her intense gaze, he looked into the trees.

"That boy, Andrew?"

"I don't know. I suppose I should have done more. I should have stayed and looked around."

Imogene waved him off. "Getting yourself killed wouldn't have been very helpful."

He looked up at the rushing clouds. "I couldn't open the door."

"What door?"

"The closet. I just couldn't turn the handle."

"It was locked?"

"No. I don't know." His voice was louder than he had intended. "I couldn't turn it and then it was all over, so quickly."

The rain eased and a bright streak opened in the clouds. For a moment it seemed as though the sun might come out, but fresh clouds closed the breach and the air was suffused with a tea-colored light. Frogs trilled, invisible in the trees. A heron flew over the uppermost branches, its head drawn back in a regal posture, and then it was gone.

"Elizabeth spoke to me," said Moss. "Afterwards, in the street." He could feel Imogene staring at him. "She warned me away. She has some vendetta against Irridis." He palmed the ocellus. "She means to kill him."

"She didn't hurt you?"

Moss shook his head. "No, it was odd, strangely formal. She delivered her message and left."

"What are you thinking?"

"I think Irridis had some kind of premonition of her intent." He faced Imogene. "Why are we really here? We could have gone anywhere."

"Because there is something I want to show you. I used to sneak away from Lamb when I was little and come here to talk to Philip. It was a place of sanity. He used to have great stories about my father, from back when John was a legit collector for the museum. One day I came by and Philip wasn't around. I snooped through the office on my own and found something interesting. I'm hoping it's still here."

Transcription from the scraplog of the *Somnambulist* for the purpose of a personal journal

Date, position, distance and wind entries omitted.

9:00 a.m. A gale blew itself out by shortly after 4 a.m. Since that time we have drifted on rough seas without the benefit of the engine. Mr. Conner and Mr. Lutes have spent the past few hours working indefatigably on the engine during which time we have moved unavoidably closer to the island of Nightjar. The water is filled with mines and debris, which we attribute to the storm. Mr. James posits that a ship has gone aground and been torn apart but there is no charted reef or sandbar in the vicinity. We must entertain that a ship struck one of the many explosive mines that plague these waters.

o

9:30 a.m. The engine is working again, though fitfully. We have determined the debris on the water to be the remains of an airship. We are unable to find identifying markers. There is a strong likelihood that it belonged to treasure seekers operating on Nightjar. Mr. James and young Charles have set out on the landing boat, to look for survivors. The state of the wreckage is no cause for optimism and while I voiced concern for Charles's wellbeing the captain permitted them to proceed. We maintain safe distance.

o

10:15 a.m. Engine failure once more and we are drifting dangerously close to Nightjar. We are well within the forbidden waters. We have seen several mines floating in the sea. The ship will flounder if the engine is not restored within the next hour, forcing us to abandon her for the island. Mr. James and Charles are on their own, as the seas will not permit them to catch us. I believe the Captain made an error in judgment in allowing them to go. I fear before the day is out my years worth of marine samples will be lost.

o

10:35 a.m. The engine is working thanks to the valiant efforts of Mr. Conner and Mr. Lutes! We are making full speed for Mr. James and Charles. They will want to continue to search the wreckage but the captain has already said that he will brook not one word of protest from either of them. We must achieve open sea before dark.

o

11:35 a.m. Remarkably, Mr. James and Charles have fished a boy from the sea. The captain says the sea is too cold and cannot explain how he could have survived. The boy was found floating unconscious and entangled in guy ropes. By all rights he should have been drowned but seems no worse for wear. His appearance is uncanny, flesh like cloudy glass. He is attended by 5 floating lights. The crew is terrified with superstitious nonsense. We can get no explanation from the boy as to how he came to be in the sea. Mr. James and the Captain are in agreement that as unlikely as it seems he must have come from Nightjar Island. An examination of the wreckage led them to conclude that it has been floating on the surface for several months. This rules out the possibility that the boy was a survivor.

Unable to land on the island, the Captain has decided that we will proceed south to the City of Steps for repairs and refueling. The boy will be dealt with there. Mr. James is vociferous in his objections, wishing to attempt landing in spite of conditions. He seeks a solution to this mystery. Mr. James and the Captain exchanged heated words during which the Captain invited him to take the skiff. The offer was declined and Mr. James has retreated to his cabin in a sulk. James will not be invited to continue the voyage beyond the Steps.

"That's all there is." Imogene refolded the sheets of paper and returned them to a tin box. They had located the journal pages after an hour of searching. A desk, its chair, several packed bookcases and a musty couch filled the office. An ivy-covered window filtered the light. Imogene had supplemented with candlelight. She sat beside Moss on the couch.

"Philip was there when Irridis was pulled out of the ocean. James must be the man who gave Irridis to John," said Moss. "James was the ship's carpenter."

"John knew a lot of questionable characters. I'll bet James absconded with Irridis and approached John with an offer. John was well known for being in the market for curiosities, no questions asked." Imogene set the box on the floor.

"Irridis told me that the exchange was to settle a gambling debt," said Moss.

Moss let his eyes wander over the backs of the books jammed into the bookcases. Under other circumstances he would have enjoyed an afternoon going through some of the titles. To Moss's surprise, Imogene leaned against him and pulled a dense blanket over them both. She laughed.

"What's funny?" said Moss.

"It's a wool blanket. You can't wash it or it shrinks into a hunk of felt like this. Who washes a wool blanket? Pure Philip." She rested her cheek on his shoulder. In a few minutes her breathing grew deeper. When he was sure she was asleep, he kissed her head.

Moss sat back on the couch with an arm around Imogene and watched the last of the candle. The flame and wick flared, melting and distorting the wax. He thought of the glow inside Irridis. Squeezing his arm between their bodies, he pulled the ocellus from its hiding place. He tossed it into the air where it spun like a coin. Suddenly cold, he pulled her closer. The candle spat and died, releasing a thin ribbon of black smoke. Outside, the wind in the trees sounded like the sea.

NORTH ROAD

Imogene drove the truck hard as they left the city. There was no sign of the car that she had seen following the day before. That morning, she had shown Moss how to refuel at a manual diesel pump on the grounds of the zoo. While he had busied himself with the task, she had filled the back of the truck with unnecessary, but convincing, research equipment, and very necessary camping gear. The scientific equipment was to support their cover story, should they be stopped, of being on a research field trip to study interstitial species of crabs in the tidal zones to the north of the city. When preparations were complete, she had walked in on him poking through cupboards in the Rhino Building looking for something they might eat.

"Don't waste your time," she said, handing him a sandwich and a flask lid filled with coffee.

"Oh," he said, pleasantly surprised. "Where did you get this?"

"It's not my first interstitial species expedition, Moss. I stowed it in the truck before I left the market. Am I not the greatest field colleague ever?"

"Insofar as my limited experience allows me to comment, yes. I don't think I have ever had a better sandwich." Moss folded the last of the bread into his mouth.

Imogene smiled. "You could have at least washed your hands first. Come on. I want to show you something." Moss followed her down a wide brick corridor hung with dead fluorescent lights and strips of crusty flypaper. She pushed a heavy door. It opened into a large room, lit from above by algae-covered skylights.

Imogene danced away from him and turned in the center of the room with her arms outstretched. "What do you think?" Her voice echoed.

"It looks like Oliver's bathroom," said Moss skeptically.

The bare concrete floor sloped toward a large drain. Green streaks covered the walls. The air was warm and damp.

"I imagine this place has seen its share of health and safety compliance orders," said Moss, leaning his head back to look at the skylights.

"It's where they used to sluice down the rhinos!" A large metal pipe stood behind her covered in cracked rubber hoses and a large showerhead.

"Charming."

"There is a natural spring underneath the building. That's why it is so hot. Before the zoo was built there was a public bath here." She was suddenly in front of him. "I thought we could have a shower before we hit the road. How does that sound?"

Moss was startled. "Um, I'm not sure." Imogene threw her head back, a smile on her lips. "We could catch something," said Moss.

"Go on," she said. "I'm listening."

"Some sort of horrible rhino disease lurking in these cracks in the floor. Bacteria can live forever in a place like this."

"Uh-huh."

"Someone might slip. You could break a leg in here."

"I guess you'll just have to watch then." Imogene began removing her clothing. She pulled her T-shirt up.

"Here, let me help with that," said Moss, wriggling it over her head.

"For safety's sake," said Imogene, from beneath the material.

"Not exactly," Moss replied.

Later, clean, dressed and warm, they had left the Rhino Building behind. With Imogene's agreement, he had put the pages of the scraplog in his bag with *The Songbirds of Nightjar Island*. Moss hoped to share the pages if they encountered Irridis on the road. Now they were headed north, traveling on a two-lane road that followed the coastline with a bit more precision than Moss would have liked, given the precipitous cliffs.

The North Irridian Sea was rough and muddy. The rain was gone but a steady wind pushed against the side of the truck, demanding all of Imogene's attention. For the first few hours they had the road to themselves, with the exception of the occasional truck thundering past in the opposite direction. By mid-afternoon they passed small groups of people carrying camping gear along the side of the road. A few miles further and their progress was slowed to near walking speed by other vehicles, trucks piled high with equipment, motorcycles, and even carriages drawn by horses. People and animals walked back and forth across the road. It was as if they had found themselves in the midst of a traveling carnival. They had no choice but to follow the group as the afternoon wore on, frustration growing as the crowd thickened. When the daylight faded in the west, stars came out and torches were lit.

In the twilight, costumed revelers appeared. A group in dark capes and high white ruffs wore curlew masks with long downward-curving beaks. Imogene pointed as a figure, easily over eight feet, strode past, his head a mass of gold scales. Red barbules dangled from the wide maw of the paper carp mask. It appeared to be handing out real eyes but when one was thrust at Moss through the window it turned out to be a sugary confection. Only after it had passed could they see the albino girl tied to his back, playing with a giant walking stick insect. Dwarves, with conical black velvet hats, above faces painted as skulls, picked their way through the crowd on stilts, flinging strings of firecrackers at the other pilgrims.

"Irridis wouldn't even be noticed in this crowd," said Moss.

On a particularly steep grade, a drunken pilgrim jumped onto the truck's foot rail, whooping as he swept a roaring torch to clear the path. Moss rose in his seat, but felt Imogene's hand on his shoulder. Eventually the man jumped or fell off. Moss sat back, rubbing his palms on his knees. At the top of the hill further progress became impossible. Traffic was at a standstill and people sat in the roadway in groups. The land to the side of the road had become an encampment filled with tents and roaring bonfires that sent plumes of sparks into the cold evening air. In spite of his wariness, the smell of roasting meat made Moss's stomach growl.

"There's no way I can get through this in the dark," said Imogene. "I'll either drive us off the cliff into the ocean or run over somebody."

"Try there." Moss pointed off the road. "There are fewer lights that way." Imogene turned the wheel and maneuvered the truck through a pasture. They rocked violently as they crawled forward. Moss jumped out of the truck while it was still rolling. Illuminated in the headlights, he guided Imogene to a spreading beech tree in a quiet corner of the field where the ground was level.

"We can camp here," he shouted.

Imogene exited the truck. Together, they surveyed the lights and fires near the road.

"Nobody will bother us here, hopefully," she said.

"I wonder what's going on."

"As long as they stay over there, I'm too tired and hungry to care." Imogene yawned as she leaned back into the cab and turned off the engine. Voices whooped in the distance. Imogene disappeared through a flap into the back of the truck. She reappeared a short time later with a roll of canvas. "Might as well build a fire and relax."

Moss gathered deadwood and made a small fire while Imogene arranged the ground sheet and carried out a hamper of food. Sitting on rolled-up sleeping bags, they ate sandwiches and shared a bottle of red wine. The damp wood crackled in the flames. When they were finished, Imogene kicked her sleeping bag flat and stretched out. She rolled a hash cigarette, which she did not light. Moss listened to the wind in the trees and fidgeted. The sandwiches had done little to satisfy his appetite, and there would be nothing else until the next town. Moss, studying an old map from the glove compartment, estimated that would be sometime the next afternoon.

"I'm going to head to one of those fires and see what's going on," he said. "Do you want to come?" When Imogene did not respond, he turned to find that she had fallen asleep. Moss pulled his coat from the cab of the truck and set off. He followed the ruts in the grass left by their tires, and climbed a slope to the road. From there, he had a view of the sea, still wild from nearly a week of storms. The sky was indigo and full of stars but the wind was biting, so he did not stand long to admire it. He walked through groups of people partying around fires, but nobody seemed interested in his presence. Buttoning his coat, he tramped across mud and weeds toward a particularly large fire. A group of about twenty people stood in a circle drinking wine out of communal bottles and poking at the mound of burning logs. The smell of cooking meat was carried by the smoke that seemed to change direction every few seconds. A metal grill had been laid over one side of the fire. It was covered in sizzling kebabs and larger cuts of meat.

"It smells good," he said to a stringy-haired youth to his left. The warmth of the fire was welcome on the palms of his hands.

"There's a pig under the coals. Some guys grabbed it from a farm in the afternoon." The teenager wore a blanket like a cape. "They're pulling it out in few minutes. Drink?" Moss shook his head at the offered bottle, which judging from the man's dilated eyes held more than wine. "Suit yourself." He took a long drink.

"What's going on here?" said Moss.

"Going on?"

"All of this. All these people?"

The man yelled at someone across the fire. "This guy wants to know what's going on." There was scattered laughter but no answer as the group on the other side of the fire struggled with someone who had decided to try to walk on the coals. Moss's acquaintance shook his head and threw the empty bottle through the flames. Moss grimaced as someone cried out. "Finch." Moss took the man's hand. It was sticky.

"Woods."

"Woods, seriously, you don't know? This is the Purge protest. Happens every year, man. We're all heading for the town of Sea Pines where there is a big festival going on. A lot of these people here, they are the actual ancestors."

"You mean descendants?" said Moss.

"Whatever, man. It was their people that got booted off Nightjar Island. You heard about that, right? Totally fucked up, man."

"How far is the town from here?"

"About another day of walking. My feet are killing me already." The skirmish on the other side of the fire took on a more serious tone, as the unmistakable thump of fists connecting with flesh became audible over loud shouts. Finch yelled encouragements and kicked the fire, sending a shower of sparks toward the combatants. His face glowed orange in the firelight. Not liking the turn towards violence, Moss swept his arm down and snagged a handful of kebabs, reasoning they would hardly be missed. He tried to melt back into the darkness, only to discover that more people had crowded toward the fire, impeding his exit. A rough hand grabbed his coat. It was Finch. "Where are you going? The party is just getting going." The man's eyes darted down at the sticks of still-smoking meat.

"I have friends I have to get back to." He pushed the man's hand away.

"Calm down, man. You're acting strange. Like all intense. Are you a cop, or what?" Finch's breath stank of wine and sinispore. Moss turned away.

"Nothing like that. I'm just a researcher. We're—I'm heading north and got stuck in the traffic." He was over-explaining and he knew it. A gap opened in the crowd and Moss stepped out of the firelight. Finch yelled something obscene after him, but Moss ignored it and moved in the direction of the truck. A few minutes later he was in an open field and the fire was a distant flicker. There was nothing to suggest that he was being followed. He bit a hunk of meat from the end of a stick.

He stood motionless, chewing. Excited voices carried over the surf and the wind. The sea was on his right and the truck somewhere to his left, invisible behind a dark cluster of trees. The land in front of him inclined toward a point where the road jogged left, away from the sea cliff. He was about to set off when something caught his attention. Silhouetted against the sky, a large carriage was being drawn along the road by a lumbering form. Moss instinctively dropped to a crouch. There was no doubt it was Echo.

The creature was hiding in plain sight, where it would be taken for just another carnival attraction. A dog, with the unmistakable shape of a rider on its back, zigzagged in and out of sight. Moss held his breath as it stopped. He had the sense that somehow it could see him in the dark. He was weighing whether or not to run when the dog and its rider turned away and disappeared from sight. Moss waited. They reappeared in front of the carriage and continued along the road.

Moss headed toward the truck. Stepping onto a slight rise, he looked back, but saw only firelight. A few strides more and something hard hit him in the back of the head. The kebabs flew out of his hands as he dropped onto his knees in an irrigation ditch. A bottle rolled along the ground a few feet away and clinked against a rock. Moss gripped the back of his head with one hand as he looked for his assailant. He was too close to the ground to see properly. His hand came away from his head warm and tacky. Watching his footing, he ran up the opposite side of the ditch where he collided with a stack of wooden boxes. The buzz from within and the vibration of wings against his exposed skin told him he had struck a beehive. Several other hives were arranged in rows.

He chose one near the middle and crouched behind it. Disoriented bees crawled over his clothing and even across his beard, but Moss remained motionless.

Several men wandered into view carrying sticks. They pushed and shoved each other loudly, between drunken swats at the grass. Finch's voice rose above the rest. Moss kept his head low and listened to them moving between the hives. He had no doubt that they were searching for him. They knocked the boxes over as they blundered forward, but veered away before they reached his hiding spot. The shouts faded but Moss waited for several minutes before standing. Even in the dark he could see that the hives were devastated. He did what he could to right them, sustaining several stings to the back of his hand for his troubles. Leaving them to their fate, he returned to the truck by a circuitous route to avoid Finch's gang. The back of his head throbbed and he could feel blood inside his collar.

Approaching the truck from sunken ground behind the beech, Moss saw a pinprick of light in the dark. Unsure if it was real, or an optical artifact—the result of being hit in the head with a bottle—he chose his steps deliberately. Moving closer to the base of the tree, Moss could see a crouched man watching the truck. The man's hand was on a rifle that leaned against the tree. Reaching into his pocket, Moss pulled out the awl. He crept up behind the man. At that moment, the stranger realized he was being stalked and turned his head. Moss leaped forward and seized the man's hair, slamming him into the tree trunk. He brought the awl up under his left ear. Moss could feel the man's carotid pulse beneath the base of his thumb.

"Stop," hissed the man. "It's me: Gale."

Moss kicked the rifle away and stepped back. Gale lay sprawled in a litter of dried leaves and beechnuts, panting heavily.

"What the hell are you doing here?" asked Moss, pointing the awl at Gale.

"Shush, there's time for that later. I'm on your side. The young lady is in trouble. Listen."

Moss could hear voices on the other side of the truck. "Get up," he said to Gale. As Gale scrambled to his feet, pulling vegetation out of his beard, Moss snatched the rifle out of the grass. It was a heavy, big game rifle that he had no idea how to use. Taking a chance, he thrust it into Gale's chest. They heard Imogene call Moss's name. Moss held the awl up to Gale's face.

"Wait a couple minutes and then follow me," he said. Gale nodded vigorously, clutching the rifle with both hands. With that, Moss left the concealment of the massive tree and rounded the front of the truck.

Imogene was lying face down on the ground with a large man on top of her. He was bleeding from a gash across his forehead. Finch and another man were kicking the fire out.

"Make sure it's all out," Finch yelled at his companion. "We don't need any witnesses." Another man, older and unshaven, kneeled on the ground near Imogene. He rubbed his cheek as if considering his options. Imogene stopped struggling. The man pulled a battery-powered torch from his sagging pants and aimed the beam in her face.

"Get off her, now," said Moss, walking into view.

"That's him," said Finch. "He's a cop. A fucking thieving cop, no less." The man with the torch turned his attention to Moss.

"Is he right?" the man asked.

"My name is Woods. That is my friend you have there. Tell that idiot to get off her," said Moss. Finch looked at Imogene salaciously. Moss lunged forward and thrust the awl into his thigh. Finch fell, screaming. The man with the torch remained where he was, impassive. Moss heard Imogene laboring to breathe under her attacker's weight. Moss strode toward her, leaving Finch writhing on the ground. He calculated that he could probably do enough damage to the older man to provoke his heavier companion off of Imogene.

"Move," he yelled. The older man laughed and raised his torch as if in surrender. Before Moss could react, the man tried to strike Imogene in the face. She twisted, anticipating the attack. The torch struck the fat man's knee with enough force to smash the light off the handle and send the bulb and reflector spinning off into the grass. Swearing, the injured man rolled off Imogene. She rolled, striking his jaw with a fist-sized rock. The shattering of bone was audible. Moss jumped at the older man hoping to knock him off balance and gain an advantage. The awl opened the man's face like a filet. He howled and met Moss with a fist in the chest. Moss stumbled away. The awl slipped from his grip and rolled into the grass. Finch had regained his feet and hooted like a hysterical chimpanzee as blood ran through his fingers. A gunshot sounded. At first Moss thought that one of the attackers had drawn a weapon. The fat man was swearing now, and running away from the truck into the darkness clutching a bloodied upper arm, his jaw gaping.

"Well, that's about enough of that, I think," said Gale. With the ornate rifle raised to his shoulder, he advanced on the man who clutched the handle of the ruined flashlight with one hand and pressed the loose skin of his cheek to his face with the other. "I'm capable of murdering you where you stand. I suggest you take your friends and leave before I am tempted." The man dropped the flashlight and ran. Finch followed, dragging his leg and crying openly. The other had already fled.

Gale lowered the rifle. Moss ran to Imogene and helped her to a sitting position. He put his arms around her. She spoke into his shoulder. Behind them, Gale lit a cigar.

"What has she got to say for herself? Is she all right?" Gale asked, issuing thick smoke. Moss inclined his head toward Imogene.

"She said thank you," said Moss.

"Happy to be of—"

"Gale, why are you here?"

"I thought you might be more grateful," said Gale.

"Give me that rifle."

With mock affront, Gale stepped back and lifted the rifle as if to present it. The stock and barrel were encrusted in golden curlicues. The trigger guard reminded Moss of the hilt on a ceremonial sword.

"Handle it with care. I'll have you know this is worth a fortune. It belongs in a bloody museum," said Gale, with a vulpine grin.

"He followed us," whispered Imogene.

A PROPOSAL

"WE NEED TO TALK, GALE," SAID MOSS.

"Yes, Moss."

With first sign of morning light they had returned to the road and discovered that it was passable. Most of the travelers had meandered into the surrounding fields to sleep, most likely due to the frigid wind coming off the sea. They continued their northward journey. Gale, citing a car breakdown, had made a request to travel as far as Sea Pines. Despite a poisonous look from Imogene, Moss had agreed. He was confounded by the enigma of Gale and wanted an explanation of why the man had followed them from the City of Steps.

"Oh yes, I know your real name." The two men sat in the back of the truck. The canvas awning shivered loudly around them. Gale sat on a crate resting his empty rifle across his knees. A hunting coat, cargo pants, and new boots that smelled of mink oil constituted a getup more suited to shooting rabbits than chasing off thugs. Moss rested on a rolled sleeping bag with his back against a metal tube that provided ribbed support for the awning. Imogene, bruised and silent, was behind the wheel, having earlier made it clear she was in no mood for conversation.

"I got shot in the leg because of you," said Moss. "I'd be dead now if that cop had any kind of aim."

"It wasn't my doing; I assure you of that. It was Seaforth's employee, Mr. Morel, who set things in motion. Habich told me that Morel had grave suspicions about your conduct for weeks. His curiosity was particularly aroused when someone brought you home, semi-conscious, and covered in blood."

"He saw that? Morel is a trouble-maker," said Moss.

"I agree. I am sorry about your leg. The detective overreacted."

"Is that what you would call it. The man was a homicidal maniac."

"From what I saw of his face after the fact, you gave a good account of yourself. You broke his nose and probably fractured his cheekbone. I'd avoid going back to the city if I were you. All that aside, I wasn't pleased that you were trying to bargain with Oliver behind my back. It was very bad form. I have a collector's instinct, eyes in the back of my head, Moss. Did you think I'd be disinterested in knowing that I was being cheated? I take my collecting seriously."

"I never intended to give Oliver the book. I was trying to bargain for something else."

"More of those interesting drawings, I would hazard to guess. I've been preoccupied by your drawing, Moss. It is how I am. When I see something that interests me I feel driven to seek it out. It's like a stone in my shoe. I become agitated at the thought of it falling into the hands of someone who might not appreciate its true value. Naturally, once I had seen the drawing I could not let it slip out of my hands. Nor the others. There are others, aren't there?" Gale took on a lofty tone. "A man of my sensibilities has an imperative to pursue the rare and unusual. How would I live with myself if I let an opportunity slip through my fingers? Unfortunately, I do not have the virtue of patience." The two men sat looking at each other as the truck shuddered. "Perhaps, if you can try to see me in a more favorable light, we might salvage something from this situation."

Moss averted his eyes. "And what would that be?"

"Before he died," said Gale, "Oliver Taxali told me an interesting story. He was convinced that he'd had a run-in with the supernatural." Gale laughed heartily. "A witch. I thought he was pulling my leg until I happened to encounter that boy, Andrew, outside the old Blackrat Bakery. It took some time to get him talking and then I couldn't get him to stop. It was quite a story. He told me of events in the Cloth Hall, that you had murdered Lamb, all of it. He seemed particularly excited about a demon, and a witch that rides a black dog."

"Andrew is alive," said Moss with relief.

"He is quite well. The witch and her companion, they have been causing you problems?"

"Make your point."

"I know they are real. I've seen them for myself on the road. The creature is pulling a large black carriage with no windows, very ominous. Now, I come to my proposal."

"So soon?" said Moss.

"There is no need for sarcasm. Simply put, I will help you dispense with these unsavory characters. I am capable. I've hunted my share of big game in the past." He patted the rifle.

"What would you expect to get out of it?" Moss fought the impulse to look at the crate Gale was sitting on, which housed the bookcase.

"The rest of the drawings."

Moss laughed.

"What is so funny?"

"Okay, for the sake of argument, how would you go about it?"

"I intend to exterminate them," said Gale, stroking the gun. "This is no time for half measures. By all accounts these are not entities to be trifled with. They are against the natural order, and I will dispatch them as such."

"Gale—"

"A phantasm, nothing more," said Gale. "It is only practical that I should come along. Whether you realize it or not, you are running out of time."

"Why?"

"We are heading north. I infer that we are following them to Nightjar Island. Confronting them there will be infinitely more complicated than dealing with them sooner. If you even get to the island, the terrain is difficult and there are many other kinds of dangers like unexploded mines, wild animals and reclusive holdouts from the Purge." Gale leaned forward. "Let me help you deal with them, Moss. Let's reach an agreement. I can see it in your eyes that you want to accept."

The man had the gleam of obsession. Moss knew that Gale had slim chance of fulfilling his proposition. He had felt the power of Elizabeth's invisible touch. Gale would turn to jelly before he could squeeze a single shell from his ridiculous rifle. Listening to Gale, Moss realized that here was a golden opportunity to rid himself of the meddler for good. With Gale poking the hornet's nest, Moss and Imogene could use the distraction to vanish into the island, to search for Memoria.

"They will be heading for the old ferry quay," said Gale. "It is the only stretch of water around the island that is even plausibly navigable."

"I've never heard of it," said Moss.

"There is nothing much left now, seawalls and old pilings. It was the point of departure for the Nightjar ferry, the closest point between the mainland and the island. The water is treacherous, full of rocks and debris from the war, unstable mines, to say nothing of the terrible currents. It would be reckless to attempt a crossing. But, there was also a tunnel there. Equally dangerous, if in fact it has not collapsed. I'd bet that the tunnel is their true destination. You cannot let them get to the island by either route. Once they are there they will vanish. You will have lost the advantage of the bottleneck. There is only one road between here and the ferry quay. We must catch them on that road."

At that moment, the truck came to an abrupt stop, sending Gale onto a pile of tarpaulins. Imogene appeared at the back of the truck. "We're here," she shouted above the roar of the idling engine.

THE INN

"WELL, I DON'T LIKE IT," SAID IMOGENE. "I DON'T CARE IF HE HELPED to scare off those idiots last night. I don't trust him. All that phony pipe and liquor bullshit. He was stalking us. Doesn't that suggest to you that he has resources? He has to be associated with the Red Lamprey." She dropped a heavy bag of clothing on the table. The room in the inn they had chosen was small for two people and smelled of the vinegar used to clean the windows. Between the few bags that they had carried in from the truck, and the traveling bookcase, there was barely room to maneuver. Moss would have slept in the truck but Imogene wanted a bath and a real bed after the assault the previous night.

"I don't trust him either, but now that he's here isn't it better to have him in plain sight?" Moss sat at a table fidgeting with a pen.

"I can't believe that you would want to have anything to do with Gale. I've met guys like Gale many times over the years. They are far more dangerous agents than the obvious gangsters. He's a threat. It's written all over his face. He'll screw us the second it's to his advantage."

Moss absently unscrewed the body of the pen. A cartridge of ink and a spring flew out. "I'm not disputing anything you're saying," he said. "But it's worth the risk. I'd rather he thought he was involved, than have him plotting behind us. Besides, he might have information we need. He claims to know how to get to Nightjar. Remember, you once said John had a back door? Gale says that there is a tunnel." He inserted the cartridge, took it out again, dropped the spring in and then reinserted the cartridge. The two halves of the pen body would not screw together properly.

"And you believe him?" Imogene challenged. She sat on the edge of a wooden kitchen chair that rocked on an uneven leg, arms

169

crossed. The side of her face was scraped from being forced to the ground and her arms were covered in bruises. Since the attack she had been distant. The easygoing Imogene from the zoo was gone. He set the pen aside.

"I don't underestimate his greed."

"You said yourself that the carriage is nearby. We need to move discreetly. Gale will do something stupid. We can figure this out for ourselves."

"Why are you angry?" he asked.

"Why did you leave me alone?" she asked, changing the subject.

"What?" Moss said, caught off guard.

"You heard me. Last night. Why did you leave me sleeping out in the open alone?"

Moss looked at her, shocked by her vehemence but glad to be finally getting to the main reason for her anger. "How could I foresee what was going to happen? It seemed safe enough. There was nobody around. You'd fallen asleep."

"I fell asleep because I thought you were there, Moss. I woke up with a pig on top of me biting the back of my neck. He would have raped me." She was shouting.

"That's not exactly fair," said Moss.

"You were supposed to have my back. Not leave me lying out in the open like bait for some crazed rapist." She was crying now and rubbing her arms as if trying to rid them of cobwebs. "I had enough of that shit with Lamb."

"This from the woman that drugged me."

"The hell with you." She shoved the table at him.

"Imogene, I am sorry," he said.

"I mean it. I can't believe you left, again."

"Stop it," he said, feeling anger rising.

Imogene came close, her face flushed and streaked with tears. "Do you want to know the real reason you're alone? It's not the mistakes you've made, or the things that have happened to you." Her voice became hoarse. "It's because you don't know how to be with people, Moss. You're so solitary, it's like your head is still in that jail." She was overheated now, jabbing her finger. "You're angry."

"It sounds to me like you're talking about yourself," he said bitterly. From the window he looked down at the inn parking lot.

A lanky teenaged girl was pegging laundry to a line. The sea wind plastered her dress to her back. A dog with long legs followed its nose through some weeds. The silence behind him felt like a leaning slab of marble. He pulled a cloth from his pocket and cleaned his glasses. The clock on the wall ticked. Wind off the sea made the walls of the inn shudder. Down in the yard the girl was reaching to the back of her mouth with an index finger as if trying to dislodge something from between her teeth. She coughed and turned scowling to look into the sky. A moment later she leaned against an old motorbike, singing to herself.

"Moss, I'm sorry," whispered Imogene. She was close behind him. "That asshole grabbed me by the hair and pulled me out of a dead sleep. When I looked around and you weren't there—" She came around the table and tried to touch his cheek.

"Imogene," Moss said, pushing her hand away. "You're right, everything you said is right."

"Are you hurt?" The look on her face changed from remorse to concern. She tried again to touch his head, but he drew back.

"I'm fine," he said. Feeling the back of his scalp, he found the spot where the bottle had struck. He curled his bloody fingers and brought his fist down on the table, leaving a smear.

"Damn it." He walked across the floor towards the door. A sinispore vial fell from his coat and spun across the floor. It was half empty. He chased it, realizing that he must look ridiculous. When it was in his hand he stopped and took a breath. Without looking at her he said, "I'm going to find Gale."

In spite of his declaration Moss had no specific direction in mind. He knew only that he had to walk, to disperse his anger. Being trapped in a room watching Imogene's mood change from anger to sadness was more than he could bear. He *was* solitary. Being alone was a punishment he had levied against himself the day he failed to prevent Memoria from falling from the wall. Abandoning Imogene probably had been an unconscious manifestation of his inability to take responsibility for another. Elizabeth had only been half right when she said Irridis could not love him; Moss could not accept love. He left the yard of the inn, hollow and furious with himself, dodging the teenaged girl as he passed through the gate. For no good reason, he turned left.

The Purge protest had taken over the area between the town's seaward-facing buildings and its crumbling seawall. Tents and carts created a backdrop for improvised street theatre and musical satire. The evening air was filled with aromatic smoke from open grills. At the front of the inn, pedestrians clogged the street. Moss shouldered through inebriated revelers until he found a natural corridor through the bodies. Here again were the costumes, but rather than seeming magical, they had sinister undertones and he averted his eyes. Having had too much of real monsters Moss could find no amusement in these forms. He was searching for a path to the relative quiet of the harbor, when an alley opened to his left. A man striding past shoved him from behind. Moss stumbled into the alley. He steadied himself and brushed dust from his clothing. The mass of bodies continued to push past the alley entrance. Turning away, he reached into his pocket and pulled out the vial of sinispore. After the scuffle with Finch's gang he had found it in the grass behind the truck. With his back to the wall he broke the cork with a thumbnail. The vial rolled in his palm and the drug sifted between his fingers. He opened his fingers and dropped the vial to the ground.

FRESCO

Moss was too agitated by his argument with Imogene to be around people. Reentering the crowd would only exacerbate his mood. He chose instead to cut between the buildings, thinking to find a quiet back route to the harbor. All hope of a simple egress was disappointed when he found himself in a courtyard garden. His first impulse was to retrace his steps but he was attracted to the quietude of the place. The winding pathway in front of him had been constructed from weathered stones. He weighed one in his palm. It was smooth and cold. Since boyhood, Moss had been a compulsive collector of stones, unable to walk on a beach without straining his pocket seams. The one in his hand was a dove-grey oval with dark feathered marks. It was pretty, and reminded him of Irridis's ocelli. He returned it to the path.

Across the garden was a deep-set door. Moss followed the path feeling very much a trespasser. Yet, the stones slid beneath his soles pleasingly. An herb garden, green despite the late season, felt welcoming. Only the praying mantis, swaying atop the seedpod of a thornapple, boxing the air, warned him off.

A horseshoe crab knocker was centered on the door. Sea air or disuse had crusted the hinge. Moss rapped lightly with his fingers, and when there was no response, he tried more insistently. Nothing. He turned the handle, though he could not imagine what emboldened him to do so. Maybe it was the spell the place had cast over him, or just simple curiosity. Regardless, he was rewarded with the unexpected sight of a chapel as the door swung in.

The ceiling was a deep indigo, punctuated with unfamiliar gold constellations. Frescoes covered the walls in three registers, depicting a picaresque narrative with repeated characters. The artist's winged monsters and grotesques reminded Moss of Imogene's tattoos and he wished that she were with him to share the discovery.

The wood floors were well swept, and emanated a smell of beeswax. Moss was puzzled by the lack of benches, but the walk to the altar provided an answer. It was designed to calm, to force a pause and transition the visitor, so that upon reaching the altar the cares of the street would have fallen away and a contemplative state reached. The transition had begun with the act of exiting the alley, where the rough brick gave way to the softer stones.

The altar was slightly raised, and supported dozens of candles. Only a few were lit. Behind the altar, an embedded grid of alcoves was built into the wall, like boxes at a post office. He calculated 144. Each alcove had a small door, though only a few were open. Moss had seen something similar in the streets of the old town in the City of Steps. It was a place to leave notes or objects of personal significance. Usually these took the form of a question, a message, or a confession on a piece of folded paper. Sometimes more substantial objects were left. It was a ritual of release. Eventually, the offerings would be taken by anonymous hands on the other side of the wall and burned in a pit. Afterwards, the tiny doors would spring open again.

The chapel was insulated by thick walls. In the silence, Moss could hear the rustle of his clothing, his breath and his tinnitus. He was suddenly aware of how much energy his senses expended filtering and sorting the outside world. His spent anger and hurt had drained him. He sat on a stool in front of the altar and contemplated the alcoves. Several minutes had elapsed when a door to his right opened admitting a man in a grey cassock. Although there was no evidence of surprise in the weathered face, the man's deep-set eyes assessed Moss carefully. He touched his beard where some red was scattered amongst the grey. He placed the empty vial of sinispore on the altar in front of Moss. "I think you dropped this in the alley." He sat on the edge of the altar. "I'm Jonathan, the caretaker of this chapel."

"I'm finished with it," said Moss, looking away from the vial.

"That's probably just as well," said Jonathan. "But it's still littering." His smile was engaging but his tone of voice was serious. In the awkward conversational silence that followed he fixed his gaze on his extended legs and battered gardening clogs. Embarrassed, Moss decided it was time to leave. As he stood, Jonathan looked up.

"Would you mind helping me out with something? It won't take long. I'm writing a chapbook on the history of this building, which I'm actually here to close up, and there's a bit about the fauna used in the mural. Do you know your birds, by any chance?"

"Some," said Moss. "In prison I used to play a game to pass the time, with an ornithologist, no less. He had a stack of cards, the kind that used to come in cigar boxes. They had birds printed on them. He'd quiz me on the names." Moss startled himself by so casually mentioning prison.

"Fantastic." Jonathan swiveled around and scanned the fresco to their right. "There." He pointed at a spot in the middle register. "What is that?"

"Some kind of chickadee. It's hard to tell from here," said Moss.

"Well, get up and have a look then. Where's your curiosity, man?"

"All right, all right." Moss was amused in spite of himself. He humored Jonathan by going to the wall. "Can't be sure. It looks like a red-breasted nuthatch."

"Wait here." Jonathan disappeared through the door and returned a minute later carrying a paint-spattered stepladder. "Try this."

"Are you serious? A person could kill themselves on that thing."

"It is quite safe. I used it just this morning." Jonathan helped Moss position it in front of the wall. Wondering what he had gotten into, Moss climbed the ladder while Jonathan held the rails. At the second to last step, Moss was at eye level with the bird.

"It is a red-breasted nuthatch," he said.

"Excellent," said Jonathan. He pulled a small notebook and a pen from the pocket of his cassock. "Now, that one to the left."

"That's easy. It's a tree swallow."

"And above that?" Jonathan gestured with the pen. "No, higher, in the vines."

"White-eyed vireo."

And so it continued for half an hour. Moss identified every bird in the mural as he moved the ladder along the wall. At times the two men debated over a particular bird, but Moss was sure of his identifications. He lectured Jonathan on habitat and voice, feeding and nesting habits. Franklin Box had been ruthless in his drills. After the last bird had been addressed, Moss turned around on the ladder. He was hot from the effort of climbing up and down.

Jonathan waved him to come down. A flash of red appeared and then vanished beneath Jonathan's voluminous sleeves. Moss pretended not to have noticed.

"Climb down. I've made a little sketch of the mural and marked all of the birds. This is fantastic. How can I thank you?"

"A drink of water. My voice is going."

Jonathan returned the ladder to its storage place. Moss was about to seat himself again when Jonathan reappeared in the doorway.

"Let's talk in here where we can sit down. Truth to tell, the chapel is a bit chilly. It used to be a school. Can you imagine, kids freezing to death during the winter." Inside the door was a hallway of rough stone. Moss followed Jonathan's broad back past several closed doors before entering a spare dining room. Jonathan invited Moss to take a chair from a wall rail and seat himself at the table. While Moss did this, Jonathan produced a loaf of crusty bread that was still warm, a bowl of herbed olive oil, a basket of boiled eggs, several cheeses, smoked fish, and fruit. He poured them each an ample glass of wine. "I hope you don't mind. I was about to have my meal when you came. Please, help yourself. It's the least I can do." Moss thanked him, thinking it was rather a lot of food for one man.

Moss tried not to steal glimpses at Jonathan's wrist. He decided to bide his time by eating. It was damned good. He smeared sardines and goat cheese on a thick slice of bread and dipped it into the oil that Jonathan placed between them.

"So," said Jonathan through a mouthful of bread. "What brings you to town?"

"Curiosity," said Moss carefully. "I wanted to see Nightjar Island from the shore." He had already anticipated this question and thought a lie close to the truth would be better than a complete fiction.

Jonathan shrugged. "I hope you're not disappointed. From the shore it's just another desolate-looking pile of rock. What's your interest?"

"I came with a woman who works for the Museum of Natural History in the City of Steps. I'm just helping her out. She's studying something called interstitial species, whatever they are," said Moss.

Jonathan stopped chewing. "She's not with you."

"We had a bit of a row."

The other man shrugged sympathetically. "No wonder you're taking sinispore."

Both men burst into laughter. Jonathan cut some hard yellow cheese and handed it to Moss. "Try this. It's exquisite. We make it where I live."

"You don't live here? Where do you live?"

"No, I am just finishing my time as a caretaker. I am locking it up tomorrow, for a long time, maybe forever." *And you didn't answer my question*, thought Moss.

He took the wedge and popped it in his mouth, nodding appreciatively. "You're right. What is it called?"

"Cheese," bellowed Jonathan, laughing. At this Moss covered his face and lowered his head to the table. He laughed until his ribs ached and tears wet his palms. He felt a heavy hand on his shoulder. He missed Imogene, who had attempted a similar gesture earlier. "You're good at naming birds, my friend, but I wonder what name have you given yourself. Could it be Stranger, Coward, Betrayer, or Failure? Those are some of the favorites."

Moss sat back in the chair and wiped his face with the rough tea towel Jonathan handed him. "Murderer."

Jonathan did not miss a beat. "You don't have the eyes of a murderer," he said around a mouthful of bread.

"I was a teacher once. In a place called the Chimneys Institute."

"I've heard of it. It closed years ago."

"During my first term, there was an incident. One of the students, one of my students, drowned in a spring flood. The investigation called it an accident, but I know if I had been there, watching, it wouldn't have happened. He was just a little boy, an annoying little kid. He was near the river because that's where he found solitude when the other kids teased him." Moss paused, waiting for Jonathan to react. The other man gestured with his hand for Moss to continue.

"A few years later, there was another incident when an artificial life-form came to the school." Moss looked at his hands.

"Go on," said Jonathan, frowning.

"It, he, looked like a boy, but he wasn't exactly, he was…something else. I don't really know what, to be honest. So, of course, the other kids took to tormenting him mercilessly. Finally, one day things turned especially bad. The kids that had been teasing the boy were killed during an outing in the woods. The result of an argument, though I didn't know that at the time. When the authorities arrived, the boy was gone. I was found sitting on a stump, in shock, with the bodies all around. I was charged with the murders and thrown in jail."

"Where were you when the first boy drowned?" asked Jonathan.

"In the arithmetic teacher's bed getting an education of my own."

"Did you know the boy was near the river?"

"No. It was after lights out. But I should have been monitoring the dormitory."

"Was that a normal expectation?"

Moss shrugged. "No."

"And the children on the outing?"

"It was an unsupervised outing. I was preparing lessons in the library."

"Not your fault then," said Jonathan. He wiped crumbs from his hands. "The stories are tragic, of course, but hardly your burden to carry alone." Jonathan poured more wine for them both. "One thing, the boy, the one you so flatteringly referred to as a life-form, was he found?"

"He showed up years later and helped me leave Brickscold, and then he helped me get back to the city. There's no way I would have made it on my own through that terrain. It's through him that I learned the truth of what happened that day in the woods."

Jonathan leaned forward and placed a strong hand on Moss's arm. "Have some more wine. I bottled it myself."

Moss drank the wine. He knew he was getting drunk, but he did not care.

"These events you mentioned, I wouldn't call them murders," said Jonathan. "Leaving aside poor judgment, real murder requires intent."

"I'm building up to that. I killed a man in the city." Moss watched Jonathan carefully. "A bastard named Lamb." Moss clearly saw his companion absorb the news. Was it anger, fear, relief, or something else that crossed his face? Moss could not tell.

"Well," said Jonathan, serious now. "I am, if nothing else, a good judge of character. You are a good man, so I say this Lamb doubtless got what he had coming to him."

The two men ate in silence for some time. Eventually, they resumed talking. Jonathan complained about the plumbing in the building, the constant running battle with mice, and his love of complex chess problems. Eventually, the conversation led to board games in general. Moss spoke of how the board games, stacked in tattered boxes, had been a solace in prison. He described the routine of his life there, some of the characters he had known, the temporary respite that sinispore brought to his alternately boring and violent existence. He spoke of his growing struggles with the drug.

It was late when the conversation dwindled to a standstill. Three empty wine bottles sat between them. Moss helped Jonathan tidy the kitchen. He dried the dishes that Jonathan washed, stacking them beside the sink. Each made a satisfying clink as it was nested in the one beneath. The dishes were stained and chipped, the glaze crackled. Moss reflected on the life of objects, how he well might live and die within the existence of a carefully handled kitchen plate. He was drunk, and his motions were slow and deliberate. He was disappointed when the work was done and Jonathan yawned in a way that was unmistakable in its meaning. The hours that they had spent talking seemed to have passed in half the time but now that it was dark, and there was little else to do but watch Jonathan drape wet tea towels over a radiator, Moss's lids felt heavy. He had not given a moment's thought to where he would sleep. Jonathan pointed at a door beside the pantry.

Moss followed Jonathan up a flight of stairs. At the top, he was shown a plain but comfortable room. A mattress on a simple wood frame was positioned in front of an open window. There was a sink in which drips from a leaky faucet had eroded the enamel to reveal the pitted iron beneath. He again reflected on the life of objects. Moss wondered where he was when the sink had been installed. Had he even been born? He sat on the edge of the bed and yawned.

"It's not much, but you should sleep well here, Murderer," Jonathan said, not unkindly.

"Moss. My name is Lumsden Moss, but you know that already." He watched Jonathan for a reaction.

Jonathan pretended to consider this with the utmost seriousness. "Not much better, actually," he pronounced finally. Both men chuckled grimly.

"I know who you are, John." Moss had not planned to reveal this until the morning. It simply came out; impulse emboldened by alcohol. The other man sat down on the edge of the bed. He looked at Moss through watery eyes.

"Of course. I guessed as much," he said. "Well, have you come to kill me?"

"No," said Moss. "I'm not here to kill you. I had no idea you were here. How could I? But since we find ourselves together, I do have a few questions."

John Machine put up a protesting hand and shook his head. "Questions are worse."

"Why?"

"I've made some terrible decisions in my life. I've abused those who have loved me. My decisions led to terrible consequences, and I never had the strength to slow their momentum. The only solution I could find was to become a ghost."

"That's not a solution, it's cowardice. Events don't stop because you've absented yourself. It just leaves other to clean up the fucking mess."

"I know that. But eventually everything falls to its level and life can continue." John shift his bulk. "I'll answer one question. Only one."

Moss shook his head, angrily.

"Ask it," said John.

"That day at the seawall was the first time in my life that I first felt implicated in death. Those other stories that I told you were horrible, but they simply confirmed what I already felt: there is a dark thread running through me. Because, John, a revelation like that isn't simply the consequence of a bad decision. It comes as a fundamental revelation of one's true nature. It poisons everything that comes after; it's bottomless."

"Lumsden. One question—"

"Did you ever love Memoria? Or was she just a meal ticket?"

John seemed taken aback. He crossed his arms and looked at the floor. "Yes," he said finally.

"Then why?"

"As you so astutely pointed out, Moss, I am a coward. Cowardliness will make a man do things he can never forgive himself for."

"You know she is alive?"

John sighed heavily. "Yes, I'd heard."

"I'm going to find her. I think she returned to Nightjar Island."

"She may have. Maybe you should leave her alone."

"You're not the first person to say that to me. I can't. Come with me, John. Make things right." Moss's eyes blazed with sudden enthusiasm. "Help me find her. We'll do it together."

John shook his head, smiling sadly. "I cannot. I am still a coward, you see. You go, if you must. I am old now. I cannot face that place again. It's haunted." His face had a sheen of sweat and his skin had grown yellow and pale. "I cannot. Forgive me."

"I don't know if I can," said Moss.

John laughed explosively and straightened up. He smoothed his robe. "I suppose it wasn't to be." He slapped his hand. "Enough bedtime stories. We've both had a lot to drink. We should sleep. I'll be gone early. I have to travel to my monastery. I won't tell you where it is. Help yourself to whatever you want, but please tidy up. The mice, you know." He backed out of the hall, closing the door behind him. "The bog is down the hall to the left."

Moss lay for some time, staring at the water-stained plaster above the bed. In the corner of the room, a spider plucked its web in silence. The house was quiet, but from outside he could hear music in the distance that seemed to thicken and run away with the wind. Once there was a loud shout from beneath his window followed by the sound of a breaking bottle and laughter.

In his cell-like room, Moss, feeling detached from the flow of his life, drifted in and out of sleep, becoming aware as he dreamed of the rain against the windows. Long thunder came, and at its end, rattled the window casements. The vibration broke the cycle of his shallow rest.

Awake now, he sat up on his pillow. The reflection of the water ran down the wall, a ghost that could not quite materialize. The evening's conversation replayed in his head and he regretted that he had told John far more about himself than he had intended. Maybe it was for the best. It had been an outpouring, like the cleansing sweat of a fever. On impulse he opened a drawer in a small bureau.

He found paper and a battered fountain pen, which was coaxed to work after a few scribbled lines.

He wrote for half an hour before he allowed himself to admit that he was writing to Imogene. Until that point he had tried to make sense of the events of the past few days. But then he found he was going further back in time, repeating the things he had told John. Finally, he expressed his feelings about her. He told her how he thought about her constantly and regretted the way they had parted. Moss had only said half of what was on his mind when he ran out of paper. He folded the sheets and put them in his coat pocket. The rest would have to wait. Outside, the windows had lightened with the coming of dawn. The house was still quiet. Was John still asleep?

Lightheaded from a blossoming hangover and lack of sleep, Moss left the room and retraced his path through the house. The kitchen was empty, the chapel, cold and still. He stood in the doorway, watching as the fog of his breath rose above him like a departing soul. The sinispore vial sat where John had put it, smooth glass against brick. Moss carried it to the compartmented wall. Among the shoebox-sized openings, he found one with an open door and pushed the bottle as far back into the cobwebbed darkness as he could manage. After a few moments of deep breathing in the chilled air, Moss made his way back up to the bedroom. He lay down on the bed to catch a couple of hours sleep before going in search of Gale. Once he located the collector he would cut him loose.

He awoke many hours later to three surprises. He was covered in a blanket, an envelope was sitting on the bureau beside the fountain pen, and the room was filled with the unmistakable smell of a building on fire.

OPERA FIRE

THE GILDED THEATRE ON THE VILLAGE WATERFRONT WAS AFLAME. Moss followed the onlookers to the promenade, arriving as the roof collapsed. Horizontal geysers of fire roared from every window. Flames twisted into the clear morning sky and black smoke rolled over the slates of nearby rooftops. Moss stood with the sea at his back watching burning paper and fabric sift out of the sky, coating the street in soft ash. People careened in panic, laden with hoses and buckets, but it was obvious to those standing with the heat on their cheeks and the flames in their eyes that the building was lost.

Moss watched the crowd in vain for Imogene or Gale, though at one point he thought that he saw Finch bobbing through the onlookers. Knowing that Gale would find the uproar irresistible, Moss plunged into the crowd in search of him.

Moss jogged along a less crowded section of the promenade that gave him an elevated view of the crowd. Voices erupted as a section of the theatre crumbled, raining bricks and statuary onto the road. While most of the crowd stepped back, souvenir hunters ran out to grab smoking debris, careless of the danger. Moss had no time for the spectacle.

He heard his name. It was Gale. The man did not seem himself. He was filthy and unkempt. Instead of his hunting coat, he wore an overcoat covered in ash. His pants were torn in several places and his hands and face were blackened with soot.

"Where the hell have you been?" he asked, coming toward Moss. "I've been all over the town looking for you."

"What happened? Were you in the fire?" asked Moss. He glanced around, uncomfortable with the attention they were attracting.

"In it? I started it, you horse's ass," said Gale.

Moss grabbed Gale and shoved him toward a staircase. He followed the man to the strand below.

"What do you mean you started the fire?"

"I found them, Moss. I found the great black horse carriage. It was hidden behind the theatre, covered by a tarpaulin. I looked everywhere but couldn't find you. What was I to do, I asked of myself. I didn't want them to slip away. I had to act. And act I did!"

Moss shook the man by the shoulders. "What have you done?"

"I waited for hours hoping they would come out. My plan was to shoot the wretched devils from a window of the building behind the theatre. But do you think they would emerge? No, the carriage just sat there. So I devised a plan. I'd smoke them out."

"Idiot," said Moss, groaning.

"Idiot? You're an ungrateful bastard. I did it for you." Gale rose to his full height with crossed arms.

"Did what? Lit half the town on fire?"

"As soon as it was light enough to see what I was doing I doused the straw around the carriage with petrol. Is it my fault the theatre was so untidy? The straw caught on to the old scenery flats leaning against the wall and before I knew what was happening the whole bloody place was ablaze. I thought that damned witch would come running out at the very least, but instead her creature came from somewhere, I have no idea where, and it pulled the carriage clear. Powerful as a dray horse. That's when I got a good look at the bloody, ah, demon, call it what you will."

"What did you see?"

"As I said, it came out of nowhere at all. It was made up of all manner of rubbish. Bones and rags, hair, sawdust, I don't know what all." Gale was waving his arms hysterically. "It had the most extraordinary eyes. Extraordinary!"

"You didn't do this for me. Do you understand me? Do you? You did this on your own. There might have been innocent people in the theatre. Where is the carriage now?"

"How should I know?" Gale sputtered, indignant. "I had my own skin to save." Moss slammed the man against a piling. He raised his fist to strike Gale but at the last second let him go.

"Stay away from me," Moss growled. "I don't want to see you again. You're out of your mind. We're finished."

Gale dusted off his clothing and spat on the ground at Moss's feet. "Finished, Moss? We had a bargain. Don't you forget it. If I don't get my prize you had better not set foot in the City of Steps again, or you'll be the one who's finished. It's no empty threat. You'll be back in the Brickscold Prison where you belong, I'll see to it." Gale laughed. "That is, unless the Red Lamprey catches up with you first. Do you think they'll let you get away with murdering Lamb? Do you? They're looking for you right now, Moss. So are the police."

Moss turned his back and walked away. Making an enemy of Gale was a mistake. He sensed that, angry as he was. Who knew what connections Gale had, or what his motivations really were? Somehow, Gale had managed to follow them this far. Yet, the craftiness behind his fortuitous appearance in the field was seemingly absent in the terrible blunder of the fire. Or was it? Was Gale leading Moss to deliberately underestimate him? Since their first meeting in the bookshop Moss had felt like he was being manipulated. It had even crossed his mind that Imogene might be right in her fear that Gale was a member of the Red Lamprey, maybe someone tasked by Lamb to keep an eye out. Moss had written off the ruby pin as a coincidence, but perhaps it was not. He had reached the foot of the stairs when Gale shouted.

"It must be comforting to be such a fool."

Moss opened his mouth to answer but then realized he had nothing left to say to Gale. His only thought was to find Imogene and continue along the north road as quickly as possible. If they could get ahead of the carriage, they could find their way to the island and Little Eye. Surely they could travel over the island's treacherous terrain quicker than Echo and the carriage. He took the stairs at a run.

The conflagration of the Opera House was likely the most exciting event the town had seen in a generation. The commotion around the collapsed structure had left the surrounding streets deserted. Moss ran to the inn without encountering a soul, arriving at the gate winded. His heart sank when he saw that the truck was gone.

Shouting Imogene's name, he burst into an empty room. It felt dim and unfamiliar. The bed was unmade and the remains of a meal on a paper plate lay on the floor. The ballpoint pen had been put back together and left on the chair arm. Moss tore the drapes open and looked down at the yard, hoping as if by magic the truck might have reappeared. Adrenaline ebbing, he tried to think. The room was untidy, but there were no obvious signs of violence. Personal possessions had been removed. Moss checked the table, hoping for a note. He was disappointed. The floor creaked behind him. It was the teenaged daughter of the inn's owner standing in the doorway, sidling from foot to foot.

"Um, sir?"

"Yes?"

"This is for you." She held out a piece of folded paper. "So, ah, that lady told me to give it to you." Moss nodded impatiently as he scanned the note.

> *Moss,*
>
> *I'm sorry that we quarreled. I was hurt. That's my only defense for the way I acted, the words I said, which I would do anything to take back. Anyway, I am not safe here. I don't trust G., and the men that attacked last night are looking for us in the town. I know you will come back, but I can't wait for you. I will continue on in the hope that you will catch up to me—I certainly can't go back to the City of Steps, we decisively burned that bridge. Lamb will have been found by now and my disappearance noticed. I will wait for you at the narrowing of the path as long as I can. If you don't come, I will try to find M. myself. There is fire at my back, Moss, please hurry. I'll watch for you along the way.*
>
> *Until then,*
>
> *Love,*
>
> *Imogene.*

Moss looked up. "Did she give you this herself?"

The girl nodded. "That's what I just said."

He pocketed the piece of paper as he shoved past her.

Outside, he noticed the old motorcycle propped against the back of the building. The girl hovered behind him.

"What are you going to do now?" she asked, eyes wide, more curious than frightened.

"Does that work?"

"Pretty much."

"Can I borrow it?"

"I expect so, if you can have it back here before my brother gets back from work."

"I will," Moss lied. "Get me the keys, okay?"

"They're in it. Always in it so they don't get like lost, or whatever."

As Moss stared at her, an idea came to him. "There isn't a gun around here that I could borrow, is there?" He grimaced theatrically, hoping it would be interpreted as an apology for the inconvenience he was putting her through.

"Yes, in the kitchen. Want me to look?" she asked.

Moss nodded with patience he did not feel. "That would be great if you could do that, thanks." He watched as she sauntered through the screen door of the inn's kitchen. When she was gone, he threw his leg over the motorcycle and kick-started the engine. It roared to life with a power that belied its dings and rust. The girl emerged from the kitchen with an ancient breech-loading military rifle dangling a canvas strap and an ammunition pouch.

"This do?" she asked. "Dad uses it to kill the rats that get into the garbage shed." Moss took the rifle from her with both hands. In spite of its age it had been carefully maintained. He checked the magazine and discovered seven rounds. He slung the strap over his head and settled the weapon diagonally across his back.

"It's perfect, thank you." He throttled the bike and it eased forward, taking a final look before heading out of the yard. The girl opened her mouth excitedly, holding both hands over her ears.

BY SEA

NORTH OF THE VILLAGE THE LANDSCAPE BECAME MORE DESOLATE with every mile. As the motorcycle clattered along the crumbling asphalt, Moss spied the odd farmhouse set in the rolling heather. Houses became less frequent as the hours passed. These outliers from the town were silvered husks, with their shingles lost in the high grass, roofs sagging inward.

Moss pulled into the driveway of a leaning homestead near the road's edge. Its boards were covered in fading graffiti. Behind the nearby milk house, he familiarized himself with the action of the rifle. He wanted to be prepared if he met any more of Finch's kind. He squeezed off a shot and nearly dislocated his shoulder with the recoil. The milk bottle he had been aiming for remained intact. Unwilling to waste any more of the precious ammunition, he balanced the rifle on the motorcycle's seat and searched for water. He had to settle for slaking his thirst with greenish rainwater from the bottom of a zinc trough. What a fool he had been to leave without the most essential supplies. Returning to the motorcycle, he remembered John Machine's envelope.

> *Dear Lumsden,*
> *I thought you would want this.*
> *John Machine.*

The black and white photograph showed two children on the canal wall at Fleurent Drain. Memoria had turned to look just as the picture was taken, her hair whipped by the wind. Moss was lying on his back with a book resting on his chest. Deeply moved, in spite of his lifelong habit of anger toward John, he folded the photograph back into the note. It was almost unbearable to look at.

A few minutes later he returned to the road feeling as prepared as he could be, which was to say, not at all.

The hours rumbled by with bone-jarring monotony. The sea was everpresent to his right while the land transformed from scrub moorland to rocky waste and then finally to an endless conifer forest. The water was no longer visible through the trees, though the air was filled with the pronounced tang of brine. An hour into the forest he was forced to reduce speed by the perilous condition of the road. Daylight faded and fog moved between the tree trunks. It was now certain that night would fall before he caught up with Imogene.

In his rush to leave, he had brought nothing but the clothing on his back and the rifle. Hoping to make the best distance possible before the fog and darkness made travel impossible, Moss gunned the motorcycle. Instead of surging forward, the engine sputtered, and then abruptly died. The motorcycle coasted to a stop. Moss lowered his feet, incredulous. He twisted the fuel cap on the tank. Although the light was too poor to see within, the metallic clang told him all he needed to know.

"Idiot!" he yelled. The trees muffled his voice. A few invisible ravens offered their commiseration. "Unbelievable. Why didn't I check the gas?" Ahead of him, the road vanished through the trees. The fog was becoming thicker by the minute. He walked the motorcycle to the side of the road and set it on its kickstand. Sabotaged through sheer stupidity, he thought.

He stood for some time, weighing options. The motorcycle's engine popped as it cooled. A barn owl watched him from a nearby tree, a mouse wriggling hopelessly from its beak. With the mist came a penetrating cold. Hypothermia could not be far behind. Rather than wait out the night at the edge of the forest, he decided to continue on foot. That way he could stay warm and with daylight, devise a proper plan. With a doleful last look at the motorcycle, he trudged along a road that had become so broken and mossy it looked like a cobblestone path to another world.

Moonlight infused the fog with a spectral glow. As the night wore on and sluggishness crept into his limbs, he had the odd sensation of walking along the sea bottom. In his half-conscious state, he imagined himself a sea creature, lumbering through diatomaceous mud in a forest of kelp. Realizing that he was falling asleep on his feet, he reached into his coat and pulled out a cigarette he had been saving. The nicotine would help fend off the drowsiness. Imogene had rolled it. He sniffed, hoping it was only tobacco.

A sharp sound came from the woods. He paused, with a match halfway to the bent cigarette between his lips. He had been hearing noises throughout the night that he had rationalized as pinecones or dead branches dropping to the forest floor. This noise had a different quality, not a thud but a crack, like weight on dry bone. Moss finished lighting the cigarette. It made him feel less alone. The issue of Elizabeth's carriage had been worrying his thoughts for hours. If she was heading to Nightjar, was it ahead of him, or behind? It was conceivable that Elizabeth on her dog, or Echo, could be nearby, in which case filling the air with tobacco smoke was probably not advisable. Surely they were behind. Echo could not move quickly. The creature would plod along in its yoke with the same relentless predictability as the turning of the earth. Although signs of Imogene's truck, or some other heavy vehicle, had been in evidence for some time, there were no carriage tracks. Areas of the road's edge were gouged by thick treads. Stones were turned through the force of mechanized wheels. He peered into the mist, not daring to call out. Then, almost as though the intensity of his concentration had induced it to materialize, a large canine form moved beneath the pines. It was gone as quickly as it appeared. It was not the muscular dog that Elizabeth rode, but a massive slinking creature with a dense coat. Wolves. Wonderful.

He had barely formed these thoughts when lights flashed through the trees, followed by the unmistakable sound of an automobile engine. Moss stood on the hump of the road and waved his arms over his head. The car rounded a bend and bore down on him, its lights blazing. The driver was not prepared for him and waited too long to brake. Moss leapt from the road and the car swerved in the opposite direction. It fishtailed and mounted the shoulder, careening into the woods before stopping inches from an ancient tree trunk.

Moss ran to the car. It sizzled on a bed of pine needles a foot thick. Light from the headlamps penetrated deep into the tangled underbrush. He tried the handle of the driver's door but it was locked. He thumped on the window. To his relief, the driver stirred and the window lowered.

"Well, aren't you a pretty sight!" said Gale.

Lumsden Moss had a headache. It had started in the back of his neck and crept slowly across his cranium to take up residence in his forehead. Gale's smugness at finding Moss in the middle of the woods, miles from anywhere, made being inside the tiny car insufferable. Dawn had come shortly after the near miss, bringing with it a thunderstorm. Constant lightning and lashing rain forced the two men to sit idle behind humid windows. Moss had refused the blanket that Gale had proposed to spread across both their knees, but begrudgingly accepted some smoked herring from a tin and hot tea from a flask. Once the storm had lessened to a shower, Moss pushed the front of the car while Gale sat inside, grinding the gears and jamming his foot to the accelerator. Finally, the tiny car had come free of its soggy prison of forest humus and leaped backward onto the road. Moss, who had narrowly missed landing on his face, climbed back into the passenger seat and stared at Gale, with thin quivering lips and crooked glasses. In response, Gale merely smiled, his own lips too red and supple with herring oil. Truly, at that moment, Moss had never hated a human being more.

For the past hour, they had driven along the coast road, finally free of the oppressive forest. Moss stared out the window in a foul temper, having wearied of staring at the burled walnut dashboard.

"The reason you haven't caught them up, the carriage I mean, is quite simple," said Gale.

"Enlighten me," mumbled Moss.

"Because they boarded a barge in the town. It is amazing how cheaply the local harbormaster was willing to oblige me with that information."

This possibility had not occurred to Moss. He faced Gale. "No hired barge will take them to Nightjar."

"Indeed not. It would be a suicidal crossing. The water is full of unstable mines. They will be making for the quay and the old tunnel I spoke of."

"Maybe Imogene will be there," said Moss. He had already told Gale about the empty room at the inn. "How far away are we?"

Gale slowed the car and pulled to the edge of the road. "Let's have a look." Both men stepped out of the car and stretched. Moss put the rifle over his shoulder.

The view was spectacular. They stood on a cliff above the sea looking out at a distant curve of land to the north that dwindled into the haze. The water was filled with whitecaps and silt upwelled by the storm. Seagulls rode the stiff breeze, rising to great heights and then plummeting into the waves to emerge with tiny silver fish.

"Look there," Gale shouted over the roar. "Do you see?" Moss strained to follow the other man's finger. His eyes traced the land's curve until it dwindled to a thin sepia line against the sea's pewter. "Out from the tip."

Then he saw it, a dark smudge on the ocean. Nightjar Island.

"Here, take these." Gale handed him a pair of binoculars.

The island was still little more than a blur as it bounced up and down in the grimy lens. Moss adjusted the focus and the island was suddenly clear. Cliffs rose out of the water, which given the distance must have been hundreds of feet high. One end looked mountainous. From Moss's perspective, it was shaped like a giant elephant molar that he had seen in John's office at the zoo. Gale took the binoculars from Moss's hands and scanned the ocean closer in.

"There! There," he burst out. He thrust the binoculars back at Moss. Moss searched water until he saw a barge churning its way north, with the carriage roped to its deck. The unmistakable form of Echo stood as still as a mast.

"If we make good speed, we should get there first. The sea is rough and will impede their progress." He snapped the binoculars into their case.

THE EDGE OF THE WORLD

It was Moss's idea to walk the remaining two miles to the quay on foot, seeing no point in announcing their arrival. As inhospitable as the landscape was, there could be other people in the vicinity. If there were, Moss wanted to be aware of them first. He also wanted to watch the barge's approach from a concealed vantage point, which would be impossible with the car.

Moss understood that the *narrowing of the path* referred to the tunnel leading to Nightjar Island. Imogene would have to abandon the truck. It would be dangerous to enter the tunnel alone. She had said that she intended to wait for him, but the appearance of the barge changed things. Imogene would not allow Elizabeth and Echo to enter the tunnel ahead of her. It was a perfect opportunity for them to lay a trap, in order to retrieve the traveling bookcase. Moss had no illusions that Imogene would survive such an encounter. Moss and Imogene had to reunite ahead of the carriage's landfall, something that seemed less and less likely.

Moss stood at the side of the road, knee deep in beach grass, keeping watch while Gale concealed the car in a willow copse. Inland, scrubby dunes rose to a distant ridge where trees clung with exposed roots. The same dunes continued on the other side of the rutted road, hiding the sea from view.

Gale emerged from the trees carrying a rucksack and his rifle.

"You ready?" asked Moss.

Gale smiled. "Yes, I'm ready. You don't have to worry about me. Whatever happens, you won't forget our arrangement? Once this Elizabeth and her demon are dispatched, the drawings and the book are mine. I expect you to honor your word."

"We're wasting time," said Moss, already stepping onto the road.

"Lead on then. What's your plan?" Moss ignored him as he struck off, scanning the dunes for movement. Gale followed, feet shuffling in the gravel.

At a bend in the road they came upon Imogene's truck pulled off to the side. Its visibility worried Moss. The scene had an air of abandonment. Around the truck, the grass was flattened. An osprey, perched on the canvas cover, took flight. It soared across the dunes to a dead tree. The cargo cover slapped gently in the wind. Moss waited, but no further movement came from the truck.

He approached from the rear, indicating that Gale should stay put and cover him. Keeping to what he judged to be a blind spot to anyone sitting in the cab, Moss ran with his rifle held in a tight grip. He dropped to a crouch beneath the tailgate and listened. The rhythmic contact of canvas against metal was louder, but there was no sound from within. He worked his way along the driver's side, keeping an eye on the mirror. Moving quickly, he stood up and thrust the rifle through the open window. The cab was empty. There were signs of a hastily eaten meal. Keys peeked from behind the sun visor, which seemed to suggest that Imogene had not left in a panic. What circumstance, then, would compel Imogene to leave the truck so exposed? Gale appeared beside him.

"There is no one in the back," Gale said. Something in the way he said this caught Moss's attention. Gale seemed to have developed a focus he had not hitherto exhibited. "Well?"

"She's doing exactly what we are," said Moss, "Walking in to avoid notice, trying to assess the surroundings." Moss surveyed the dunes. "The wind is coming off the water. We'll climb up there, and avoid the direct route to the quay." He pointed to a trawler that lay on its side, half buried in sand. "That way, toward the mound behind the wreck. We should be able to observe without being seen ourselves."

Halfway to the boat, Gale touched Moss's shoulder. He pointed to a spot on the other side of the road. It was just possible to see an old panel van pushed into the scrub.

"Company?" asked Gale.

The two men waded through the grass, taking care to skirt the jagged debris that seemed to jut from the sand at every conceivable angle.

"It's from the war," Gale said loudly.

"Keep your voice down."

"These beaches are filled with shrapnel from the mortaring of the station that used to stand here. It's probable that the sand is still full of live explosives, so keep your wits about you. Are you sure you want to go this way?"

Moss continued walking.

"You first then. It's your party. If you hear a click, don't lift your foot up until I'm well clear."

They passed the trawler, plodding through cascading sand to the crest of the dune. A stinging wind buffeted them at the top, and the sound of the ocean rose sharply, like a rhythmic electronic static, almost unbearable at its crescendo. Far out on the black water, beyond a flock of bobbing gannets, a house floated. Silver windows glinted on walls stained black by the sea. It tumbled over and over in the wind-driven swell, top-heavy and disintegrating. A gust of wind hit Moss full in the body. He turned his face away; he had never been able to breathe easily in high wind. Holding the rifle between his knees, he covered his ears until the whine of his tinnitus was foregrounded against the muted ocean's roar. The familiarity of its pitch enabled him to draw down his mounting nerves. As he caught his breath he watched Gale, who stood a few feet way, picking sand out of his eyebrows. The air stank of organic decay. Moss gradually took his hands away from his ears, able now to tolerate the noise. The house was gone, if it had ever truly been there.

They took advantage of a band of twisted conifers to reach a high point from which they could see the quay. It extended into the sea like an arthritic finger of masonry. Irridis stood on a seawall that ran along the shore, his head wrapped in black cloth. The ocelli encircled him at intervals of several feet. Moss could see Gale in his peripheral vision, examining his face for a reaction. Imogene was further away, still on the seawall, but where it continued on the other side of the quay. She watched the water through a pair of military binoculars that Moss recognized from the truck. She lowered them to her chest and whistled through her fingers to Irridis. Imogene pointed out to sea, her hand like a pistol. He nodded slowly, but did not turn to face her. He was already aware of what she had seen. Moss had been so focused on his friends that he had not fully attended the appearance of the barge. The carriage could be clearly seen lashed to the deck with heavy ropes. Echo was stationed at the bow, a monstrous figurehead. Irridis took a faltering step forward.

The boat angled dangerously in the swell, heaving the carriage against its restraints. Waves sluiced across the deck. Shredded tractor tires chained to the side of the barge would be the only cushion against the ancient stone quay.

Gale stepped forward, leaving the cover of the trees. Moss pulled him back.

"Not yet," he said. The barge was closer to shore than he expected, and Irridis seemed to be committed to a confrontation.

Gale looked as though he wanted to say something to challenge Moss. Instead he drew back several feet. Moss, retreating, joined him behind the trunk of the largest tree.

"They are waiting for the barge," said Moss. Through the filter of branches, the boat appeared toy-like against the sea and the darker mass of Nightjar Island in the distance. "How far is the tunnel from here?"

"A mile, maybe less."

"Why aren't they hiding?" asked Moss, not expecting an answer.

"The woman is," said Gale. It was true. Imogene had moved into the shadow of an old crane raised on a circular concrete block. She stood motionless, clinging to a rusted wheel twice her height. Gale handed his binoculars to Moss. "Your friend doesn't look so well." Even without the binoculars, Moss could see that for himself. Irridis had followed the wall and stepped onto the quay. He walked a few steps and dropped to his knees as though praying. The ocelli tightened their circle.

"What's he up to?" asked Moss.

"When they move that carriage onto the quay, that's our opportunity. We need to hit them before they get oriented but not before the barge backs out. We need the water behind them." Gale was drawing diagrams in the sand. Moss ignored him.

"He's planning to confront them," said Moss.

"That would be a big mistake. He's no match for that creature. I've witnessed its strength. It will tear him apart."

Water flowed onto the mudflat around the quay, joining tide pools and covering barnacle-encrusted rocks with startling power. The barge wallowed. There appeared to be only two crewmen aboard. They moved along the length of the deck, preparing to dock. Smoke, pouring from a single funnel, was swept ashore by the wind. Moss noticed a third man in a wheelhouse that was little more than a shed of corrugated metal.

Moss left the trees and slid down the seaward side of the dune, making his way toward the quay. His sternum felt tight. He held the rifle with both hands to stop them shaking. Gale had ceased to exist for him and he could not have cared less if the man was behind him, or not. The gravity and horror of what he now planned to do was his alone to experience. He would stand with Irridis.

The ground became firm. He ran along the foot of the dune and dropped to a crouch behind the seawall. Imogene was less than thirty feet away but so focused on events unfolding on the quay she had not noticed him. The barge had reached the quay and heaved against the masonry. The sound was deafening. A blast of water shot high into the air, raining down on Irridis. He seemed oblivious. The carriage pulled against its ropes. Echo leaned into his yoke. One of the sailors ran to the edge of the boat and leaped onto the quay. Another threw him a rope. Hoisting it over his shoulder, the first man jogged alongside the barge. The third sailor could be seen moving frantically in the door of the hut. Smoke billowed from the funnel as the engines stopped, dampening the ship's momentum. Finally, the barge settled against the quay, crushing the tires with its edge. The sailors tied off on two dock cleats. When the ropes were secure, they bounded onto the ship's deck and dragged a metal plate forward to bridge the space between the barge and the quay.

The sailors shouted instructions at one another. Fear was evident in their expressions as they fought to work against the unstable conditions. They worked methodically to free the carriage, unfastening ropes and kicking chocks from behind the wheels. As the ropes fell away, Echo surged against the yoke. The carriage moved forward. The sailors deliberately looked away as they worked. Twenty feet away from Echo, Irridis now stood with his arms at his sides. Above his head the ocelli burned in the sour light like drops of molten silver.

A large wave struck the boat with concussive force. Echo heaved again, drawing the carriage behind him. It lurched agonizingly across the metal plate onto the quay. As soon as it was clear of the boat, the sailors were freeing the ropes from the cleats. Propellers churned and the barge reversed in a cloud of diesel smoke, abandoning the connecting plate, which tumbled into the dark water. The sailors did not turn to observe the calamity of their departure.

The carriage rolled further onto the quay. The suspension and iron-shod wheels creaked ominously beneath the cab. Seaweed trailed from the carved ornamentation. Steam rose from every surface as though the carriage had been lifted from the bottom of the sea. Irridis walked to meet it.

There was no time to run. Moss raised the rifle to his shoulder. He held his breath and took aim at Echo, tilting his head and lining up the sights along the barrel. His hands sweated on the stock and he had to reassert his grip. He put a slight pressure on the trigger. The high, steady tone of his tinnitus was like something threatening to burst from his skull. At his back, an engine roared. Moss ignored it, thinking it an acoustical quirk caused by the retreating barge. Imogene screamed. Lowering the rifle, Moss turned. Imogene's truck hurtled along the road toward them, ahead of a long trail of dust. It was unmistakably Gale behind the mud-spattered windshield. He was steering the truck toward the quay, but he was going too fast. In moments, he would hit Irridis. Moss fired wildly at the truck, but the shot was wide. His second bullet caused the windshield to explode into thousands of granules, but failed to halt the truck's momentum.

"Move," Moss yelled to Imogene. He ran, waving his arms and shouting, but his voice was lost in the sound of the truck mounting the quay. He tripped and landed in stony sand. Imogene disappeared behind a wall of dust. Gale had lost control. The truck skewed hard to the left. Carried by momentum, it rolled onto its side, crushing the cargo cover and sending crates and equipment tumbling into the water. A large section of aged quay, unable to bear the assault, gave way beneath the truck as it came to a standstill, its cab submerged, wheels spinning in the air.

Moss froze. It was Imogene's screams that refocused him. On one side of the ruined quay Echo fought to pull the carriage onto a stable surface. It had pitched at a dangerous angle and for a moment seemed poised to fall into the water. Suddenly it was righted, with a shower of rust from its ancient suspension.

Irridis lay unmoving on the ground in front of Echo. He had been struck by the truck or flying debris. Moss watched in horror as Echo's coat opened and Elizabeth unfurled from a nacreous void within the demon's body. She moved with single-minded purpose toward Irridis. Clutched in both hands was a sword. When she reached him she straddled his legs and tore open his coat. She brought down the blade without hesitation, thrusting it into his stomach and driving it up through the torso as though gutting a fish. Fluid sprayed across her face. Imogene screamed, but Moss could not see her. Irridis thrashed wildly on the weathered stone as Elizabeth thrust an arm into the wound she had created. Moss ran toward them, shouting and hurling stones. Her task complete, Elizabeth staggered away from Irridis, holding a black organ that trailed a convulsing filigree of white tissue in one hand, dragging the sword with the other. For the first time, she looked at Moss. Even from a distance he could see the triumph in her face as she watched him hurl stones, tears flowing down his cheeks. Moss faltered. With the strength of an ape Elizabeth leapt onto the carriage and vanished into an opening in the top. Echo, who had remained motionless throughout, shoved Irridis's body to the side and dragged the carriage around the overturned truck to dry land.

Moss thought only of his friend. Clear of the sand, he quickly covered the distance to the quay heedless of the shattered masonry and jutting rebar. Irridis lay on his side, barely breathing. The ocelli hovered in the air above him, forming a circle.

"Irridis," said Moss. He did not know what else to say. It was obvious his friend would be gone in seconds.

"Moss, I remember everything now. The name she spoke in the Cloth Hall, it made me remember who I was," said Irridis. Moss took his hand, but Irridis pulled it away, pressing it to his wound. "No time for displays. I need your help."

"Anything," said Moss, stung. The hand had been as cold as the sea.

"Take the dark stone to my sister's grave in Little Eye."

"Sister?"

Irridis closed his eyes and shook his head with a barely perceptible movement. "Aurel, in Little Eye. It's very important."

"Irridis, what sister?" Moss yelled, rolling Irridis's head into the palm of his hand. "What stone? I'm confused." Moss shook Irridis, but his friend was dead.

As Moss lowered Irridis's head gently onto the ground he felt movement against his skin. Despite his grief, he snatched his hand back and wiped it vigorously on his sleeve. Something was rising out of Irridis's exposed skin. It was a kind of steam or fine dust. Moss pulled back, but the dust had already settled in the hairs of his hands. It tingled. He could feel it in his eyes, reddening his eyelids, making them sore and heavy. In a few moments, Irridis's body had become less distinct, as if it were expanding outward in the form of fine particles. They entered Moss's windpipe, causing him to choke. In a panic he tried to stand, but could get no further than his hands and knees. When he tried to call out, he found that his voice had vanished.

Imogene ran to Moss, calling his name. Moss scrambled to his feet. Irridis's clothing littered the ground but the body was nowhere to be seen. Nor was there any sign of the mysterious dust. Disoriented, Moss ran to the edge of the quay and frantically searched the roiling waters, but he could only see debris from the truck. He climbed around the rubble created by the crash, supporting himself on rebar that cut into his skin. He shouted the name of his friend until he was hoarse. When he came dangerously close to falling into the water, he clambered back to a place of greater stability. He stared at the sea in disbelief, afraid of seeing Irridis under the surface, afraid of not seeing him. He remembered the way the ghostly powder had stuck to the hairs on his hands. Desperate for any confirmation of what he had experienced, he examined them closely. There was nothing. He turned away, shaking in the wind coming off the sea, which was almost unbearable. Imogene waited nearby, her hair tangled and wet, her face stricken with an expression that mirrored his grief. Without a word he approached her. After a time, she gently pushed him back.

"We've lost him," he said, fighting tears.

"Moss. Look," she said, looking past him.

"What?" he said. Her eyes darted to the side, and she stepped away. Turning his head, he became aware of the dark ocellus suspended in the air to his left. It had somehow worked itself free. Barely breathing, Moss extended his arm, palm up. The stone gently descended into his hand. It pulled against the cage of his fingers, toward Nightjar Island.

INSIDE OUT

GALE WAS WAIST-DEEP IN THE FREEZING OCEAN, MUMBLING LIKE A madman. His arms were filled with items that had spewed from the truck. Moss had no idea how the man had survived the catastrophic wreck, but wished he had not. He cradled the rifle that he had retrieved from the sand, noting that it still held several rounds.

"There was nothing you could do," said Imogene. She stood on the seawall, with the traveling bookcase at her feet. They had pulled it from the water after a fruitless search for Irridis. Her hair was stiff with brine and sand.

"I know," said Moss. He was deep in thought and had been able to do little in the past hour but stare across the water to Nightjar Island.

"I found him here," said Imogene. She smiled. "He drove himself here in an old bread van. Can you imagine? He was surprised to see me alone, I think, and he didn't say much, only that he wanted to get to the monastery at Little Eye. He was looking for the tunnel Gale told you about. She stabbed him, you know, after Lamb barged in at the Cloth Hall. He was very weak. I think he knew he had very little time left."

Moss did not respond immediately. "I wonder how he knew about the tunnel?" he said finally.

"It's on the maps."

"What maps?"

"He told me that he went to your old house after he left the Cloth Hall to look at some old maps." Imogene shrugged. "When I told him I'd seen Elizabeth's carriage leave the town by boat, he insisted on waiting to meet it."

"He wanted to confront them?" asked Moss.

Imogene shook her head. "No. That's what I thought at first too, but he wanted to talk to Elizabeth. He had questions he wanted answered about his past. He thought that he could reason with her."

"But why?"

"I tried to talk him out of it." Imogene sat down on the wall, fighting her tears. Moss sat beside her. "I'm all right," she said. "Oh damn, here he comes."

Gale walked up the incline from the water's edge and dropped a pile of items onto the ground.

"A treasure trove," he said. The man's color was not good, his face was drained and his eyes were red with broken vessels. His beard was speckled with algae. The left side of his torso was slick with congealing strings of blood. Moss reached down and picked his shoulder bag from the litter of junk at his feet. It was dry.

"Where did you find this?" Imogene took it from him with both hands and pulled out *The Songbirds of Nightjar Island*.

"Ah, I found it in the truck," Gale said, panting. "Dry as a bone after all that carry on. You can't have it. It's mine, according to the terms of our deal. Now then, that box, the contents are also mine. We had a bargain. Tell her, Moss." He pointed at the bookcase.

"Go to hell," said Imogene. She moved in front of it. "After what you did? You'll never see them. You get nothing." A quivering smile crossed Gale's lips. His mouth was full of blood-smeared teeth.

"Oh, I shall. We had a bargain. Our bargain. Tell her," he insisted, looking at Moss.

"There was no deal. You made that assumption," said Moss. He moved toward Gale, fists clenched. "All you've done here is make things worse. You're an idiot, Gale. You helped the very people we were trying to kill."

Gale's mouth fell open. "But what about everything I've done for you?" His voice was shrill, pleading. "You'd still be lost in the woods if not for me. At the very least I've pushed things to a head, frightened them off. Surely that is worth the reward." A wave of pain crossed his face. "Oh dear, I must sit down. So dizzy." Gale staggered back a few steps and fell to a sitting position like a toddler. Without warning, he lunged at the bookcase, missing it by a wide mark. "Lovely," he said, pawing at the sand with his fingers. "So lovely." He fell sideways. Sand trickled from his closed fist.

When Gale had stopped breathing Moss crouched at his side and searched through the man's pockets. From inside the blood-stained jacket he pulled a large leather wallet. Its surface was weathered and contoured to the shape of the documents within. He opened it expecting money or personal papers.

"What is it?" Imogene asked, alarmed by his expression.

"He was a cop, a detective. Look." He opened the wallet again and displayed to her an ornate printed document. A black horse, emblem of the City of Steps Police Department, was centered on the paper.

"That means?"

"It means he was playing us the whole time," said Moss. He looked down the dunes, half expecting to see a contingent of police lined up along the crest. "He must have been biding his time, using us to see what he could uncover."

"Or using his investigation as an excuse to secretly add to his collection," said Imogene with disgust.

Moss returned to Gale's pockets. This time he pulled out a black notebook, which was hinged at the top edge and held with an elastic band. He thumbed through the pages, confirming his suspicions, stopping here and there to scan a passage. Imogene moved impatiently behind him.

"Well?" she asked.

"He was making detailed notes. See, it starts here with a statement that the bookseller Oliver Taxali admitted under interrogation that certain contraband, rare books, were sold to Judge Habich Seaforth." Moss moved quickly through the pages. "Here, it says, blah, blah a representative of Judge Seaforth hired Lumsden Moss, a fugitive from Brickscold Prison. Moss operates under the alias of Joseph Woods. Moss appears to acquire contraband antiquities on behalf of Judge Seaforth." Moss put the notebook and wallet in his coat pocket. "He seems to have gotten the wrong end of the stick, as they say."

"Maybe it was Seaforth that was the center of his investigation?" said Imogene.

"Maybe at first. I wonder if he thought he'd stumbled across something much more interesting, something of a more personal interest. He was definitely acting alone the last few days. Like a man who saw something he wanted slipping away."

"No sane person would do this," said Imogene, looking around.

"I wonder at what point he figured out who I was," said Moss.

"Never mind that now," said Imogene. "He can't cause you any more grief."

Moss looked up at her. "I'm not so sure about that. There's no way to know who he's told about us, or if he was working with someone."

"I know," said Imogene. "By now the Red Lamprey has probably figured out Lamb is dead, and the police have no doubt found whatever is left of Oliver. Going back was never an option, was it?"

"Burned bridges," said Moss, quoting her note. He rolled Gale over with his foot so that he did not have to look at his face any longer. "We're going to find Memoria, and I am going to take this ocellus to Little Eye. I owe Irridis that."

"The season is changing. We don't have the right gear."

"Are you saying you don't want to go?" asked Moss.

"Hell no," said Imogene gamely. "You forgot the third thing."

"Third thing?"

"We have a witch to kill." She pointed to the traveling bookcase. "But first we need to burn that, because come what may, there's no way she's seeing that shit again."

They built a fire in the shelter of the seawall using driftwood collected from the shore. Moss opened the traveling bookcase and removed the drawings. These he placed safely inside his shoulder bag along with *The Songbirds of Nightjar Island*. When this was done, Imogene helped him heave the case onto the fire. He half expected to see a howl of evil spirits rise up in the flames, but in the end there was just a lot of black smoke, and popping. While it burned, Moss collected Irridis's clothing from the quay. He set them on the flames, along with Gale's papers, and turned to the problem of what to do with Gale's corpse.

Burning the body would take too long and require far more wood than they could reasonably collect. In the end, they opted for burial in a remote spot far back from the beach, using a camp spade retrieved from the wreckage of the truck. By the time Moss was finished, Imogene had put together a couple of packs for their journey.

THE HARROWING

Yellow jackets led Moss and Imogene to the tunnel entrance after several hours of searching. Wasps bustled from a hole in the ground, hidden among clumps of goldenrod. Listless in the fall air, they flew only a short distance and scrambled in the surrounding weeds. Investigation revealed their nest to be tucked into a ventilation shaft where an odor of rotten eggs drifted from a grate. Close by, they found railroad tracks under a mat of bindweed. The rails ran between retaining walls to a tunnel mouth. *Nightjar*, in soot-blackened letters, was carved at the apex of the entrance. A barrier of rebar had once been welded in place to prevent access, but this had been forcibly removed and lay to one side.

Imogene lit a hurricane lantern salvaged from the truck. A few minutes of poking around was rewarded by the discovery of a brakeman's lantern lying on its side against a wall. Moss poured some kerosene from their lamp into the one they had found. The globe was cracked, but when he lit the wick, a red glow filled the tunnel. Looking down the track, they could see circles of daylight spaced along the receding ties. These came from identical shafts to the one utilized by the wasps. Beyond the daylight, the tunnel followed a downward grade and the air became damp and cold. Moss looked at the dripping ceiling and imagined the weight of the sea above.

"Well?" said Imogene, dubiously.

"It's the only way," said Moss.

It was no easy walk. Flooded zones of icy water were common, submerging sections of the track. They negotiated these by using fallen debris as stepping-stones. It was difficult to imagine how Elizabeth's carriage had passed this way. It would have taken great strength, yet the ruts were there as evidence, filled with oily water.

Fear of encountering the carriage in the tunnel was the source of a brief argument between them. Their hushed voices echoed off the bricks. Moss wanted to douse the lights and use only a small flashlight from the truck. Imogene was against it. It was decided that without a substantial light to guide them, the risk of a fall or some other kind of mishap would be too great. A compromise was struck and the hurricane lamp was put out. They continued in a bubble of red from the brakeman's lantern.

With the issue of the light resolved they walked as briskly as they could. They walked side by side, at first lost in silence, each deep in their private thoughts. But after a while they took each other's hands and talked in a hush of the past days. Water dripped on them incessantly and a breeze pressed their clothing to their bodies with gentle persistence. An hour passed, then another. Moss shivered uncontrollably for a time, but then that passed as well. Without warning, the tunnel turned to the left. Moss, who had been trudging with his eyes fixed on the track in front of him, daydreaming of being a boy and reading in a tree, heard his name.

He stopped, realizing that Imogene had released his hand. He lifted the lantern above his head. The tunnel had widened to a large natural chamber. Imogene stood beside the track, arms folded. The swinging red glow passed over dozens of skeletons lying on the ground. The skeletons were dressed in decomposing wartime uniforms. Spent canisters of gas lay in profusion. Some were clutched in the gloved hands. Suicide, thought Moss. He set the lantern down and embraced Imogene. They held each other, and over each other's shoulders absorbed the pathos of the place until, by unspoken agreement, they could bear it no longer and continued on.

A mile or two down the track, they discovered crates of munitions, leaking drums, reeking pools of oil, and pieces of machinery neither of them could identify. Aware that their lantern could trigger an explosion, they did not dally. Further on they shared a roll of biscuits that had survived the crash, and wished for something to drink. Moss thought about how they would supplement their supply of food when they exited the tunnel. They had little, a few cans and an assortment of dried foods crammed into the packs they carried. Imogene had purchased some supplies in the town, but most of it had been lost when the truck had disgorged its cargo into the sea. *I'm not turning away*, had become his mantra, but a cup of coffee would have been marvelous.

More dead. More rusting munitions. Neither one of them had a watch but together they estimated they had been walking for six hours. As they pressed on, Moss thought about all the things one could do in six hours that did not involve walking in ankle-deep ice water.

Eventually, they came to a dry spot and decided to rest. Moss made Imogene lie down first and covered her with their only blanket. With her head resting on his lap, he sat in the red light and wrote in the margins of *The Songbirds of Nightjar Island*. The pages felt damp. He idly stroked Imogene's head. Her hair was stiff between his fingers. Her ear was red. He tried to move a strand from her cheek but it stuck to the skin. She did not move. She might have been dead. He was relieved when she opened her eyes for a moment and looked around without properly waking. He lay down beside her and tried to make sense of Irridis's dissolution. Over and over he relived the violence of Elizabeth's actions. Imogene squeezed his hand.

"I saw your father," said Moss. He told her everything.

"I'm not surprised he is still alive. Anyways, he's been dead to me for years," said Imogene coldly. "He's right, you know."

"About what?"

"He is a coward."

The end of the tunnel came unexpectedly after several more hours of walking. The ground sloped upwards and the air became slightly warmer. A bright circle appeared. It was almost painful to look at after hours in the near dark. Now that they had a visible goal, they doused the lantern. Closer to the entrance, they hid both lanterns in an alcove and piled a rotten tarp over them.

"I don't believe it," said Moss, stepping out of the tunnel.

"Snow," said Imogene.

Moss walked back to the fire. They had discovered a tiny caravan in a clump of trees about a mile from the tunnel mouth. It had long since been stripped of anything of value but had the welcome advantage of being nearly undetectable from any direction due to the bowl-like depression it sat in. Moss had been checking to see if the smoke was visible. Although the landscape appeared deserted, they did not want to take unnecessary risks. Imogene warmed a can of baked beans over the flames. The snow was falling in fat flakes that melted on the ground almost immediately.

"You know when the temperature drops tonight this is going to accumulate," said Moss, looking up into the sky. He stuck his tongue out to catch a snowflake. It slipped under his glasses and into his eye instead.

"It's pretty," said Imogene. "These are ready."

"I'll bet they left the railroad tracks and took that road over there to the north. Absentia is in the north. I think we should head east to the center of the island. That's where we'll find Little Eye."

Imogene nodded. "Is this insane? What if they didn't go north? What if we miss the monastery? This island is vast."

"It looks a lot bigger than it did from the shore," said Moss.

"How long do you think it will take, to get to Little Eye?"

"Three days maybe. Depends on the terrain."

"And if we run into Elizabeth and Echo?"

"Then we have to be prepared to fight."

"She wants the bookcase. If she thinks we're here, she'll come after us sooner or later."

"Yes she will."

"We're going to be out of food pretty soon," said Imogene. She handed Moss a spoon. "What do you mean, prepared to fight?"

"No hesitation," said Moss. Since their exit from the tunnel Moss had been thinking about Elizabeth's threat outside the bakery. "We need to be as ruthless as they are. More so, if that's possible."

Through the night they slept together inside the caravan, covered in their blanket while outside the snow fell. Imogene woke him at dawn.

"Look," she said. He followed her out of the caravan. The ground was blanketed with white. The sky was slate. Several feet away, the ground was covered in boot prints.

"Whoever it was," said Moss, "was out here within the last couple of hours."

"Elizabeth?"

"The footprints are too big."

The temperature rose slightly by mid-morning, causing the snow to melt off the macadam of the road, making it easy to follow. They walked side by side, sharing stories and eating the rest of the biscuits they had started in the tunnel. They scanned the landscape constantly, but saw no sign that they were being followed.

Imogene pointed at the ocellus that followed Moss everywhere. "I've never understood what those things are. That time John brought Irridis to the house when we were small, he had them even then. My mother, Sylvie, was scared to death. That's why he was sent to sit in the garden. She wouldn't let me be out there with him, even though I wanted to. I had to sneak out the back door while they were arguing."

"Sometimes they seem to have a mind of their own," said Moss. "This one certainly doesn't have much to say."

"You know what ocelli means, right?"

"John called them that. Irridis called them stones."

"Ocelli means *little eye.*"

"I know, I looked it up," said Moss. "I think John made a connection between Irridis and Little Eye a long time ago." During the trip through the tunnel, they had discussed the revelation of Irridis's sister, but with nothing to go on, the conversation had gone in circles.

"So do I. How's your aim?" asked Imogene.

"Pardon me?"

"Your aim. Look over there," she said, pointing. Moss shielded his eyes to block the glare. "Wild turkeys. I count ten of them."

"What am I supposed to shoot them with?" said Moss. "This rifle I have is shit."

Imogene laughed. She dropped her pack on the road and detached a wrapped bundle. It was Gale's rifle. "This!"

Moss smiled, deciding not to jeopardize Imogene's revival of spirits with his gloom. "I'm not shooting with that."

"Why not?"

"On aesthetic grounds."

"Would you rather starve?"

They lost an hour chasing a turkey with a near supernatural ability to sense their presence. Moss finally attempted a shot. A piece of bracket fungus, attached to a tree at a point twenty feet above the bird, dropped through bare branches. It hit the ground with a thud. The bird moved a few feet away. Moss swung the gun around and fired again, this time surgically removing the turkey's head at the base of its neck.

In a nearby stream Imogene removed the organs and skinned the bird while Moss built a fire. They cut the meat into strips and cooked them on green branches. After they had eaten their fill, they wrapped as much as they could in a piece of cloth and stowed it in Moss's pack. By the time they were finished, the afternoon was late. The sky had begun to darken, and the snow, which had held off most of the day, began to fall again.

They followed the road until well after dark with the snow swirling around them. Moss walked in a mental fog. When he stumbled on a hidden root, he looked behind him to see how Imogene was making out. She was gone.

DOGS IN THE DARK

HE KEPT TO THE TREE LINE. THE WOODS ACTED AS A BREAK AND prevented the feeling of tumbling that he had when he looked into the snow. The trees were visible, black in the glow of the fallen snow. The sky had taken on an orange cast. He shouted her name as he walked back the way he imagined they had come. To his left the trees seemed to breathe as if they were aware of this man in their midst. Wrapped in a coat, hands under his arms, he plodded with great effort. Snow stuck to his boots like wet pastry. He stumbled forward leaving the trail of his breath, while behind him the woods seemed to wrap around to prevent a retreat.

The snow changed to rain, varnishing every surface. The ground under his feet was a brittle crust. Leaves rattled. In the woods every branch was soon coated in a layer of ice. Overburdened, deadwood crashed through the trees.

He stopped beneath an oak that still had many of its leaves. Moss shook his hands, to work blood into the numb fingertips. He looked up. Owls, dozens of them, left the tree and swooped down over the field to be absorbed into a rising fog. Moss blew into his palms and yelled her name again. He heard her voice faint in the distance. The cold forgotten, he ran recklessly over the snow.

"I'm here, I'm here," he shouted. He found her at the bottom of a hill. The ice on her coat crackled like eggshell when he put his arms around her.

"Come on," he said. "We have to keep moving." She remained where she was, shivering violently.

"How are you with animals, dogs specifically?" She gestured back the way she had come.

"You saw a dog?" he asked.

"More like twenty," she said. "I ran down here. I thought it might help to get out of sight. But I'm realizing that probably wasn't a good idea."

"I didn't see any dogs. Follow me. Stay close," said Moss. He started to take the lead.

"Hang on. I think we should go that way." She pointed west. "I saw a sizeable house standing on a tree line. It didn't look too far away. Moss, I'm cold," Imogene said. Her hair was plastered to her head, and tangled in ice. Moss looked at Imogene's bluish lips and glittering skin. She would not survive long in these conditions. A sudden dread passed through him as he realized how easily they could die here. "Moss, I'm really cold and I'm afraid of those dogs." Her teeth chattered. She flicked a droplet of snot from her upper lip with her tongue and smiled distantly, and then passed out.

There was no time to react. Her legs folded and she tumbled forward onto her side. She came back to consciousness, but she was unable to help herself. Taking care not to fall, Moss put his arms under her knees and back. He lifted her gingerly, letting her head fall against his collar.

"Stay with me," he said as he climbed the hill. Imogene mumbled into his neck. At the top, she jerked in his arms. For a moment he thought she was having a seizure, but soon realized that she was trying to remove her jacket. Moss slipped and fell forward, landing on top of her. Imogene's head plunged beneath a snowdrift. She was unconscious again. He tried to wake her by rubbing her cheeks, but it was hopeless. Once again, he picked her up. He ran with her in his arms but he had lost his sense of direction and could not see the house. Swearing, he turned and ran in the other direction. He stumbled and nearly repeated his fall. "Which way, which way?" he shouted to the night. A cold wind blowing across a field of snow was the only response. Then he saw it, a blocky mass against the sky.

The dog between Moss and the front door of the boarded-up house stood motionless. It was taut animal with a black mask and scarred muzzle. The hair on its nape was raised, but its ears were flat against its skull. There was no mistaking the intent of the deep growl in its barrel chest. Moss stood, feet and knees aching from the burden of having carried Imogene for half a mile on icy footing. He longed to lay her down, to ease the tightness in his back, but he feared that to do so would invite an attack. Her words rang in his ears, *more like twenty*. Were there more out beyond the limits of the snow's glow, nineteen skulking monsters like this one? Or had she, like him, been confused by the cold?

The dog crouched and circled around behind him. When he took a step to readjust his grip on Imogene, the dog peeled back its lips. Its teeth were ivory. One incisor was broken. Moss thought of the rifles and only realized then that Imogene's pack had been left behind.

"Get out of here," yelled Moss. The dog barked and snarled. Several more dogs emerged out of the night. Most, like the first, were large specimens, but there were smaller ones too, yipping at the fringe of the circle. Imogene murmured. Moss secured his hold. He walked forward, expecting to be attacked at any moment. Right away, there were noses at the back of his legs, one pushing against the healing wound on his calf. A sharp whistle came from behind. Moss whipped his head around but there was nobody in sight. Perhaps he had imagined it. The pack of dogs broke off, following the unseen leader into the brush.

Moss climbed the wide steps to the front door. It was boarded over but with a few kicks, he was able to shatter the rotten wood. He carried Imogene into the dark and propped her against the first few steps of a staircase. He positioned her head against the newel post with his pack as a cushion. When he was sure she would not slump forward, he returned to the door and barricaded it the best he could with the broken timber. Before putting the last board in place, he peered outside. A thin human form was visible for a second before it vanished into the storm.

"Great," he muttered as he jammed the last piece of wood into place.

Even in the poor light, it was obvious that huge sections of the floor had decayed and fallen in. Moss stayed near the walls of a large drawing room and tried not to think about what lay below. He carried Imogene to the north end of the room and laid her on the tiles before an enormous fireplace. She was unmoving and her hands were as cold as stone. He wrapped her in the blanket and layered all of the clothing in his pack over her. When this was done, he set about building a fire with wood gathered from the room. Soon, there was a blaze on the ceramic firedog. Moss returned to Imogene and positioned her so that she was safely away from the direct heat but still within the warmth. Sitting cross-legged beside her, he held her hand and fed the fire pieces of dry rotted kindling. Outside the house, the pack of dogs barked, until a faraway whistle silenced them.

HOUSE OF THE PUPPETEER

When daylight came, Moss ended an hours-long debate with himself and mounted the stairs to investigate the rest of the house. He had vowed to the unconscious Imogene that he would be gone no longer than five minutes at a time. It had been a night of almost overwhelming tension, not knowing what or whom lay in the rest of the dark rooms. As soon as his eyes could distinguish the surroundings, he had kissed her cold forehead, banked the fire and retraced his steps to the stairs.

Nothing in his imagination could have prepared him for what he found. There were eight rooms on the upper level filled with dust-covered puppets and sets made of every conceivable material. Many of the sets—shops, drawing rooms, opera stages—lay in near ruin, the result of age, rain that had come in through the roof or, to judge by the droppings on the floor, curious raccoons. Puppets in elaborate costumes hung clipped to wires that crossed from one side of a given room to the other, or mashed into drawers and cupboards. Watchmaker's tools lay scattered across benches. Strips of cloth moldered in heaps around sewing machines fused with rust. Antique cameras nodded on tripods and lenses peered out of warped cardboard boxes. In the last room, he found a bed amid the clutter. After he had cleared the debris he found a serviceable mattress underneath. In a nearby cedar trunk, he located several blankets that had survived in a near miraculous feat of preservation.

He made the bed as best as he could and lit a fire in a small hearth. When the room had warmed, he carried Imogene up the stairs and laid her in the blankets. No longer needing the clothing to warm her, he made a pillow of it and put it under her head. She had been unconscious for hours, and he feared that she would not last the night. As he lay down beside her, he promised her that he would never leave her side again.

At mid-morning the sun made its way across the room. Shadows moved over the faces of the puppets, momentarily imbuing them with life. It was a progression that must have played itself out on many such days in the years since the house had been abandoned. It was obvious that the puppeteer had left in a hurry. The evictions from Nightjar Island had been swift and brutal, nowhere more so than in the rural areas where the same families had lived for centuries. Moss could only imagine what it would have been like for the puppeteer to be marched away from his life's work at the end of a gun, if indeed, that is what had happened.

By mid-afternoon the room had once again grown dim as a new snow front moved in. Moss ate some turkey and crackers from his pack. In the early evening he climbed back into the bed with Imogene and watched the firelight play on the walls.

During the day, the dogs and the whistling had receded from his mind like the memory of a disturbing dream. Now that it was dark again, he did not relish the resumption of those eerie noises. When they came an hour later, he felt the full weight of his previous dread settle over him. Somebody was out there, and they knew that he was in here with Imogene. He had little doubt that the person had seen him carry Imogene inside. Was it Elizabeth? Echo? He climbed out of the bed and looked out the window. There was no sign of life in the barren landscape behind the house. He let the musty curtain drop and returned to the bed. This time he did not get in, but instead took up a position at the end. If someone tried to enter the room, he would see them and strike first.

Hours passed and he heard no more whistling, though the dogs cried mournfully in the dark. He was feeding broken pieces of a tiny stage set into the fire when he heard the wood barricading the front door fall in. Moss rushed to the top of the stairs and looked down. A hand holding a lantern was thrust through the opening and then withdrawn.

"It's warmer in here," said an old woman's voice.

"Be careful, the floors are rotten," said a man.

"It's not the first time I've been here, you. Hold the light up, or I'll walk into a wall," said the woman.

"Who's there?" called Moss.

A tiny woman wrapped in a huge scarf, wearing a man's hat and boots, looked up the stairs with pursed lips and a wrinkled nose. Her glasses glinted in the lantern light. In her hand was a black physician's bag. A man stepped into the space behind her. He made certain the woman was safe before he too looked up. He was dressed in a knee-length worsted wool coat with a hood. His leather boots rose above his knees. Moss recognized him immediately from the shipwright's house, the night he saw Echo. Both of the visitors breathed white vapor into the air.

"My name is May," said the woman. "Where's the girl?"

Something in the certainty of her tone made him feel it would be ridiculous to do anything but to state the truth. He took a chance. "Up here."

"Then I'm coming up." With this declaration, May ascended the stairs with the grace of a junebug, all flailing arms and false starts.

"Careful, May," said the man.

"Master Crow, you're more of an old woman than I am."

Moss watched as the two climbed to the landing. He stepped back from May while she regarded him as though he were another one of the fantastical puppets adorning the wall behind him. Up close May looked to be in her late eighties. Moss had never seen a woman so minutely wrinkled. Moss interrogated Master Crow with a look.

"Later," the man said. "First we'll see to Imogene."

"Well, where is she?" May looked down the long corridor to the room lit with firelight. "Never mind." She pushed past Moss with the air of a woman who was used to being obeyed. Master Crow politely waited for Moss to follow before falling into line. Once in the room the old woman removed the scarf from her head and draped it across the foot of the bed. Nonplussed, Moss stood to the side as she opened Imogene's eyelids, looked in her mouth and checked her pulse.

"I think she has hypothermia," said Moss. May looked at him as though he was an imbecile, then looked at Crow. She opened her bag and pulled out a stethoscope and listened to Imogene's chest. May smelled her breath and looked at the palm of her hands. She reached once more into her bag and pulled out a bottle filled with some kind of dried herb. She handed it to Moss. "What is it?" he asked.

"Tea. I'd kill for a cup."

"May—" Moss began. It felt odd to use her name with such familiarity, when he had only met her five minutes earlier. He felt Master Crow gently take the bottle from his hand.

"If it was hypothermia, she would have died hours ago," said May.

"Then what?" asked Moss.

"How well do you know this young lady?" said May, stroking Imogene's hair.

"Well enough," said Moss. As he said this, he realized how little he did know.

"Right." May sat on the edge of the bed. "Forgive me, I'm old and nobody offered me a chair." She glared at Master Crow, who, having found an old kettle, was presumably heading off in search of water. She returned her gaze to Moss. "So you don't know if this has happened before?"

"What has happened before?"

"She's been drawn away."

"What does that mean?"

"I've seen it before. It means that someone pulled her out of her body into another."

"Impossible," said Moss.

"It's as I say. She may not even have known it was happening. Master Crow said that she fell unconscious because of the cold. At that moment she would have been weak, no resistance. Somebody took advantage of that and pulled. She left her body behind like a loose slipper."

"To where?" asked Moss, unsure how long he could tolerate this nonsense. Master Crow reappeared with the kettle packed with snow. He cleared a spot on the coals and kneeled down to tend to the making of tea.

May shrugged. "It's anyone's guess. There's no use trying to understand it."

"Who might have done this drawing?"

May chewed her bottom lip. "Well, the Black Carriage has returned. So I think we can guess." Moss, his head abuzz, wandered around the room distractedly. He came to a desk covered in papers and books. A circus elephant's head made of silver sat on a round wood base. Moss picked it up and weighed it in his hands. There was a tiny monkey on the elephant's head. It opened to reveal a hidden inkwell. The ink had dried long ago. He set it back down.

"What can I do for her?" asked Moss.

"You have to keep her here," said Master Crow. He gave May and Moss a cup of tea each. Moss looked at the china cups, curious where they had come from, but he was too preoccupied to ask. "If you don't, the others will kill her. In their eyes she will be seen as tainted. Bad luck."

"The others? There are more of you?"

"Well of course there are more of us," said May. "Do you think an old woman like me would be wandering around this forsaken island alone?"

"May, there's no call to be unpleasant," said Master Crow. "There is a small community about five miles from here. May is one of the elders. They are survivors of the Purge. Many in the community have died mysteriously of late and they believe it is the influence of a witch that lives in the monastery, in the flooded forest. I know, it sounds like a ridiculous fairytale. But they have suffered real loss and live in unmitigated terror of her. One of the men lost a daughter this way. If they see Imogene they will not let her live. Superstition runs very deep here."

From this explanation Moss understood that Master Crow was concealing their previous interactions. Master Crow was, after all, the person who had identified Echo in the shipwright's house. He sensed that Master Crow's relationship with the survivor community was provisional. Moss thought back to the footsteps outside the caravan and wondered how long Master Crow had been following them. Had he tailed them from the City of Steps? Did he know Irridis was dead? Did he know about the dark ocellus?

The tea was scalding but Moss drank it quickly. He had never been so thirsty. "The witch, her name is Elizabeth?" he asked.

"That's not her real name," said May, sipping her tea rather loudly. "But I won't speak it. You are right. She goes by the name of the wretched girl whose body she inhabits, Elizabeth. Jansson's poor little girl; so lovely, before she drowned."

The blood was rushing in Moss's ears as he looked down at Imogene. How had Elizabeth taken her so deftly?

"What a night," said May. "The wind's howling." She handed her teacup to Master Crow and lowered herself into the chair he had found for her. She winced. "Oh, my feet."

At that moment, Imogene shot forward in the bed and screamed. Moss threw his empty teacup at the ceiling. Master Crow jumped backwards, lost his balance and careened into a stack of theatre models. Imogene beat her head with her fists until Moss grabbed them and forcibly held them to his chest. She screamed again, eyes darting wildly around the room.

"Good God," said May. "What a carry-on."

TRAPS

MOSS WAS ABOARD A SHIP LOCKED IN A FROZEN OCEAN. OUTSIDE every window of the house was an expanse of white, broken only by islands of trees. In the far distance the hills were like the coast of a country never visited. Completing the effect, the house even creaked like a ship when the wind was up.

May and Crow had left in the morning on a dogsled. Imogene had come around gradually under May's ministrations and calming hands, while Moss and Master Crow had watched from the bedside. Eventually, she had fallen into a deep but natural sleep. May had carefully instructed Moss not to press Imogene on what had happened, fearing that it might bring back the trauma. Moss understood this but was left wondering what Imogene had experienced.

She woke in the late afternoon. The temperature had risen, bringing wind that howled in the fireplace. Moss emerged from a spiral of dark thoughts—he had been thinking about Irridis's murder—to find her watching him.

"I'm afraid you'll think of me differently now," she said.

"How do you mean?"

"Moss, what are we?"

Moss fidgeted under her gaze. He shrugged. "What are we?"

"Do you love me?"

"Yes," said Moss, without hesitation. It was true. He had known it since that terrible night when he thought she was going to die.

"I love you too." Imogene looked down. Tears followed the contours of her cheeks.

"You don't look very happy about it," said Moss.

She looked up. "I'm going to tell you what happened to me. I hope you feel the same way after." Moss reached over and put two oak bannister rungs in the fire.

"Shoot," he said.

She looked at him oddly, and began.

She had never been cold before. Oh, she had been cold, of course, but compared to this, it was nothing. The air penetrated her clothing as though it were tissue paper; it chilled her muscles and bones. The worst of it was the shivering. Imogene understood the mechanisms of hypothermia. The shivering was a harbinger of much worse to come. Even this knowledge, though, was not as painful as the fear and concern in Moss's eyes. What fools they were, being out here, unprepared, chasing monsters in the dark. Elizabeth would kill them in a heartbeat. If Memoria was alive, how could they hope to find her amid this encroaching danger? What they both feared in their hearts was inadvertently leading Elizabeth to Memoria. Memoria had been kidnapped from Little Eye at the same time John had taken that vile bookcase. Unspoken between them was the fear that Elizabeth was not after the bookcase alone and that there was a connection they did not understand. And then there was the gross assumption. Why would Memoria speak to them, even if they could find her? This was a woman who did not want to be found, if indeed she existed. It had occurred to Imogene that Memoria was a creature whose only existence was in the minds of trauma-tized men. Was she a person, or a dark reflection? After Irridis's death, Imogene's misgivings had begun to run deep. Elizabeth was a monster. Imogene, no coward like her father, was nevertheless no slayer of monsters, not even close. If she were, she would have killed Lamb herself many years ago.

"Moss, I'm really cold and I'm afraid of those dogs."

She'd always been afraid of dogs. Sometimes it seemed as though the entire city was full of them, dogs running wild. In the city it was possible to stay out of their way, but here there was nothing but open ground. She licked her lip. And it was as though this minute action triggered a cataclysm. Suddenly she was falling. Something was pulling her. Terrified, she jumped clear and ran. She felt light, the way you feel in the spring when you put on shoes after months of boots. She thought herself to the edge of the woods. That is how it felt, a wish granted before it was expressed. Her toes barely touched the thin film of ice. Was she flying? Looking down she could see that she was naked. Her breasts and stomach, thighs and feet were like smoke coiling in the transparent membrane of her body. How strange! Beneath the trees she stopped and looked back. What had happened? Moss was standing over a woman's body. He picked her up. *He's afraid,* she thought. *He thinks that I've died.*

Don't wait, said the trees. *Move,* said the grass. *As fast as you can,* said the half-awake moles beneath the ground. The wind itself called her on. She rose into the air, arms outstretched like wings, one foot drawn up like a dancer, and turned. *Make haste from here,* said a voice from above. She looked up and for second saw the moon through the shredded clouds. *Go.*

Into the thicket she fled, like a hare, like a doe, like a bird. She felt as though she was all of these things at once. Branches and thorns that should have shredded her flesh passed straight through her without so much as the rustle of a dry leaf. She flowed around every tree trunk as she hurtled deep into the woods. Sticks tinkled like tiny bells. She was not so much propelled as lifted; in the way that John had lifted her once, when she was five. He had held her by the hands and spun her so quickly that if he had let go they both would have spiraled off into the rose garden.

A small clearing appeared in front of her. There was something there, unmoving. It was orange. A fox. It lay on its side with its coat broken in a way that left no doubt that it was dead. Without thinking about it, she jumped into it.

Imogene had no idea how or why she had done this thing. Going into the fox had been instinctive, like burrowing into a hiding place to evade a pursuer, but once she was inside, she was seized with terror. The aching hunger that had just a moment ago caused the fox to die was now her hunger. It pervaded her being, and pushed her toward despair. Was she trapped? Stuck? She lifted her head and stood gingerly, grasping with frozen footpads to find a grip on the ice that covered everything. Her ears pricked. Moss was shouting out beyond the trees. She shook and filled the air with droplets, as her body heat melted away the ice. She could not return to him, not like this. He would not see her.

On a hidden road that ran for a few hundred feet in the woods, she caught a mouse. It was still moving as she swallowed it.

The ice rain turned back into snow. It sparkled in her fur as she trotted down the middle of the road. She heard something, a clink of metal against stone. There it was again. She followed the sound to an open place in the woods and sat in the shadow of a tamarack.

Elizabeth's carriage formed the backdrop to the scene that was unfolding. Its heavy wheels were caked with mud. Along the side was evidence of events at the quay, a deep gouge in the side panels that ran from front to back. Echo stood in the space protected from the wind by the body of the carriage. The organ Elizabeth had cut from Irridis floated in the air, emanating a faint light. It moved slowly, filaments snaking around each other. Imogene thought of the jellyfish in the great aquarium in the Cloth Hall repository. Whispers. Before it stood Elizabeth. Her hair, knotted and unclean, hung down, covering her bowed head. Imogene could not hear and moved closer, slinking against the trees until she was only a few feet away from Elizabeth's tattered hem.

"Do you remember the names of my deaf sisters, Violette, Charlotte, Anna, Magda, Chella and Allison? They gave their lives to watch over you. They've all gone. You outlived them all. Now it's just me. I'm sure the Sisterhood of Little Eye didn't expect me to be the last Attendant," said Elizabeth. She crouched down and hissed at the floating organ. "You should never have lived. They should have killed you all those hundreds of years ago when they found you and Aurel bewildered and frightened on the heath." Elizabeth walked around the black organ. "After they killed Aurel you seduced them with your wonders, didn't you. You maintained your childish form, never growing, so they would pity you. But you were a toxic prize, one that they couldn't turn away from. They called you Starling, the Terrible Angel. Keeping you imprisoned was a fatal error. I have no remorse for trying to kill you after everyone else was killed, and none for finishing the job now. I will bring you back home to Little Eye, Starling, and bury you with your dead sister." Elizabeth motioned to Echo. He shuffled forward ponderously, leaving deep impressions in the pine needles beneath the snow. The girl stepped back as Echo lifted the organ. He carried it to the carriage where a perfectly square panel slid aside. A thin white arm emerged and took the organ. The arm withdrew and the panel closed with a loud click.

Imogene did not have long to think about what she had seen. Elizabeth turned suddenly as if she had heard something. The child's eyes flitted around the clearing and landed on Imogene.

"Little fox," she whispered. "So you came." Imogene felt herself held by Elizabeth's eyes. Her legs felt paralyzed. Elizabeth moved closer, the hem of her dress dragging through the slush. "Little fox, come here and I'll burn you like I did your mother." Warmth spread through Imogene's body. She panted, unable to move as Elizabeth's finger found the soft down behind her ears and stroked it gently. "Life is full of little twists and turns." Elizabeth stopped her hypnotic stroking and smacked Imogene on the muzzle so hard that her teeth cracked together. She seized Imogene by the scruff. "Burn, little fox," Elizabeth spat. Imogene buried her teeth in the girl's hand. Miraculously, it was enough. She twisted from the grip of the small hand, hit the ground and ran. Elizabeth's laughter followed.

Imogene followed a deer trail back through the woods. Behind the clouds the sky lightened. While she had listened to the bizarre conversation, the temperature had steadily dropped and now the snow had begun anew. A sparkling dust fell through the trees. Crows cawed overhead. Ice fell from the branches. The ground was sharp and painful against her feet. She slowed to a trot only when she was convinced that she was well away from Elizabeth and her companion. The deer path carried her out of the woods to a leaning wire fence. A plan of sorts had formulated in her mind. She would look for the old house that she had seen and see if Moss had taken shelter there. Beyond that, she had no idea what would come next, but at least she would be near him.

The fence was too high for her to jump, so she looked for an opening underneath. She found one. It was a low, fur-lined dip through the snow and the grass that grew thick against the fence. Rabbits had probably made the hole. Without a further thought, she slipped through. She realized her mistake immediately as a wire snare closed around her body. The more she fought, the tighter it became.

The hours wore on. For a time, the light brightened. Snow drifted. Imogene lay on her belly unable to extricate herself. The grass around her was covered in a bloody slush. In her attempts to chew through the wire she had cut her tongue and gums. Breathing was difficult. She took the air in sips. She had tried to jump from her fox body, the way she had jumped from her own. But she did not have the trick of it, or her pain had so stolen her concentration that she could no longer envision it. She was snared.

In the night, footsteps came through the creaking snow from behind. Imogene was too weak by this point to raise her head. She simply whimpered and lifted her ears. A boy came over the rise. He was bundled in a patched coat and scarf. He pulled a small sled where a selection of rabbits, a mink and another fox lay in a frozen heap. At the front of the sled was a lantern that threw wild shadows. His body language conveyed that he had not expected to find a living animal, even one so close to death. Moving stealthily, as though she might vanish on him, the boy released the sled and lifted a rifle to his shoulder. He aimed carefully and pulled the trigger.

"Do you still love me?" asked Imogene.
"Yes," answered Moss.

MAPS AND LEGENDS

A THAW CAME ON THE OVERNIGHT WIND OUT OF THE SOUTHWEST. They woke to the sound of running water as the ice softened. Moss untangled himself from Imogene and left the warmth of the bed to look out the window. The path across the fields behind the house, snow-packed the previous day, was now a ribbon of red earth. A boy on a pony and a man walking to the side made their way toward the house.

"Company," said Moss, pocketing the ocellus.

"My name's Jansson. We are here to take you to May." The man was sandy haired. The nail on his left thumb was bruised a deep plum. He wore work clothes, farmer's clothes. His homemade sweater was full of unraveling holes and his boots were military issue. The gaze of the slight boy that accompanied him was fixed on the pony's mane. He had indoor skin and a blue vein that ran up from his jaw line to the corner of his mouth. On his head, hair like milkweed silk wafted in the breeze. He was blind. Jansson fixed a slipping blanket on the boy's shoulders as he spoke.

"Come with us," said the boy.

They all turned as Imogene came out of the house. Her hair was uncombed and her lids were still puffy from sleep. She had wrapped herself in a blanket. Jansson seemed to bristle as he took in these details. His inspection stopped at her long feet where the tip of a tattooed green tendril ended in a spiral.

"Why?" asked Imogene.

"It's easier to reach now that the snow is melting," said Jansson.

"Where are we going?" asked Moss.

"To the Oak Hall. It was decided at a meeting. Master Crow said no harm would come of it. They thought that you should come to see the maps." Jansson's eyes bored into Imogene.

"Is everything all right, Mr. Jansson?" asked Imogene.

"It's the boy. He asked to have a puppet. May said he might have one, for coming."

"Puppets," said the boy.

Imogene led the boy, Luther, on his speckled pony, while Moss and Jansson walked behind. Luther clutched a puppet under his blanket so that the wooden face with eyes made of black coral peeked out like a second rider. For Moss, the puppet's face bore an uncomfortable similarity to Lamb's. Moss and Imogene had packed everything they could into Moss's pack and shoulder bag. They would not be returning to the puppeteer's house. It took several hours to reach the village. During this time Luther talked to Imogene in an unending stream. Jansson said little. He seemed a practical man who commented that he sacrificed a good day's work to fetch strangers. His only wish was to dispense with the task and return to his field.

"What's he saying?" asked Moss as they walked along a stony road. They had just passed through a deserted village that had been largely overrun by vegetation. Damaged walls showed signs of an armed conflict. Moss sought a distraction.

"He's telling her fairytales. He's memorized all of those old stories."

As the afternoon faded, they came to a small collection of buildings separated from the surrounding fields by dry stone walls. The air smelled of sweet wood smoke. Jansson led the group to a house significantly larger than the others. A sign on the door said Oak Hall. Inside was a rustic meeting place. The walls were covered with chore lists of names grouped under houses; blue house, yellow house, green house. Moss and Imogene stood in the hall, stamping off the cold, while Jansson took the pony to a barn. Luther vanished with his puppet.

"Now what?" asked Imogene.

"Now, you eat," said an unfamiliar voice. It belonged to a man in his thirties with long brown hair. He looked like a recipient of Jansson's hand-me-downs. "I'm Grove. The others are in the back." Jansson returned and seemed content to hang back after the two men exchanged what seemed to Moss to be significant looks. At the far end of the hall they passed through a door to a second, smaller room. Approximately thirty people sat at long tables eating, while other men and women served food from steaming bowls. The air was filled with the fug of boiled vegetables. At the far end there was a kitchen where mealtime activities were in full swing. Grove directed them to an empty section of table. Moss felt surreptitious glances on him but when he looked at the others he was greeted with noncommittal nods or the occasional, tentative smile.

"Visitors are rare here. They have a natural curiosity about you," said Grove.

"That's one word for it," muttered Imogene.

They sat down and were immediately served. The walk had made them ravenous and they ate without speaking. Halfway through their meal, chairs scraped the floor as others rose to leave the room or pitch in with cleanup. It was not long before they were nearly alone. Grove produced a pot of coffee from the kitchen. When everyone had been served, he turned to Jansson.

"Thanks for getting them," he said. Jansson nodded and left the table, leaving his coffee untouched.

Grove turned his attention to Moss and Imogene. "You should be aware that there was a very loud meeting in this room. Many of the people eating in here tonight were of the mind that you should have been driven away. May and Master Crow were successful, just, in convincing them that you should be brought here."

"That's not very comforting," said Moss. "We won't be staying."

"They are frightened. There is a rumor that the witch known as Elizabeth has returned. These people believe this is attributable to your presence. To put it bluntly, your presence at the puppeteer's house was seen as a bad omen. Infant mortality is extremely high in our village and in lieu of a scientific explanation there are some, less educated, who fall back on superstition. It's a small subgroup but despite their beliefs, these people are our friends and family and we must respect what they believe."

"Then why invite us for dinner?" asked Imogene, shaking her head.

"The reason you have been asked here," said Grove patiently, "is to be given what you need to continue your journey. In other words, we will supply you. We are not bad people, merely cautious. In exchange, we ask that you never return, or mention our existence. You cannot settle here or in the puppet maker's house."

"What gives you the right to be here? Nightjar Island is forbidden territory," said Moss.

"These people are survivors of a dirty war. The soil is contaminated with chemical agents, but it is their homeland. Their families farmed here for generations. They have nowhere else to go."

"How did they survive the Purge?" asked Moss.

"That, I'm not prepared to tell you," said Grove. "You never know what the future holds."

"Fair enough. It must be a hard life," said Moss.

"People don't live long here," said Grove. "There are far more females born than men. There is a sickness that claims most in their early adulthood. I won't lie, it can be hard." He turned to Imogene. Although till now his demeanor had been calm, resignation passed over his face. "Some of the people believe you to be like Elizabeth."

"Why?" asked Imogene. She looked at Moss, frightened.

"A combination of things. The fact that you were drawn, the tattoos—"

"This is bullshit. We don't need your help," said Moss. He stood up. "We'll leave now. It was never our intention to stay."

"Wait," said Grove. He turned toward the door. "Okay, come in."

A large man with grey hair, who Moss had seen at dinner, came through the door holding a rifle.

"Damn," said Moss, looking at Imogene.

Luther rushed around the man in a nightshirt. In one arm was the puppet and in the other a cookie tin and a cardboard chessboard. He sat down opposite Imogene. Moss was amazed by the familiarity with which he did this. This was truly Luther's home.

"Imogene will stay here and play chess with Luther," said Grove. "You will come with me. In less than an hour, you can both be on your way. You will be provisioned."

"I won't leave Imogene here," said Moss.

"It's okay, Moss," said Imogene. "I'll play chess with Luther. Go see what they want."

"Okay," said Moss to Grove. "Let's go." The man with the rifle sat down at the table and lit a cigarette. Imogene took the cookie tin from Luther. She took a different colored pawn in each hand.

"Pick a hand," she said.

"Left," said Luther. He sat the puppet beside the board, a silent witness.

Moss was uncomfortable leaving Imogene, but he followed Grove through the kitchen knowing that the alternative would force a confrontation. He wanted to learn more, and in his gut did not believe she was in danger with Luther present. At the back of the kitchen they passed through a door to the outside. A path lined by weak electric lights led to an adjacent building. It was smaller and much older than the other building. The walls were built of field-stone and its roof edge was covered with grass. It looked one with the landscape.

In the confined space of the corridor Grove asked Moss to remove his boots. At first Moss thought this was to prevent him from running, but then he saw six other pairs of boots along the wainscoted wall. Grove removed his footwear and waited while Moss unlaced. In socked feet, both men entered the main room. An aged boardroom table dominated the space. Most of the chairs were empty. Five seated people turned their heads. The sixth, May, sat at the end of the table knitting, counting stitches. Master Crow was at the opposite end. He nodded at Moss. Two women and two men comprised the remainder of the group. In the center of the table sat a black, aerodynamic object. Its fire-blackened form reminded Moss of a ray. Copper wires protruded from the region that would have been the gills. The object had been mounted on a circular wooden base. Between the spreading "wings" there was a deep hole, just wide enough that if Moss had wished, he could have inserted his finger.

"No one knows," said one of the men, seeing his curiosity. "A scavenging party brought it back from the island's interior."

Moss remained standing. The group waited patiently until May had finished her row. Moss marveled at this but realized that it was a show of respect. May finally sighed and put her knitting on the table.

"Cable stitch patterns will be the end of me," she said to nobody in particular. She suddenly focused as though only now realizing there were seven other people in the room shifting uncomfortably. "Dr. Grove, thank you for bringing our visitor to the meeting. You have explained the predicament that we find ourselves in?"

The doctor nodded. "Somewhat."

May turned to the four people Moss had not met. "This is Jason, Adrian, Susan and Sara." Moss acknowledged them each in turn. "Mr. Moss and Dr. Grove, please make yourselves comfortable." When they were settled, May pushed her knitting to one side and clasped her hands on the table. "Our group is made up of determined people, and they are bound together by hardship." Moss looked at the faces around the table and wondered what their individual stories were.

"How many are you?" asked Moss.

"What you saw at dinner," said May, "plus a few more who are foraging in the city. This number is half what it was five years ago."

"The doctor mentioned an illness," said Moss.

"That is correct. Adrian will explain."

Adrian was a melancholic-looking man with sharp features and mechanic's hands.

"Thank you, May. The group was fairly stable up until fifteen years ago. Just the usual illnesses you'd expect in any small, closed community."

"What happened?" asked Moss.

"On a day not unlike this one," said Adrian, "one of our foraging parties went to a region at the center of the island. Typically, we keep to the coastal areas, as travel is easier and things are not so overgrown. A few of the younger members were keen to see the remains of a crashed aircraft known as the Crucible. We had heard that the Crucible contained functional communications technology that we might make use of. Well, they did find it after many days in the dense forest. In the end nothing workable was salvaged. They brought this as a kind of souvenir of their adventure." Adrian indicated the artifact on the table. "It's what it looks like, a relic of technology, which we can never hope to understand. Anyway, the party went further into the forest, to a large flooded region. At an abandoned monastery known as Little Eye, they came upon something extraordinary. A boy, lying in a shallow hollow in the ground, covered in leaves and soil. He was curled up in a ball, like a hibernating animal, with roots entwined around his limbs as though he had been there for years. When they freed his body, he woke up."

"What did he look like?" asked Moss, heart pounding.

"Like no boy we'd ever seen," said Adrian. "He was beautiful, intelligent and as transparent as a jellyfish. Two members of the party took him for something supernatural and attempted to kill him on the spot. They died immediately, pierced in a dozen places by the glowing stones, which floated around this boy's head and appeared to do his bidding. Terrified, the remainder of the men retreated. The next day they attempted to return but try as they might, they could not find their way." Adrian put his hands into his lap. "The boy appeared in their camp and told them that he could guide them out of the forest. He was true to his word but on the way back to the village, several of the men died of a hemorrhagic fever."

"What's a pity is that they didn't all die before they got here," snapped the woman named Sara.

"Forgive the outburst, Mr. Moss," said May. "Sara lost her son last week."

"After the remaining men returned to the community, many more people died of the sickness. It was believed that the boy had brought the illness with him, maybe deliberately."

Jason, the man who had first spoken to Moss, continued. "Weeks later, someone in the village took it upon themselves to lead the boy to the sea during a gale. He took the boy on to a flat promontory in the night. The boy was washed into the ocean by the violent surf and never seen again."

"If you don't know who did it, how do you know what happened?" asked Moss.

"I witnessed it," said Master Crow. "But the night was such that it was impossible to make out the man's face."

"Then how do we know it wasn't you?" sniped Sara.

"Silence," said May. "What's done is done. We all have our suspicions who it was."

"Jansson?" Moss did not know why the farmer's name came to him so readily. The others did not respond, but glances were traded.

"Shortly before the boy appeared in our midst," said Adrian, "there was an accident. Jansson's daughter Elizabeth fell into a well and drowned. She was a beautiful girl and her loss was sorely felt. She was laid out in the Oak Hall awaiting burial when something horrible happened." The man paused and gave a nervous laugh. "Everyone in there felt a presence in the room. It passed from person to person. Each time it left someone, they fainted to the floor."

"It moved like an invisible wave," said May. "Until it reached the dead girl. Only those grieving behind the table were unaffected. When it reached the child, she became animated. She climbed down from the table and walked out of here into the woods as calmly as a princess."

"Jansson was devastated. We believe that when Jansson saw this boy, and the destruction he purportedly brought upon us, he believed it to be connected with what happened to his daughter.

"I can't tell you if that is true, or not."

"It doesn't matter what is true. What matters is what people believe," said Grove. "You and Imogene were seen long before you reached the puppeteer's house. We know you also possess one of the strange stones. This is reason enough to banish you, given our history." Moss looked sharply at Master Crow, but the man was staring at the machine on the table. Was he friend or foe?

May said calmly, "These people are probably doomed, most of them anyway, but unless they think the group is of a like mind it will be impossible to maintain cohesion. People like Jansson must not be given the means to tear the group apart. You must sleep for a few hours, and then leave before morning, or I cannot assure your safety. I am sorry. Adrian, be a dear and collect the maps from the other room."

THE SILO

"I'LL WALK WITH YOU," SAID JANSSON. "MY FARM IS UP ON THE rise." He stood by the door in a coat that smelled of tobacco, and a hat with earflaps. It was not yet dawn. A single bright star shone through a gap in the clouds. Moss did not answer, too busy jamming last-minute items into his pack. Imogene was also silent as she hugged herself in a warm, patched coat and stared off into the fanned-ink darkness of the distant tree line. A few minutes earlier, Moss had noticed the man looking at Imogene. He could not tell if it had been a look of reproach, or something else. Jansson moved away and busied himself with his pipe.

"Do you hear me?"

"Thanks, but it's not necessary, Mr. Jansson. We'll manage," said Moss. "I'm sure you have better things to do." He cinched the drawstring on the pack and then hoisted it over his shoulders.

"I'm going up there anyway. There's a shorter path that will save you slogging through a cow pasture full of mud and horse shit."

"Imogene," said Moss. She turned and, seeing Moss ready to depart, picked up her own pack. "Fine, Mr. Jansson, lead the way." There were no others in the yard.

They followed a track that led them away from the buildings to the scrubland behind. Moss and Jansson walked in front, while Imogene fell in behind. She had also been aware of Jansson's attention.

"This island is an evil place, no question there," said Jansson.

"Places aren't evil, people are," said Moss. He wondered how far Jansson's farm was.

"You're talking about the witch?"

"Just speaking philosophically, Mr. Jansson."

"She's not human. But I'll grant that you do have a point about people being evil. A man has to be careful who he keeps company with."

Moss stopped and turned to Jansson. "Is there something that you want to say to me?"

Jansson kept walking. "Just passing the time," he said. "Don't get yourself all worked up." Moss let Jansson take the lead and fell into step with Imogene.

"For a forbidden island, this place is pretty crowded," said Imogene. She drove her walking stick into the muddy ground. "It seems to have a high per capita rate of crazy."

"It's like any island, I guess," said Moss. "Everything is condensed." He continued walking beside her. It was now an hour past daybreak. Jansson walked in front, out of earshot, chewing on a cold beef sandwich that he had pulled from his pocket.

"Why is he here?" asked Imogene. "How far can his farm be? We've been walking for ages."

"I don't know." Moss dropped his pack and sipped from a canteen. Imogene stopped to wait.

"Ask him where Memoria is," she said. "I bet these people know."

"Already have," said Moss. "Says he doesn't know. Never heard of her."

"I think he's lying. A woman traveling alone on this island would not be a secret for very long." Imogene lowered her pack to the ground and sat on it. "You said they were spying on us the whole time."

"The same thought crossed my mind." Moss wrapped his fingers around the ocellus, which he had been keeping discreetly out of sight. It was smooth and pleasant to the touch.

"Let's lose him. This can't be the only way," said Imogene.

"What is he doing now?" asked Moss. Jansson had stopped. He was probing the ground with a long stick.

"Poking a stick into the dirt," said Imogene. Moss did not answer. He looked at the ground to either side of where they had just been walking.

"Don't move," he said.

"What is it?"

"Right there. Do you see it?" Moss directed her gaze to a spot about ten feet away.

"I don't see—" Her eyes grew wide. "Is that a landmine?"

"It's an antipersonnel mine," said Moss. "Designed to blow your legs off. When I was a kid, I found a few of them on the beach. That one looks old. Jansson led us into an old minefield."

Imogene looked around the field. "How many?"

"Hundreds, maybe. There's no way to tell. Most of them would be buried under years of grass. That one must have been pushed up by the frost."

Moss cupped his hands around his mouth. "Jansson! This is a minefield." The man was quite far ahead. He acknowledged Moss with a shrug and a wave. "Jansson!"

From the top of a hillock Jansson shouted back. "We know what she is." He pointed at Imogene. "Some of us don't agree with May. It's not right to let her go free. It's begging for trouble. I'm putting an end to this nonsense. Good day now." His shock of white hair blew up in the breeze like a cockscomb. He turned his back and lit his pipe. Moss yelled after him, but he wove an irregular path, with his hands in his pockets.

"He's bluffing." Imogene locked eyes with Moss. "Moss, right?"

"I'm not sure he is. I can see the edge of another one, there. Pick up your pack. We'll go back the way we came. We can retrace our footprints. The ground is soft enough." Moss led them slowly back along the muddy track. Imogene walked in his footprints, hands resting on his pack. In twenty minutes they reached a rocky outcrop. They followed the stony, well-used path at its base, away from the field. Rounding a corner, they ran into several men with rifles, nervously waiting where the outcrop sunk into the ground. The group was monochrome in the dawn light. They scrambled to block the path.

Moss and Imogene stopped. One man with severe overbite lifted his rifle to his concave shoulder and pointed it at Imogene.

"You can't come back this way. That was the arrangement."

Moss looked past the men to see if there were others nearby, or if the group was acting alone. A figure on a bicycle tottered toward them along the winding path. It was unmistakably Master Crow. Everyone turned at the contraption's clatter and bell dinging. Nobody spoke as Master Crow rode up, breathless, and dismounted. The bicycle shuddered down a fence post despite his efforts to lean it carefully.

"Bernard, put that thing down," he said. "You're not going to shoot an unarmed woman."

"You know what she is, Master Crow, and she's not coming back to Oak Hall." He lowered the gun slightly, uncertain. "Don't look at her directly."

"Jansson led us into a minefield up that way," said Moss. Several of the men smirked knowingly. "We don't want to go back to the hall. We just want to go around it the other way."

"What's the matter with you?" said Master Crow, to the men.

"You know. You saw it yourself." Bernard lowered the gun with a warning look at Moss and Imogene. He walked closer to Master Crow. "She was drawn, and she came back. You wouldn't come back the same from something like that."

Moss and Imogene looked at each other.

"What would you know about it?" said Master Crow.

"What are you saying?"

"I'm saying not everyone is as big a fool as you, Bernard Foster."

"We'll see who's a fool," said Bernard. He turned quickly and, raising the gun, fired at Imogene. Imogene had already begun to turn. The bullet missed and tore into her backpack. Moss leaped forward and shoved Bernard's rifle barrel skyward. He brought his knee up, driving it solidly into the man's abdomen. Bernard dropped the rifle. Moss shoved him backwards as Imogene rushed for the weapon. There was a second shot. Bernard jolted and reeled back along the path. Someone had shot Bernard from a distance. He took three steps and crumpled sideways. The rest of the men broke ranks and ran for cover.

"Run," yelled Master Crow. Moss grabbed Imogene's hand and pulled her off the path, away from the direction of the minefield. They ran for the concealment of a birch copse. Another gunshot cracked and echoed. One of the escaping men sprawled on the ground. Moss and Imogene ran with Master Crow close behind.

"Who's shooting?" panted Imogene.

"I couldn't see. They must have been on higher ground," Master Crow said. "Maybe from the silo. They would seem to be on your side, whoever they are."

"Keep going," said Moss over his shoulder. "It won't be long before those men regroup."

They stopped to catch their breath under the cover of the trees. The sun illuminated the upper branches, but the underbrush remained deep in shadow. Moss stood at the base of a large tree and scanned the area they had come from. In the distance, Bernard Foster lay on the ground, unmoving. It was not possible to see the other fallen man. The silo Master Crow had mentioned was washed in gold against the sky, but there was no discernible movement. For a moment, Moss had half expected to see Gale, until he remembered the man was dead.

"Shit, that was close," said Imogene at his shoulder. Moss turned and grabbed her.

"Are you hurt?" He stuck his finger in the hole in her pack.

"Just shocked. These people are insane."

"They're scared," said Master Crow. "Bernard had two children. He knows what happened to Jansson's daughter."

Imogene strode over to Master Crow and pointed a finger in his face. "Do I look like I am in the mood for a fair and balanced discussion? If I hadn't turned, that asshole's bullet would be lodged in my liver."

"I'm sorry," said Master Crow.

"Stay away from me." Imogene walked back to Moss. "So?"

"Now we head into the center of this island and try to find Memoria before anyone else gets there first." He pulled the ocellus out of his pocket and tossed it into the air. It spun like a top before coming to a rest directly above him.

"What about him?"

"I'm coming with you," said Master Crow, watching the glowing stone. "I can take you to Little Eye." He looked meaningfully at Moss. "You're not the only one who made a promise."

CRUCIBLE

AFTER THREE DAYS OF HIKING THEY CAME UPON THE WRECKAGE of the Crucible. A concave shell of grey metal was wedged between the two sides of a gorge, with a deafening river fifty feet below. It formed a shallow bowl for a mirror of stagnant water. Imogene said it looked like a bridge, but to Moss's eye it looked more like a piece of art. It was difficult to imagine the craft that would have incorporated so unlikely a shape. It would have been dangerous if not impossible to access the wreckage as it lay at least thirty feet below the level of the narrow path they had just negotiated.

Moss and Imogene sat on a rock ledge with their feet dangling over the void. On the other side of the gorge, the trees were sparse and the forest floor was littered with leaves and needles. The sun felt good on their skin. All around them, birds gathered in noisy groups or flitted from tree to tree. The air smelled of pine resin. Master Crow had climbed the higher ground behind them to see what could be seen. They had grown used to this quiet man. He had proven to have a reliable instinct for the best trail. Master Crow's chief concern was that men were following them from the Oak Hall. Moss had seen no evidence of this but was grateful for the other man's vigilance.

"There's more of it down in the gorge," said Moss. Imogene had leaned back on the carpet of needles, using the edge of her pack as a pillow. She had taken off her jacket and pulled her T-shirt up, letting the sun warm her stomach. She murmured sleepily. Moss ran his fingers lightly across her skin tracing the curve of an inked line. Imogene smiled.

"Be good," she said unconvincingly. Moss lay down beside her and rested his cheek on her stomach. It was firm and warm. He could feel her heartbeat and it made his own quicken. "How long do you think Master Crow will be gone?" Moss felt her fingers on his neck.

Dead pine litter crackled behind them. Moss sighed. He sat up and turned around, expecting to see Master Crow. Instead, he saw Jansson crouching a mere twenty feet away. Moss shook Imogene. She sat up quickly.

"What? What's the matter?" she asked.

Realizing that he had been spotted, Jansson stood up, grinning, and walked toward them. Moss and Imogene stood up. Out of the corner of his eye, Moss could see Master Crow scrambling down the hill behind Jansson.

"What do you want?" asked Moss. Jansson walked toward him shaking his head with a disappointed expression. He held a rock in his right hand. His fingers were whitened in a tight grip.

"You're right, you know," Jansson said. "It is people who are evil. And there's none more evil than her kind."

"Back off, asshole," said Imogene. Moss tried to keep her behind him but she was having none of it. She stepped around him. "What do you know about me?"

"Imogene," said Moss. He held out his hand.

Jansson came closer. The spot on his lip where the stem of his pipe habitually rested was glossy and purple. "It's your kind that took my little girl. You and your demented magic. You should be burned. You're a disease."

Moss put himself between Jansson and Imogene. "She had nothing to do with what happened to your daughter," said Moss. "Let's keep our heads and talk."

Jansson flinched. Moss saw what was coming. Something in the other man's stance, the movement of muscles in his shoulder registered in Moss's mind. "Imogene, get down," he yelled. It was too late. Jansson hurled the stone. It split into two halves against Imogene's head and flew out over the gorge. There was no blood, just a red mark that started to immediately swell as she staggered into Moss's arms.

"What have you done, you crazy bastard?" screamed Moss. Jansson lunged at Imogene, grabbing at her hair. Moss swung, landing a fist in the base of Jansson's skull. Still holding Imogene, the man staggered back toward the ledge.

"Stop." Moss leapt forward, grabbing wildly at Jansson's legs. Imogene was limp. "Jansson, please," begged Moss. "Please." Jansson fell backward, taking Imogene with him. Moss raced to the edge and would have followed them over if two arms had not seized him around the waist and flung him to the side.

"Moss! She's gone," said Master Crow. Moss broke free of Master Crow's arms. Looking down he could see Jansson's body lying submerged in the water pooled in the Crucible's wreckage.

There was no sign of Imogene. She had fallen into the rushing cataract.

Moss implored Master Crow, "I have to get down there."

"She couldn't have survived. There are too many rocks, Moss."

"I am not leaving her." Moss grabbed Master Crow's arm. "Help me get down there."

"Okay," said the other man. "It won't be easy."

And it was not easy. The gorge was deep and fissured. Using roots and branches as handholds they descended a steep path, barely maintaining their footing on the rocks. Moss pushed himself forward heedless of the danger. Master Crow moved at a more deliberate pace, but always keeping his companion in view. The enormity of what had happened hit Moss in waves. He would not accept that Imogene had been killed. When Master Crow finally fell behind, Moss shouted at him to hurry, accusing him of not trying hard enough. Half an hour after Jansson's attack, Moss jumped from a rocky outcropping nearly twice his height, onto a loose pile of shale. Bloodied and frenzied, he rushed up to his waist in water that took his breath. He stumbled on rocks yelling Imogene's name. There was no answer except the ceaseless roar of the rapids.

They walked the river back to the shadow of the Crucible's wreckage. Moss felt the stones shifting beneath him in the current. The water was like a living thing that wrapped itself around his legs in an effort to twist him from his feet. He did not belong in this element, but he could not bear the thought of Imogene being alone in it. He surveyed the steep walls of the gorge. The entire landscape seemed to be arrayed against him. He stopped in the cold shadow of the aircraft, soaked. On the bank, Master Crow sat with his elbows on his knees, his head hung.

Master Crow eventually built a fire in the shelter of a rusting jet engine. In failing light, he climbed the side of the gorge to where they had left their packs. Moss was awoken when three packs struck the ground several yards away. Master Crow was invisible at the top. Moss could see only see a river of stars defined by the trees. A few minutes later Master Crow yelled down, but it was impossible to hear what he was saying. Moss threw deadwood on the fire and fell back to sleep. His dreams were full of the images Imogene had related in her story of the fox. The floating organ, once part of Irridis, eluded him as he tried to steal it away from Elizabeth. Moss woke shouting in the dark and did not sleep again that night.

At first light they divided what they needed from Imogene's pack. In one deep pocket Moss found a cube of hashish. He stowed this and some of her clothes into his own pack, wrapping *The Songbirds of Nightjar Island* and the drawings in one of her shirts. When they had finished their task, Moss hid Imogene's pack under a pile of stones.

"We'll head downstream," said Moss. "Maybe we'll find her if there are shallows." Master Crow nodded.

"Are you sure you want to find her?" asked Master Crow.

"Yes," said Moss. "She might be injured."

They hiked for hours shouting Imogene's name, through a mist that slowly thickened. They scanned the water, checking protruding logs that might have snagged her clothing, but it was futile. There was no way to see all parts of the river. Some bends concealed deep pools where the water appeared almost black, while other areas were geysers of white foam against the rocks. Imogene's body might have been in any of these.

Toward the end of the morning they came to a horseshoe-shaped falls that dropped nearly a hundred feet. In the distance, the landscape flattened out. The river was lost in a sea of trees. Moss sat down on a slab of shale.

"Look down there," said Master Crow, dropping to his haunches beside Moss. Moss followed the line of the other man's finger. At first it looked like another mass of blackened rock at the edge of a pool fed by the falls. The fog thinned to reveal the form of Elizabeth's carriage. Echo stood several feet away, swaying from side to side.

The sight of the carriage immediately returned Moss to his dreams of the previous night, and Imogene's account of her meeting with Elizabeth in the woods. One image pushed itself to the forefront, a white arm emerging from the carriage to take the glistening organ.

He suddenly knew why they had not been able to find Imogene's body.

"She's in the carriage," said Moss, with conviction. "The river has swept her right into the witch's arms. We have to get her out."

HEART'S DESIRE

"You can't be sure." Master Crow watched the mist swirling around the base of the falls. Echo vanished, reappeared and vanished again. He knew what Echo was and it terrified him. Deep within his stomach, the glass pupa that had lain there since he had stolen it from the witch, so many years ago, shifted as if coaxed. It wanted to join the other pupae that were inside Echo. They were the demon's life force. He knew the demon felt it too, a stirring from Master Crow's proximity. It was swaying in the mist, surely feeling the same tug in its belly.

"I am," said Moss. "Elizabeth has been stalking her from the start. Waiting for her chance, like a spider. It's punishment for her father's actions."

Master Crow accepted this. Moss looked terrible. The skin on his hands and face was crisscrossed with welts from tearing down the side of the gorge. Master Crow wondered whether the man would survive the island. Moss would not be the first who had gone mad obsessing over their heart's desire in the wooded depths of Nightjar Island.

"What do you think he's doing?" asked Master Crow.

"Waiting. Guarding the carriage. I don't see Elizabeth or her dog."

They waited for an hour at the top of the falls, keeping a careful watch on the carriage and Echo. Elizabeth did not materialize. The relentless cascade of water was ever changing and yet unchanging.

"How important is this to you?" asked Master Crow. Moss, who had been silent, looked up sharply.

"If you want to go, go," said Moss. "I won't hold it against you."

"That's not what I meant."

"I won't leave here without her."

"There's no possible way that she can be alive. It was too high a fall. As I said at the time, too many rocks," said Master Crow.

"Maybe," said Moss. "But I won't leave her body in the hands of these monsters." He paused. "Whatever the cost."

"I know, my friend." Master Crow put his hand on Moss's shoulder. He closed his eyes and absorbed the sound of the falls, the cool damp on his skin and the rich, sweet smell of pine resin. The pupa tugged.

"I think I can draw Echo away, for a few minutes anyway."

Moss patted the hand on his shoulder. "Thank you."

"Wait here. When you see Echo move away, you should take that path to the left. It looks like the quickest route down the falls. On the other hand, I am now going to go down through the trees so that I'm not seen."

"Be careful," said Moss. "Elizabeth could be nearby."

Master Crow winked. "Moss, I've never had anybody to love, you know. Nevertheless, I understand regret. I'm sure that Imogene would not want you to bring yourself further pain. There are many ways to honor the dead. One way might be to simply go on, and leave her be. Don't do anything that you might later regret. Life is long and though it might not seem it now, this is not everything. Not everything is focused on this one point in time. Life is ahead of you. I can see it in your eyes."

"Be safe," said Moss firmly. Master Crow looked at Moss for a few seconds, hoping he would change his mind, hoping that there would be some dimming of his resolve. When it did not happen, he pulled his hood over his head and ducked into the trees.

Echo stood motionless on an expanse of black slate of a type that had once been described to Master Crow as mudstone. The mudstone crumbled beneath the creature's feet, and though not visible from where he stood, Master Crow knew the stone was filled with fragments of trilobites and brachiopods. These were remnants of the ancient world before the age of man and machines. They made for a rich mud.

Echo was wrapped in his heavy coat from which innumerable fine polyps waved, thriving in the moist air. The polyps reminded Master Crow of hair-like worms he had seen writhing in the ruined ponds in Absentia. Echo's skin was a rind. Where it was visible, it was thick and scarred. His feet were three-toed stumps, like those of a rhinoceros, with curiously light-colored nails. Of his face, Master Crow could see only a single eye. It was unexpectedly small given the creature's size, surrounded with thick folds and pleats of coarse skin fringed with long bristle-like lashes. Echo's unwavering gaze seemed to be weighted with a fathomless melancholy. Behind him, the falls thundered. Master Crow resisted the temptation to search for Moss on the upper rocks.

There was no doubt that Echo had seen him. The creature stopped its rocking. Master Crow abandoned the pretense of hiding and left the shelter of the trees. He climbed over the uneven shale. It tilted under his feet and he nearly fell into a pool. The vibration of the falls shook his body. He reached Echo, soaked and short of breath. As he lifted himself onto the cantilevered slab he was conscious of the water churning, endlessly braiding into dark hollows beneath. Echo stood at the opposite end, his back to the falls. The black carriage was several yards away on the firm ground of the true bank. Behind it, the forest was a near-black wall, broken only by the red flashes of a cardinal swooping from tree to tree. He approached slowly, unsure of how he would play his only card. He cleared his throat, about to speak, but Echo interrupted.

"Crow." The creature blinked. Steam rose from its body and sparks were carried on its breath. Master Crow's legs trembled. In the back of his mind, he wondered if these were his last moments alive. This was a place of staggering beauty, a place where you could hear the planet's blood and see its jutting bones.

"Yes," said Master Crow. He had to shout to be heard. Echo's voice had come to him as a voice at his ear.

"Have you come to return what you stole?" asked Echo. Master Crow felt a shift in his stomach. "To finally free me from this."

It was not what he had expected. Uncertain how to respond, he said, "Free you?"

"I was bound to this body without my consent. Only you can undo it."

Master Crow was taken aback. "Me, how can I undo such a thing? I have no skills in the magical arts." The pupa in his stomach fluttered like something on the verge of panic.

"It need only be shattered, but it must be given freely. Would you return the glass to me?" A plume of sparks showered the wet rock

247

and sizzled at Master Crow's feet.

So this was the day he would return the pupa, the day he would cease to be human, or even cease to be at all. He had wondered about it countless times; what kind of day it would be. He had known from the first, of course, that when the time was right he would return what he had stolen, and with each tug in his body the pupa nagged. He could barely remember what it had been to be a crow. He had changed so much. His old life was but a memory of a memory. The thought of giving back, of sacrificing what he had become, terrified him. But though he had grown used to his human form, he had always felt like an impostor. To die pretending that he was other than what he had been born as was to betray himself. Yes. He looked up at the sky and smiled. In his mind he saw the boy, Monster, Starling, Irridis. Back in the City of Steps, Irridis had come to Master Crow. Irridis had made him promise to help Moss, perhaps foreseeing just such a day. How beautiful it was now to be able to atone for a crime and fulfill his promise at a stroke.

"Yes." He jammed two fingers to the back of his throat. "Yes." Tears sprung from his eyes. The pupa pushed at the top of his stomach. He doubled over and howled. Something inside tore and a bubble of blood appeared in the corner of his mouth. It was happening too fast, he had to draw the creature away from the carriage. He turned to run. His boot slipped on algae and he fell heavily on one knee. The pupa was in his esophagus. With one hand he clawed at his neck, with the other he tried to crawl toward the edge of the rock. Echo moved behind him.

"The seventh glass can end this." The roar of Echo's voice had become one with the falls. "Please." And then, like a burning ingot, it was in the back of Master Crow's throat. He rolled on his back, unable to scream or breathe. He drove two fingers into his mouth and felt its smooth surface. Ribbons of blood followed his fingers when he pulled them out. Fists balled at his temple, he rolled over and banged his head on the rock. The glass pupa skittered across the rock toward the water.

"No!" roared Echo. "Catch it! Smash it!"

Master Crow struggled forward, gasping for air. His fingers found the pupa in a small depression. He beat it against the ground until his knuckles were raw and bloodied. Suddenly it burst into a cloud of powdered glass. He heard a wail begin behind him but the fate of Echo was no longer his concern. His hands shook. He felt his teeth shatter as the front of his skull elongated. With every reserve of energy he had left, Master Crow crawled to the edge of the mudstone and threw himself into the churning river.

Moss watched from high above the falls in disbelief as the body of Master Crow fell into the water and was swept from view. A sound came from Echo that raised the hair on Moss's arms. The creature's great head tilted forward. For a moment, Moss expected it to howl again but it did not. Echo's form collapsed inward as though the damp of the air were dissolving it. The coat fell away like a sloughed skin. Sticks, bones, paper, shells and animal remains sagged and fell to the ground in clumps. All of it burned in a column of blue fire. And then, Echo was gone, leaving behind a smoking mound.

THE HAND OF DARKNESS

THE CARRIAGE WAS LARGER THAN IT HAD LOOKED FROM A DISTANCE. Its windowless bulk sat atop an undercarriage designed to carry a great weight. The heavy wheels had torn deeply into the bed of moss they now rested on. The carriage body was constructed from wood that felt as hard as iron beneath Moss's fingers. The joins were as tight as those of a ship. It seemed more tomb than carriage, and yet, Moss reasoned, there had to be a way in. He circled several times, examining the intricate carving that covered every inch of the carriage's surface. Scenes of erotic and even demonic revelry encrusted the wood with bewildering complexity. It repulsed him, and for the first time, he wished that Gale had been successful at setting it ablaze.

After checking the falls and the woods to be as sure as possible that there was nobody watching, Moss climbed the carriage. He hoisted himself up on one of the high rear wheels, using the spokes for leverage. From there it was an easy matter to climb onto the top, using the carved grotesques as handholds. Filthy, soaked and feeling half mad, he crouched on top of the carriage and searched the surrounding area for movement. Still, there was no sign of Elizabeth or her damned dog.

At the middle of the roof there was a brass handle with a butterfly key at its center. Halfway into the turn, his hand met some resistance, but when he applied more pressure, there was a distinct click. Moss opened a circular hatch and turned his head away when an odor of decay rose from within. It was dark inside the carriage. Moss relied on the shaft of meager daylight admitted by the hatch to guide him. A ladder of bone and brass led into a strange cavity that was part bedchamber and part grave. The walls were lined with silks and dark velvet. With a start, Moss realized that the space he

250

was in far exceeded the outside dimensions of the carriage. Moss moved stealthily, his pulse throbbing in his ears.

The sword Elizabeth had used to eviscerate Irridis was mounted in an alcove ornately embellished with carved wood. The floor was also wood, so highly polished it reflected the interior like still water. At one end of the space, there was a built-in bed with the curtains drawn. Someone lay behind the cloth, sleeping, judging from the sound of the breathing. He forced himself to ignore the sound for the moment. Imogene lay on the floor in front of it. She had been bound in muslin and red string. There was a strong scent of wild herbs and disturbed fungus in the air. Moss stroked her cheek through the thin material. To his eyes, she did indeed look like a spider's prey. She had a slow pulse. Tears of gratitude sprang to his eyes as he pulled her to him.

"I'm here," he whispered. He lifted her, surprised at how light she felt. Getting her up the ladder was an awkward task, but he managed it. Clasping her to his body, he climbed out of the carriage and slid to the ground. He carried her a few feet away and with great gentleness he placed her onto a bed of pine needles. Working quickly, he removed the cloth. She breathed more evenly.

He returned to the carriage and once again dropped into the small room. As he approached the drawn curtains of the bed a hand slipped out. It was a female hand, long-fingered with bluish nails that had become overgrown. The skin was as white as a beetle grub. Heart pounding, Moss quietly eased the sword from the wall. He lined up the tip with the body behind the curtains. The pale fingers moved, slowly, as though testing the air. Moss's arm shook violently. Gritting his teeth, he prepared to stab through the cloth. This was the real Elizabeth, the monster who cast herself into the body of a drowned girl, the monster who murdered Irridis.

He felt hot breath on his neck. He turned quickly but there was nothing there. The sound of scrabbling came from outside the carriage. The white arm swiped at him blindly, leaving red welts across his hand. Then it had him, firmly. Its strength was astonishing. The fingers closed around his wrist until he felt the bones grinding together like rocks. Something invisible and hot snaked into his open mouth. He gagged, unable to breath. A second hand appeared from behind the curtain. It drove its thumb into the roof of his mouth and pale fingers sought his eyes. Turning his head, Moss tightened his grip on the sword. Knowing he was seconds away from death, he drove it through the curtain into what lay beyond. There was an ear-piercing scream and the hands loosened their grip. On the third thrust, the blade returned covered in blood. The hands fell away and Moss flew backwards, letting the sword clatter on the floor. He gasped for breath. The noise from outside the carriage stopped.

In a few seconds Moss had recovered sufficiently to stand. Picking up the sword, he pulled the curtain back with its tip. A woman lay bloodied among the silks. Her hair was the longest Moss had ever seen, white and twisted in knots. Her eyes were the palest blue. Moss dropped to his knees and took the motionless arms in his hands. He stretched them out in the weak light. Fine white scars covered each of them, like bracelets of thread. It was Memoria. She screamed and tore her hands free. The force of it pulled Moss forward. Memoria scrabbled over him and tumbled to the floor of the carriage. He grabbed for her ankle, but she rolled away. She pounded the floor with a fist, and a hidden trapdoor dropped her out of sight. By the time Moss reached it, the door had sprung back into place. He hit it numerous times, but it would not open.

Stunned by what he had seen, Moss climbed out of the carriage into the cold, rain-washed air. It was only when his feet hit the ground that he realized that he had brought the sword with him. Memoria was nowhere to be seen. Glancing at Imogene to satisfy himself she was safe, he hastily bound the sword in a shirt and lashed it to his pack. Behind him, the carriage loomed. Whatever had been scrabbling from the outside was also gone. Maybe it had been an illusion. The clearing was still. He searched the nearby woods for Memoria without success.

Dazed, he walked back to the spot where Master Crow had confronted Echo. Moss did not understand what had happened here. He knew only that Master Crow had sacrificed himself in order to give Moss a chance to save Imogene. By what path the man had reached this decision it was impossible to say. Looking into the water running beneath the rock, Moss realized that an incomplete understanding would just have to be good enough.

Moss found six glass pupae in the pile of detritus left by the dissolution of Echo. He washed them clean in a puddle and held them up to the light. For a moment, he considered slipping them into his pack, but then changed his mind. He did not want them. Despite Echo's terrifying presence, there had been a profound sadness about the creature. One by one, Moss dropped the stones into the water. They flashed momentarily before being swept away. He dropped to his knees and bowed before the falls. Head pressed to the stone, he slowly allowed himself to confront the implication that it was Memoria in the carriage. She was the witch all along. He rolled over on his back and let the rain mix with his tears.

Fearful of her return, he rose. He walked slowly back to where he had left Imogene. She was gone. He ran around the carriage shouting her name, until he heard her voice calling to him. He followed it to a deep recess in the rock. Imogene squatted on the ground, gently moving strands of black hair from Elizabeth's grey face. When Moss climbed down to them, he noticed that Elizabeth's fingernails were torn and bloody. Splinters from the carriage were embedded in the pads of her fingers.

"I found her face-down," Imogene said. "She's dead."

"Imogene." It was all he could say as he seized her in a tight embrace. He held her for a long time. "It was Memoria in the carriage," he said as he released her. "She was the witch."

Imogene looked at him, confused. "Moss, how?"

"It makes sense. John took her from Little Eye, the same place he found the bookcase. It was there all the time."

"I woke up in the carriage after Jansson carried me off the cliff," said Imogene. "I saw her. It was horrible."

"She got away."

"Oh god."

"We need to look for her, search the woods. I injured her."

Imogene shook her head, resolute. Her face was bruised from the fall but she did not seem seriously injured. "No. We have to bury Elizabeth. We have to bury them both. Elizabeth and Jansson."

"What?"

"Jansson was only acting out of grief."

"He was a murderer," said Moss, incredulous.

She took his hand. "If we don't treat him with dignity, we'll carry hate for him for the rest of our lives. He wasn't a monster, however much we want him to be."

"I won't. He tried to kill you, Imogene," said Moss bitterly.

"Yes. But in his mind, he had a reason, a real reason, Moss. He was a misguided idiot, but not a monster. We need to respect his humanity. Please, for me."

"It will be difficult to get the body," said Moss. He looked off into the trees on the other side of the waterfall where a piebald crow had alighted on tamarack branch. It bobbed up and down.

"We have rope."

The crow cawed loudly, dipping its head.

"I think that bird is telling us that it's time to go," said Moss. The crow walked back and forth on the ground, impatient.

Retrieving Jansson's body was dangerous but they were careful and methodical. The hard work of climbing into the gorge to retrieve the body and the digging of the grave gave Moss time to probe his anger, and if not forgive, at least begin to form an understanding of events. It was hot work, with only the camp spade and their bare hands to break the earth. As they rolled Jansson into the ground, Moss pulled a gun from the man's boot and put it in his own coat pocket. In the end when both Jansson and his daughter were buried together, Imogene scattered the ground with autumn flowers. Afterward, they washed in the river and ate a wordless meal by a fire.

"The third thing," mused Imogene.

Moss pulled the ocellus from his pocket.

They returned to the carriage. Moss entered a final time, to look for the organ Memoria had taken from Irridis. He found it among the bedsheets, half eaten. When he climbed out, Moss locked the opening in the top and threw the butterfly key into the falls.

LITTLE EYE

"Hopeless." Moss flattened the map against the ground where he had pieced the tattered sections together. At Oak Hall, May had handed him the map in a battered file folder held together with an oxidized rubber band. The map's folds had long since surrendered, leaving Moss with a stack of rectangular pieces. He had tediously ordered them over the past few days, comparing the result with the topography of the landscape. It was late morning. The early chill had retreated before the sun. They had paused beneath an apple tree, which still had a few leaves. The air was sweet with ferment.

"I think you have that part on the left upside down," said Imogene.

"No, look, this fits here," said Moss, pointing to a blue squiggle that ran across both pieces of paper, before he saw her amused look.

The map represented territory that had existed years earlier. Since the Purge, the process of ecological succession had subsumed most human traces with relentless efficiency. Small towns, and the roads connecting them, were disintegrating beneath trees and brush. Occasionally, subsidence of the soil or a geometric outcrop would reveal signs of earlier habitation. Tantalizing as they were, these clues proved difficult to reconcile with the tattered map. They knew which direction they needed to go, but they were also aware that days could be wasted placing confidence in the vagaries of the landscape. There had been no sign of Memoria. If she had survived, she would still be formidable, and she would also be traveling to Little Eye. Moss was distracted, thinking of Memoria thrashing in her own blood.

"Moss?"

"There's nothing to go by beyond this point." He cleared the hoarseness from his throat. Since the struggle in the carriage, he had fought depression. Finding Memoria alive, and seeing what she had become, had been hard. He often found himself longing for the oblivion of Seaforth's brandy. Imogene knelt beside him.

"I think we're about here," he said. He circled an area on the map with a stick. "The center of the island is low wetland according to this."

"The swamp."

"According to May, that is how we'll find Little Eye." Moss carefully stacked the pieces of the map. "We should get moving."

Two hours later, they found a hare shredded to ribbons in a gully. Footprints that may or may not have been human surrounded it. The carcass's skin was already a stiff parchment. When Moss flipped it with a stick, the underside was alive with maggots. It was an old kill, but the discovery unsettled them.

In unspoken assent, they continued with greater urgency. Imogene led. She wore patched army fatigues, pilfered from a cardboard box in the Oak Hall, and a black T-shirt. As she scrambled along a deer trail, her shirt rode up, exposing a goblin within a vortex of flowers in the small of her back. It watched him with hard eyes until she disappeared around a bend in the trail.

He stopped to adjust his pack. Imogene shouted down from the top of an incline.

"Moss, I see something."

The crow that had become Moss's constant companion glided past him, up the trail. Envying the bird its wings, he climbed over tree roots to join. She stood at the foot of a blackened monument. The stone man had been sculpted with a military greatcoat, goggles, and an aviator hat. He stood with one arm cradling a large book and the other lifted to the sky. The hand of his upraised arm was broken off at the wrist. He stood on a base of limestone that bore an epitaph reduced to a meaningless pattern of lines and depressions.

The crow flew to the top of the statue's head. Imogene looked up, shielding her eyes from the sun. Walking had made her lean and strong, returning the vigor she had lost during her ordeal in the snowstorm. She turned toward him, blinking as her eyes adjusted.

"That bird is trying to tell us something," she said. It hopped in a circle like a broken weathercock.

"One of us should climb up," said Moss. "It'll give us a better perspective."

"Are you insane?" asked Imogene. "At least let me go. I'm light. You could lift me up to the top of the base."

Moss put his shoulder to the cool limestone and made a foothold of his hand. "Be careful," he said.

"You're not even going to try to talk me out of it?" Imogene stood in front of him.

"I've learned not to argue with crazy people," said Moss.

She gripped his shoulders and lifted one booted foot into his hands. "On three." They counted together. Moss heaved her skyward. He endured a succession of kicks to his shoulder, neck and head. She whooped. Moss walked down the steps and turned to observe from a less punishing angle. Imogene was adroitly scaling the giant stone aviator.

"Hidden skills?" he yelled up.

"Break and enter training, courtesy of one Mr. Lamb," she shouted.

"Of course," Moss muttered. The crow left its perch on the aviator's head and flapped, cawing, to a nearby chestnut tree.

"Wow, it's a much different world up here." Imogene hoisted herself the remainder of the way. Using the book as a platform for her feet, she wrapped an arm around the aviator's neck. "Whooeee!"

"Okay," said Moss, backing up. "That's far enough." He caught his breath as Imogene jumped and threw one leg over the statue's shoulder. A moment later she sat astride the figure like a child watching a parade. The toes of her boots were wedged into the folds of the coat. With one hand clutching the man's nose, she pointed with the other.

"I can see the center of the island," she yelled. "I can see Little Eye."

Her words had a galvanizing effect. Moss felt the depression shift like a slab of marble.

They slid down a skree-covered decline. It was all that remained of the ancient crater wall. The air at the bottom was dank. They marveled at the profusion of insects despite the late season, and the din of the frogs and birds. Using the sword, Moss whacked a path through dying weeds. As the crater wall at their backs darkened in the fading light, they followed a natural trail into the forest. The shadows lengthened, but Moss and Imogene continued moving. When something crashed invisibly through the underbrush, Imogene stopped.

"Probably a deer," said Moss, in response to her unasked question. The sound had reminded him of the wolf he had seen on the night his borrowed motorcycle failed on the north road. Ten minutes later, they passed the weathered turrets and barrels of abandoned artillery equipment, bleached like gigantic vertebrae. In places the track skewed into a ravine or dropped into a flooded sinkhole, but it always resumed further on. Eventually they came to the edge of a great swamp. The track vanished gently beneath a plane of sepia-colored water.

The swamp stretched into a forest of the oldest looking trees either of them had ever seen. Misshapen trunks twisted out of the water on gnarled and blackened roots like an army of monsters supernaturally frozen in the midst of a battle. The labyrinth of forms dissolved in phosphorescent haze and darkness. Somewhere in that darkness lay Little Eye, the island within an island.

"It's like the entrance to hell," said Moss.

"With mosquitoes," said Imogene, slapping one from her arm.

"Well, we can't go any further tonight," said Moss. Imogene was already gathering wood for a fire.

The crow woke them at dawn with raucous cries. Blearily, they kicked the remains of their fire into the swamp. The sky beyond the tree canopy was yellow and threatening. They searched the shore in the hopes of discovering a raised piece of land that would allow them to make an inroad. After an hour of fruitless wandering, Moss, who had been scanning the canopy, touched Imogene's shoulder and directed her gaze. An interruption in the pattern of branches had caught his eye; short boards lined up side by side. It was a path through the treetops, suspended by twisted boughs and knotted ropes. They visually traced it over the water to a point where the everpresent haze swallowed everything.

"It looks pretty old," said Imogene. "Do you think it will support our weight?"

Moss looked at her with a raised eyebrow. "You scurried up our aviator friend."

"I didn't scurry," she said, punching his shoulder. "I don't scurry."

Moss rubbed his shoulder. "It's all we have. I think we should give it a try."

Imogene climbed with the same agility she had shown at the monument. Moss envied her, even as bark rained down on his upturned face. When she reached the dangling footpath she shouted down.

"Come on, it's an easy climb."

It was not, but in a few minutes, hands scraped and bleeding, he had joined her. Balanced astride an enormous limb, he shook the weathered ropes skeptically. The slatted path was slung from tree to tree as it disappeared over the swamp. It vanished in a tangle of limbs that became too confusing to differentiate.

"Suicide," he said.

"It's stronger than it looks," said Imogene. She stood further along the same limb.

"I'll go first. If it supports me, you should be fine," he said. Imogene rolled her eyes and appraised him sadly. "Or you could go first," he added.

She left the relative security of the tree and lowered herself onto the nearest section of boards. Holding tightly to the ropes, she tried her weight. The structure creaked and swayed, but held.

Imogene looked at him and laughed nervously. "Come on," she said. He waited until she had reached the next tree and then followed. They agreed to maintain twenty feet between them as a precaution. Imogene tested every footstep before committing her entire weight. Several rotten boards dropped into the water below. They rested at each new tree to catch their breath and assess the path ahead. In this way they soon lost sight of firm ground.

Periodically, the path drooped to within a few feet of the water. In these places they saw lugubrious carp moving through the murk, trailing plumes of silt and tadpoles in their wake. There were also signs of past human presence, crumbling foundations, rusting farm equipment, and the hull of an overturned boat, furred with algae. These artifacts depressed Moss. He was relieved when the path took them into the higher reaches of the trees. The crow flew ahead, its caws absorbed by the relentless background din of amphibians. If Moss and Imogene were forced to slow their progress, it perched and waited for them to catch up.

They saw Little Eye for the first time in a sifting rain. The main monastery house, a towering edifice rising out of a mass of lesser buildings and wreathed in ivy, dominated the small island. The surrounding structures tilted against each other like blocks left by a retreating flood. Moss and Imogene crouched side by side, sheltering in the trees. She put her hand on his shoulder, for balance. On impulse, he pressed his lips to her fingers. Leaves rustled against the masonry as a few birds hopped through the knotted stems, but there was no movement to suggest habitation.

"This feels like a trap," Moss said.

Imogene dropped back on her heels and faced him. "Why are you here?" Moss stared at her. "I know why I'm here. Why are you here? Because if you go in there, you have to be sure it's what you want."

Moss was thoughtful for a moment. "I don't think it was an accident that Irridis came into my life when he did—he saved my life. He asked me to return the ocellus to Little Eye. Of course, he'll never know now, if I did it or not. You see, I owe it to him to do this, but not because he asked me to. I'm doing it because he can't do it himself."

They crept along the path toward the edge of the island. The boards were slippery and cracked in places. In spite of the danger Moss was looking forward to having earth beneath his feet again. The suspended path ended in a tangle of ropes at a platform in a large willow. Moss dropped to the ground to observe the monastery. Imogene landed behind him with a thud. They followed the shore to get away from the tree path—always fearful they were being followed—ducking behind cattails. Imogene put her finger to her lips and pointed toward the ground. The footprints of a large dog had churned up the mud.

"Let's see if we can find an unlocked door," he said. At that moment, the ocellus began to glow.

THE TADPOLE

"God, what a place," said Imogene. "You can taste the bitterness in the air." With Moss leading, they climbed a sloping path where marsh marigolds gave way to lady slippers and ferns. The ocellus punctuated the air above his head. The rain had eased, leaving the sound of dripping vegetation and the enervating trill of frogs. Moss scanned for any sign of Memoria or her dog. Little Eye was the heart of her world. She would not have left it vulnerable. Jansson's gun rested in Moss's peacoat pocket.

Little Eye felt timeless, its season out of synch with the rest of the world. Overhead, the sky was filled with breaking clouds. It gave Moss the impression of looking up from the bottom of a deep well, a sensation familiar from the exercise yard in Brickscold Prison. At the top of the path, the crow balanced on a post, watching their progress, its feathers glistening with dew.

"It's the fungus," said Moss. "Don't brush against it. Try not to breathe it in." Moss sensed that the plants were a first line of defense, intended to confuse and deter visitors. It was simple enough to spot and avoid the commonplace species of poisonous plants and fungi. It was the unfamiliar organisms that disturbed him most, a thread-like moss with minute bulbs the color of blood, the reeking orange slime running down a rock wall.

Imogene stepped over lichen that undulated on a rock like crests of fine lace in a breeze.

"Moss, I hear a dog panting," she said.

Moss turned around and coaxed her forward. "There's no dog, Imogene. It's a hallucinogenic effect of the plants. I feel it too. Keep walking. Don't stop for anything."

Moss probed the path with a stick, not fully trusting his eyes. Imogene trailed, distracted by the plants that moved on either side of her in rhythm with her breathing. Beneath an umbrella of spiny leaves, something caught her eye.

"Lamb?" she said. "Why are *you* here?" In the shadow of the leaves, Lamb's head, wrapped in a filthy blindfold, bit into the earth, grinding the soil in his stained teeth. She wanted to warn Moss, but when she looked again the head was gone. Moss took her hand. Without realizing it, she had stepped off the path.

"He's not here," said Moss. "Don't let go of my hand."

She looked at the dark ocellus suspended above Moss's head. It struck her as malevolent, of this world, not hers. She nodded to reassure Moss that she understood, but she was unable to formulate a reply.

At the top of the slope, they pushed through a copse of silver maple and ash to find the buildings of the monastery in front of them. Trees grew from under paving stones and out of gutters. Sour light glinted off veins of metal in the old stones. The crow flew past them toward the highest point of the Little Eye monastery, swooping over the roofs of the surrounding buildings. Imogene felt no desire to see what lay behind the walls.

The effects of the plants dissipated. Sitting on a slab of rock, they shared a bottle of water from Imogene's pack and discussed where to go next. Irridis had not told him the location of Aurel's grave. They could search for days and be no closer to finding it. Although the island was not large, no more than a couple of acres, the architecture of Little Eye was interlocked and dense, a puzzle of crumbling masonry, alleys and staircases. Seeing it before him in its entirety, Moss felt dread. What if, coming this far, he was unable to fulfill his promise to Irridis? What would they do with the ocellus? The mute buildings of the monastery offered no ready answer.

He struggled to imagine how an ordinary life could ever have been lived here. These stones, and the ground beneath them, embodied an awful history of unimaginable crimes that seemed the very denial of life. He tried to see Memoria, the little girl he had known in the City of Steps, surviving on God only knew what, among these ruins after the massacre of her people. He tried to see Irridis, sleeping for years like a hibernating animal, in a shallow hollow. The water ate at his stomach like a lump of salt. The crow screamed from the top of the monastery, deciding their direction.

They passed under an arch, chosen because it was wider than the others, and wordlessly climbed to the top of a narrow staircase. Moss was acutely aware that they could be trapped if someone came up behind them. The stairs opened onto a courtyard bounded by windowless walls covered in marks, systematic but indecipherable. Moss commented that whoever had made them would have had to work from a high ladder.

"What is that?" asked Imogene, stepping into the courtyard after Moss. Moss picked an object from a wire stand. It was a fetal form made of green glass. In his mind he saw the glass pupae, picked from the remains of Echo, tumbling in the cold water of the river. It moved in his hands like a waking baby. Moss cried out and instinctively flung it away. The thing landed on the wet flagstones and exploded in a cloud of granules.

"What the fucking fuck," said Imogene, jumping back.

"This place," Moss said, "it's like something malign inhabits every molecule, and is desperate to be released."

"I'd like to be released," said Imogene. "When I was in the carriage, I had dreams. Dreams that went on forever, level after level, and they felt like this place. If you weren't here, I swear I'd think I was still dreaming."

Moss turned to look at her, but she was craning her head at the charcoal symbols covering every inch of the walls.

"Let's go," he said. He walked toward another staircase, past unfinished assemblages of glass, rusted metal, bones and dried seedpods. "We shouldn't linger." Imogene followed, skirting the same objects. They climbed the second set of stairs to a flat rooftop. From there they could see the swamp surrounding Little Eye and the crater wall in the hazy distance. A path ran along the spine of the roof, leading to a set of carved wood doors set into an uninviting portico. They had found an entrance to the central building of the monastery.

Imogene leaned against the parapet looking toward the crater wall. Moss placed his hands on her shoulders and she turned to face him. Her features were faded in the morning light, her lips and eyelids nearly colorless.

"Turn around for a second," she said. He did as she asked, and felt her tugging something from his pack. When he turned back, she was holding Memoria's sword. He shrugged off the pack and leaned it against the parapet. He walked toward the doors, but Imogene hung back. Moss turned to see her still standing by the parapet, the forest behind her. The grip of the sword was settled in her right hand. Its tip rested against the ground.

He walked back. "What's the matter? Aren't you coming?" She met him halfway with an embrace, pressing her cheek to his chest. She pushed him away. Her face was serious. Moss started to speak, but she cut him off.

"I'm waiting here. I've had enough of dark places." She swept her hair over her head, and drew a deep breath. "Don't make me or I'll have to stab you." She smirked. He felt the sword dig painfully into the toe of his boot. He pressed his forehead to hers. She pushed him away with the tip of the sword. "Stop it. I'm going to keep watch out here. You saw the dog's footprints. We both know Memoria is in this monastery, either in there, or out here. We have to be prepared for either possibility. I'd rather die in the daylight, thank you very much."

The rooftop was suddenly flooded with sunlight. Moss was taken by its transformative effect on Imogene's skin. It drew out some freckles on her face. Her lips, chapped from the journey, regained some color. He stroked the bruise above her left eye; caused by the stone that Jansson had struck her with or by her fall into the gorge.

"Did you plan that?" asked Moss. They both laughed.

He knew that she had come this far for him alone. Despite her bad temper, her ability to get under his skin, and her occasional, well more than occasional, foul mouth, he glimpsed for the first time a life beyond present circumstances, one not haunted by Memoria, or even Irridis for that matter. Moss could not bear the thought of leaving her alone on the rooftop, but this time it was what she wanted. He would not convince her otherwise.

"I'll hide myself and yell bloody murder if I see anything," she said. "I promise. Then you can come and save me, if you want."

He laughed. "Try not to hurt yourself with that thing then."

"Go fuck yourself, Moss."

"If you see anything—"

"Go."

Moss put his hands on the doors and pushed. They opened into a dark interior. Eddies of dust rose into shafts of light falling from openings between the rafters. Pigeons burst into the air, and resettled on high ledges, clucking and cooing. The age of the buildings settled around Moss, deep silence, and the smell of ancient wood. Moss pushed the doors shut behind him.

Once his eyes had adjusted, he became aware of seven figures facing each other in a circle. His hand felt for the gun, but there was no response. As a group they floated, unbound by gravity, toes drawing cursive in the dust. He released the gun. They were too still to be alive, yet Moss had the sense that they were uncannily aware of his presence. He stepped into the circle, accompanied by the ocellus. Wood faces looked down, blank but aglow with a luminescent, milky wash. Their hands, positioned in a suspended discourse, were articulations of tarnished brass and silver. Insects had made lace of once-beautiful gowns. He had no doubt that these creatures were Memoria's handmaidens. Their suspension was proof of her presence, as was a commencement of soft canine panting.

The dog that Elizabeth had ridden, crouched, muscles tight-packed, in a trapezoid of daylight. Blood and foam flecked its snout. It watched Moss intently. He heard a young Memoria in his head. *In mythology there is a dog that guards the entrance to the underworld.* Here he was. Moss's pulse drummed in his inner ear. To deliver the ocellus home meant dealing with Memoria. He would not turn away from the creature that had been the cause of Oliver's death, the creature that had murdered Irridis, and haunted Imogene. His heart threatened to burst with the tragedy of what she had become, raised from death in his hopes, to a wraith, pale and raving. And now, closing a terrible circle, she would die at his hand. Moss met the dog's eyes. There was a score to settle here. This time he would not falter.

"Where are you?" The words reverberated, but no answer came. The dog soundlessly curled its dewlaps from yellowed canines. Its eyes took on a fixed stare. The creature was dying. Perhaps it had shared a symbiotic relationship with Elizabeth, or perhaps it was the victim of some injury visited by Memoria.

"You don't belong here. Why did you come? I told you to let it go." Her voice animated the air like the flutter of wings.

Moss spun. "Why are you hiding? Are you afraid, without your creatures to protect you?"

"I told you to stay away."

"Why did you kill Irridis?" Moss persisted. The dresses on the suspended forms rustled on currents of air.

"It was a necessity, a duty I was born into."

"Was it duty to torment Imogene?"

The voice laughed cruelly. "That was the price of John Machine's wickedness."

"How could murder be a duty?" Moss played for time, turning in a circle, trying to discover where Memoria was hiding.

"I was the last *Attendant* of Little Eye. The last in a long tradition, always a child of magical propensities, each ritually deafened to prevent them falling under the sway of Starling's voice. It was an honor."

"How did that become murder?" Moss became aware that the dog had ceased to breathe.

"In the evening before my deafening was to take place, a regiment came. They raped and massacred the sisterhood to which I belonged. I hid and survived, eating insects and drinking water from the swamp because the cisterns had been poisoned. I knew I had to leave but it was forbidden for Starling to leave Little Eye. So I decided to free myself of the burden of duty." The voice seemed to flow across the room. "I stabbed him and hid the body in a shallow in the earth. I was interrupted in this task when John Machine arrived, full of his lies and empty promises. I didn't know I'd failed to kill Irridis until that day in the Cloth Hall."

"When you tried again."

"Where is it?" asked Memoria, with impatience.

"What?"

"Aurel's dark stone."

"Hidden," said Moss. *Among the pigeons*, he thought.

"Nothing is hidden forever," said the voice. The tone of her voice told Moss she was tiring of the conversation. A cicada whine reverberated through the room. It took Moss a moment to realize that it came from the floating women. Something moved around Moss's limbs like tentacles. He swatted at them, remembering how easily she had entered his body as he stood in the closet in the Blackrat Bakery. The air grew colder. He saw a flash of silver, like a fish catching the light in dark water. Memoria appeared several feet away, coalescing out of the air. She was emaciated and wore a white shift with long sleeves. It was rent and bloody. The skin of her face and neck were colorless. Moss could see the ghostly movements of the bones beneath her skin. The dust made vortices in the air behind her. He could see that supporting and concealing her broken and wounded body had taken a disastrous toll on her energies. All trace of the child he had known was gone.

She let a drop of spittle fall to the ground. It was a perfect sphere of lightless black. It landed audibly, leaving a black circle no larger than a penny. Moss felt a movement in the air, a stirring of his clothing, and heard a low whistle coming from cracks in the wall. Without looking down, Memoria placed a yellow toenail at the edge of the circle and pulled, expanding its circumference to that of a teacup. The wind increased, tugging insistently at his clothes and hair. Dust and feathers vibrated and tumbled toward the black circle.

"I mean to have it," she said. Smiling at him, she pulled the circle further. He looked up as pigeons fluttered the air, confused and panicked by the force pulling them from the rafters. The air rushing into the black circle grew shrill. The dog's body slid. The ocellus appeared amid the birds. Breathlessly, Moss fought to free Jansson's gun from his pocket, but he fumbled. It hit the floor and rattled toward the hole. The ocellus moved inexorably toward Memoria's upraised hand.

Moss leaped forward even as Memoria's fingers were closing around the ocellus. He seized her around the waist and threw her to the floor. She landed on top of the hole with a curdling scream. Moss brought his foot down on her wrist. The bones snapped like sticks and her hand flew open, sending the ocellus across the floor. Moss scrambled and seized it in his fist. He heard Memoria rise behind him. The wind had ceased. Throwing himself forward, he grabbed the gun.

Memoria crossed the space between them and slashed his face with the pale fingernails of her remaining hand. He was raising the gun when he was suddenly pulled backwards by the mechanical women. Fighting himself free, he pulled the trigger, and saw Memoria convulse. Brass fingers curled into his mouth and nostrils. Nails scratched his face in a horrifying repetition of Memoria's attack in the carriage. He was wrenched from his feet and landed on his back with such force that he felt all of the vertebrae in his back pop like a string of fireworks. Screaming, he fired several shots in rapid succession. One of the bullets tore through the nearest face, exploding it in a shower of wood and carpenter ants. One of his legs came free. It was all he needed to push himself to his feet. Slashing spasmodically, a creature drove at his eyes. He ducked and fired blindly. Another tore at his thigh like a frenzied animal.

Imogene ran through the doors and came up behind two of the creatures that stood to the side, swaying, their arms flailing without control. She moved with the grace of a cat. In one clean arc she swept the sword through their necks. One of them dropped into a kneeling position and remained still, its head lolling on a wire. The other's head toppled and thumped across the floor. The body remained upright. Face contorted with revulsion, Imogene kicked it between the shoulder blades and impaled the monster from behind. Moss watched in awe as she pulled the blade clear. Three remaining sisters flailed on the ground kicking their legs and screaming. They smashed their heads against the flagstones until they disintegrated into splinters and fell still.

Moss ran for the doors that had been flung open by Imogene during the attack.

"Moss," Imogene shouted after him. He burst onto the roof and stopped short. Several feet away, Memoria's body was hunched on the ground, her entrails pulled through a hole in her back. Her head lay several feet away.

Imogene appeared in the doorway holding the sword. "I killed her," she said.

AUREL

"She came out of the door," said Imogene. "I thought she'd killed you." Moss stood on the roof looking up. The ocellus hung in the air. In spite of the horrors of the last few minutes they were no closer to fulfilling their purpose. They had been looking at the monastery; perhaps they should have been watching the ocellus more closely. Maybe it was the only way to pierce the illusions of the island. He spat a mouthful of blood on the ground.

"She would have," he said.

"I'm sorry."

"She would have killed me. What you did," said Moss, still watching the ocellus, "was what had to be done. It was necessary. I don't blame you for that. The Memoria I thought I loved, the girl who fell off the seawall, died that day. The thing that replaced her was a vile simulacrum." He looked with loathing at the emaciated form on the ground and rocked it with his foot. "Maybe she was never real. Maybe she was simply the corrupted root of this, monster. What do we owe the people we once loved if they're revealed to be something else? I don't know."

Imogene dropped the sword and covered her face with her hands. "I didn't even have time to think."

"And for that I think we should be grateful."

"Look."

The ocellus was moving.

They followed the ocellus to an alcove that collected shadows and dead leaves. A door had been left ajar. Inside, a staircase spiraled downwards, exhaling a dank odor that Moss found anything but inviting. It was lit by a faint bioluminescent slime that seeped through the walls. The way was narrow. Moss followed the now faintly glowing ocellus. Imogene followed with the crow balancing on her shoulder, poking at shadows with the sword. The staircase was filled with recently torn cobwebs; otherwise it looked as though it had been unused for years, maybe centuries. After several turns, Moss slipped, barely saving himself by grabbing the curved railing at the last second.

"Watch your step," he said. "The ground is wet."

"Disgusting," said Imogene.

"Did you see that?" A reflection of light had caught Moss's eye down the curve of the stairs. It had been so subtle that until it occurred again he was not sure it had been real. "Hey," Moss shouted. He ran carelessly down the steps.

"Moss, what the hell are you doing?"

Moss reached the spot where he thought he had seen the light, but there was nothing there. He looked over his shoulder to make sure Imogene was following him and then plunged down the stairs again. After a few more turns they came to the bottom. Instead of a door, there was an arch made of thick roots. In the back of his mind, Moss wondered how long someone would have had to spend to train the roots into such an elaborate form. As he moved closer, he realized that the roots were alive and moving, slipping through loops and knots. The arch had opened for the ocellus and it was now closing. Without thinking, Moss jumped through. The arch became a rapidly narrowing aperture. Imogene thrust her arms through. Moss grabbed her wrists and pulled, but the roots closed around her elbows until all he could see was her forearms and hands flailing in a wall of tendrils.

"My arms are breaking," she screamed. Moss grabbed her hands and pushed them back through the opening. For a second he could see her eye appear at the shrinking hole and then suddenly he was alone. He kicked the wall of roots.

"Imogene," he shouted. "Imogene!" There was no response. He tried to pry the woody tendrils apart, but they had formed a tight, impenetrable barrier. There was no choice but to continue. Several feet away, something rustled. A figure stepped forward, tearing its body free of centuries of cobwebs and grasping roots. The ocellus dimly lit its oversized head. Moss held his breath as it ambled toward him. At first he thought it suffered from some kind of affliction that caused its skin to hang in shreds. It took him a moment to realize that the creature's skin was a rind of thickly layered paper, teeming with sowbugs and millipedes. Its eyes were embedded in dark sockets; the mouth was a ragged slit lined with tiny teeth. The creature shuffled on hoofed feet trailing filthy peelings. It came to a stop close enough to Moss that he could smell its mildew-laden exhalations. "Is Aurel buried here?" said Moss, wishing he had the sword. He settled for the gun, which he pulled from his pocket.

The creature moved its mouth for sometime before whispering, "Not here, but I can take you there."

"How far?" asked Moss.

"Not far. Don't be frightened," said the creature.

Moss's only options were to remain, or follow this strange individual. He wondered fleetingly if Irridis had been aware of what he had asked of his friend.

"You won't need that here," said the creature. Moss was startled. He had forgotten that he was holding the gun. Nodding, he tossed it onto the floor.

"Where is the grave?"

"This way." The creature cupped the ocellus with long fingers and took several steps. He stopped and looked over his shoulder.

"Are you coming?"

"Yes," said Moss.

The paper creature proceeded with an odd side-to-side gait, leading them on a wandering path of passages, empty rooms and staircases. Moss gave up trying to memorize the way after a few minutes. Convinced they had just passed through a room for the second time, he gave in to impatience.

"Where are you taking me?" Not thinking, he tried to grab the creature by a peeling shoulder, but his fingers dug deep into the decaying paper.

"As it happens, we're here," it said, stepping back, appearing only mildly inconvenienced. It peered back at Moss with unblinking black eyes. They stood in front of a high, partially draped door. "Are you sure of this? Are you sure this is what you want? Perhaps you would rather simply leave well enough alone. We are made of such delicate fiber." It twitched its head to the side. In the soft light of the ocellus, its hands were bejeweled with restless insects. It opened its fingers and released the ocellus.

"Open the door," said Moss.

"I hope you find what you're looking for." With this, the creature pulled back the drapery. The door opened with a whisper.

They stepped through the door into the base of a wide sinkhole. Concave walls of limestone soared up around them like a melting cathedral. The floor was a sea of ferns. In the center, partially obscured by a veil of drizzle, Moss could see a stone bust. It was obviously ancient, marred with cracks and crusted in lichen. He walked toward it through knee-high fronds, followed at a slower pace by the paper creature. The bust—one head with two androgynous faces—rested on a plinth of fossil stone. Moss circled it under the creature's watch. He had no doubt that their destination had been reached. Elated, Moss looked up. A circular patch of sky was filled with darting swallows. Running water had cut deep fissures into the steep limestone walls. Although Aurel's grave was a place of great peace, it was also a place that was disappearing. Frost and rain would eat away at the collapsed cave, until one day it would be just another steep-walled ravine. Moss was humbled by this thought. It asserted a true perspective. Existence was a fragile thing; their time was brief.

He had been standing for some time, letting the falling water cleanse his face, when he realized the paper creature was no longer moving. It had expired on a mossy slab, away from the light, having completed its brief task of guiding Moss to the cave. Its form had already begun disintegrating into a pool of water. Moss wondered how many years it had waited, dormant, in the silence of the tunnel. Remembering the disturbed cobwebs in the entrance, he wondered if Memoria had come here. He thought not. It was more likely that she had intended to, but was interrupted by their arrival.

"Moss." Imogene stood in the doorway that led into the cave. Her face was sweaty and her hands were covered in scratches. She still held the sword that she had used to decapitate Memoria. "Do you have any idea how hard it was to cut through those roots? They kept growing back. It was no easy task following you through all those twists and turns back there either." She followed Moss's path of trodden ferns to the bust, pausing momentarily to take in the pulpy form on the slab. "So this is it? Aurel's grave." She pointed at the ocellus that floated above the statue.

"Yes," Moss said, as he leaned against it. Running his hands over the bust, he wondered what he was missing. Why would Irridis have wanted to risk his life, and Moss's, to bring the ocellus to Aurel's grave? Moss worked on the principle that it was a symbolic gesture. He had heard of just such a tradition in certain religions. Setting stones on a grave was a way of remembering and marking the dead. But this seemed so unlike Irridis. What bothered him was that the ocellus was not inert; it was the epitome of condensed energy, like an egg or a seed.

Moss turned to Imogene who had pulled a hood over her head and sat on the ground at the statue's base. "Do you have your penknife?"

She opened her eyes, lulled by the sound of the rain, almost to sleep. "What? Do you want to leave your initials?"

"Imogene."

"Okay, fine." She pulled the small knife from her pocket and handed it to him. Moss opened the blade and picked at the crust of lichen on one of the faces. Imogene stood up, curious. "What are you doing?"

"I want to see what's underneath." As he cleared the lichen, a weathered green stone with metallic flecks emerged. The eyes had carved pupils, which had not been visible before. Encouraged, Moss continued his scraping. He worked his way down the slender nose to the lips. Here, the knife blade slipped into a black hole. "There's an opening. Why would a bust have an opening?" When he was finished they could see that there was an elliptical space between the upper and lower lip. Moss was pondering this discovery when Imogene snatched the ocellus from the air and inserted it into the hole. The fit was near perfect.

"I wonder if we get a prize?" she said dryly.

"Shit," said Moss, pulling her back. Honey-colored ooze flowed from the opening.

"Uh-oh," said Imogene.

Moss and Imogene stood back as they watched the ooze flow down the bust and spread across the ground forming branches and tendrils.

"What's happening?" asked Imogene.

He shook his head. "Help me clear the ground." Working just ahead of the flow, they tore up ferns and threw stones to the side, heedless of the cold and wet. The flow thickened and darkened.

"Look," said Moss, pointing. "Something's changing, branching inside of it. They're spreading." A universal natural pattern emerged. They were the self-similar patterns shared by rivers, geologic faults, coastlines and leaf veins. At first, the structures, nodes and branch points emerging from the earliest sections were easy to follow, but the transformation soon became exponentially more complex.

"We're seeing a birth," whispered Imogene. "This is why Irridis was so desperate to return the ocellus. God, it's magical."

"This is not a grave," said Moss, shaking his head as he looked up at the statue. "It's not magic, though. It's hiding some kind of technology. Irridis must have come to understand this. It's not technology from our world."

"When I was drawn, Elizabeth—Memoria, I mean—said that the sisters had found Irridis and Aurel on the heath hundreds of years ago." She frowned. "Moss, why would—"

"I don't know."

Bones formed from knotted thickenings in the gelatinous form. They lengthened and widened at the joints. Webbed networks of nerves, veins and arteries spread over through the growing form. Then came the organs, some familiar, others not.

Hours passed. Imogene wept as she pointed at the creature, for now there was no question of the humanoid form lying in the torn ferns. Pricks of lights had begun to run along its branching pathways. Limbs had sprouted fingers and toes, and a head had grown, like swelling bud. Dark globes appeared in a translucent eggshell skull, darting beneath the eyelids like those of a disturbed sleeper. Then, the growth slowed. The form darkened. The creature opened its mouth and a vapor rose into the air, spiraling and twisting. It dissipated, settling over Moss and Imogen like fine pollen, as they watched, unable to move or speak. And like characters in a fairytale, they fell into a deep and dream-filled sleep.

Moss opened his eyes. The sky had grown dark. A slender figure stood over him. Five points of light glowed in a circle around her head. He was dreamsick and could not seem to rouse himself. He was only dimly aware when the figure closed his eyes with graceful fingers.

"Moss, wake up." He opened his eyes to find the cave lit with slanting morning light. The air was filled with steam rising from pools of water. Imogene kneeled beside him. "It's gone." There was regret in her voice. He sat forward. A flattened bed of ferns was the only evidence the creature had ever existed.

"I saw her," Moss said, remembering. "I woke up and she was there, but she did something to me, made me fall back asleep."

"What did she look like?" asked Imogene.

Moss thought for a moment. "Beautiful." It was the only word he could think of that came remotely close to what he had seen.

"Well," said Imogene. "She stole my sword, my coat and some clothes out of my pack. I'm not sure what that says about her character." Her voice trailed off.

Moss looked through his pack. A moment later he turned to Imogene with a broad grin. "She took the drawings too."

A figure in a long coat strode out of the tunnel mouth that led from Nightjar Island to the mainland. Her head was covered in a hood. Black lenses, found in the dead city, protected her vision from the light that shot through the trees. On her shoulder, a piebald crow maintained sure balance. A sword was tied to the pack on her back.

Aurel walked through a wood, surrounded by glowing ocelli. She soon found herself at a seawall where nearby, an overturned truck and the ruins of an old quay lay half buried in tidal ooze. Across the channel, Nightjar Island slid behind a wall of mist. She would never return there. Aurel walked over the dunes and found a rutted road. It was not much, but it was a beginning.

EVENING

EVENING CREPT OVER NIGHTJAR ISLAND, AFTER A PROLONGED LATE afternoon thunderstorm. The buildings of the village cast elongated blue shadows. Gold light raked the furrows, mounds and sprouting vegetables in the gardens. Steam rose from the fur of motionless rabbits, driven from their flooded burrows. A dead apple tree, split by lightning, burned furiously. Its spark-laden smoke rose into the clear sky, where the first stars had already appeared.

At the foot of the silo, a long-legged dog raced to the end of its chain and snapped back onto its haunches. Its barking spread to several other locations around the village like a musical round. Two individuals emerged from the woods onto the packed mud path that ran toward the gardens. The tallest, a man with a beard and scraggly hair, rolled a cigarette as he walked. A woman walked behind him warily taking in the surroundings. Her hand trailed over the high weeds.

They proceeded, unchallenged, to the Oak Hall. As they came closer, a curtain was pulled back from a window and a face appeared in a triangle of darkness. Raised voices could be heard from within. Several men had followed Moss and Imogene from the outskirts. They kept their distance, but there was no mistaking the fear in their faces. Moss handed the cigarette to Imogene who took a practiced drag and handed it back. The smoke was pale blue against the deepening shadows of the buildings. A door opened and several people stepped out through, clustering on the porch. They stood in a patch of sunlight and shielded their eyes with the their hands. They waited, stern-faced and still, like figures in an antique tintype. Several of the men were openly armed. Finally, the group parted and May pushed through, clearing the way with an ivory-headed cane.

"Lumsden Moss," she said. "I didn't expect to see you again. We assumed the worst."

"May," said Moss, nodding a greeting. "We've come to tell you that Elizabeth is dead. The monastery at Little Eye is empty."

"I know. Some of our men found her carriage when they were out looking for Jansson. They burned it."

"We saw the smoke," said Moss.

"You've brought Imogene back here," said May. Two men raised their rifles. Moss thought he recognized them from the group that had tried to shoot Imogene.

"Easy," said Moss, meeting their gaze. "We're not here to cause a problem." They begrudgingly stepped out of the way so that May could move closer. The man on the left, in threadbare pants and a muddy barn coat, looked uncertainly at the other man. Moss wondered if they were father and son. The older man, in fatigues and T-shirt, seemed ready to kill Moss where he stood.

"Be careful, May," blurted one of the women in the doorway. A child with a dirty face peered around her skirts.

"May," warned another woman. The older man walked down the porch steps and put the end of his rifle at Imogene's temple. His hands trembled.

"What the hell is this creature doing here?" he growled. "Are you out of your mind, bringing her back to where we live?" He glanced at Moss.

"I'm no more of a creature than you are." She turned away from the man and addressed herself to May, her posture and expression neutral. In the darkening garden, fireflies pulsed. Moss had been nervous about returning to the village with Imogene. It had been her idea to confront these people directly. During the journey from Little Eye, they had argued about this approach, sometimes angrily, with Moss advising that it would be tantamount to suicide. Imogene firmly believed that dispelling the mystery around herself would create an opportunity to lessen their fear. Moss thought she was being naïve.

"I know who you are," said May. "You are John Machine's daughter. Did you know that your mother once lived here?"

Imogene looked around as if searching for something in their faces. "No, I didn't."

"He came here years ago, a soldier. He was traveling alone, and fell into some trouble. We helped him, but he repaid us by taking away one of my daughters, Sylvie, to the City of Steps. I never saw her again."

"I didn't know any of this," said Imogene. "If what you say is true, then you're my grandmother."

May held up her hand. "Oh, it's true. Tell me, girl, why have you come back?"

Imogene, relieved by the abrupt return to the purpose of their visit, quickly refocused. "There's something I need to tell you."

"What are you talking about, witch?" said the man with the rifle. Moss noticed a couple of people on the porch roll their eyes.

"Brian, let her speak." May pulled a shawl around her shoulder.

"Some of you think that the deaths of your loved ones are somehow attributable to the supernatural," said Imogene. A murmur ran through the group. Somebody recited a prayer.

"Not everyone," said a woman on the porch.

Moss stepped toward Brian and pulled the barrel away from Imogene. "Listen to her," he said. The man twisted the weapon out of Moss's grip and returned it to Imogene's head. Moss pulled his hands back, shaking his head. Imogene turned quickly, startling even Moss. She faced the man and moved the barrel to the corner of her eye.

"If you want the best chance of a clean kill, this is the recommended target area," she said. "Are you really man enough to murder me at close range in front of these people?"

Several seconds passed, and then Brian, sweating and laughing uneasily, took a step back. He lowered the gun. "Crazy bitch."

Imogene turned back to May. "The reason your people are dying has nothing to do with the supernatural. It's due to a neurotoxin. Scavenging around the wreckage of the Crucible, they exposed themselves to a toxin used during the fighting. The Crucible was an aircraft being used toward the end of the war. It was designed for the express purpose of cruelly and indiscriminately dispersing the toxin. It went down with its full payload, but as a result of the crash, the ground soil at the main site is still a high-risk zone."

"I don't believe you," said Brian.

"You are not that stupid," said Imogene. Brian gestured at her obscenely, which earned him a few scattered laughs. Others attended Imogene's words closely.

Moss reached into Imogene's rucksack and pulled out a thick

folder of yellowed papers tied with string. He handed them to May.

"Military documents. We found them in Little Eye with other things left behind. It's all there, everything she just told you and a lot more."

"Go on," said May.

"The problem was well known. We also found a supply of the antidote. We've hidden it. We'll tell you where it is, but there is a price."

"Here we go," said Brian.

"Let us stay in your community," Imogene said. "I want a chance to prove to you that I am not what you think I am. I have a lot of knowledge that you need."

"Like what?" asked Brian.

"Well, farm management for a start. The layout of this garden is all wrong."

"May?" said Moss.

"Well, she has some courage, I'll give her that." May sighed and took the folder from Moss's hand. "Come inside. It's getting dark and I have a lot of questions." Some of the crowd erupted in protest. Brian stalked off, swatting tomato plants with his rifle butt, swearing and shaking his head. May put up her hand.

"Enough," she said. The crowd quieted, with some residual grumbling. May looked up at Imogene, hands on hips. "If we don't take you in, then what?"

"Then most of you will die, directly or indirectly. I am asking that you let me stay. But if that is not the will of the group, I'll leave the island with Moss and you'll never see me again."

"I believe you mean what you say. Why would you want to help us?"

"The people who lived on Nightjar Island were unfairly treated. Everything was taken from them. I think you deserve, we deserve, a better future than picking through the rubble of our city."

"I agree," said May.

May sighed. "Well, I can't make the decision for the group. They're going to have to speak for themselves on this one. You will have to accept the will of the community."

"I've said as much," said Imogene.

May faced the group. "Show of hands from those who want her to stay." Two thirds of the hands rose slowly.

"That's it then," said May. "You're going to have to convince the rest of them eventually, which won't be easy, but for now we'll have you."

"Thank you," said Imogene.

"We never really had a choice," said May. "It'll take time for some of them to figure that out." She clutched her cane and suddenly looked very old.

"What's going on?" asked Luther, who appeared from around the building. "I've never heard Brian so pissed."

"Your mouth, Luther," said May.

Following the group into the hall, Moss passed a cluster of children at a long table. They were reading aloud from a battered school textbook.

Moss turned to May. "Where's their teacher?"

"Gone," she said. "Dr. Grove was the most recent to succumb to the illness." She followed the others into the adjoining room where coffee and sandwiches were already being prepared. Through the door, Moss could hear snatches of a conversation. An elderly farmer and Imogene were discussing the salinity of the local soils.

"Do you mind if I join you?" asked Moss. The children said nothing. Moss sat down and took one of the old textbooks from a pile. A girl with blond hair decorated with ribbons pushed her book toward him. Her finger marked a place in the story.

"What's your name?" asked Moss.

"Emily."

"Hi Emily, I'm Lumsden."

She pointed to a line in the book. "Do you know what this word is?"

"Yes, I do," said Moss with a grin.

THE SONGBIRDS OF NIGHTJAR ISLAND

Moss looked on as Mr. Tern, Head of Collections, raised the lid of the rosewood display case. The glass rattled and the hinges made a high-pitched sound. The air was tainted with the bitter-tasting dust of the storeroom. Tern had offered an unconvincing apology for the state of the room, something about changing exhibits and the tastes of modern audiences. A quiet zoo of rare animals filled the small space, wrapped in sheets of cloudy polyethylene and brown paper. Rough shelves bowed precariously beneath the weight of specimen jars. Moss, put off by the milky eyes of something suspended in a tincture of its own flesh, focused his attention on the object of his visit.

The forged volume of Franklin Box's *The Songbirds of Nightjar Island* rested on the bed of felt where Moss had placed it three years earlier. He eyed it critically. It was faultless. The glue had held and the dyes had faded to the degree expected. There was nothing to suggest that it was not the book once owned by the mad ornithologist. Even the fine dust and the speckled shell of a museum beetle inside the case conspired to give an air of authenticity. A note-perfect performance, thought Moss with a mixture of pride and shame.

In the year since Moss and Imogene had said goodbye to Nightjar Island, he had put his hands to more constructive purposes. With the help of a few taciturn workmen, he had turned John Machine's abandoned chapel into a library. In the evenings, still covered in plaster dust, Moss taught a reading class for the local children, and even a few of their parents. His hands had developed calluses, their creases ingrained with dirt. The nail on his left thumb was dark, the result of a badly timed hammer blow. Before leaving to come to the city he had prepared a garden for winter, laid a wall of reclaimed brick and repaired the roof slates. When he was not working on the building, or teaching, he wrote. It helped with the depression and anxiety that dogged him, appearing without warning, several times a month. Imogene had told him that happy endings were bullshit. She was right, of course. Haunted by what he had seen on Nightjar Island, Moss had started to read the histories left behind in the monastery at Little Eye. His research was the main reason he had come back to the City of Steps. He was taking advantage of a few balmy days to visit the archives before the inevitable autumn rains and winter. He had begun writing a history of Nightjar Island that would probably never be read. It did not matter; the act of writing was enough.

"Judge Seaforth must be a forgetful man not to remember that he'd sent you here on a previous occasion," said Tern. He folded his arms and then immediately unfolded them and smoothed his jacket pockets.

"The judge has a bad memory." Moss shrugged. "If we could at least go through the motions of verifying the edition is the correct one, for the sake of saying we did, I'd be much obliged." Moss adopted the body language of the long-suffering personal secretary.

"As you wish, sir." Tern made a show of consulting his watch and then stepped away from the case with his pale hands clasped over his stomach. At that moment a woman stepped into the storeroom. Her amber eyes took in the crowded collection before settling on the two men. Her velvet-trimmed coat could not conceal her pregnancy.

"Hello," said Tern, raising his hands in exaggerated surprise. "How can I be of assistance?"

"The women's lavatory?" she asked in a stage whisper. "This is clearly not it." The mere mention of the women's lavatory was enough to redden Tern's cheeks. He turned away from Moss and gave Imogene such elaborate directions she could have found the public lavatory in a blindfold. Moss took advantage of the distraction. He lifted the forged book out of the case and slipped it into his overcoat pocket. He replaced it with the original, which had been his companion for three years. In the process, it had become a different book. The cover was stained by ocean brine; the pages were marked with the penciled notes that Moss had kept during his search for Memoria and the fulfillment of his promise to

Irridis. Filled with Moss's hopeless drawings and pressed botanical specimens, it was considerably thicker than it had been on the day he had whisked it from under Tern's nose. One day maybe someone would pull it from the case and read his ramblings, but until then it would rest in the quiet of the storeroom, its secrets hidden. Imagining his future reader's perplexity, Moss smiled and closed the lid.

"Thank you, Mr. Tern," said Moss. The other man whipped his head around as Imogene disappeared through the door. He glanced at the case perfunctorily, nodded, and then gave Moss a sly look.

"Did you see her?" Tern asked. "What an eyeful!"

"You have no idea." Moss grinned. Tern's mouth opened as he cocked his head in a way that reminded Moss of Morel's dog. "Well, thanks for your help." Moss started to walk away but was stopped by Tern's hand on his shoulder.

"I'm sorry, I've completely forgotten your name. Was it Wood, Woods, something like that?"

Moss shook his head thoughtfully. "No, my name is Lumsden Moss."

ACKNOWLEDGMENTS

I would like to thank my dear friend Hans Rueffert for reading and encouraging *Necessary Monsters* from its earliest beginnings. Thanks to Mark Teppo at Resurrection House for giving *Necessary Monsters* a home and great editorial advice, and to my agent Martha Millard for her assistance and support. Special thanks to my wife Elaine for reading uncountable early versions of *Necessary Monsters*, offering invaluable suggestions, and for her unwavering support for all my creative endeavours—to say nothing of supplying endless cups of tea.

ABOUT THE AUTHOR

Richard A. Kirk is a Canadian visual artist, illustrator, and author. Richard has illustrated works by Clive Barker, Caitlin R. Kiernan, Christopher Golden, China Miéville, the rock band Korn, and others.

Richard's work is drawn from an interest in the forms and processes of the natural world. He explores these themes through the creation of meticulous drawings, which often depict chimerical creatures and protean landscapes. Metamorphosis is an underlying narrative in all of Richard's work.

CPSIA information can be obtained
at www.ICGtesting.com
Printed in the USA
LVOW13s0004070517
533573LV00001B/1/P